HER
FEUD

BOOKS BY EMMA TALLON

HER FEUD

EMMA TALLON

bookouture

Published by Bookouture in 2024

An imprint of Storyfire Ltd.
Carmelite House
50 Victoria Embankment
London EC4Y 0DZ

www.bookouture.com

ISBN: 978-1-83790-361-0
eBook ISBN: 978-1-83790-360-3

To my bright warm sunshine and my sparkling star,
Christian and Dolly.
You're my whole heart, today and all days.

ONE

A streetlight flickered in the dark residential street as its inhabitants slept soundly behind closed curtains and drawn blinds. The old Victorian houses stood silent, two militant rows lining the long straight road, their red bricks dimmed to a bruised grey in the moonlight. Somewhere in the distance a cat shrieked, the sound carrying through the air in the unusually quiet hour.

It was a reliable logic that explained London's quietest hour. Up until 2 a.m., the city was still crawling with people out for a good time – those still young enough to not need eight solid hours of sleep to function the next day. After 4 a.m., the roads would begin to busy with trucks and delivery drivers. A little later, runners and cyclists, the disciplined early risers of the world, would trickle out onto the paths. But at 3 a.m., for the most part, the city was empty – the only people lurking in the quiet, those who were up to no good. Those who thrived in the darkness and wanted no witnesses.

Hidden in the shadow of a large tree, a man leaned against the trunk, his brooding gaze trained on the house across the street. There was nothing special about it. Other than being a corner house connecting a side road to the main street, it was the same as all the others. The front door opened straight onto the pavement with one window beside it and two above. The same moss-covered tiles blanketed the roof and the same black guttering framed its edges. But still the man stared, his intense gaze slowly roaming over each brick with a strange and dark fascination.

The fractured tinkling of broken glass cut through the silence, and his eyes darted to the side, his expression alert and his stance tense. Several minutes passed and nothing happened, but still he stared into the darkness, waiting for something.

Dragging his gaze away briefly, he pulled back his black leather glove and checked his watch, before swearing under his breath. With a quick glance down the deserted road, he stepped off the pavement and started towards the house, but as he moved, a long shadow suddenly stretched out from the side road. He paused and tensed, peering into the darkness, but as the man attached to the shadow came into view, he instantly relaxed.

They met silently in the middle of the street, then moved together to the front door.

'It was more secure than I'd anticipated,' the other man whispered.

'You fitted them up OK though?' he checked, glancing back over his shoulder.

The reply was a swift nod. 'You ready?'

'I've never been more ready for anything in my life,' he growled.

Unzipping his dark jacket, he pulled something out of the inside pocket. The sharp, acrid smell of petrol filled the air the moment he unwrapped the carefully sealed bag, becoming stronger as he fished out the soaked rags inside. Beside him, the other man produced a sheet of bubble wrap, and, holding the letterbox open with one hand, spread it around the edges, creating a protective funnel. Careful not to let any of the potent liquid touch the door in any way, he pushed the rags through and they dropped with a dull thud onto the floor inside. The bubble wrap was pulled away and cast aside into the road.

'How long?' he asked.

'Two minutes,' came the whispered response. 'Maybe three for the bigger ones.'

He nodded. 'Move back.'

Pulling off his petrol-soaked gloves, he shoved them into one pocket then pulled a matchbox out of the other before striking a match. The momentary flare, as it ignited, emphasised the hard lines of anger and hatred etched deeply into his face, then he pushed open the letterbox and dropped it through. He paused only long enough to check that the small flame had caught the rags, then turned and ran up the road towards his partner in crime, who was already a fair distance ahead of him.

When they reached the mouth of an alleyway that ran through to the road where they'd left their vehicle, they stopped and turned to watch. At first nothing happened. Then a flicker of orange appeared and grew quickly brighter in the downstairs window. Thick black smoke began seeping through the cracks of the old wooden window frames and a dull boom sounded, followed by the shattering of glass as all the windows burst outwards, littering the road with hundreds of sharp, shiny shards. They glittered against the dark tarmac as they reflected the growing flames that reached out and licked the outer walls.

The two men watched as the inferno grew, their eyes gleaming with tense anticipation. Windows began lighting up all down the street, shortly followed by front doors opening and sleepy but horrified residents running out into the street with cries of fear and shock. Men began shouting to each other as they worked out who needed to do what, but as they moved towards the house, they were suddenly blown back with force by a large explosion.

Debris flew through the air and littered the road, and half of the side wall crashed down in one large chunk as the raging fire took over the entire building. As the nearest neighbours fled their homes, the first sirens began to wail in the distance.

'Come on.' The other man gripped his arm, pulling him away. 'We're done here. It's over.'

'Oh, it's far from over, brother,' he replied, a cold glint in his eye. 'This is barely the beginning.'

TWO

Checking her watch as she walked out of her bedroom and down the hall, Lily sped up her pace slightly. She fastened the buttons on the cuffs of her black satin blouse as she nipped down the stairs, then pushed her hands back through her thick, gravity-defying halo of blonde curls, in an attempt to smooth them down. They immediately sprang straight back to the same position, as stubborn and untameable as the woman they belonged to.

The smell of freshly brewed coffee hit her senses at the same time she noticed the sound of voices coming from the kitchen, and she turned expectantly towards it as she reached the downstairs hallway.

'Oh good, you're here,' she said, accepting the cup of coffee her eldest son, Cillian, held out towards her as she reached him.

She checked her watch again and twisted her mouth to one side as she debated whether or not she had time to sit down.

'Don't sweat – we've got loads of time,' Cillian said, catching her expression.

Lily looked up into his handsome face and cocked an eyebrow. 'Your version of plenty and my version of plenty are two very different things, Cillian Drew. You'd be late to your own funeral.' But despite her protest, she slipped onto the bar stool next to Billie, his fiancée, who was quietly pulling an expression of agreement.

Cillian feigned shocked offence, throwing his arms in the air in a gesture of defeat. 'I don't know, you meet a girl, think she's alright, and the next minute she's ganging up on you with your own mother!'

Billie laughed, and Lily rolled her eyes with a good-natured grin. She sipped her coffee and watched her son over the rim, feeling the familiar pang of loss his handsome face incited in her these days. She'd been lucky, as a mother, that neither of her twin sons had grown up and flown the nest as soon as they'd found their wings, the way so many did. For nearly thirty years they'd been in her life almost every single day. Though it hadn't really been down to luck. She'd worked hard to keep them there.

For them, she'd built up a number of successful, lucrative businesses from scratch. For them, she'd taken a knife and carved a thriving empire out of London's dark underbelly, staining her hands with its blood over and over again to do so. And it had taken everything she'd had. Blood, sweat and tears had been only the very tip of the iceberg. Because Lily Drew had come from nothing.

Orphaned as a teenager with a young brother to raise and no home or money, she'd had no head start in life. No money, no safety net to catch her if she failed. She'd learned young how to survive and thrive by any means necessary, and when she'd had her children, she'd sworn they would never know the same hardships she'd faced. That was what had driven her every move since the day they were born.

But despite all she'd created, her other son, Connor, had left her anyway. Left all of them. His twin brother, his cousin, his family firm, the firm built on all the bones she'd broken with her bare hands – his own goddamn inheritance. Feeling the bitterness rise, Lily tried to turn her thoughts away from him. Today was Sunday, the Lord's day. And while she couldn't afford Him the full day off from the murderous thoughts that came with lingering on that for too long, she'd at least show Him the respect of not bringing them into church.

'Have you spoken to Scarlet?' she asked, pulling out a cigarette.

'She's not coming today. She's too under it,' he replied, watching her light up with a slight wistfulness before pulling a toothpick out of his pocket and placing it between his teeth. 'She's at the factory.'

Lily frowned. 'I thought she was going over to sort all that last night?' She took a deep drag and savoured the feel of the smoke filling her lungs.

'She was there most of the night by the sound of it. She's gone back to carry on.' Cillian shrugged and looked over to the TV as he sipped his coffee, tuning into the morning news.

Lily pursed her lips. With Connor gone, Scarlet and Cillian had been picking up the slack, but they were already spinning as many plates as they could manage. Now they were stretched too thin, and although they'd taken it in their stride without a word of complaint, it was beginning to show.

'You got any decaf, Lil?' Billie asked, standing up and walking around the long white marble breakfast bar towards the cupboard.

'Decaf?' Cillian repeated with a frown. 'What's the point in that? Drinking decaf is like jumping in a river to get dry.'

'It's not!' Billie argued.

'At the back on the left,' Lily replied absently, the name of a familiar street catching her attention on the news.

'I like the taste. I'm just having a bit of a detox.' The glass bottom of the coffee jar chinked against the worktop as Billie shut the cupboard door.

'... *the fire started in the early hours of this morning and is being treated by the police as arson. Fragments of several small home-made bombs were discovered inside, and it is believed the fire was started by the front door before spreading through the rest of the house.*'

Lily eyed what was left of the charred, smoking house behind the reporter and shook her head as she took another drag on her cigarette. 'What a mess,' she mused.

'*Two men are being treated for injuries following the blast, and though it caused no fatalities, an older set of human remains has been found within the wreckage of one of the fallen walls.*'

Lily's arm stilled, the coffee cup she'd been about to drink from suspended in mid-air as the reporter's words sharpened her attention.

'Whose car are we taking?' she vaguely heard Billie ask behind her.

'I'll drive Mum's,' Cillian replied.

The reporter was still talking about the police investigation, but Lily tuned her out, her eyes now scanning the scene behind.

'My bag's still in our car. Will you grab it?' Billie asked him.

Lily placed her coffee on the breakfast bar and took a couple of steps towards the TV, to get a closer look.

'Sure, we need to get going now anyway. Mum?'

She heard Cillian's words, but she wasn't really paying attention, and as the reporter shifted slightly, she finally saw it. Her eyebrows shot up, and a stab of foreboding pierced through the bottom of her stomach.

'Mum?' Cillian repeated.

'Hm?' Lily tore her gaze from the screen, smoothing her troubled expression as she turned towards him.

'We going then, or what?' he asked.

Church. 'Yes,' she replied. 'Yes, let's go.'

Cillian paused, his sharp perception as on point as ever. 'You alright?'

'I'm fine,' she replied, a forced briskness to her tone. 'Let's go.' She gestured towards the hallway and raised her eyebrows.

Billie led the way, and Cillian peeled off after her, grabbing Lily's car keys in the hallway on the way out. Picking up her bag, she slowly followed them, her eyes drawn back to the littered street on the news, where a sheet of bubble wrap, partially trapped under a brick, gently danced in the breeze.

THREE

Cillian bowed his head and reeled off the words he'd committed to memory at just four years old, as the priest, Father Dan, dragged them through the final prayer of the service. He stared down, unseeing, at the small red-and-black flagstones beneath his feet, his mind elsewhere.

It had been nearly two weeks since he'd last seen Connor. It was the longest they'd ever spent apart since the day they'd been conceived. They'd argued that day and hadn't parted on the best of terms. And maybe he was to blame for that, but he just couldn't understand *why*. Why Connor had left them. Why he'd teamed up with the man they both hated most in the world. He'd thought Connor had been happy with his life. *Their* life. The one they'd always shared. But his brother hadn't been able to give him an answer, and he'd grown frustrated.

Now, they were barely talking. The only time they spoke was when it was about work, which had to be continued as Connor slowly unwound himself from all the threads of the family firm. For the first time ever, Cillian had no idea what his brother was doing. Whether he was OK. Whether he was happy. And it bothered him more than he'd ever realised it could.

Aware suddenly that the low murmurs of the congregation had stopped, Cillian lifted his head and pretended to listen to the service. He hadn't heard a word Father Dan had spoken in years, but the Drews were always afforded the respect of being shown to the front row when they attended Mass, and being right under the keen eye of an Irish Catholic priest who loved any excuse to send a boy to extra Sunday School sessions had been enough to help him hone his skills of fake attentiveness.

There was a shift in the room and people began to leave. Cillian followed his mother and aunt out of the pew and into the central aisle behind Father Dan.

'He's intense, isn't he?' Billie remarked, nodding towards Father Dan.

Cillian grinned. 'You don't know the half of it.'

'Oh yeah?' She glanced at him, intrigued.

Cillian leaned a touch closer and lowered his voice. 'When we were kids, running riot, driving Mum up the wall, ignoring every threat, as kids do... if Mum reached the end of her tether, she'd threaten to tell Father Dan. And d'ya know what, it bloody worked – he used to scare the shit out of us.'

Billie stifled a snort and put a hand over her mouth. Lily glanced back, and Cillian squeezed his fiancée's hand, shushing her under his breath.

'Button it, you,' he warned jokingly, glancing around to make sure no one else had heard his confession. 'That's my deepest darkest secret right there, alright? So that's between us – you don't tell another soul.'

Billie grinned. 'I know for a fact *that* ain't your darkest secret, Cillian Drew,' she declared quietly.

'From the law? No. But from the rest of the world, it really is. Our world anyway.'

He tilted his chin to acknowledge the nods from two men

waiting in the pews further back. No one behind them would exit their pews until the Drews had passed. It was a basic mark of respect.

'Fear is weakness, Bills. And in this game, none of us can afford to show an ounce of it. Not even through a funny childhood story.' He turned to her, catching her bright blue eyes with a smile. 'You're the only person in the world I'll ever trust with secrets like that.'

Billie's face lit up, and she squeezed his hand. 'I love that I'm that person for you.'

'Me too,' he replied, meaning it with every fibre of his being. He squeezed her hand and nodded back to a couple of people offering their respect.

'Did she ever actually do it?' Billie asked.

'Hm?' Cillian replied.

'Your mum. Did she ever actually follow through and take you to Father Dan?'

'Oh. Yeah. She did, once or twice. We weren't stupid enough to keep pushing after that.'

They reached the door and Cillian eyed the priest standing up ahead, remembering how terrifying the man had appeared in his youth.

'He looks more like a pro-boxer than a priest,' Billie commented.

'Actually, he was, back in the day. Semi-pro anyway,' Cillian told her. 'He used to train at the club. Taught me a lot of what I know.' He tilted his head wryly. 'Boxed some sense into me more than once too.'

Lily turned to look back at them, beckoning them to join her and his aunt Cath. This was the first time Billie had ever been to church with them. Not that he expected her to come at all. In truth, he only came each week out of respect for his mother. He didn't need a weekly sermon to remind him he was going to hell one day. But this week, after they'd discussed having the wedding here, Billie had asked if she could come along to meet Father Dan and get a feel for the place.

'Father Dan, this is Billie, Cillian's fiancée,' Lily said, wrapping an arm around Billie and propelling her forward as they reached her.

'Ahh, Billie, it's great to meet the woman that's going to finally make an honest man out of this one,' Father Dan said, the Irish accent still prevalent in his deep booming voice, despite the decades he'd lived in London. 'Are you from the area?'

It was a loaded question, and Cillian could see the steeliness behind the welcoming smile. He groaned internally.

'Yeah, born and raised,' Billie replied sunnily.

'Is that so?' Father Dan replied with apparent surprise. 'How is it that we've not met before? Are your family not Catholic?'

Don't tell him. It's a trap...

'Actually yeah, my family is Catholic,' Billie admitted. 'We just don't really go to church.' Her smile faltered as she realised her mistake.

Father Dan's expression turned stern as he eyed her. 'Well, I hope that's going to change now that you're thinking of entering into the covenant of holy matrimony, young lady. It's not a decision to be taken lightly, a promise such as this, made in the house of God.'

'N-No, of course not,' she stuttered. 'We're in this for life.'

'Then I expect to see you here each week, with your future husband,' he warned, holding her gaze until she flushed pink and blinked. 'And I'll enrol you both in pre-marriage counselling.'

'What?' Cillian exclaimed. 'No, we're good, Father—' he began to argue, but Lily cut in.

'It's a standard process if you want to get married in the church, Cillian.' She caught his gaze with a look that told him to back down.

He stepped back and forced a grim smile. 'Right.'

'Well, that's settled then,' his aunt Cath said chirpily. 'Have you thought about when you want to get married yet?'

'As soon as possible really,' Billie said, before Cillian had a chance to reply.

Her answer surprised him. They'd only been engaged a couple of weeks and hadn't discussed things like that just yet.

'Well, you may have to wait a while,' Father Dan replied. 'Because other than a cancellation the Thursday after next, the wedding calendar is booked up for the next eight months.'

'Eight months!' Billie exclaimed. 'Christ!' Her eyes widened as she realised what she'd said. 'Oh God, I'm sorry, Father. Oh shit...' She clapped a hand over her mouth, her expression growing more horrified as Father Dan's darkened.

Behind her, Lily closed her eyes and tightened her jaw, and Cillian could almost hear the curses that must have been running through her head.

'Eight months isn't that long really, when you think about it,' Cath said hurriedly in an attempt to distract the priest from Billie's blasphemous verbal diarrhoea. 'With all the planning that comes with a wedding. You've got to sort out so much. There's the suits and dresses, the venue for the reception, the flowers, the cake—'

'I don't need eight months for that,' Billie cut in suddenly. 'Two weeks is just fine.'

'*What?*' Cillian asked, moving towards her and placing a hand on the small of her back. 'Bills...'

'No, I mean it,' she said with certainty. 'I don't need months to muck about with frills and fancies. I just want to be married to you. Father Dan, can we take that cancelled spot?'

His bushy eyebrows rose in surprise. 'There wouldn't be enough time to read the banns. They have to be called three Sundays in a row, by law,' he explained.

'Is there no way around that?' Billie pressed.

Cillian frowned and studied her eager face. 'What's the rush?'

'Why not?' she countered with a shrug. 'I don't care about all that other stuff. I ain't getting married so I have an excuse to sip champers in dress shops or have cake tastings every weekend. I'm getting married because I want to be your wife. Your family. Because I want to grow old with you.'

Father Dan's severe expression softened slightly. 'And *that*, young lady, is exactly the right reason for wanting to be married.' He twisted his mouth to one side for a moment in contemplation. 'There is a way around the banns. *Not*,' he added sternly, 'that I approve of it under normal circumstances. But I've known you since you were a wean, Cillian, and He Himself knows you need a good woman by your side to keep you out of trouble. Other than your mother of course,' he added with a nod to Lily. 'So I'll allow it. You'll need to apply for a special licence. I can talk you through it all.'

'Thank you, Father!' Billie exclaimed, turning and wrapping her arms around Cillian with a small sound of glee.

'But where would you hold the reception?' Cath asked, sounding aghast at the idea of throwing a wedding together so quickly.

Cillian wasn't sure he disagreed with his aunt's reaction. He'd only just proposed two weeks ago. He'd assumed Billie would want to take her time planning the perfect day, sharing all her ideas with him while he smiled and nodded along. He hadn't expected it all to be done and dusted in less than a month.

'I guess we could use the function room above the pub,' Lily said hesitantly. She turned to him then, concern hiding within a small frown. 'If this is definitely what you want to do?'

'Er...' He scratched his neck with his free hand as he tried to process all that had happened over the last few minutes. 'Well, yeah, 'course it is. That's why I proposed after all.'

Billie looked at him, her big blue eyes holding his quietly. These eyes didn't beg or plead with him, the way so many others had in the past. Billie was too proud for that. But he could tell how much she wanted this.

'Thursday after next it is then,' he said. 'Book us in, Father.'

Father Dan grinned widely, his blue eyes twinkling as he slapped a heavy hand on Cillian's shoulder. 'Well, congratulations to ye both. I have to say, I wasn't sure I'd live to see the day you or your brother would walk down this aisle, but I'm very glad I have. Where is young Connor anyway?'

Lily visibly tensed at the mention of her other son and, as Cath and Billie both glanced at her, the silence became awkward.

'Avoiding his sins, I reckon, Father,' Cillian said with a forced smile.

'Well, I want to see you *both* in church next week,' the priest replied, looking unimpressed. 'So you just make sure he's here. We'll need to talk him through his duties as best man. I'm assuming he's your choice?' Though it was a question, the priest didn't pause for the answer. It was already a given. 'Because being a best man isn't just for the wedding; his role is to help you both through married life.'

'I'll make sure he's here,' Cillian promised.

But as he watched his mother's jaw tighten, Cillian wasn't sure how easy that was going to be, and it dawned on him suddenly that there was very little chance their family issues were all going to be solved in two weeks.

He looked down at Billie and felt his heart sink. He wanted to marry her. He wanted to give her the wedding she wanted – and he was prepared to do almost anything to do that. But there was no way in the world he was getting married without Connor by his side. No matter the consequences.

FOUR

Scarlet rubbed her forehead back and forth, feeling stressed. She was in over her head and no matter how she looked at it, or how many late nights she pulled, she couldn't get back on top of things. Throwing her pen down in frustrated defeat, she sighed and slumped back in her office chair.

Paperwork was scattered all over her desk in multiple layers. All of it should have been done already, but she was just stretched too far. With Connor gone, she and Cillian had naturally shared the load, but neither of them had the time spare around their own workload, and that was the one problem nothing could fix.

There was a knock at the door, and she looked up just as it opened and Isla poked her head in. 'This a good time?' she asked, in her soft Mancunian accent.

Scarlet glanced down at the desk and then back up to Isla. 'Actually, yes,' she replied. 'Come in.'

Isla came in and took the seat the other side of the desk, crossing her slim legs and pushing her blonde locks back behind one ear.

'I like the hair,' Scarlet said, nodding towards it.

'Oh, thanks,' Isla replied with a wide smile.

She'd grown it out over the last year, her previous shoulder-length straight bob now replaced by a longer, softer style.

'Does Connor like it?' Scarlet asked innocently.

Isla thought nobody knew of her infatuation with Connor. She was a skilled liar with a poker face that could win Oscars when she needed it for work, but when it came to her feelings for Connor, all those skills seemed to disappear. She mooned after him like a schoolgirl with a crush. Isla thought her secret was still hers, but everyone knew. Everyone, that was, except Connor himself.

Connor was blindly oblivious to his adoring fan. And that was mainly because while Isla silently pined for him, he was distracted by his ongoing unsuccessful attempts at wooing Sandra. The one woman he'd ever pursued who had no romantic interest in him whatsoever. It was a frustrating love triangle to watch, in Scarlet's opinion. But it wasn't her place to get involved.

'Connor?' Isla looked away with a nonchalant shrug. 'No idea. Haven't seen him.'

Isla pretended to study something outside the window, and Scarlet allowed herself a small smile.

'So what's up?' Scarlet asked.

'There's been a fire at the factory in Manchester.' Isla's brow furrowed into a frown.

'How bad?' Scarlet asked, her expression mirroring Isla's.

'Bad,' Isla confirmed. 'It was in the middle of the night so no one was there. Half the building was already up in flames before someone noticed, and by the time the fire engine got there, the rest was gone too.'

Scarlet's eyes widened in shock. 'Shit.'

'Yeah.' Isla pulled a grim expression.

The implications of what this meant for them began to race

through Scarlet's mind, and she exhaled slowly. 'Shit,' she repeated. 'At least no one was hurt though.'

'Not physically, no,' Isla replied.

Scarlet nodded.

Isla had joined the firm a couple of years before, the first outsider to be allowed into their close-knit firm since Lily and her brother Ronan had first formed it decades before. She'd been on the run from a violent gang leader from her estate back in Manchester, who'd forced her into an abusive and controlling relationship from a young age. He'd made sure she had no money to her name and no way to escape. But Isla was smart, and when the opportunity had arisen, she'd run away to London and sought out the Drews, offering them her skills and loyalty in return for a job and a safe haven. Lily had taken a chance on the young woman, and they'd dealt with Isla's ex, making sure she'd never have to fear him again. They'd dealt with his wife too, but not in quite the same way.

Jazmin had been the real brains behind the crooked businesses they'd run on the Manchester estate. Sensing that she was getting sick of her husband and his selfish, philandering ways, Scarlet had convinced her to help the Drews get rid of him, and to partner up on a new business deal that would benefit them both. It had been a win-win situation. The Drews were able to stop the risky truck heists they'd been pulling for the real stuff, getting knock-off goods at a low price from Jazmin instead, and Jazmin's business had doubled overnight. But in return for such cheap pricing, the Drews gave her their protection and support with anything concerning the factory. Which meant that this had now become a headache for them all. Another headache to add to the growing unmanageable pile.

Scarlet rubbed her temple then wiped her hand down her face. 'OK. Was it an attack or accidental?'

Isla deliberated for a moment. 'They traced it to a loose wire in one of the machines, said it was an electrical fault.'

'But?' Scarlet could see the doubt behind Isla's deep brown eyes.

'But the wires could have been tampered with,' she added. 'Jazmin's had some issues lately with another firm in the area. They think she's getting too big for her boots.'

'And is she?' Scarlet asked.

Isla shook her head immediately. 'Nah. She's just doing well. They're local bully boys who don't like seeing a woman do well. They're too lazy to try and keep up with her, but they *are* dangerous. It could be them.' She shrugged.

Scarlet rested back in her chair, turning the situation over in her mind. 'We need to stick with the assumption it was an electrical fault. She's an ally, so if it turns out to be more, we'll obviously help, but we don't have the manpower or time right now to look into maybes. She'll be covered by insurance for the building and machinery, and we'll set up a meeting soon, to talk about what that means for supply. We'll have to ration what stock we've got left, tell the traders to go slow. How much have we got?'

Isla shook her head with a look of helplessness. 'A month maybe, if we're really conservative. But she's not going to be back up and running in a month.'

Scarlet cursed. This was the last thing they needed right now.

'I'll see what I can do about getting some sort of temporary production going up there, check out her other sites, see if I—' Isla began.

'No.' Scarlet cut her off sharply. 'No. Jaz will have to figure this out on her own. I'll call her myself, sort out what I can, but I need you here.' She sighed and gestured to the mess of paperwork. 'It's something I was going to talk to you about anyway. With Connor gone, we're stretched to capacity. *Past* capacity,' she corrected. 'I need you to take over some of this.'

Isla nodded, but her expression was troubled. 'Do you really think he's not coming back?' she asked.

Scarlet heard the hope in her voice and felt her guilt push down a little heavier in her chest. It was her fault Connor had left the firm. Not that anyone else knew that. She shook her head.

'Sorry, Isla, no. I don't think he's coming back any time soon.'

Isla's face fell and she looked away, trying to hide it. 'Well, that's a shame,' she said. 'For your aunt, I mean. For all of you.'

'For all of *us*,' Scarlet said with a sad half-smile. 'Things are changing, and Connor's absence affects us all. I'll go over things with you properly later, but for now can you take these?' She rummaged through the mess on her desk until she found the pile of papers she was looking for and handed them over to Isla. 'You've done these before. I need you to get that all through the system at *our* factory and then log everything in the books. Both books, you understand? The auditable ones and the real ones.'

'Yeah, 'course. No problem,' Isla said, taking the papers and standing up. 'I'll go over and get started now.' She turned towards the door then paused, looking back. 'Do you think maybe if Connor knew how much he's needed, he'd come back? I mean, you're all so close, surely he wouldn't want to see you struggling because of him?'

Scarlet sighed. 'He's got to make his own choices and for his own reasons, Isla. We'll figure it out, this end. We just have to get straight first.' She gave the other woman a tight grin of what she hoped was encouragement.

Isla didn't look convinced, but she nodded anyway and continued out, closing the door behind her.

Alone once more, Scarlet dropped the smile and rested her head on the back of the chair. Isla wasn't the only one who missed Connor. Workload aside, they were all used to seeing him day to day. Now his absence felt unnatural, and it had left a gaping hole in all their lives. But whose fault was that? *Hers*. Another ripple of guilt ran through her, and she shifted uncomfortably in her seat. Connor had only left because of the weight of her secrets.

She picked up her phone, scrolled through her regular contacts and hovered over his name for a moment, then moved down to Joe's number instead. She pressed the call button and it was answered in two rings.

'Yes boss?' he asked dutifully.

Pushing the guilt aside with difficulty, she forced herself to focus on the present.

'Meet me at The Hideout. I've got a job for you.'

FIVE

Flicking his cigarette away agitatedly, Connor blew out the last of the smoke in his lungs and glanced back through the window of the greasy café he stood outside. His gaze instinctively moved to the cheap plastic clock on the wall, the red second hand ticking impatiently away, telling him that the afternoon was nearly gone. Four thirty-six. Soon it would be the evening and then another Sunday would be gone. Another Sunday he'd spent away from his family.

His brown eyes slipped from the clock towards the four men in the corner, sitting around a table. They were the only ones inside. No one would disturb them. Even if the closed sign on the door didn't deter people, the two men blocking the door would. And Connor didn't need to put any extra effort into ensuring his expression was dark and unfriendly today.

'Got somewhere to be, 'ave ya, sunshine?' the man standing the other side of the door asked sarcastically.

Connor shot him a dirty look and pulled out another cigarette, ignoring the jibe. As he lit it, he tried to imagine what they were all doing right now. Lunch would be over and they'd probably be sat with a brandy. A whisky for his mother, if she was particularly stressed. Cillian would be making them all laugh with some anecdote.

He turned his back to the other man and stared stonily down the road. It wasn't that he was feeling sorry for himself. He'd known this would be a possible consequence of going to work with Ray.

It had never been an option before, leaving the firm. There had never even been a discussion about what he and Cillian might want to do next: their lives had been planned out for them pretty much since the day they were born. Lily had spent her life building them an empire to run and rule, and he'd always been grateful for that. He wasn't blind; he knew how much she'd sacrificed to do that. But after everything that had happened, he couldn't look her or Cillian in the eye every day. Not while the secret he carried for Scarlet was still so fresh. Not while it was all he could think of. He could hide his feelings from most people, but not from his twin. Cillian would know he was hiding something, and then he wouldn't let it go until he'd uncovered it.

Being a twin was so much more than just being a sibling. They were their own people, but they were also one and the same. It was like they had their own frequency, and all their thoughts, their movements, their silent understanding of each other on a deeper level than any other, all travelled along it. They'd never been able to hide their feelings from the other halves of themselves. So until he worked out a way to make peace with what he knew and put it far enough behind him that there was nothing for Cillian to see and dig into, he needed to stay away. For Scarlet's sake. For all of their sakes.

The door suddenly swung open behind him, and he turned to see Ray exiting the café, with Benny – one of his men and Scarlet's current boyfriend – right behind. Benny glanced back into the café as he buttoned up his suit jacket.

'What they doing?' Ray asked, his voice a low rumble. He

walked away without turning, and Connor fell into step behind them.

'Nothing. They're scared,' Benny replied. 'Dan looks like he's going to throw up.'

'Well, that says it all,' Ray responded grimly. 'It was all a front then, like I thought.'

The four of them crossed the road and got into Ray's car. Connor slipped into the back seat wondering what the meeting had been about. As he was only there to make up numbers and in case the need for muscle arose, he hadn't been told.

Benny started the car and pulled out into the street, and Connor watched the side of Ray's hard face from behind as he stared out of the window.

'Burn them to the ground,' Ray eventually said.

'Boss?' Benny queried with a quick glance at him.

'The kitchens. Burn them down. Tonight. Get everyone out first though. Ain't no need for anyone else to be harmed,' Ray clarified. 'Pull the sleeping beauty.'

Connor's eyebrows shot up in surprise. He might not know what had happened, but he knew what kitchens Ray was referring to, and they weren't the kind you found in restaurants. The two men Ray had met today ran one of the few successful drug factories in the country. They sold exclusively to Ray after he'd helped them make the transition from two men cooking up gear in a council-flat kitchen to running a full-on production in two fully kitted out off-grid locations. What could they possibly have done to anger Ray enough to burn down the source of his own supply?

'Connor, Brendan, be ready to go at midnight. Black camo, no faces,' Ray ordered.

Connor frowned. Black camo was the term he used for what they'd always called heist hear. Black clothes and leather gloves. And no faces meant balaclavas. This was serious.

'What they done?' he asked.

Next to him, Brendan snickered and shook his head. 'Christ – you don't ask, boy, you just *do*. Thought you were supposed to know the score?'

Annoyance flashed across Connor's features. 'If I'm burning someone's gaff down, I wanna know why,' he retorted sharply. 'I ain't *no one's* mindless minion. And watch who you're calling boy.'

'You *what?*' Brendan shot back, pulling himself up to full height in his seat. 'You jumped-up little—'

'Hey,' Ray cut in with a growl. 'I didn't bring you here to bicker like fucking schoolgirls. Shut up, the pair of ya.'

Ray leaned his elbow on the door and rubbed his forehead. Benny kept his gaze fixed on the road, wisely staying out of the conversation. Connor clenched his jaw and stared out at the road, supressing the urge to punch Brendan in the face.

When Ray had announced Connor was joining the firm, there hadn't been a great response from his men. Everyone knew who Connor was – he was one of the infamous Drews, a respected member of an ally firm. Many of them had worked alongside him, at some point or another, when the two firms teamed up. But Connor wasn't joining them as a Drew. He was joining them as Ray's son. As – in status, even if not in name – a Renshaw. And this was a situation none of them had ever expected to arise.

Ray had always been a lone wolf. He had no wife – because Lily had refused time and again to marry him and move down south. He'd had no children until recently, when he'd found out that Connor and Cillian were his. A fact Lily had kept hidden, until Cillian's life had hung in the balance and she'd needed Ray's blood to save him. So unlike most other firms, Ray's business model wasn't based around it working for family. It ran on loyalty and time served. It was a simple, fair hierarchy where everyone understood their place. The men in his inner circle had earned their way there. Those at the very top had worked their way up with the unspoken knowledge that they would take over one day. Because who else would?

Yet suddenly, Ray had pulled in this newfound son. A seasoned underworlder, in all fairness – but not one of them. Connor hadn't earned his stripes and climbed the same ladder they had, and neither would he have to. Ray had projected him not quite to the top, but not far off. Connor had been placed right into the inner circle, and it had caused quite a stir, even among those who'd previously liked him.

It was very clear how the men felt about it, but for the most part, Ray ignored it. At times he cut in with a curt shutdown, as he had just now. When one man had outright voiced his disapproval, Ray had publicly demoted him and reminded him – none too gently – that this was *his* firm. *He* was the boss here, and if any man decided they didn't want to follow his instruction, then they would no longer be welcome. It had been enough to deter anyone else from voicing the same concerns, but it hadn't dispelled the bad blood that was circling around Connor's arrival.

'Drop us all home,' Ray instructed Benny. 'Then send Rick out for everything we need and tell him to drop it by the house. You two, get some rest for the next few hours. It'll be a long night. Benny, you as well, then meet me at eleven to prepare.'

'Yes, boss,' Benny replied with a nod. He turned off the road, changing course towards Connor's flat.

Connor opened his mouth then closed it again. Ray hadn't answered his question. He still had no idea what these people had done, and that didn't sit well with him. He had no qualms about pulling this sort of job, but he needed to know it was justified.

A stab of frustration shot through him. Lily would never have expected him to do something like this without giving him a good reason. But as he was swiftly learning, Ray ran a very different firm to his mother's.

Fifteen silent minutes later, the car pulled up outside Connor's block of flats, and he immediately relaxed, glad to be back in familiar territory.

Benny caught Ray's eye. 'You OK to drive back?'

'Yeah, go on then,' Ray replied.

Connor opened the door then paused as Benny twisted to face him.

'Any chance you could drop me over to your cousin quick?' Benny asked.

''Course,' Connor replied reluctantly.

Gritting his teeth, he stepped out of the car. The last thing he wanted to do right now was run Benny around, but he couldn't exactly say no. He waited, kicking at a loose stone on the edge of the path, as Ray slipped into the driver's seat and pulled away.

Benny walked over, looking down at his phone as he sent off a text.

'You need to get your keys?' he asked without looking up.

'Nah, they're on me. Let's go.' Connor walked over to his car. 'Where you meeting her?'

It suddenly struck him that Benny may well be headed for Lily's house, and his stomach constricted. Lily was furious and she'd made her stance clear – Connor had abandoned them and that was the ultimate betrayal. She was ignoring him completely. If he turned up there now, at best it would be painfully awkward. At worst it could unfold into an explosive scene.

'The pub,' Benny said over the roof of the car as he opened the door.

Connor slipped into the driver's seat and exhaled in deep, silent relief. Even if Lily was there, he didn't need to go anywhere near the actual building.

He started the car, suddenly aware that Benny was watching him from the side.

'What?' he asked with a frown, his tone brusque.

Raising his eyebrows slightly, Benny looked away. Connor pulled out of the car park and swung the car into the throng of traffic crawling down the main road.

'Dan and Eric made a deal with a large crew over in Bristol,' Benny said, breaking the silence. He shook his head. 'Arranged to sell them everything they've got, all the stock from the last month of production.'

'Ray's stock?' Connor asked, confused. 'Why would they do that? What were they planning on telling him? Surely they ain't stupid enough to think he wouldn't find out?'

'Yeah, *our* stock,' Benny replied, putting emphasis on the subtle correction. 'And they weren't planning on being around when Ray found out.' He shifted in his seat. 'They'd asked for the money early this time. Gave some spiel about equipment needing replacing and cash flow. They planned on taking that cash from Ray, selling the stock – and most of the kitchen equipment we kitted them out with – to their new benefactors, and then disappearing. Apparently, the Bristol firm were going to hide them in their new underground lab for a while. They wanted the two of them to set it up and run the operation.'

'Sneaky bastards,' Connor replied in disbelief. 'Double the money on the drugs, and I bet the kit was worth a fortune.' He shook his head. 'They'd have made out with a nice little bubble there.'

'The story about needing the cash early was what tipped Ray off. It didn't add up,' Benny continued. 'So we did some digging and found out what they were doing. Today was just about checking one last bit of information.'

'Why burn the kitchens though?' Connor pressed. 'That don't hurt them; it wasn't their money that went into it.'

'It hurts 'em plenty.' Benny's tone darkened. 'You heard Ray. We're pulling the sleeping beauty.'

Connor paused, reluctant to admit that he didn't know what that meant. Each firm had their own codes for things, making it possible for them to discuss subjects freely without outsiders understanding, but each time he had to ask, it just highlighted the fact he wasn't really one of them.

Benny waited for a moment, then realisation flickered through his expression. 'You ever heard of mivacurium?' He raised an eyebrow, and Connor shook his head. 'Surgeons use it when they operate. It's half of a two-part anaesthetic. On its own it paralyses the body but not the mind, so surgeons add a second drug to knock 'em out.'

Connor thought back to Ray's earlier instruction. *Pull the sleeping beauty.* The dots suddenly connected.

'You're giving them that and leaving them in there to burn,' he said flatly.

'No,' Benny replied. '*We* are giving them that and leaving them in there to burn.'

Connor locked his jaw grimly. These wouldn't be the first people he'd killed and would unlikely be the last. But when he'd done it before, it had been to protect his family. The people he cared about most in the world. This time it was for Ray. And though he'd fully committed himself to this decision and would do what was required of him, he didn't feel that same loyalty or sense of rightness about it.

'How'd you find out?' Connor asked, changing the subject.

'That don't matter.' Benny dismissed the question. 'What matters is that they were about to steal a lot of money and goods and screw our whole E operation. So now you know. Alright?'

They'd reached the pub, and Connor pulled up on the road just outside the car park. Benny got out and shrugged on his suit jacket.

'Thanks,' Connor said, seeing the information Benny had

just given him for what it was. A subtle offer of help. 'I appreciate that.'

Benny leaned on the roof of the car and ducked his head back in. 'Yeah, well...' He trailed off and squinted through the back window. 'Just keep it to yourself.' He tapped the roof twice and straightened up. 'And be ready for twelve.'

He shut the door, and Connor's gaze slipped over to his brother's car on the far side of the car park. He felt an almost physical pull to his twin, but things were too strained between them right now, and even if they weren't, he'd clocked his mother's car, too, next to Cillian's.

Feeling lonelier than ever, Connor pulled away from the kerb, an uneasy sense of dread settling in as he turned his mind to what lay ahead of him tonight. It was one thing doing this sort of thing with people you trusted, but he was heading into this among people who wanted him to fail, and that made things a lot more dangerous. A lot could go wrong on a job like this. If it did, who would stick around to help him out? Or, the thought suddenly occurred to him, would someone use that kind of opportunity to leave him behind and get rid of him for good?

SIX

Mani Romano wheezed heavily as he walked down the road towards his sister's sprawling family home, feeling angry that he'd not been able to park closer to the house. His bushy eyebrows knotted, and his already drooping mouth turned down even more.

'Man of my age coming to visit and they don't even make space?' he muttered. 'No fucking respect for elders these days.'

In truth, Mani wasn't old at all, but anyone watching him wouldn't have been able to tell. The layers of excess weight that sagged around his middle and multiplied his chin, along with his sparse grey hair and the pallid skin that resulted from his unhealthy lifestyle, made him appear a good decade older than his sixty-odd years.

He was alone this morning, which was unusual for him. Like most leaders of London's criminal firms, he usually travelled with at least one of his men. More if there was a suspected threat. Most of the time he kept his son, Riccardo, by his side. The boy was set to take over from him one day, and for the last few years, Mani had proclaimed that he was semi-retired, there in an advisory role more than anything. Not that there was any truth to this. He still ran the firm with a stubbornly iron fist, unable to let go and trust the next generation. Today though, he'd come alone on purpose. And slipping away from Riccardo and his men hadn't been very hard, under the circumstances.

Mani had spent the night at the police station, after being detained for questioning the day before. A very uncomfortable night that he hadn't seen coming and which he was furious about. After they'd let him go this morning, he'd slipped off without telling anyone he was out. Because today he wanted to speak to his sister's boys alone.

Eventually reaching the sweeping front garden that was his sister's pride and joy, Mani scowled at the cars lined up next to each other on the drive, purposely banging against one or two of them as he passed. When he finally reached the door and pressed the bell, he was thoroughly hot and bothered, despite the early winter chill.

The door opened, and a tall man with dark hair, olive skin and attractive, well-defined features looked down at him in surprise.

'Mani,' he said in a deep, rich voice. 'What an unexpected surprise.'

Mani pulled out a handkerchief and patted the sweat from his forehead. 'Yes, well. It wouldn't be, Alessio, if you ever answered your phone,' he replied waspishly. 'Is this any way to treat your uncle? Move aside. Pour me a drink!'

'Come on in,' his nephew said.

It was said much less enthusiastically than Mani considered respectful, but he let it go. There were bigger issues at hand. He made a beeline for the casual lounge, where he could hear voices. Inside, his other nephew, Antonio, sat on one of three long sofas circling a wide wooden coffee table. Several of their men sat around him, discussing something with urgent tones. Mani scowled as he caught sight of Maria, his niece, sitting between two of the men, leaning forward and listening intently. She shouldn't be here. This type of business was not for women.

The discussion abruptly stopped as he entered the room, and all eyes turned to him. Antonio's gaze almost immediately flickered past his uncle to his brother, his frown deepening.

'Uncle.' He stood up. 'How are you?'

'I've been better,' Mani replied. 'But you're in the middle of a meeting.' He gestured around the room and held his hands in the air in brief apology. 'Carry on, *vai avanti*. I'll wait in the library.'

'Mani, what a nice surprise!'

He turned at the sound of his sister's voice and saw her hurrying through the house towards them, her hands in the air and a wide smile on her face.

'Hello, Elena,' he replied, kissing her on each cheek as she reached him.

'Alex,' she said, looking past him to her eldest son. 'Why don't you take your uncle through to the library and see what he needs, eh?' She looked back to him. 'I take it this isn't a social call?'

'It is not, I'm afraid,' he replied, hiding his irritation at the shortening of his nephew's name. He didn't agree with it. The boy's name was Alessio, not Alex. Alex didn't even sound Italian. This side of the family were starting to forget their roots.

'Of course,' Alex replied smoothly.

He ushered Mani through to the library, a room Mani had always privately mocked. They had no need for a library. He'd never seen any of them read even one of its many books. Though it did double up as an overly large office, so at least it got some use.

Alex took the leather chair behind the large chestnut desk, a seat that had belonged to his father before he'd passed away several years before. It had irked Mani that arrangements had not been made to hand his brother-in-law's firm over to him to manage, until his nephews were better placed to take over. This had grown into a larger firm than his own and though, in his opinion, that was all down to luck, he'd always felt bitter about it.

Mani took one of the matching leather tub chairs on the other side of the desk. Antonio took another, and it was then that Mani noticed Maria had followed them into the room. She moved to take the last seat, and he put a hand out to stop her.

'Maria, get us some drinks, will you? Grappa, if there is some. Whatever brandy you have if not,' he ordered.

Maria paused, one hand on the chair, then with a tight-lipped smile that didn't quite reach her hazel eyes, she turned and walked away to do his bidding. Mani waited until she'd left the room before speaking again with a shake of his head.

'Is there still no one on the horizon to marry that girl?' he asked the two men with a raised brow. 'Eh? Surely you can find her someone with your standing and her looks?'

Alex sighed. 'She'll find someone in her own time, Uncle, I'm sure.'

'But time is exactly what she doesn't have,' Mani argued. He tutted. 'What is she now? Thirty-two? Thirty-three?'

'Thirty-three,' Antonio replied, looking towards the long bay windows on the other side of the room, apparently uninterested.

'Exactly,' Mani told him. 'She is already in the winter of her child-bearing years. She needs a man *now*, before it is too late. She needs a family to occupy her too. A woman with nothing to keep her busy ends up in all kinds of mischief.'

'What can we do for you, Uncle?' Alex said, ignoring this.

Mani sighed but dropped the subject. He wasn't here to save his niece from becoming a spinster; he had much bigger problems.

'There have been some concerning developments

concerning an old enemy,' he said gravely. 'It's something you need to be aware of and prepare for.'

Both men frowned, and Alex leaned forward on the desk as the door to the library opened once more.

'What developments?' he asked. 'And what enemy?'

Maria laid a tray down on the desk with a bottle of grappa and four glasses. 'Enemy? What's happened?' she asked, her dark brows knitting together in concern.

'There is no need to worry, Maria,' Mani replied sharply. 'Your brothers and I will sort it out. Go and see if your mother needs any help in the kitchen, eh?'

Cold impatience flashed across Maria's face, and Mani was reminded how beautiful his niece was. Her golden-brown skin was flawless, high cheekbones dominating the shape of her face, and her strikingly bright hazel eyes were framed by thick dark lashes. She'd highlighted her long jet-black hair and wore it loose with soft waves. She was a touch taller than Mani thought attractive for a woman, but she had a good-enough figure that he'd wager most men would overlook it. Perhaps he would suggest some men to Elena for her, when he had the time.

'My mother is fine, thank you, Uncle,' Maria replied tersely. 'But it seems the rest of us may not be. So please continue.'

'Maria...' Mani said, tutting exasperatedly. 'I've told you before, this is *no* place for a woman. This is business, now please go along and help Elena. Or anything else, I don't care what, but I need the brains of *men*. Men who know what they are doing. Men who don't possess the simpleness and softness of women. Now please *go*.'

Alex made a sound of exasperation. 'Whoa, OK, that's—'

'Don't,' Maria cut him off sharply. 'It's a waste of time.' She sighed and rubbed her forehead with a look of exasperation. 'I'll be in the lounge.'

Picking up the bottle of grappa, she poured herself a large glass then took it with her out of the room.

Mani waited until the door closed then dived straight back to the point. 'Have you heard about your great-aunt Giulia's house?' he asked.

'Of course. It would be hard to miss. It's been all over the news,' Antonio replied.

'Do you know what they found inside?' Mani watched as the brothers shared a look.

'We do, but the body wasn't one of ours. We assumed it was yours,' Alex replied.

Mani reached for the grappa and poured himself a large measure. 'Not exactly.'

Alex frowned. 'Who else would put a body in Great-Aunt Giulia's wall?'

'Well, I put it there, but it wasn't mine.' Mani tipped half the contents of his glass into his mouth and then exhaled heavily. 'Ten years ago we made a move to expand our territory. There was a small firm next to ours, three brothers running it. It was an easy takeover. We knew of a hit they were planning and got intel about when and where. We got there early, set up a camera and hid.'

He downed the rest of his drink, then rolled the empty glass around in his hand, eying the bottle of grappa. Antonio got up and poured him another one, nodding at him to continue.

'The brothers turned up and things got heated between them all, then eventually they shot the guy and put him in a body bag.' Mani sipped his drink this time, savouring the fiery liquid as it warmed his throat.

'And then?' Alex urged.

'We surrounded them. We had more men, more guns. We took the body and gave them a choice – leave the country and start over elsewhere, or have the body, recording and their gun dropped off to the police.' Mani shuffled in his seat, feeling uncomfortable as both brothers raised their eyebrows.

'That's a dirty move,' Alex said, his disapproval clear.

'It was,' Mani admitted, holding his hands up in acceptance. 'But those were different times, and it isn't one I'm proud of.'

Alex eyed him for a moment. 'Go on.'

'Finn, the one holding the gun, was too close to the water. He threw it in before we realised what he was doing, so then we only had the body and recording.' Mani shrugged. 'It was unfortunate, but he was gloved anyway. Before the shooting though, one of the others had grabbed the man they'd killed by the neck and spat in his face. He *wasn't* gloved, so his DNA was all over the body. They had no choice – they took the offer and moved to Spain.'

Antonio tilted his head. 'Wait, is this the turf you gained and then the Drews took from you?'

Mani's face clouded over. 'Yes,' he growled. 'They took it back for their friends, they claimed. Though even now they run it as their own. Pious fucking vultures.'

Memories of Lily and Ronan Drew storming his office with a small army and forcing the handover flashed through his mind, and his anger began to swell.

'So it was the body you took from the Logans?' Alex asked, pulling him back to the point.

'Yes.' Mani pushed his hatred of the Drews to the side. 'And I fear the Logans are behind the fire. They must have somehow found out and set fire to it, to burn out any last traces of their DNA. After ten years, any left would have been fragile.'

'But the recording, surely you kept that somewhere else?' Alex prompted. 'Surely they wouldn't be so stupid as to uncover their own victim when their enemy holds the footage of them pulling the trigger?' Alex searched Mani's face. 'No, Uncle. You're being paranoid.'

'I'm *not*,' Mani insisted. 'Yes, the footage is in my personal safe. But it's useless. When I watched it back, it hadn't captured anything that would stand up. The lens was blurred. No faces, no features. But I *know* it's them. They left a calling card.' He rubbed his heavily lined forehead, stressed.

'What kind of calling card?' Antonio asked.

'The Logans always liked a petrol bomb. They hit many places in their time, always the same way. A sequence of small explosions to ensure maximum coverage. And they always used bubble wrap as a funnel for the initial ignition. They left the bubble wrap behind. That's their calling card.'

Alex looked at Antonio, who pulled a grim expression.

'So you believe they're back,' Alex stated. 'How could they know the body was there?'

'That's what concerns me. There's no way they could have known. The only people who knew were myself, Aunt Giulia and the seven there that night. Aunt Giulia wouldn't have told a soul, four of the men there that night are dead and the other three I trust implicitly. Even if I didn't, it's too dangerous for them. It makes no sense.' Mani sipped at the grappa again, his eyes darting between his two nephews.

'No one else knew – at all?' Alex checked.

'No one. Not even your father. They knew we took over and that we lost it to the Drews, but the details were never spoken about.'

There was a short silence as the two younger men processed the information. Alex picked up the grappa and poured generous measures into the remaining two glasses, passing one to Antonio, then sipping from his own before replying.

'I'm sorry to hear of your troubles, Uncle,' he said carefully. 'We'll ask around, see if we can find anything out for you.'

Mani nodded. 'Good, good.' He shuffled forward on his seat and eased himself up, placing his empty glass back on the tray. 'Keep in touch. And watch yourselves. We may run two separate firms, but we are one family. They're unlikely to note the difference.'

Leaving his nephews in the library, he paused only to say

goodbye to his sister and niece, then swiftly departed, thinking the conversation over on the long walk back to his car. This visit had been successful. The Logans may be a small firm, but they had a lot of friends here still, and they were ruthless men with a grudge that had been building for ten years. Mani wouldn't be able to win whatever fight was coming on his own. He needed the strength of his late brother-in-law's firm behind him – and it seemed he'd got it. Not that he'd ever thought he wouldn't have. They were family after all.

His phone rang, and he pulled it out of his pocket.

'Riccardo.'

'Where are you?' came the irate response. 'I came to the station to find out what was taking so long to release you; they said you left nearly two hours ago!'

'I had some business that couldn't wait,' Mani replied vaguely. Riccardo would need to be told but not over the phone. 'Meet me at the café; I'll fill you in.'

'You have a car?' his son asked.

'Yes, I'll be there in half an hour,' Mani confirmed.

There was a short pause and then a sound of irritation. 'Ach... Next time, take someone with you.'

'Eh, I'm still the head of this firm – watch yourself,' Mani retorted sharply.

There was a tightness in his son's tone when he replied. 'Yes, of course. See you there. We have a lot to discuss.'

'What?' Mani asked, glancing behind him to make sure he was alone.

'The house – it's empty. As in *empty* empty.'

Mani's step slowed to a stop. 'What do you mean?'

'They're not just keeping a low profile. All the clothes are gone, the fridge is empty and the gas is switched off. No clues left behind,' Riccardo replied.

Mani bit his lip and squinted into the distance. 'Where the hell are they?'

'I think he's taken them underground,' Riccardo said.

Mani shook his head. 'No. He was happy to do the job; it was a simple one for him. And good money too. The threat to the girl and her mother was just a precaution.' He frowned. 'And he was too hard to spook. It makes no sense.'

For months they'd been running a scam on the Drews, syphoning off thousands from the profits of their underground fight nights as revenge for the many wrongs the other firm had done to them. They'd lived in grudging harmony for most of the last decade, after agreeing to a truce. But a few years before, when Mani had loosened the reins on the firm and allowed his two sons some more responsibility, his younger son, Luca, had tried to sneak in and take over some of the Drews' protection clients. It had been a stupid move, but when the Drews had caught him, they'd inflicted a harsh punishment. The situation had escalated, and the resulting blow had left Luca in a position that lost him the respect of all the men in their firm – and, indeed, the rest of the underworld. Only the strongest of men could recover from a situation like that, and Luca was sadly not among them. In one blow, the Drews had stripped the credibility of one of his only two heirs. And that had been the last straw.

Over the last few months, the Romanos had gathered information on all their fights and had run their own bets with better odds, stealing their business from right under their noses. Mani had been smart about how he'd gone about it, hiring a man unknown to the underworld. A man who'd been part of the most elite group of marine commandos in the country. He ran the bets and was then set, once the Drews finally clicked, to kill them off one by one. Mani had ordered him to hit Lily last, so that he could watch her fear and devastation as everyone and everything she loved was taken from her. And once they were gone, Mani was ready to claim their territory as his own.

But Robert, the man he'd hired, had disappeared into thin

air a couple of weeks ago. They'd searched high and low and found nothing. To ensure things went to plan, as Robert was an outsider, they'd made it clear that they knew where his ex lived with their daughter, and that they would pay the price if Robert decided to back out of their deal. But he'd never thought he'd need to use it. Robert was a professional. They'd gone over there a couple of times, but no one had been home, and today, after two weeks of no contact, he'd lost patience and sent Riccardo to break in and dig around. To hear they'd disappeared was concerning.

'You're sure the Drews haven't cottoned on?' Riccardo asked. 'Perhaps they caught him.'

'No. They're clueless. You were there when we went to her casino night; you saw that curly-haired viper. Pouring us drinks, asking after my health...' Mani trailed off with a sound of disgust. 'They don't know a thing.'

'Then I don't know what to think,' Riccardo admitted.

Mani pulled a grim expression. 'We need to figure it out and get this plan back on track.' He started walking towards his car once more with a grimly determined expression. 'I'm done waiting. We need to speed this up. It's high time we wiped those smug bastards off the face of the planet and make sure that by the time anyone realises what's happened, they're nothing but dust.'

SEVEN

Connor turned over in bed, his body still heavy with sleep. He lay with his eyes closed for a few minutes, allowing the cogs in his brain to start up at their own pace as he turned over the events of the night before in his mind. He'd been anxious, going in there surrounded by frenemies – men who could have been tempted to throw him under the bus, had things gone south – but luckily it had all run smoothly. When they'd arrived, the two condemned men were already trussed up in the back of a van, and when they'd stormed the underground kitchens, the workers running the late-night production line had scattered without a fight.

He'd watched the two struggling men slow to complete still-ness as the drug Benny administered took swift effect. Their bindings had been removed, and they were placed against the wall facing the open door, one last mockery in the last minutes of their lives. They made no sound, but their eyes were wide open, the raw fear and desperation there louder than any words could have been.

They'd left no trace behind. As per Ray's instruction, they'd arranged a number of chemicals around the two men, then tipped over a barrel of one of the more flammable liquids. They waited for it to spread down towards the entrance, then after placing a load of cigarette butts they'd found around the corner there, they'd dropped a lit match. The place had gone up in seconds.

After that, they'd cleared their tracks in the usual way – careful routes, burned clothes – and the first tinge of daylight had begun to water down the darkness as he'd finally collapsed into bed.

He wasn't working today. Other than Benny, Ray had told all of them to take the day off. Deciding to use the day to do absolutely nothing, Connor turned back over and buried his head in the pillow, allowing the fuzziness of sleep that still clawed at the edges of his mind to pull him back in.

It was just as his consciousness was about to slip into the comfort of nothingness that a sound jarred him awake. For a moment he didn't react, not quite with it, but then some instinct tugged at his brain in warning. He lifted his head and squinted towards the bedroom door.

What was that? He'd probably just imagined it, he decided. His mind was playing tricks on him.

Laying his head back down, he closed his eyes but listened out for a few moments more, just to be sure.

Chink.

Connor sat up, alert now, twisting his body around and swinging his legs out in one swift, silent movement. He tensed, his sharp brown eyes shooting to the partially open door. Whoever that was wasn't here for a friendly visit. No one ever broke in somewhere because they had *good* intentions.

Careful not to make a sound, Connor quickly threw on a pair of tracksuit bottoms and dropped to the floor, pulling out the bottom drawer of his bedside table. With one eye on the door, he reached in and grabbed the switchblade taped to the back. He tested the weight and stood up, then approached the door cautiously, adrenaline coursing through his veins. He had no idea who was out there, but that didn't matter. Whoever it was, he wasn't about to make this easy for them.

Checking the hallway was empty, he slipped out and padded silently to the corner that led off to the open-plan living space beyond. His heart thudded in his chest, and he steeled himself, raising his switchblade in readiness before peering round with a grim, wary expression.

As his eyes scanned the room, his gaze narrowed and his brow furrowed. The big leather recliner that usually faced the coffee table in the middle of the room had been turned to face the windows, and steam from what had to be a hot drink drifted up from one side. They'd come alone, he realised. But his mind wasn't eased by this. That sort of confidence was usually paired with a gun. Which meant his one hope was to disarm them with his knife before they realised he was awake.

He moved slowly, his heart beating hard against the wall of his chest, and his survival instincts took over. He mentally calculated the distance between them. *Fifteen feet. Twelve... Ten...*

'Of all the things I thought I'd uncover by snooping around in here, the fact you have an actual subscription to *Good House-keeping* magazine was definitely not one of them.'

Connor released a heavy breath and sagged in relief as the soft Mancunian accent registered.

'What the *fuck* are you doing, Isla?' he demanded accusingly, flipping his blade away and slipping it into his pocket as he rounded the chair. 'Seriously, I was about to put a *knife* to your throat.' He put his hands to his face and rubbed his eyes with a groan of annoyance.

Isla smirked, amused, and closed the magazine on her lap.

'No you weren't,' she replied. 'You're not as ninja as you think. I heard you from the door.'

'That ain't the point,' Connor replied, angry now. 'You don't break into people's homes while they sleep. I thought you were here to do me harm – and with good reason! There are enemies everywhere – you *know* that. What are you even *doing* here?'

'Sorry. I didn't mean to scare you. I came by to talk to you. I saw your car and figured you were here, so I came up. Then when you didn't answer, I called your phone, and I could hear it ringing inside, but you still weren't answering, so then I started to worry that something was wrong...'

She put the magazine down on the coffee table next to her drink and stood up, clasping her hands together awkwardly. 'I'm sorry. It just didn't seem right, and I knew if I didn't check and then found out later that someone had you tied up in here or something and I'd just left, I'd never forgive myself. So I broke in and found you asleep, then figured I'd just wait until you woke up as I was already here.' She twisted her mouth to one side and shrugged.

Connor shook his head, his frown relaxing and his anger seeping away. Running a hand back through his shock of dark hair, still messy from sleep, he glanced back towards the front door.

'How'd you even get in? That door's practically impenetrable.' Which was exactly the reason he'd had it fitted. But apparently it couldn't even keep a skinny five-foot-nothing little imp like Isla out.

A smile briefly fluttered across her face and then she turned her deep brown eyes away. 'It's a skill of mine.'

Connor nodded. Isla had lived in the underworld for many years before she'd joined their firm. Some of it they knew about – the parts they needed to. The rest she mainly kept to herself. One thing he'd learned was that her skills were vast and finely tuned.

He scratched his head. 'I'd offer you a drink, but I can see you've already helped yourself.'

'Tea,' she confirmed, picking the cup back up and taking a sip. She watched him over the rim, relaxed again now that he was too. 'You're out of sugar.'

'Right. I'll get some,' he replied, bemused.

Isla took another sip, and her eyes flickered down to his torso. Realising he was still barely half dressed, Connor padded back to the bedroom and slipped on his gym hoodie, zipping it halfway up.

Isla was staring at the cover of the magazine she'd been reading when he returned, and she looked up at him with a quizzical expression. '*Good Housekeeping* though? *Really?*'

'What, a bloke can't have an interest in his own home? They have good life hacks and tips in there,' he replied, crossing his arms over his middle defensively. He shrugged and sniffed. 'And I like the recipe pages. Everyone has to eat.'

Isla's face softened, and a smile began to spread before she swiftly contained it. 'Oh, I totally agree. I think they're great.'

Connor tilted his head in moody acknowledgement. 'Well, don't go telling no one,' he said gruffly. 'That's personal. And it wouldn't do me any favours.'

Yawning, he walked to the kitchen area on the far side of the living area and turned on his coffee machine. He hadn't had enough sleep or caffeine to be dealing with anyone right now.

'What did you want to talk to me about?' he asked, pulling a mug out of the cupboard.

Isla walked over and hovered on the other side of the long breakfast bar. Her smile disappeared and a more troubled expression replaced it.

'Your family think you're not coming back,' she said, a touch reluctantly.

'I'm not,' he replied, working to keep his voice steady as his heart dropped. 'Not for a while anyway.' He turned his back to her to make his coffee, hiding his misery.

'What's a while?' Isla asked. 'A week? A month?'

'I'm not sure, but definitely longer than that.'

'But they *need* you,' she retorted, sounding distressed. 'Things are falling apart without you.'

Connor laughed, the sound coming out more bitter than he'd intended. 'They don't need me, Isla. Cillian and Scarlet were already running anything that Mum wasn't, long before I left. And they've got the men. They've got *you*,' he added. 'There's nothing I was doing that you and the others can't do.'

'That's not true,' Isla argued, shaking her head vehemently at him as he turned back to face her. 'And I know you know that. Scarlet and Cillian are stretched too thin now they've taken on your jobs too. Because they *can't* trust most of it to anyone outside the family, and the parts they can, they don't have the time to teach people. I'm picking up as much as I can, but they're struggling, Connor.'

'They'll be fine,' he said, brushing it off. 'They're good at this. Trust me, it might seem chaotic, but they'll figure it out.'

'Don't you *care* anymore?' she demanded, her cheeks flushing red as she stared at him accusingly. 'They're your family – and they're *good* family. Family that love you, who always protect you no matter what. Don't you *want* to help them and be part of it all?'

Connor faltered, surprised at the sudden turn in the conversation.

'I'd kill to have the family you do,' she continued. 'And you just walked away from them. I don't get it.'

The stark reminder of all he was missing was like a wire barb to the heart. 'That ain't your business,' he snapped.

'Actually it is,' Isla retorted, sticking her chin out stubbornly. 'I might not be part of your family, but I'm part of the firm. What about your brother? Or your mum?'

'They're *fine*,' Connor snarled, louder this time as his temper took hold. 'And you're *way* out of line now. You don't speak for them. If they want to speak to me, they know where I am, but they *haven't*. Because they're more than capable. They always have been. It's just business.'

'Right, because they're the only people it affects, yeah? And it's all just about work for you, isn't it?' Isla shouted back miserably. 'What about the fact someone they love dearly has just up and left them, eh? The people who *love* you, who're used to having you in their daily lives suddenly have to accept that you've just pissed off and left them without a second thought, do they?' Her eyes glistened as they filled with angry tears, and she leaned forward. 'How do you think that feels? For your mum, for your brother, for *me*.'

She caught herself, suddenly pulling back and pressing her lips together tightly. It took Connor a second to catch up with her reaction, and his frown deepened.

'For *you*?'

Isla stared at him, her expression trembling with a mixture of anger and hurt and horror, then without another word, she turned and fled.

'Isla!' Connor called after her, but she didn't stop.

As the front door closed behind her, he lifted his arms and dropped them in defeat, utterly flummoxed. Isla *loved* him? He knew she'd always seen him as a friend, but *loved*? He thought back to a conversation he'd had with Cillian. He'd teased him about Isla once. But perhaps it hadn't been a tease at all; perhaps he'd been serious.

And was it true? he wondered. *Were his family really struggling?* Guilt flooded through him as he thought it over. He knew his mother would be too proud and stubborn to tell him if that *was* the case, but surely Cillian or Scarlet would speak up if they needed his help. *Wouldn't they?*

Placing his freshly made coffee on the counter, Connor

exhaled heavily and pinched the bridge of his nose. Every fibre of his being wanted to call Cillian and ask him directly. But he couldn't. Things were so strained between them, and what difference would it make? If it *was* true and Cillian hadn't told him, he wouldn't admit it now. But still, he was worried.

He picked up his phone, opened his texts and found the last message from his brother. His thumb hovered over the keypad, and he stared down at the flashing line in the empty content bar for almost a full minute. There was so much he wanted to say that he either couldn't or wouldn't, and the words circled around and around in his head almost screaming in their intensity.

I miss you so much.
I wish I could come back, but I can't.
I did this for your own good.
I did it because I love you.
I feel so lost. I'm so unhappy. I wish Mum would talk to me.
I've never been so lonely.

But he would never say any of that. With deep sadness etched into his face, he began to type.

Hitting the gym at 4 p.m. Need some practice if you're up for a spar.

He pressed send, then grabbed his coffee and sat on one of the bar stools. He slumped forward glumly, propping himself up on his elbows and resting his head on his fists. It was only just gone twelve. He had no idea what he was going to do with the rest of his day. He knew he wouldn't sleep now, not after Isla's visit.

His phone vibrated beside him, and he grabbed it quickly, opening Cillian's reply with bated breath.

Sure. See you there.

His heart lifted instantly, and he closed his eyes in relief. Nothing had changed, but he was at least going to see his brother today. That was something.

EIGHT

Scarlet pressed the pause button on the remote just as the man they'd been following on the CCTV tape turned his face into full view.

'There,' she said, her deep red lips hardening into a grim line. 'That's him.'

Lily narrowed her eyes at the screen, taking another drag on the cigarette. She leaned back in her leather office chair and crossed her slim legs.

'I don't know how we missed him,' she mused.

'They came at strategic times, always with a crowd.' Scarlet shrugged. 'It's not something we thought to watch for.'

'No.' Lily furrowed her eyebrows and took one more drag of her cigarette before stubbing it out. 'We'll have to deal with him as well. Make an example. But not yet.'

He was one of Romano's men who'd come along with Riccardo to their matches. They'd always arrived at the busiest time, and now it was clear that it was so this particular man could veer off unnoticed, once inside. He'd been spying on their betting booth and collecting information.

'We need to move soon.' Scarlet pulled out the seat on the

opposite side of Lily's desk and sat down, resting her elbows on the arms of the chair and lacing her fingers together. 'They must know by now that Robert's gone. It's only a matter of time before they start suspecting our friendly façade is fake, or before they try something else.' She shook her head, her grey-blue eyes roaming the face on the screen. 'Who is he anyway?'

'Andre. He does a lot of intel gathering for them. Not bad with a security system either,' Lily replied.

'So he's their Bill?' Scarlet queried.

'No.' Lily's reply was instant. 'He's not a patch on Bill. That's like comparing a twenty-year-old Ford Fiesta to a brand-new Rolls Royce.'

The corner of Scarlet's mouth hitched up in a brief half-smile.

Bill Hanlon was their go-to man for anything to do with information, security or black-market tech. He contracted through the underworld with any firm on the same side as the infamous Tylers, who he was loyal to above all, and had been instrumental in many of the Drews' grifts over the years.

'We will make a move on the Romanos,' Lily said, answering Scarlet's earlier concern. 'But we need to talk to the Logans first. We're meeting with them in a couple of hours. They're running against them too, and I think it would make more sense to run together. Our interests are aligned, and we could do with the numbers.'

Scarlet nodded dutifully while she wondered whether to voice her concerns. It was all well and good that the Logans were here now, but they lived in Spain and would return there after this play was run. What then? The Romanos had loyal men and were connected by blood to another much larger firm.

'We could do with the numbers, yeah. But I'm guessing whatever they have in mind is big, and big comes with consequences,' she replied.

Scarlet assessed her aunt, trying to gauge her mood. Lily

was the one person she respected more than anyone else in the world, but she was also someone Scarlet had learned to tread very carefully around. She didn't want to touch a nerve, but the path they were about to go down was dangerous for all of them, and they needed to make sure they were adequately covering their backs.

'We have the numbers to protect ourselves,' Lily replied. 'The entire underworld has seen our growth this last year. This allegiance will help us get what we want without stretching those of us holding up the businesses too far, and then the men who now work for us will make sure we're protected from any fallout. But I'm sure it won't come to that.' Lily reached for her packet of cigarettes and lit another one. 'The appearance of strength often does more than the muscle behind it. That should be enough of a deterrent.'

'What about his niece and nephews?' Scarlet countered. 'It's family. It doesn't matter how strong we look, they'll *have* to do something about it.'

Lily's mouth twisted, and she shook her head with a thoughtful wince. 'I don't know. There's the chance they could look the other way. They're family, yes, but the two firms are completely separate. Mani's sister married into that firm, and she's always stayed out of it. Her husband never had much time for Mani. Still, there was never any bad blood.' She took a thoughtful drag and blew the smoke upwards towards the ceiling. 'Realistically we can't gauge it. We've never done business with any of them so don't know them well enough to predict their move.'

Scarlet frowned. 'So what, we just wait and see if they want to come at us down the line?'

'We prepare for every outcome.' Lily raised her eyebrows with a grim expression and spoke frankly. 'We're lucky we stumbled across their plan. If we hadn't, we'd all be dead by now. They weren't testing the waters; they hired a trained killer to fleece us and take us out. We're already on borrowed time. As you pointed out yourself, they'll regroup and try again soon if we don't strike first. The fact we don't know whether or not another firm will take offence is the least of our worries right now.'

'I know,' Scarlet agreed. 'But it's still a worry we need to think about.' She took a deep breath before speaking her next words. 'We have allies, Lil. We don't need to prepare for the fallout alone.'

Lily immediately tensed, her chin lifting and her mouth pursing into a cold hard line.

Scarlet continued quickly, knowing her time to do so was coming to a close. 'I know you're still angry, but Ray has always been our closest ally. Together, we—'

'*Together* is what this family unit was before Ray slithered in and stole a piece away for himself,' Lily snapped, her deadly tone so low and angry that it was almost a growl. '*Together* is what this firm would still be, had he not worked tirelessly for months trying to convince one of my sons – *either* of them, that is; he didn't care which – to leave us and put their skills, that *I* taught them, to use in his *own* firm.' White-hot anger flashed across her face as she stared at Scarlet across the desk. 'The son I brought into this world. *I* carried, *I* raised, *I* protected.' She bit her top lip and shook her head, looking away. 'Ray isn't an ally; he's a snake in the grass.'

Scarlet shook her head back. 'No, Lil,' she said quietly. 'He hasn't done this to hurt you. His way of going about it was shitty, but he didn't have bad intentions.'

Lily stood up and slammed her hands down on the desk, glaring down at Scarlet. 'This ain't *Dr Phil*, Scarlet. We're not here to talk about our feelings and debate intentions; we're here to run a fucking business.'

Her loud outburst quietened, but the cold intensity in her eyes and words remained. 'You're a clever girl and that's why your opinions are welcomed and valued in the firm, but issues surrounding my sons and their father are *my* business, and mine alone.' Without breaking her cold glare, she stood up straight and put the cigarette still balanced between her fingers to her mouth. She sucked in a deep breath full of smoke and blew it out slowly. 'While I'm the head of this firm, Ray isn't up for discussion.'

As Lily turned away to shake the moment off, Scarlet shook her head. Lily was a strong woman – the strongest she knew – but sometimes that strength was her own undoing. She'd had to fight behind impenetrable armour for so long that sometimes she placed the wrong people on the other side of it.

She didn't blame her. Lily was only human, and humans made mistakes. But this mistake was beginning to cost them much more than they could afford. How much more would it cost before she finally woke up to the risk she was forcing them all to take? Or was this the mistake that would eventually cost them everything?

NINE

Crossing her arms over her chest as she looked out into the back garden, Lily took a deep drag on her cigarette. Sometimes it felt as though her chest was just a hollow void until she filled it with smoke. It was a space that used to be fit to burst with all the emotions and responsibilities that came with her children. She used to think it would remain that way forever, yet here she was, not even fifty years old, and she was down from three of them to only one.

Her only daughter was dead. Her youngest son had abandoned them. Only Cillian was left, and he was on the cusp of settling down with Billie. They'd have children of their own someday, and then he would be too busy to make time for her anymore. Who would she have then?

Catching her maudlin thoughts, she chastised herself. She was being pathetic. She had a lot in her life – and even if she didn't, she didn't really expect her children's lives to revolve around her. All she'd ever wanted was for them to be happy and safe, and to be able to support them from the sidelines. That was her job after all. But it *had* been a difficult couple of years, and the hollowness Ruby's death had carved out in her chest never seemed to diminish.

Right now, more than ever, she needed to keep her sons close. She needed to protect them. It was the only way she could keep moving forward and ease her constant fear of losing them too. But Ray had taken Connor from her, and with him the ability to do just that. She had no idea what danger surrounded him now. And Ray couldn't keep Connor safe the way she did. *Nobody* could protect her sons the way she could. No one would go to the same lengths. And so she wandered this big empty house most nights, unable to rest. Unable to let go of the worry that something bad was going to happen to Connor, and that she wouldn't be there to stop it. Just as she hadn't been there for Ruby.

The grief threatened to engulf her again, and Lily squeezed her eyes shut for a moment, before opening the back door and stepping out into the cold. The icy air hit her body like a wall, shocking her system just enough to jolt her out of her spiralling thoughts. She took a deep breath in and focused on the meeting ahead.

The Logans would arrive any moment. Cillian, Scarlet and Isla too. And this was a meeting she really needed to go well. She wasn't blind to the precarious position they were in. The worries Scarlet had voiced earlier in the day had been keeping her up at nights long before now. But Scarlet didn't know as much as she thought she did. She didn't know Ray like Lily did. Closing her eyes, she raised her tired pale face to the sun and pushed her tight blonde curls back off her face.

A sound behind alerted her to the fact she was no longer alone, and she turned expectantly.

'Hey.' Scarlet stepped out and wrapped her arms around her slim frame, rubbing her upper arms against the cold.

Lily stubbed her cigarette out in her garden ashtray. 'Is Cillian with you?'

She walked back inside, holding the door for Scarlet.

'No, he's picking up Isla.'

They went through the house to the kitchen, and Scarlet cast a furtive glance at Lily's face as she passed her. 'You OK?' she asked, turning the coffee machine on.

'I'm fine,' Lily replied. 'Update me on the factory. I meant to ask you earlier – has it got any better with Isla helping out?'

Scarlet pulled a tight expression. 'Ye-es...'

'But?' Lily prompted with a frown.

'But things up north aren't going well,' Scarlet admitted grimly, pulling all of Lily's best mugs out from the back of the cupboard. 'So sooner or later we're going to have to send her back up to help Jaz sort things out. And with Isla gone, we'll be back at square one.' Scarlet turned her troubled grey-blue eyes towards Lily. 'I think we need to consider promoting Joe.'

'No.' Lily shook her head and pursed her lips. 'Connor won't stay with Ray. He'll be back; we just need to keep the businesses running between us until then.'

'Lil, he can't turn back now,' Scarlet said, grimacing. 'The whole underworld is watching him.'

'Right now, sure, but they'll lose interest soon,' Lily argued. 'Whatever carrot Ray dangled will lose its charm, and he'll come home.'

Scarlet shook her head. 'There's no carrot Ray could dangle that would ever be juicy enough to entice him away if he didn't want to leave. You know how stubborn he is.' She turned away. 'Whatever his reasons, Connor wanted to go.'

Lily frowned as Scarlet's words brought forth a realisation. She was right. Not about Connor wanting to go; Lily knew him: he loved his family too much to want to leave. But there *wasn't* anything Ray could offer that would entice him away. No amount of money or power in the world was worth more to Connor than his family. All this time she'd assumed Ray had lured him away with something too good to turn down, and been so caught up in her rage that she hadn't paused to consider that it could have been something much darker. Did Ray have something over him? Was he threatening him? Her blood ran cold. That *had* to be it.

A car pulled up on the drive, and a second later, the front door opened. Filing this horrifying thought away to deal with later, Lily smoothed her expression just as Cillian and Isla walked in.

'The Logans have just pulled up on the road. I left the door open,' Cillian said, pausing to peck her on the cheek before reaching past her to take the mug of coffee Scarlet held out to him. 'Ta.'

'Great. Good.' Lily nodded. 'Isla, did you find anything?'

Isla's brown eyes glinted with promise as she nodded. 'I certainly did.'

'Good. Save it for now; let's see what they're thinking before we share anything,' Lily ordered.

'Got it.' Isla slipped over to the side of the room just as the three Logan brothers appeared in the hallway.

Lily plastered on a wide smile and walked across to them. 'Finn, Sean, Cormac, it's good to see you.'

'And you, Lil.' Finn met her with a warm half hug and a kiss on the cheek.

They all greeted each other with the ease of old friends, and Scarlet busied herself making everyone coffees as they caught up.

Sean took a sip of his. 'Mm, this is good stuff.' He nodded to her appreciatively.

'Well, it's no Black Ivory, but it certainly tastes good to me,' Cillian replied wryly.

'Eh? What's that when it's at home?' Cormac asked.

'Don't worry – you don't want to know,' Cillian replied with a grin.

He caught Lily's eye, and her mouth briefly hitched in

shared amusement. Their latest mark had been a very odd snobby woman who only bought coffee beans collected from elephant dung, as it was the most expensive coffee in the world.

'Right,' she said, looking around the room. 'Let's take this through to the office, shall we? This way.'

She led the way through the house towards the large second reception room she used as a home office and comfortable meeting room.

Settling into the high-backed armchair she favoured, Lily crossed her legs and laced her fingers together over her knee as she waited for everyone else to be seated. The knee-length black leather skirt and turtleneck she wore was her usual signature look, but today the stark contrast with her unusually pale complexion lent her an extra hardness, along with the dark rings below her eyes and taut stress in every feature. Something she felt acutely aware of as she caught Finn assessing her thoughtfully. He looked away and cleared his throat.

'Right. We all know why we're here.' He sat forward, resting his elbows on his thighs. 'We're in the unique position of sharing the same enemy at the same time, and we're both looking to collect their very hefty dues.' He shared a grim look with his brothers. 'The Romanos fucked us over ten years ago. Took everything from us. Our territory, our businesses, they drove us out of our homes and even the fucking country.' His lip curled in disgust. 'Our hands were completely tied. If we'd fought back in any way, we'd currently be enjoying a very long stretch at Her Majesty's pleasure, but things have changed.'

'How so?' Lily asked, reaching for her cigarettes.

She offered one to each of the brothers. Finn accepted and stood up to light hers before his own.

'Bill Hanlon sent us the piece of the puzzle we've been missing all these years,' Sean replied, his craggy voice softened by the same Irish accent his brothers had also somehow failed to lose, despite the fact they hadn't seen Ireland in decades.

Lily frowned. 'The house?'

'You caught that?' Cormac asked with a proud smirk. 'You always were sharper than any other tool in this city, Lil.'

'What house?' Cillian asked, confused.

'Well, your calling card was hard to miss,' Lily replied with a wide casual shrug.

'The way Mani forced us out went against all our ways,' Finn explained, directing his words towards the three of them who hadn't been around at the time. 'We had a situation that needed to be dealt with. It had gone too far to do anything other than kill the man in question. The whys don't matter.' He scratched his head. 'We had it all set up, got there, did what we needed to, then before we could clean up, Mani and his men appeared.'

'They had us surrounded,' Sean continued. 'Took the body and hid it, then threatened to drop it to the police if we didn't up and leave the country for good.'

'*What?*' Cillian's face was aghast.

Scarlet's eyes widened in shock, then she frowned. 'What proof did they have that it was you though?'

'Finn did actually cotton on just in time to chuck his gun in the river,' Cormac answered. 'He was gloved up too.'

'But Sean wasn't, and his DNA was on the body,' Finn continued. 'He'd got angry and grabbed the guy. Spat in his face too.' Sean had dropped his gaze, and Finn looked over to him sympathetically. 'It wouldn't have been an issue if things had run to plan. We'd have covered those tracks one way or another. But when Mani showed up...' He held his hands out hopelessly and sighed.

'So he had the body, Sean's DNA and some footage of the three of us walking into the area,' Cormac summarised. 'That was more than enough to put us away.' He shifted in his seat. 'He hid the body and gave us the ultimatum. Pack up and get out of the country within forty-eight hours or he'd drop everything at the nearest station. We had no choice. We sold the houses from Spain, but other than that, we lost everything.'

'That's *awful*,' Scarlet said.

Sean nodded at her. 'We had contacts back here covertly looking for the body, including your aunt. Your dad too,' he added with a sad smile. 'But they had to tread carefully so he wouldn't spook and carry out his threats. No one ever found anything.'

'Until now,' Finn said in a brighter tone, patting a sombre-looking Sean on the back. 'Bill sent word a couple of months back, an envelope containing the location of the body and a few other gems. No idea how he finally got it, but you know Bill.' He shrugged and sat back.

'He has his magical, mysterious ways. We mere mortals don't need to understand them,' Cormac added with a chuckle.

'So whose house was that?' Lily asked, curious about the details.

'The house belonged to Mani's aunt Giulia,' Sean said quietly. 'Well, technically Mani, but she lived there. She was having some work done inside back then, and Mani hid the body bag in a wall cavity. She died a couple of months back. Perhaps her death caused some chain reaction that opened up the information, I don't know. But the house then sat empty after she passed. So we set some charges and laid a strategic trail of fuel, and burned it down, body and all. After all these years traces of my DNA would still be there, but the fire would have got rid of that.'

'You said they had camera footage,' Cillian interjected. 'What happened to that?'

'They do,' Cormac confirmed, 'but apparently our faces never show. Bill confirmed it's in his home safe but that it's not something we need to worry about.'

Lily propped herself sideways on the arm of the chair and leaned her chin on her free hand. She watched the brothers thoughtfully, wondering how Bill had managed to see that tape.

'Does Mani know you're here yet?' she asked. She tapped her cigarette lightly on the crystal ashtray by her side.

'He'll have guessed by now,' Finn answered. 'But no, not for certain.'

She nodded. 'So now you've destroyed what Mani was using to keep you away, what's your plan?'

If she didn't like the sound of the Logans' plan, as aligned as they were, they would branch off and do their own thing. But she really did hope that wouldn't be the case. They'd be stronger together.

Finn caught Cormac's eye and scratched the back of his tanned neck before answering. 'Our focus was getting rid of that evidence first. Now we've done that, we have the time and space to work out the next stage.'

'We're gonna wipe them out though,' Sean added, leaning forward with a hard seriousness in his clear blue eyes. 'The whole firm. They took our lives from us. From our children. There's no outcome here where they get to continue theirs.'

Lily's brows twitched upwards, and she took a moment to digest this. Of the three brothers, Sean had always been the quietest, using his words sparingly, as if each one cost him something. So when he made statements like this, there was no doubt that he meant every word.

'Wiping out an entire firm, especially one the size of theirs...' She shook her head as she tried and failed to imagine a way in which they could pull that off. 'They've grown since you left,' she warned. 'Considerably.'

'We're aware,' Cormac told her.

There was a long silence in the room, and Lily took a couple of slow drags on her cigarette, blowing the smoke out in a long, thin plume before stubbing it out. Wiping out a firm entirely meant killing each and every man who worked for them. Mani and Riccardo had signed their own death warrants as far as she was concerned, perhaps a couple of the others working closely with them, but the rest of their men should be allowed to slink away into the shadows. The price the Logans wanted to exact for their revenge was too high.

'A lot of the men who work for the Romanos now weren't around back then,' she said, looking at each of the brothers in turn. 'Wipe out the core and you'll have balanced the scales. There's no need for such a drastic removal.'

Finn shook his head with a resolute expression. 'They removed *us* completely, Lil. After we make our move, however we do it, there will be no one left to remember they even existed.'

'You want to wipe them from our history,' Scarlet stated.

'Exactly,' Cormac replied.

Lily held Finn's gaze as her mind worked overtime. She couldn't take as big a risk as the Logans were suggesting. The Romano firm was spread too wide to take out in one blow, which meant those they didn't hit straightaway would turn and defend with a vengeance. But how could she convince them to pull back on this? After ten years of exile, she could understand why they felt the way they did, even if she didn't agree with it. It was obvious that the reason they hadn't made a solid plan was because they didn't have the numbers to pull it off. They needed the strength of this partnership too. But turning them down wouldn't be enough to deter them. She knew Finn too well. They'd just go ahead anyway, and that still wouldn't end well.

At best, the brothers would get themselves killed and leave the Romanos on such high alert that she'd never get close to them. At worst, her family would be pulled into the fight anyway, through association. It was a foolish idea fuelled by emotion rather than logic, but they didn't care about logic after so many years banished from their home. They just wanted revenge, no matter the cost.

An idea came to her, and she sat forward, squeezing her gaze. 'What if you could erase them from this city *and* from our history without spilling one drop of blood?'

Finn looked back at her warily. 'How?'

'You do exactly what he did to you,' she suggested. 'We find something to hang over his head that's bad enough to force him to leave. To force *all* of them to leave. Him, his family, his closest men.'

Finn pulled a dismissive expression, and Cormac followed suit. Sean's expression remained sombre and unreadable.

'No, *listen*,' she urged. 'Death is too easy for them. They aren't like you. You three got thrown into the darkness and you just dusted yourselves off and learned to make fire. But Mani – sure, he had it in him to build a firm up when he was younger, but he's old and his health is failing. He had a heart attack last year and has been in and out of hospital ever since. Now don't get me wrong, that old dog still has a hard bite *here* with all the resources he's built up, but elsewhere he wouldn't stand a chance. He hasn't the energy or strength to start again. And his sons are nothing without him. Riccardo's handy with his fists and does what he's told, but he's just a party boy underneath. Hasn't had an original thought in his life. And Luca's a wet blanket; my boys stripped him of his cred years ago. Which is partly why we're in the position we're in,' she admitted. 'But those two couldn't build a sandcastle, let alone a new business.'

She exhaled slowly, her hope growing as she saw that Finn was listening with a touch more interest. 'If *they're* cast out the way you were, they'll not only lose everything, but they'll never recover. They'll spend the rest of their days in a country they don't want to be in, without money, or status, or power. They'll suffer slowly and painfully, and Mani – that arrogant underhand back-stabbing bastard – will have to watch as the life he spent so many years building crumbles to *nothing*.'

Lily sat back and waited, knowing she'd piqued their interests now. There was a long silence as the brothers mulled it over.

'What's to say we could even dig up anything big enough to pull that off?' Finn asked. 'We'd be pinning this entire plan on something we don't even know if we can get.'

'And yet it's *still* a more viable plan to get out of this victorious and alive than *your* idea,' Lily countered, fixing him with a piercing gaze.

'A second ago Mani was a sick old man, and now you're afraid of him?' Cormac challenged.

Lily flashed him a dangerous look. 'I'm not afraid of *any* man,' she shot back. 'But a wounded bear is a dangerous creature. You *wound* Mani's firm, he'll send whoever's left to finish us all off in any way they can. And he can be vicious when provoked, as you well know. I don't fancy our chances of coming out of that unscathed. And I *will not* put my family at that sort of risk when there's a better way.'

She took a deep breath. 'If we do this, by the time we hit out, it will be too late for him to strike back. His hands will already be tied. We'd win a much greater revenge without inflicting one physical blow. And if we can't find anything, what will we have lost by trying?' She widened her eyes in question.

A polite cough pulled her attention towards Isla, who up until now had sat silently listening from the side. The girl pulled a big brown envelope out of her handbag and held it out to Lily.

'Actually, if that's the way you're thinking of going, then I have something you're going to want to see...'

TEN

Isla waited patiently as Lily opened it and cast her eyes over the various pictures and notes inside. She frowned then lifted her head and raised a questioning eyebrow at Isla.

'I've already been digging around to see what I can find, these last few days,' Isla explained, looking around the circle before directing her gaze back to Lily. 'Mani isn't so easy to find dirt on. Or dirt that would stick anyway,' she corrected. 'There are plenty of stories, like with any firm, but nothing usable. Riccardo, on the other hand, isn't so careful.'

'Oh?' Cillian shuffled forward in his seat, watching her intently.

Isla gestured towards the papers in Lily's hands. 'What's there isn't enough on its own, but it should lead us to what we'd need.' She tucked a stray lock of golden hair behind her ear, and her expression darkened. 'Riccardo is known for liking rough play in the bedroom.'

'Don't we all?' joked Finn.

Lily didn't laugh, instead turning one of the photos towards him. 'I don't think your version of rough play is quite the same as his.'

Finn's grin immediately dropped. 'Christ,' he muttered.

Isla eyed the girl in the photo, the swollen bruises and bloody cuts all over her face, and felt her hatred for Riccardo rise. She, more than anyone else here, understood what it was like to be in the clutches of men like him. Men who got off on using their power over weaker beings. Who enjoyed seeing their pain. She swallowed and looked away.

'This girl was a prostitute,' she continued. 'Her name was Mandy.'

'Was?' Scarlet picked up on her choice of words quicker than anyone else.

Isla nodded. 'She disappeared a few weeks after this and was never seen again. The injuries were from one of Riccardo's house parties. She was hired to attend along with a few other girls. Very well paid too. He took her and another girl off somewhere with a couple of his friends. A housemate cleaned her up after, but she refused to talk about it, then when she disappeared a few weeks later, one of the other girls found a second phone in her room. These pictures were on it, dated back to the day after that party.'

There was a short sombre silence.

Scarlet shook her head grimly. 'Who gave you these? Was there more?'

'I can't share that,' Isla replied firmly.

It had taken a lot to track down anyone connected to Mandy, and when she had, the woman hadn't wanted to talk. She'd had to work very hard to get her to open up at all.

'This is awful, but how can we *use* it?' Cillian asked.

'Mandy is just one of many,' Isla told him. 'He's actively avoided through the escort community; it's only the new girls who don't know of him or the ones desperate for the money who go to these parties now. It's why he pays so well, to lure them in and to buy their silence.'

Lily shook her head with a grim expression. 'Even if we

could get one of them to talk, which I doubt, it wouldn't be enough. Mani would just have her killed, and even if we could hide her, this wouldn't bother them. They'd call our bluff and take it on the chin.'

'It's just not that big a threat,' Scarlet agreed with a sigh as she flicked through the pictures. 'They'd know they could just annihilate her in court. She's a sex worker. Their lawyer would claim she was blackmailing him, and that with so many clients, the bruises could have been from anyone. They'd say that she's depraved and her choice of work shows her character.' Scarlet shrugged apologetically, passing the file on to Cillian. 'Even if there was proof, they'd easily prove it was an agreed transaction. It would be thrown out.'

'I get that. But it's not just prostitutes,' Isla replied. 'That's just how I got my lead into all this. Apparently there are always normal women at these parties too. If he can get them to pass out, he takes them away and, well...' She trailed off. 'You get the picture.'

'I still don't see how we can use this,' Cormac said, declining the file as it reached him. 'No thanks. I don't want to see that.'

'Well, that's because I haven't got to the good part yet,' Isla told him. 'Not that *good* is the right word,' she added. 'He films it. All of it. Every time. Has a room set up with a mattress and a camera that's linked to a laptop next to a bunch of external hard drives. Several people reported the same thing.'

Lily's eyebrows shot up with a spark of interest. Isla nodded, knowing exactly what she was thinking, because it had been her first thought too. If they could get hold of those hard drives, footage of him raping and beating multiple women, they would have exactly what they needed. Riccardo would be facing endless sentences with no chance of worming his way out of it.

'In his flat?' Cillian asked.

'That's what it sounded like. But apparently he always

blindfolds the girls who are awake and dizzies them before he walks them through. Which was the odd part.'

'Did you say he's got a flat?' Finn asked, directing his question to Cillian.

Cillian nodded. 'Yeah, but none of the others live in the same building. That we know of anyway. He rents it.'

'Maybe he rents more than one. Maybe he keeps his nasty little hobby in another dwelling so it don't get stumbled upon by a guest or in a raid,' Finn suggested.

'Makes sense,' Lily agreed. 'We all keep our homes clean against raids; this would be no different.'

'How many flats in the building?' Cormac asked.

Cillian grimaced. 'It's a high-rise.'

'It wouldn't be far,' Scarlet interjected. 'If these girls are being walked through blindfolded, he won't risk going far. But I still don't see how we can find it on the quiet. He won't have rented it under his name or anyone closely linked if it's a hide-away.' She leaned on the arm of the chair and strummed her perfectly manicured red nails on her cheek as she stared off through the wall.

'If we work out a way to pinpoint it, then I think it's worth giving this a go,' Finn said, turning to his brothers. 'What do you think?'

Isla sat back and waited to see what the others thought before saying any more. She knew how Lily liked to play the game. She only revealed what she absolutely needed to, even with friends.

'I think I'd like to carve Mani up like a Sunday roast, slowly and painfully, myself,' Cormac said in a grumpy growl. 'But I do see the merit. It's cleaner on everyone. And I appreciate your feeling of protectiveness over your family, Lil. If I had kids or a wife to think of, I'd feel the same.'

'Cormac, the terminal bachelor,' Finn joked.

'Yeah, well, not all of us were as lucky as you two,' he shot back. 'Women worth their salt, who'd put up with this life, are hard to come by. And when you do, they're either taken or a bloody enemy.' He rolled his eyes with a dramatic sigh, and there was a short round of laughter.

'Sean?' Lily asked.

Sean nodded. 'I can't promise I won't throw at least a little punch once we get there, but I'm on board. It does extend the suffering, I suppose.'

'It will,' Lily promised him.

Isla smiled. 'I have an idea as to how we can find the flat, or wherever that camera room of his is hidden.'

'How?' Scarlet asked.

'I noticed Riccardo has a type,' Isla said, leaning forward and running a hand back through her hair, to give it some volume as it fell back in flicky waves around her shoulders. 'All his women are slim blondes; most have brown eyes.' She pulled her shoulders back and posed. 'For most of the time I've worked for you, I've either been up north or in the background. If I changed up my style a bit, I don't think he'd ever recognise me. With some planning, we could set me up to meet him as if it was random, and I'll get myself invited to one of these parties.'

'After all you've seen him do to these girls, you want to volunteer as *bait*?' Cillian asked, his expression alarmed.

Isla turned her gaze to Lily, to see what she thought of the suggestion. There was concern in her frown but also the recognition that this was probably the best opportunity they were going to get.

'Yes,' Isla confirmed determinedly. 'I want to volunteer as bait.'

ELEVEN

Cillian walked into Repton Boxing Club and scanned the area for his brother. Connor was sitting on one of the benches to the side of a ring, wrapping his wrists. He was absorbed by the task, frowning at the bandages and unwrapping the last round to redo it a little looser, as Cillian made his way over. He cast a critical gaze over his brother, taking the opportunity to study him before Connor realised he'd arrived. He looked unhappy. The corners of his mouth drooped, along with his shoulders. Cillian frowned as worry momentarily replaced the hurt and confusion that had lingered since his twin had left them.

'Alright?' he said as he reached the bench.

He unzipped his gym bag and began to pull out his gloves. Part of him wanted to grab Connor in a bear hug and squeeze him so tightly he could never leave again. An equally large part wanted to punch the shit out of him for going in the first place and shutting him out. At least he'd be able to satisfy one of those desires here today.

'Yeah, you?' Connor made a sound of exasperation as he unwound the bandage for the third time.

Cillian tutted and took it from him, expertly rewrapping it

in seconds. This wasn't Connor's domain really. They'd both boxed as teenagers, but Connor had taken his foot off the pedal in their early twenties, returning only occasionally to spar as a workout. It had been Cillian whose love for the sport had pushed him through continued training until he was unrivalled by anyone else in the club.

He'd seen straight through his brother's message. Connor hadn't come here to work out; he'd come because it was the only common ground he could still reach out on. Cillian hoped against hope that the unexpected meet meant he was looking for a way back in. Things just weren't right without him. This was Connor's home, his family. His firm. And Lily, although she'd never admit it, was a mess. She'd already had to live through losing one child, and although Connor was far from dead, Cillian wasn't sure Lily would be able to properly make that distinction if he didn't return soon. Her nerves were already hanging by a thread.

'So, how are ya? How's things?' Cillian asked as they finished gloving up.

'Fine,' Connor replied with a slow nod, not meeting his eyes.

You're not fine, you lying twat, Cillian thought irritably. 'Good,' he said curtly. 'Me too.'

Except for the fact you left without so much as an explanation after we've lived as practically one person for the entirety of our twenty-nine years on this fucking planet, you absolute arse, he added silently.

'Good. Well...' Connor shifted his weight awkwardly. 'Pads or spar?'

'Spar,' Cillian said decisively, jumping up and weaving through the ropes.

He looked around the gym and caught a few furtive glances, but everyone swiftly turned away. Clearly the fact Connor had left to join another firm hadn't gone unnoticed, and this public meeting between the two of them was making people uneasy.

The door to the office at the far end of the gym opened, and Jimmy, the general manager, stepped out. He didn't look over, but as he wandered through the room and casually leaned against the wall not too far away, Cillian knew he was placing himself there in case intervention was needed. Not many people could get away with jumping in between them, but Jimmy had been their first coach, raising them in this gym since they'd been just a pair of gangly kids, half his height.

'Ready?' Connor asked.

Cillian turned and took a stance opposite his brother, then both of them began to move.

'When was the last time you were in the ring?' Cillian asked, watching his brother's footwork.

'Probably the last time we were here,' Connor replied, taking a shot.

Cillian blocked it easily. 'It shows.'

Connor ignored the insult and doubled down on his efforts to land a punch. Cillian blocked and ducked, then shot a jab into Connor's midsection.

'Agh.' Connor jumped back with a sound of frustration, repositioning himself.

'I'm not even trying yet – you know that, right?' Cillian asked drily.

'Yeah, well, I'm just warming up,' Connor muttered. 'Not all of us have the time to train down here every morning.'

A sharp stab of annoyance shot through Cillian's core, and he darted forward, dealing Connor a swift right hook, much harder than the friendly jab before had been. As Connor let out a sound of pain and gritted his teeth, Cillian held his stare coldly.

'*Some* of us *make* the time to train. Some of us get here at half five in the morning because they don't have any other time to do it,' he said in a low warning tone. 'Some of us work round the clock, looking after the family and the family businesses. The only things that actually *count* in life.'

Connor made a sound of derision and shook his head. 'You have no fucking idea.'

His response only angered Cillian more, and he pulled his fist back, slamming it into Connor's chest viciously.

Connor flew back with a yell of pain, just managing to find his footing as he hit the ropes. Cillian glared at him, and his mirror image glared straight back as both of them gave in to their anger. With a roar, Connor dived forward, and the pair slammed together, punching and kicking each other, the rules of boxing abandoned. The gloves came off, and one skittered out of the ring as hard blows were dealt and taken.

'You're a fucking psycho,' Connor yelled as Cillian pulled him into a headlock, punching his shoulder again and again.

'*You're* a fucking deserter,' Cillian yelled back as Connor managed to flip him over and punched him back furiously.

They continued their struggle on the floor, attacking each other with all their pent-up frustrations for another few seconds, before Jimmy and David Higgs, one of the coaches, grabbed them from behind and began prising them apart. It wasn't easy, the brothers straining against them as they each tried landing one more blow, but eventually the pair were separated.

'Hey, hey, Cillian, *stop* this. Come on – easy now. It's done. It's done.' Jimmy's voice by his ear was authoritative but quiet as he pulled Cillian back and locked his arms around him.

His voice eventually cut through the red haze clouding Cillian's mind, and he stopped struggling, allowing Jimmy to lead him away to the side. Jimmy's tight grip remained for another few seconds until he was sure Cillian wouldn't make to break away again, then he released him with a loud breath of relief.

Across the ring, Connor struggled in David's grasp for a few moments longer before giving up. David and Jimmy exchanged a grim look, and then David shook his head as he sat Connor on the stool in the corner. He patted Connor's shoulder reassuringly then stepped away with a sniff.

Cillian placed his hands on his hips and turned in a slow circle, catching his breath after the furious exchange. His anger still ran raw through his veins, but he had a hold on it now. As he faced a grim-looking Jimmy once more, he nodded.

'It's OK. We're done,' he said, still a little breathless.

Blood trickled from a split on Connor's swelling bottom lip, and he immediately felt guilty. He hadn't meant to hurt him *that* badly. Suddenly aware of a throbbing above his temple, Cillian reached up then winced as his touch sent shooting pains through a small gash there. He pulled his hand down and stared at his bloody fingers in surprise.

'Yeah,' Jimmy said, raising his eyebrows and moving his disapproving gaze back and forth between them both. 'You both inflicted some real damage. Dave, can you grab the first aid box?'

'Nah, we're fine,' Cillian said, raising his hand to stop the man, but Jimmy shook his head resolutely.

'No. You know the rules.' Jimmy nodded at David to carry on. 'You get it in here, it's treated in here.'

He looked around the room at all the men pretending they weren't watching. 'Well you certainly put on a show, that's for sure.' He let out a long, slow sound of annoyance then turned his back to the room. 'I don't know what's going on between you, and I doubt I need to. But in all the years I've known you, as snotty-nosed kids, angry skinny teens, young men working to make their mark – through all of that I have *never* seen you turn on each other. Not *once*.' He eyed them both with hard accusation. 'I *would* say the pair of you need locking in a room until you sort this out, but after what I've just seen, I'm not sure how many bloody pieces you'd come back out in.' He shook his head. 'Go and sit in the locker room while I go find some antiseptic. *Go on.*'

Cillian bit his tongue and nodded, knowing Jimmy had every right to be as pissed off as he was. Anyone else caught letting rip in the ring the way they had, flouting the rules of boxing and bare-knuckle attacking their opponent, would have been thrown out and most likely banned for life. Jimmy couldn't do that to them. Aside from their status, they owned the club. But that didn't change the fact that Jimmy's rules were to be respected. He'd more than earned that right.

Cillian jumped down and walked through to the changing rooms, aware of his brother just a couple of steps behind. Inside, he took a seat on the nearest bench and leaned back against the wall. Connor sat beside him, and there was a long silence as they each tried to decide where to start.

'What's going on with you?' Cillian asked eventually. 'I just don't get it.'

'I know you don't,' Connor said tiredly.

There was another long silence before he continued. 'A lot has happened in the last couple of years. I can't explain it, but I just needed to get away and have some space from everything for a while. The opportunity with Ray gave me a way to do that. That's all it is. And I know that's hard for you – it's hard for me too. I hadn't realised I'd be ousted from the family *completely.*' He exhaled slowly and closed his eyes for a moment. 'I didn't realise I'd spend my Sundays watching café fucking doors for Ray, instead of sitting round Mum's table with you lot. But it's done now. And I need to see it through. Can you understand *that?*'

Cillian listened to his words, hearing the truth in them. But though he knew his brother was being honest, he still couldn't shake the feeling that he was missing something. He sighed.

'If that's what you need, *space...*' He mashed his lips

together as the idea settled like a bruise on his heart. Whatever else was going on, he'd never thought his brother would ever need space from *him*. 'I can't pretend to understand it. But if you need it, I can respect it.'

It was hard to say those words to Connor. He just wanted to shake him and force him to talk, so that he could protect him from whatever was upsetting him so much. The way he always had done.

'Thanks,' Connor replied, turning to him with a sad half-smile. He winced as the action pulled at his split lip.

Cillian grimaced. 'Sorry 'bout your lip.'

Connor shrugged. 'Sorry 'bout your head.'

They both managed a small grin this time, though Connor was careful to keep it to the lesser-damaged side of his mouth.

'Listen…' Cillian lay his head back against the painted brick wall but tipped it towards Connor with a sideways glance. 'I'm getting married.'

'Yeah, I was around for that, remember?' Connor reminded him. 'I have only been gone a couple of weeks.'

'No, I mean we've set a date.'

'Oh, congrats. When's the big day?' Connor glanced at him expectantly.

Cillian unzipped the pocket of his gym trousers and pulled out a toothpick, placing it between his teeth. 'Next Thursday.'

'*Next* Thursday?' Connor repeated in surprise. He sat up and faced Cillian properly with a frown.

'Yeah.' Cillian shrugged and raised his eyebrows with a brief shake of the head. 'I know – it's nuts. But it's what Billie wants, and Father Dan had a cancellation, so here we are.'

Connor nodded and fell silent, looking troubled.

'I'm not getting married without you beside me,' Cillian told him. 'I don't care what's happening. You're my best man. In general,' he added. 'So tell me you'll be there.'

'Of course I will,' Connor replied immediately. 'That goes without saying. But what about Mum?'

'Don't worry about Mum,' Cillian told him. 'I'll talk to her. It's my wedding. Everyone will behave and get on or... Well. There ain't no *or*.'

Connor nodded. 'OK. What do you need me to do?'

'Well firstly you need to come to church on Sunday. Father Dan's on the warpath, and he wants to talk to you about your duties.' Cillian grinned wickedly as Connor groaned, then he glanced though the partially open door into the gym to check Jimmy wasn't just outside.

'Secondly...' he continued, standing up, 'as you started this little dance today, you can stick around to get the rest of the lecture and take the flack.'

'*What?*' Connor looked at him in alarm as Cillian moved towards the fire exit that led to the car park behind the building. 'Where you going?'

'Home. I've got shit to do.' He paused by the door, twiddling the toothpick between his teeth. 'But I'll speak to you later.' He looked back at his brother, still feeling the distance between them but glad that it was starting to get a little shorter. 'We'll sort out the details for all the wedding stuff, yeah?'

''Course,' Connor replied.

Cillian nodded then glanced up at the door as he heard Jimmy's voice approaching. 'Grab my gloves and bag when you go, will ya?' he asked quickly. Then with a cheeky wink at a bemused Connor, he pushed through the fire escape and slipped out into the car park.

TWELVE

Billie woke up and reached out for Cillian, but instead of meeting a warm body, her hand found a cold emptiness in the bed next to her. She half opened one eye and looked around, then sat up with a tired yawn. Glancing at the clock, she frowned. It was nearly eight, which meant that even if he'd gone out early to the gym, he should have been back by now. And she was sure he'd said he'd miss this morning, to give Jimmy time to cool down after he'd given him the slip the day before.

Slipping out from the cosy warmth of the bedcovers, she groaned, feeling utterly wretched and exhausted still, then wrapped a dressing gown around her body and walked through to the lounge. Cillian sat in the armchair by the window, a coffee cradled in his hands and a troubled expression on his face as he stared out, unseeing. He roused as she slipped her arms around his neck from behind and leaned down to snuggle her face into his neck. He leaned his head on hers and reached up to squeeze one of her hands.

'Sorry, did I wake you?'

'No,' she mumbled, kissing him a few more times before letting go and walking around the chair to place herself on his lap. He moved his cup to make space for her and loped his arm around her legs as she pulled them up. 'I missed my morning cuddles though.'

'You know for a hard little nutter who doesn't flinch at anything, you're a right soppy bird at times,' Cillian said with a teasing grin.

She swiped at him playfully with a narrowed gaze. 'Watch it, you. Just because you've got those pretty eyes and perfect dimples in your perfectly carved mug, it don't mean your charm will always save you from a *hard little nutter* like me.'

'It does though,' he argued with a cheeky wink.

Pulling a witheringly unimpressed face, she looked him up and down. 'It don't actually.' She paused, and the corner of her mouth twitched. 'It's the abs that save you really.'

'Right...' he said, mischief flashing in his eyes.

She shrieked as he grasped her waist and began tickling her.

'You forget one thing, Billie Anne Archer. I know I can overpower you with one hand.' He continued mercilessly as she tried and failed to wriggle out of his grasp. 'And I'll take this opportunity to remind you that I'm not just a piece of meat for you to ogle.'

'*Stop*,' she begged through breathless screeches of laughter. '*Stop!* Don't – Cillian stop, I've got a bad *stomach*.'

'OK fine, you can ogle me. You win,' he joked, setting her free. 'You OK?'

'Yes, fine. Something I ate. You cheating bastard,' Billie accused, pointing her finger in his face. 'I told you before, that ain't playing fair.'

'All is fair in love and war, Billie. Don't you read?' he replied loftily.

'Yeah?' She raised her eyebrows. 'What book's that from, hm?'

Cillian winced. 'Umm, I think it was a Superman comic, back in '64, '65...'

She shook her head. 'Oh, stop it.'

'Well, nobody reads books anyway,' he said with a grin, glancing over to her current read on the windowsill. 'Except you, that is.'

'And most of the rest of the world,' she added with a grin.

He smiled back at her, his gaze roaming her face for a moment, then as the moment passed, the weight of worry settled back into his expression like a wet grey cloud.

Billie ran her hand lightly over the back of his neck. 'What's wrong?'

Cillian ran the side of his forefinger across his lips, something she often noticed him do when he was anxious. 'The meeting with the Logans yesterday...'

'I thought you said it went well?' she asked, surprised. 'That you were going to work together on this?'

'Yeah, it did. We are,' he assured her. 'But I just don't like how we need to do it.'

Billie frowned. 'Do you want to talk about it?'

They worked as a couple because from the off, Billie had known and not cared about who Cillian was. She accepted every part of him, the good and the bad. She had no romantic notions about his life, no illusions of grandeur. She trusted in who he was rather than judging what he did, lied for him when he needed her to and trusted that he'd share whatever she needed to know.

Cillian exhaled heavily then stayed silent for a few moments before answering. 'Riccardo has a dirty secret we could use against him to force Mani to move his family out of the country.'

Billie tilted her head with a look of grudging admiration. 'Do what he did to the Logans. Poetic justice.'

'Right. But to find where he keeps the proof, our best option is to send Isla in as bait.'

'OK. Does she not want to do it?' Billie asked.

'It was her idea,' he replied. 'But it's not a good one.'

'Why?'

'Because his dirty secret is that he likes to beat the shit out of conscious women and rape the unconscious ones,' Cillian said frankly.

'Oh.' She pursed her lips.

'Yeah.'

'There's no other way?' Billie asked.

'Possibly, but this is the most direct route and the most likely to work. But if she gets into a bad corner and we don't know where she is...' He trailed off with a shake of his head.

Billie nodded, understanding his worry. No matter how hard she was, how seasoned she was in their way of life, physically Isla was short and slight. She could easily be overpowered.

'What's your mum's take?'

'Mum's for it,' Cillian replied. 'She sees the danger but Isla's willing, and it's our best shot. She says we'll take precautions.' He shrugged helplessly. 'It's going ahead anyway.'

Billie nodded again, biting the inside of her lip. 'Then you need to just trust in that. Lily always takes the safest path for you all. She weighs up the risks, and her decisions have always seen you through. Even in your darkest moments.' She reached up and pushed a dark lock of his hair back off his forehead to sit back neatly with the rest of it.

'That's true,' he said quietly. 'Anyway, I have more pressing issues to deal with. Like a wedding *next week*.' He laughed with a small groan. 'I still need to find a suit. You got a dress yet?'

'Not yet, but Scarlet and Isla are coming dress shopping with me tomorrow. I've asked them to be bridesmaids,' she replied with a warm smile.

'That's nice.' He held her gaze, a question in his own, then looked away.

'What? What is it?'

'Nothing.'

'Don't lie to me,' she admonished. 'Speak up.'

He moved his gaze back to hers. 'Are you *sure* you want us to rush this? I mean, it's supposed to be the best day of our lives and we're rushing it through like the world's going to end. We're missing all the build-up – no engagement party, no hen or stag parties...'

'Is that what this is about?' Billie asked, cutting him off. 'That you ain't had a stag?'

'No! I couldn't care less about that. I just feel like we're missing out on a lot by rushing through it. Like *you're* missing out on a lot. Don't you want to go on dates to cake tastings and pick the perfect band? I mean, we're having a knees-up in our own pub for Christ's sake.'

'I feel like *you're* the girl who's been secretly planning her wedding since she was five,' Billie joked.

Cillian sighed. 'I just don't want you to look back in years to come and wish we'd enjoyed this time more, you know? We're going to be married for the rest of our lives. We don't need to rush the wedding.' He touched her face, looking at her earnestly. 'I ain't going anywhere, Bills. You do know that, don't you?'

'Of course I do,' she said, putting her hand on his and casting her eyes down.

'And finding the right dress surely don't happen in a week,' he pushed gently. 'I mean, you'll look amazing in any dress. You'd look like a princess in a bin bag, in my opinion. But don't you want to find that one perfect dress all you girls seem to talk about?'

She let out a short laugh and looked up at him again. 'Ahh, babe...'

She bit her lip and felt the butterflies fly around inside as she geared herself up to tell him the real reason she was so desperate to rush things. Taking his hand in hers, she studied it for a moment.

'I'll be happy with any dress. All I care about is walking down that aisle and becoming your wife. Mrs Billie Drew. In all the ways I can. Heart, soul and name.' She smiled as he pulled her hand towards his mouth and kissed it.

'That's all that matters to me too,' he said softly. 'That and your happiness. I don't care about the rest.'

'Good,' she replied, love shining out of her bright blue eyes as she stared at the man she loved with every ounce of her being. She rubbed his hand, keeping it between hers. 'Plus,' she added, 'the only dresses I'll fit in soon are the ones they make for hippo weddings at the zoo.'

'I don't think they perform hippo weddings anymore,' Cillian replied, automatically jumping on the opportunity for banter before processing her actual words. 'Banned them after one of the brides ate the vicar.'

Billie waited, amused.

'Wait, hang on.' He frowned in confusion. 'What you on about?'

The butterflies fluttered upwards in a thrill as she watched him slowly connect the possible meanings behind her statement. His eyes darted from her face to her stomach and back up again, a cautious question dawning. She moved his hand down to her stomach, already hardening into a small curve now that she was thirteen weeks along – a fact that had taken her aback considerably when she'd initially found out.

'You... Are you...?' His eyes moved back to her stomach as she pressed his hand down, and his jaw dropped.

'I found out last week. Friday. I've been waiting for the right time to tell you,' she whispered.

Cillian had frozen in shock, his mouth open and his eyes wide. She watched him, the butterflies of excitement fluttering more uneasily now. Was he upset? Happy? Angry? She couldn't tell. The seconds passed painfully slowly as she waited for a reaction – *any* reaction, until eventually she couldn't take it anymore.

'Cillian?' she asked. He didn't move or seem to even hear her. 'Cillian?' Her voice was louder this time, and it seemed to finally reach him.

He took a deep breath in and shook his head. 'This is...' He ran a hand back through his hair, still staring at her stomach as though he'd never seen one before.

Billie felt her heart rise to her mouth, and for a moment she thought she might actually cry. He wasn't happy. He didn't want this. He didn't want their baby. As the first tear began to swell in her eye, she tried to blink it away. She wasn't going to do that. She wouldn't let him see her cry.

He glanced up at her and immediately looked horrified. 'Oh no, Bills, no, don't cry! I'm over the moon! I'm in absolute shock, but this is...' He looked down again at her stomach, a wide smile of wonder lighting up his whole face. 'God, this is the best news I've ever had.'

'Really?' Relief flooded through her, but rather than disappear, her tears just seemed to multiply and flood down her face.

'Really!' he replied firmly, wiping her tears away with his hand. 'Billie, this is *amazing*. Oh my God, there's a little you growing inside there! A little *us*.' He stared down at her stomach again, the wonder on his face growing with every passing second. 'Bills, this is the best thing you've ever given me.'

She laughed through her tears and looked down to their hands entwined on her stomach, and when she looked up again, she saw something she'd never witnessed before. His cheeks flushed red and his forehead crumpled upwards before a tear fell down his cheek. He wiped it away with a shake of his head.

'Christ, look what you've done to me,' he joked.

Billie didn't respond, amazed at his emotional reaction. Instead, she just gripped his hand and put her forehead to his, and they spent the next few minutes just staring at where their future child lay hidden inside, growing steadily. Eventually, Billie broke away, looking up at Cillian with a contented smile.

He touched her face. 'You found out Friday, you say?'

She nodded. The last few days had felt like an eternity, but they'd been so busy that this was the first time they'd sat and had a proper conversation that hadn't been rushed or on the phone, since she'd found out.

'Anyone else know?' Cillian asked.

'No, 'course not,' she told him. 'I wouldn't tell someone else before you. There is more to tell you though,' she added.

His face drained of colour, and his eyes darted a little more cautiously towards her stomach now. 'It's twins, ain't it?' His voice was low with fear, and he quickly changed it to a braver, more upbeat tone. 'If it is, then that's great. Two for the price of one, and of course money's no issue – you know that, right? You could have ten in there and we'd still be fine. I mean, maybe not mentally...' He laughed now. 'But physically at least. But twins, that's great. That's really great. You never know, we might get a boy and a girl. Both at once. Save you having to go through it all twice and all that.' He nodded at her encouragingly as he rambled on, and she couldn't help but laugh.

'Babe, it ain't twins.' She chuckled. 'But I love you for that speech.'

'Oh thank *fuck*,' he breathed. 'I'm honestly happier than you can know about this baby, but I don't know how I'd handle two.'

'Well, your mum did a pretty good job of it,' Billie reminded him.

'Yeah, but she's a bloody warrior,' Cillian replied, the corner of his mouth hitching in a half grin. 'I'm a mere man don't forget. I ain't got the superpowers you lot do.'

'*You lot?*' Billie queried.

'Women. You have all those extra senses going on, don't ya?

That all-seeing eye and sonar hearing and shit. And you can multi-task – you ever seen a man successfully multi-task?' He raised an eyebrow.

Billie shook her head with a grin. 'You'd have figured it out.'

He ran a hand through his hair and rested his head back on the chair before suddenly lifting it again. 'But, hang on, how do you know it's only one for certain?'

'OK, so, as it's getting colder now, I pulled out all my winter clothes Friday morning while you were at the gym, and I was trying to put on my favourite jeans, but they wouldn't do up, right? And I knew I'd put on a couple of pounds lately but thought it was just bloating, you know?'

'Yeah, I figured it was just a bit of winter weight,' Cillian agreed.

Billie bristled and pulled back, and he realised his mistake immediately.

'No, I mean...' He floundered. 'That didn't come out right. What I meant was, like, that you seemed like you felt more, like—'

'Stop talking, Cillian,' Billie ordered drily. 'You ain't helping yourself.'

Cillian drew his lips into his mouth between his teeth for a second then expelled a long breath. 'What I *really* mean is I think you're the sexiest woman in the world, whatever you weigh, and to be completely honest, I've been more distracted by your boobs lately than anything else. And now I guess we know why.' He shrugged.

Billie's icy demeanour melted, and she nestled back into his arm before continuing her explanation. 'Well, anyway, they wouldn't do up, and no matter how much I tried to suck my gut in, it wouldn't move. So then I started really looking at my body and noticed, well, yes, my boobs.' She rolled her eyes as he pulled an appreciative expression. 'They do seem a bit bigger. And they're sensitive. And then I realised they have been for a while, but I'd been too busy to wonder why. Anyway I did a test after you left for work, more to count it out than anything. I didn't think it would come back positive, because we're always so careful.'

Cillian began to nod but then paused and tilted his head to the side with a wince. '*Most* of the time we are. There've been a few times we got carried away.'

'True,' she admitted. 'I still didn't believe the first test though, so I went and got a bunch more. After eight positives, I did one of those expensive ones that tells you how many weeks, but it only goes up to *three plus* as the max and it said three plus. So then I rang the doctor and managed to get an appointment. He confirmed it and then started asking me about my periods. That's when I realised I hadn't had a proper one since summer.'

'Billie!' Cillian exclaimed. 'Surely that was a pretty clear indicator?'

'Well, no,' she argued. 'I'm not that regular, so it weren't out of the ordinary. But the doctor said we needed to do a scan ASAP to see. He sent me straight over to the hospital for a scan, and that confirmed I'm already three months.'

'Three months?' Cillian's eyes widened. 'Shit, OK. So only six until you give birth then. Wow. OK.' He swallowed and nodded as he took it all in.

A smile spread across her face, and she slipped off his lap, nipping around the chair towards the bedroom. 'Wait there. Hang on.'

She ran to her dressing table, opened her make-up drawer and retrieved the slim envelope she'd stashed there on Friday, before running back to Cillian.

She retook her seat on his lap and opened it, holding her breath in anticipation as she slipped out the shiny black-and-white images. The paper they were printed on was so thin she was scared it would tear and ruin, so she held the precious pictures of what she'd affectionately coined her little blob very carefully by the corners.

'Oh wow,' Cillian muttered, leaning closer as he tried to work out what he was looking at. 'That's her?'

'Or him,' Billie responded. 'I just call them little blob for now.'

'That is exactly what she or he looks like,' he agreed with a grin. 'Little blob it is.'

'See here.' Billie pointed to one of the white outlines. 'This is little blob's head. And this here, look – that's the little heart.'

'That's incredible,' Cillian said quietly.

'It is.' Billie looked up at him and smiled. 'And now you see why we need to get married next week. I want to be your wife before little blob arrives. And then we'll be the perfect family.'

'We really will,' Cillian murmured, pulling her close to him as they both stared at the fuzzy black-and-white shapes. 'Me, you and baby Drew. I can't think of anything more perfect in this world, Billie.' He squeezed her tight and kissed her head. 'I'm going to be the best husband and father I can be. That I promise you, with all my heart. I'm going to give you both everything. I'm going to give you this whole fucking world.'

THIRTEEN

'That was a good call about the weight,' Lily remarked as she and Scarlet slipped into her car. 'I hadn't thought about that. Well done.'

Scarlet smiled, taking the compliment and mentally filing it away with the other treasured comments her aunt had bestowed on her over the years. Lily didn't part with compliments like that unless they were well earned, and as such, they still held impact, even now.

Outwardly she shrugged as though it was nothing. 'It only occurred to me this morning when I picked up Mum's hairspray instead of mine. I knew without looking because of the weight difference, and it made me realise it would be too easy a tell down the line if these weren't the same.'

They'd just stepped out of a meeting with a man they were about to enter a new business arrangement with. An old friend of Lily's had opened a pepper spray factory in France and was open to going off book, making his the first legal pepper spray manufacturer to offer this. Pepper spray was currently illegal in England, classed as a section five weapon and weighted with the same legal penalty as a gun. And while there was no doubt some logical reason for the severe legal weight attached to it, this just didn't sit right with her aunt. It was a self-defence tool. And if the government weren't going to allow those who felt vulnerable access to it, then they sure as hell would. And they'd disguise it perfectly too.

Now, following their successful negotiations, the Drews would be the first underground importer of pepper spray cans, designed to look and feel exactly the same as a common brand of hairspray. It didn't change the legal threat. If caught with it, women could still suffer the penalties. But it made it easier to obtain and easier to hide, even in plain sight.

'We need to set up some meetings, spread the word that we have exclusive import rights and will be selling in bulk,' Lily said as she turned onto a dual carriageway and put her foot down. They whizzed past the other cars on the road as they headed back towards The Hideaway. 'How soon can you start setting things up?'

Scarlet considered this. 'I honestly don't know,' she answered frankly. 'I know we need to get things moving, so we're ready when the first shipment arrives, but we have *no* time.' She pulled out her phone and scrolled through her calendar, scanning the full blocks for anywhere she could create a space. She paused on the following day. 'Who's coming to the gambling night tomorrow? Is there anyone there we'd pitch this to?'

Lily twisted her red lips to the side. 'The Tylers might be coming,' she said. 'They'd be a good first hit.'

Scarlet made a sound of agreement. 'We should make a list of the other London firms we want to talk to, see where else we can cross paths. Cos's firm would have the set-up for this sort of distribution. And of course R—' She halted abruptly, stopping herself just in time, but Lily still caught it.

'Ray will *not* be on this list,' she said coldly.

Lily's knuckles whitened as her grip tightened on the

wheel, and sadness washed through Scarlet, along with a fresh wave of guilt. Lily had no idea why Connor had really left. While Ray had made him the offer, it was *she* who'd caused Connor to leave his family and the life he loved so much. And now Lily was suffering for it, feeling betrayed not only by her son but by the man she'd been in love with for over thirty years.

Scarlet watched her subtly, in her peripheral vision. Lily had always enjoyed her own company, a fiercely independent woman who was confident in her own skin. But she'd always been secure in the knowledge that her family were around her, and Ray had always been there for her to turn to, an anchor of love and support whenever she needed. Now one of her children had left her, shattering the sense of security she'd felt in her family's future as a united whole. Without Ray, Lily no longer had anyone to turn to, to support her through it. And it was all Scarlet's fault.

Turning away, she looked out of the window thinking back to the conversation she'd had with Cillian the day before. Connor hadn't found his feet yet within Ray's firm. The men still treated him as an outsider, according to Cillian's source. He'd confided in her that part of him hoped this would eventually wear Connor down enough to make him return, but all she'd felt was sadness for her absent cousin. He'd done so much for her, sacrificed so much to keep her safe. There had to be something she could do to help him in return.

Her phone buzzed in her handbag, and she pulled it out to look at the screen. It was a message from Benny, asking how her day was going. Staring at it for a moment, she bit her lip then sent her reply.

Good thanks. Are you free to meet? MB in 20 mins? X

She locked the screen and looked back over to her aunt. 'Don't disown me for asking, but have you actually *talked* to Ray about all this with Connor?' She watched Lily's expression harden. 'Things might not be exactly how they seem, that's all. It might be worth just hearing what he has to say.' She mentally winced and braced herself for Lily's wrath. 'You can always kill him afterwards,' she joked, a weak attempt to lighten her suggestion.

Lily drew in a deep breath, but the cutting reply Scarlet expected never came. She waited, glancing sideways a couple of times. But Lily simply expelled the air slowly and turned the car into the factory car park. As she headed towards her parking spot next to Scarlet's, she nodded, her expression hard.

'Perhaps you're right,' she said, her tone cool and even, making it hard for Scarlet to read. 'Perhaps I should have a little talk with Ray.'

'Yeah,' Scarlet agreed, wary and confused by this calm response. She narrowed her gaze as she flicked another glance Lily's way. *Why did this feel like a trap?* She continued cautiously. 'Maybe arrange a sit-down. Have a drink and talk it over.'

'Mm,' Lily murmured in agreement, nodding as she focused on backing the car into her space.

Scarlet frowned, feeling unnerved.

'You're completely right, Scarlet,' Lily said resolutely. 'A nice chat is exactly what Ray and I need.'

Briefly widening her loaded smile, Lily turned and got out of the car. Scarlet stared after her, her eyes widening in alarm as warning bells jangled through her body. She had no idea what Lily was about to do, but she was familiar enough with her aunt's ways to know that this calm reaction to her suggestion meant something very, very bad indeed.

'Shit,' she breathed, unbuckling her belt and opening her door.

What the hell had she just done?

FOURTEEN

Scarlet pulled the belt of her tailored woollen coat a little tighter and pushed her hands down deep into the pockets. Her breath briefly shadowed the air each time she exhaled, and the cold wind bit sharply at her face, raising her long raven hair and whipping it around in all directions.

She pushed it out of her face and checked for traffic before nipping across the road between cars as she made her way towards the Millennium Bridge. The wind increased as she reached the river, and she tilted her head upwards, embracing the cold rush. She quickened her pace on the bridge and gazed out at the glittering peaks on the murky brown water below as the sun briefly peeped through the blanket of grey above.

Benny was waiting for her at exactly the halfway point, leaning on the metal handrails and staring down at the river with a serious brooding frown. A smile warmed her face as she saw him and drank in his handsome face, rich brown skin and sculpted features. The sight of him instantly lifted her heart, just like it always did. Her gaze moved across the smart navy coat covering his suit to his tensely hunched shoulders. He looked as though he was carrying the weight of the world there.

As she neared, Benny clocked her and stood up. He turned to face her, the frown swiftly hidden. She wrapped her arms around his middle, meeting his kiss, and allowed her body to relax into his for a few moments. He hugged her back then tucked her windswept hair behind her ear.

'You're a sight for sore eyes,' he told her.

'Ditto,' she replied.

He stepped back and picked up the two takeaway coffees by his feet. He handed her one and hitched an eyebrow. 'Feeling Irish or not today?'

Scarlet debated it for a moment. One wouldn't hurt. 'Yeah, go on then.'

Benny pulled a small bottle of whisky out of his pocket and poured a measure into each one before slipping it away. They both turned to face the river and leaned on the rail.

'So,' Benny prompted, 'what's going on?'

Scarlet took a sip from the cup in her hand before answering. 'I need to ask you a favour. A big one.'

'What kind of big favour?' Benny asked, his tone level.

Scarlet sighed internally and stared into the distance to where the buildings grew smaller and disappeared behind the line of bridges dotted all the way down the river. She and Benny didn't talk about Connor. It was a difficult subject to navigate. Up until recently, there had been clear lines in their relationship. She and Benny lived and worked in the same dark underworld. They understood what could be shared and what privacies needed to be respected. Their firms were on good terms, but there was a clear separation, and that was what made their relationship easy.

But now the clear lines of their firms had been broken, and this new knotted mess of interests and issues was entirely new ground. Connor was a Drew, her cousin, her blood. He was an integral member of both family and firm. But his loyalty had now been pledged to Ray and *his* firm. He was theirs now.

Except he would never really be theirs. He would always be a Drew. And wherever he was, she would always have his back. Even if that meant crossing some lines to do it.

'I know the men aren't taking to Connor's arrival well,' she said. This much was common knowledge and, as such, not off limits. 'Tell me how bad it is.'

'That's true,' Benny confirmed. 'And to be expected really. Ray's set-up has never been about blood; it's always been about those who prove their worth. You work hard, you get rewarded. The more you prove yourself, the higher you rise.' He let out a grim sigh. 'His core men worked damn hard to get there, and over many years. Not one of them was born to it the way you and Cillian were.'

Scarlet drew back and fixed him with a cold stare. '*Excuse* me?' she asked, her tone sharp.

'It ain't meant as an insult.'

'I worked damn hard to get to where I am too,' Scarlet continued in a hard tone, pushing back off the rails. 'You have *no* fucking idea what I've done to earn my place, to earn the respect of the people around me...'

'Hey, I know.' Benny twisted to face her, reaching out to pull her back towards him. He stared down at her seriously. 'I wasn't putting you down; I'm just explaining the differences.'

Scarlet exhaled heavily through her nose as she turned to lean back on the rail.

Benny followed her gaze down the river. 'These men, some of them have been with Ray since before Connor was born. They bought their tickets opening night under the promise that if they climbed the ladder the way Ray told them to, the show would be theirs one day. So they climbed and they bled and they fought and got dirty, and they kept going. Now they're there, at the top, and Ray's opened the back door to some kid who hasn't paid the same dues.' He grimaced and shook his head. 'You can see how that's upset things, I'm sure.'

Scarlet's forehead furrowed into a deep frown of concern. 'I didn't know he had people set to take over like that.'

'Who else did you think it would go to?' Benny asked. 'He never had a family. That he knew of anyway.' He rubbed his chin. 'It was the only way to ensure loyalty.'

Scarlet glanced at him. 'You've worked hard to get up that ladder too,' she pointed out. 'You're in Ray's inner circle. Is that how *you* feel?'

Benny smirked, amused. 'No. I do understand how they feel, but I was never in the running to take over – not for a few decades at least. There are too many others ahead, no matter how high I rank, so it don't make a difference to me.'

Scarlet nodded and took another few sips of her coffee, glad of the whisky and its warm kick. 'What's your take? Does he stand a chance?' she asked, her grey-blue eyes troubled.

Benny made a sound of reluctance, but she ignored it and waited for his answer. She wouldn't retreat from this conversation gracefully. Connor was too important.

'Alright, look... If he could prove himself a decent leader, show some sort of win, it would help him gain their respect. Help grow their trust. But he's just shadowing and following orders right now. He don't know enough yet for Ray to give him responsibility for anything. It'll take time.'

'He doesn't have time,' Scarlet replied bluntly. 'With that much bad blood, if he continues to just follow, they'll find a way to push him out. You know that.' She looked down at her cup and swirled the liquid around. 'The weak are always weeded out one way or another. It doesn't matter who he is. And Ray can't protect him and expect him to earn his place at the same time. He needs a way in *now*. Even if it's just a boot holding the door.'

'I'd love to tell you I know of a way, but I don't,' Benny replied.

'Well I do,' she said. 'But I need your help.' She turned to meet his gaze cautiously. 'I've never asked anything of you before that could affect your work life.'

He took a half step back with a look of grim reluctance, and she reached out to grip his arm.

'*Please*,' she urged. 'Just listen. We've always kept a distance between whatever's going on in the firms and our private life, I know. We agreed on that from the start.'

'*Yes*,' he reiterated strongly. 'We *did*. And there was a reason for that, Scarlet.'

'Safety,' she said with a nod. 'I know. So we never put ourselves in a compromising situation where our loyalties could be questioned. And I would never do that to you,' she stressed. 'The firms come first.'

There was a short silence as they stared at each other, their minds both circling the dark side to that agreement. The side neither of them had ever voiced out loud. Their firms had always been close, so even if their individual goals weren't aligned, they'd always sat on the same side. But the day the tables truly turned, when one of Lily and Ray's fallings-out became permanent and turned them into true enemies, both of them were set to lose.

Scarlet broke away first, casting her troubled gaze over the moody churning waters below. She pushed her windswept hair back off her face before turning back to Benny resolutely.

'I won't lie to you, what I'm asking means you'd have to take a course you wouldn't consider otherwise,' she said. 'But it's not something that could put you in a compromising position. And I know I'm asking a lot here...' She shook her head sadly. 'But he's family. And I owe him.' She looked away from the question her admission sparked in Benny's eyes. 'I can't tell you why, but I do,' she said. 'If I could help him myself, I would, but I can't do Jack shit from my side of the river. I have no sway down there. You're my only way.'

She held his gaze with a deep intensity, willing him to help her. Willing him to see how much this meant to her. Willing him to be swayed, just this one time, by his love for her rather than his own needs and goals.

He closed his eyes and exhaled heavily before wiping his face and turning away in a wide, slow circle. She could see how much he hated being put in this position, and she hated herself for doing it. Benny had spent too many years working his way to where he was now, making all the hard sacrifices, learning never to sway from the path he'd plotted. Not for anything. Except now Scarlet was asking him to do just that. To play this next move in protection of the other side's chess piece instead of himself. A piece that was already surrounded with little chance of survival.

Reaching full circle, he stared out at the river, a deep frown etched into his face as he finally answered her. 'What *exactly* did you want me to do?'

FIFTEEN

Ray jolted awake, feeling disorientated. His room was still in total darkness. *It's the middle of the night,* he realised as his wits slowly gathered. *What woke me?*

It took only a fraction of a second to cycle through these dazed thoughts and reach the realisation that something cold and hard was pressed up against his throat, and that a good chunk of his hair was gripped tightly in someone's fist.

Not my first choice of wake-up call, he thought wryly.

'Always good to see you, my love,' he said out loud, the same wryness colouring his words.

'You lost the right to call me that the day you stole my son,' Lily hissed in his ear.

She hadn't been pressing the blade hard enough to hurt before, but now that suddenly changed, and Ray tensed, well aware of how dangerous Lily could be when she wanted. His face contorted, and he silently cursed.

'Now, now,' he continued in a low, easy tone. 'I've already had a shave today; I don't need another.'

'I don't know,' she replied, matching his mocking tone but somehow managing to sound much deadlier. 'I think you might have *missed* a bit.' She twisted the handle with a swift flick, and the end of the blade nicked him viciously.

'Ow!' Ray exclaimed, biting his lip to stop himself cursing her out loud. 'Can't lie, Lil, you'd make a shit barber.'

He tried to move, shuffling and twisting his body away, but she yanked him back, reminding him how surprisingly strong she was for such a slight person. Ray let out a low chuckle and narrowed his eyes as he slowly moved the hand she couldn't see up towards his pillow.

'Scarlet suggested that you and I should have a little chat,' Lily said in a low, angry voice. 'That I should come and hear whatever poor excuse you'd peddle for slithering into my family and luring my child away from the firm I spent his whole life building for him. And I thought, *yeah*, why not? So...' The dark, angry edge to her words became calmer again. A tone Ray had learned to fear much more than her outbursts. '*Here I am.*'

'Mm. You'll have to remind me to thank Scarlet for that stellar suggestion,' he replied, his dry humour beginning to wane.

'The only reminder you need is whose family you decided to fuck with,' Lily replied, her tone hard. 'Because you've clearly forgotten. Either that or you've suffered some sort of brain damage, because *my* family is the one thing I will happily kill for. Kill, maim, torture, I don't really care which,' she hissed, yanking his head back once more. 'Any will suffice, to protect them.'

'A trait of yours I've always greatly admired, you crazy fucking psychopath,' Ray replied through clenched teeth. 'Except what exactly do you think you're protecting them from?'

'*You*,' she growled back.

'From what? The job I offered him that he willingly accepted? The firm I'll hand down to him one day that can be merged with yours to become the largest firm the city's ever seen?'

'I will *never* merge my firm with yours,' Lily shot back hotly.

'*You* won't, no,' Ray agreed. 'But your boys will. *Our* boys. One day they, and Scarlet, will be running the show, and they'll come together. I'm giving them the opportunity to create a fucking *empire*, Lil.' His voice grew stronger as he urged her to see it. 'Not just one firm, one territory. With our firms united, they'd run half the damn city for God's sake!'

'Shut up,' Lily warned as he raised his voice.

'Why are you here, Lily?' he asked, shifting his weight carefully. 'I'm assuming it's *not* to kill me.'

'And why would you assume that?' Lily asked, her voice playfully low again.

Ray chuckled, her tone putting him on edge but not quite overcoming his trust in the logic of the situation. 'No, you can't put me off that easily; you forget how well I know you,' he told her. 'If you really wanted me dead, you'd either have cut my throat in my sleep or had me taken somewhere you could draw out my pain uninterrupted. So the fact I'm still here and you're all alone tells me this is a slightly friendlier visit.'

'You think this is *friendly*?' Lily spat, moving the blade further up his neck and pressing it hard enough to make him wince.

'I did say *slightly*,' he reminded her.

'What do you have on him?' Lily asked, finally jumping to what must have been the point of all this.

Ray frowned, confused. 'What do you mean?'

'You know *exactly* what I mean,' she accused. 'Neither of my boys ever warmed to you, no matter how hard I tried to change that over the years. And I *did* try, whatever you might think.'

Ray resisted the urge to snort. That argument could be started another time.

'They didn't trust you, and they still don't. I *know* they don't,' she added vehemently. 'There's no reason on earth that either of my boys would willingly leave us to join you. So you must have something over him, some threat, and I want to know what it is *right now*. Because I swear to God, if you don't release my boy, I will tear you into a hundred fucking pieces in the most painful ways I can come up with.'

Ray's anger swelled at her words. 'Are you fucking *serious?*' he demanded, his deep, gritty voice booming loudly around the dark room. 'They're my *sons*! You may not have given me the chance to raise them, but they're *still* my blood. I've done a lot of shady things in my time, but I would *never* blackmail my own children for Christ's sake! I'd never force those boys to do *anything*! Jesus *Christ...*' He squeezed his eyes closed for a moment as he tried to contain his outrage.

'All I've done is offer them a choice, an option. And when they told me no, I accepted that. I kept the offer open, but that was it. And you're sat here accusing me of holding Connor hostage?' He laughed, the sound bitter. 'Go and ask him *yourself*. Go on, go ask your son whose choice this was and look him in the eye. You'd know already if you'd bothered to talk to him at all these last few weeks.'

He ignored her sharp intake of breath as he turned the tables, too outraged to continue playing her game.

'You haven't seen this precious son of yours *once* since he came to work for me. You think I don't notice him moping about each Sunday? You think I don't see you *punishing* him, the same way you're punishing me? And you're doing that because deep down you know *damn* well this was his choice. But his reasons are his own; I don't know what they are either. So if you want to know, go and ask him.'

Lily's breathing grew steadily angrier as he talked, and the knife was already as tight as she could pull it without drawing blood, but he knew already that she wasn't going to use it for anything more than the nicks she'd already inflicted. He knew her better than she knew herself, in some ways. And he knew why she was really here, even if *she* didn't. She was here because she needed to blame him to ease her pain. She was here because she wanted to set him on edge, remind him that she could get to him anywhere at any time. But mainly she was here because she wanted a fight. An outlet for her rage. Well, now she'd got one.

'You *don't* get to talk to me about my relationship with my son,' Lily seethed, her voice shaking with anger. 'You don't get to have *any* say in my family after you went behind my back the way you did.'

Ray tried to nod, not really managing it, trapped as he was in her iron-like grasp. 'Alright,' he said. 'You're right. The way I approached it could have been better. I wanted them to think it over on their own, without you immediately knocking the idea out of their heads and blacklisting the idea.' He exhaled tiredly. 'But I never wanted to hurt you. I love you, Lil. You know I do. I love every damn side of you, from your whip-smart perfect side to your crazy fucking wildcat side and all that's in between. I mean, it's certainly never boring. I never know if I'll be woken up by a kiss or a death threat.' He grinned devilishly in the dark. 'It kind of turns me on.'

'I really don't know what drugs you've taken that make you think you're in any position to joke right now,' Lily replied, her tone just as angry as before, as his attempts to defuse the situation fell flat.

'Oh, Lil.' Ray rolled his eyes. 'You're my only vice, you know that. Well, you and the fags. And the whisky,' he added as an afterthought. 'But not drugs – you know that ain't my bag. It's the knife I've had aimed at your gut for the last five minutes that gave me that confidence to joke.'

He waited in silence as she shifted to look down at the knife he'd carefully slipped out and positioned to his own advantage.

She couldn't do anything about it without moving one of her hands, and if she moved one of her hands, he could twist out of her grasp. She was trapped.

'Did you really think I wasn't expecting you?' he asked calmly. 'I've had that under my pillow for weeks. I have to admit though, your timing threw me off. I thought you'd come way before now.'

She cursed and muttered something under her breath. Knowing his time with her was coming to a close, he tried one last time.

'Look, you have two options here. You could back off and slip away. I won't stop ya. *Or* you could lower your blade and just kiss me, the way I *know* you want to.' This time his words were not aimed in jest; instead, his deep gravelly voice softened with emotional sincerity. 'All this fighting with you just pisses me off – I *love* you, Lil. I don't want this, and I know you don't either. Not really. Put that away and stay with me tonight. Come back to me.'

His muscular arms ached to wrap themselves around her slight body and pull her against his chest. He missed her more than he could put into words. He hated it when the connection between them was broken like this. They were one and the same, him and Lily. It had always been the two of them, ever since they'd met as street-hardened kids. It had always been *her*.

'Well, there's always the third option,' she replied. 'I *could* just slit your throat right now and take the risk with your blade. It doesn't look that big.'

Ray resisted the urge to make one of the many obvious jokes that immediately sprang to mind. 'You could. But then *you* ain't that big either. I reckon it would still do the job,' he countered, unfazed.

Lily fell silent, and he held his breath. Her words meant nothing, he knew that. They were just one last show of bravado while she decided what to do. As the moment stretched on, his confidence grew. His words had won her over. She was caving and this was just her stubborn way of making him wait, he was sure of it. But then suddenly she pulled back, her hand and the knife slipping away from him in a movement so quick he almost missed it. And then, to his surprise and deep, hollow disappointment, Lily was gone.

SIXTEEN

Lily walked out of the small antique shop, and the door clanged shut behind her. Frowning at the black clouds threatening a mid-morning tantrum above, she turned and walked briskly towards the main road. She lit a cigarette and took a deep drag as she walked, willing the nicotine to ease some of her stress, but it didn't seem to be helping this morning. Her black stilettos tapped out a sharp, angry rhythm on the pavement, and her face pinched into a hard glower as her dark feelings towards Ray consumed her once more.

None of it made any sense. Ray *had* to have been lying last night. Because she *had* asked Connor, back when he'd first told them. She'd asked him to help her understand and begged him to reconsider. There was no reason for him to want to leave them. *Was he bored?* she'd asked. If so, they could solve that there. He could do anything he wanted, head up a new branch of the firm, lead a fresh new grift, take over one of the existing businesses, but he'd told her that he simply wanted to work for Ray.

That she'd known was a lie. Her sons were stubborn men,

set in their ways and not easily swayed. Ironically, just like Ray. The man they'd spent their whole lives openly disliking.

She blew her smoke out sharply. The fact Ray had been ready for her, that he'd expected her move, really stung. She'd been accused of many things throughout her life, but predictability had never been one of them. Perhaps she was losing her edge. Perhaps that was why he was doing this.

Over all the years she'd loved Ray, she'd always kept him at a careful distance. He was larger than life, enigmatic, colourful, powerful, and he could be incredibly kind and loving. But he was also ruthless and unpredictable, and once his mind was set, he couldn't be contained or controlled.

Ray did love her. But that wouldn't stop him bulldozing her firm to the ground if he decided it was in his best interest.

Reaching the front door of a small greasy caff, she took one last long drag on her cigarette before dropping it to the ground and crushing it with her shoe.

The first few heavy drops of rain pelted down on her jacket as she entered the caff, and she turned her thoughts towards their other troubling issues. Inside, a group of tradesman sat eating a late breakfast to one side, and two old men nursed mugs of tea over a crossword on the other. Cillian sat at the far end of the room, leaning back against the wall, watching her thought-fully as three of their men chatted around him.

She made her way over, and the men fell silent as she took a seat.

Cillian glanced over her shoulder to the woman behind the counter. 'Another coffee, love. Strong one. Cheers.'

Lily checked no one was listening then addressed the small group of men with a grim expression. 'The Romanos are coming tonight.'

Ever since they'd bought the pub, the Drews had run regular gambling nights on the floor above. They were completely off book and only open to those in the underworld.

An unregulated, unwatched casino night where London's faces could relax and bet their ill-gotten gains without fear of it being noticed by the wrong people. Tonight was one of these nights and the Romanos had been an unexpected last-minute confirmation.

'What?' Cillian said with a dark frown. 'They have some fucking nerve.'

'They still think we're in the dark,' Lily replied. 'So they're keeping up appearances.' She twisted so she could keep half an eye on the room as she talked and crossed her slim legs. 'Mani isn't coming, just Riccardo and a couple of his men.'

'They'll be on a big one then,' Cillian said, his deep brown eyes zoning out as he rubbed his chin. 'It's an ideal set-up, but we haven't sorted a tracker or anything yet.'

Joe frowned. 'Tracker for what?'

Lily looked around at the three other men. Of all who worked for them outside of their inner circle, they trusted Joe, Danny and Ben the most. It was why they were here now.

Lily bit the inside of her cheek. 'The three of you know what we're facing right now with the Romanos,' she said levelly. 'And that we need to make a move before they realise we're clued up.' They each nodded. 'We're going to work with the Logans to bring them down. *All* of them.'

'The whole firm?' Danny asked.

She nodded, and the three men exchanged looks of unease.

'We're not taking them out,' she assured them, understanding their reactions entirely. 'That ain't the plan. We're doing something a little different. A little off book.' She met Cillian's gaze. 'We have some dirt on Riccardo that's bad enough to use as leverage against them all. If what we know came out, his life would be over. He wouldn't get out of the clink until he was an old man – if he got that far. Mani, for all his many faults, has always been a devoted family man. He'd lose everything before letting that happen. Which is exactly what we plan to take from him. *Everything*.'

'Mani forced a dirty takeover on the Logans, ten years ago,' Cillian explained, seeing the confusion on their faces. 'That's why they moved to Spain. He exiled them by holding the proof of one of their murders over them, threatening to send it to the pigs.'

'Dirty cunt...' Joe murmured, looking unimpressed.

Lily nodded. 'Exactly. We've always respected the unspoken laws of our world, but for them, after all they've done, we're making an exception.' She waited and watched their expressions closely.

There were very few rules in their way of life, but the ones they *did* have were set in stone. They were free to make moves on other firms. Kidnap, torture, kill, steal, overthrow. It was basically Wild West mentality. Take what you want – but make the move and it's win or be killed. It was that simple, at face value. But one of their most resolute laws was that the *actual* law should never be involved. To grass someone up to the police was a sin of the highest degree. It went against every code that protected their way of life. But their rules were supposed to be mutually respected, not manipulated for personal gain.

After a tense silence, Joe spoke first. 'The rules are there to protect those who follow them. Way I see it, Mani lost his right to their protection the day he did that to the Logans. Dirty players like him deserve everything they get.'

Ben nodded. 'Yeah. I agree. He can't expect to be included in a code he don't keep. He ain't really one of us after that, which makes him fair game. What's the plan?'

Lily turned her piercing gaze to Danny. 'Where's your head at?'

'I don't like it, but I'll do it,' he answered honestly. 'My loyalty's yours; you know that. I just worry about how this will affect us – after.'

'It won't be common knowledge,' Cillian told him. He pulled a toothpick from the breast pocket of his suit jacket and slipped it between his teeth. 'The only people who'll know the full extent of it are those of us in on it and the Tylers. This ain't to be discussed outside that circle.'

'The Tylers?' Joe asked, surprised.

'After we pull this, I want the Romanos out of the country quickly,' Lily explained. 'The threat will be enough to ensure the win, but those boys of Mani's have hot tempers and they're known for reacting without thinking. To take out the risk of any stupid, hot-headed moves when we strike, I want them smuggled straight out to the mainland. They'll be blindfolded before being taken, so won't know the Tylers are involved, and our silence on Riccardo's dirt and whereabouts will be reliant on their silence about our involvement too.'

'So long as this is kept between us, there's no reason for anyone to link us to the Logans' attack on them at all,' Cillian said to Danny. 'Them striking back like that is fair game. It's an eye for an eye. Won't affect their credibility at all.'

Danny nodded, his expression serious.

'Our whole aim is to protect the firm,' Lily reminded him. 'Make sure they can't strike out at us again.'

'And punish the cunts for stealing and trying to kill us of course,' Cillian added darkly.

'Yes, that too,' Lily agreed. 'But my point is that we're not doing it this way to take what's theirs. The sole reason for going off book like this is that it's a viable way to pull it off without an all-out war. No one wants that. This way will be quiet and controlled. No bloodshed. Plus, the Logans are moving back in. They'll be taking over, round there.'

Joe raised his eyebrows with a low whistle. 'They'll be busy.'

'They will. But they're well prepared,' Lily said with confidence.

'They need our manpower to pull this off,' Cillian told

them. 'And we need a way to get rid of the Romanos for good. Until they're out of the picture, we're all just sitting ducks.'

Danny nodded again, a resigned agreement lifting his expression. 'What do we need to do?'

'What we found is useless without the proof, which is currently hidden somewhere in Riccardo's building,' Lily replied, pausing as her coffee arrived. 'Thanks.' She watched the waitress walk back behind the counter. 'We have a plan to get in, but it means Isla running point on a plan that's unpredictable.'

She saw the tightness in Cillian's expression and understood how he felt completely. She didn't like it either, but it was the best shot they had. Danny's reaction surprised her though. His head snapped towards Cillian, and his face widened in shock.

'Really?' he asked, a clear undertone in his voice. 'You're sending Isla *there*?'

Lily frowned, and her sharp eyes flicked over to Cillian. He held Danny's gaze grimly as they shared some silent exchange, then he turned to meet hers. There was a short pause as he tried to work out how to frame his next words, but Lily was already a step ahead.

'You knew about him already,' she said in quiet surprise. She glanced at Danny and frowned. 'You both do. Is it really that common knowledge?' The idea that it was and that the rest of their world hadn't batted an eyelid made her feel sick.

Cillian shook his head. 'No, it's not common knowledge, but there's always been rumours, and a few people, me and Danny included, saw some of it first-hand. We got invited to one of his parties, years ago. We were maybe eighteen – it was back before any of the big fall-outs. Before the Logans.' He looked away with a grim expression. 'We weren't there long. I kicked off at him after he started slapping this bird about. But there was too many of them and only two of us. In the end, we had no choice but to back off and leave.'

Lily sat back and watched the pair of them. They looked uncomfortable and ashamed. 'Don't do that,' she ordered with a frown.

'Do what?' Cillian asked.

'Beat yourselves up. It was what it was.' Lily sighed, itching for a cigarette. 'You were outnumbered, young and naïve. And he's a fucking menace.' She bit her lip. 'Look, I don't like sending Isla in either, but unless either of you look good in a wig and make-up, she's the best option we've got. And we're running out of time. Their last plan to take us out failed, but that was down to pure luck. We can't afford to wait for the next one.'

Cillian made a sound of grudging agreement. 'I just wish we had time to get her rigged up with a tracker.'

'Well, we don't,' Lily replied heavily. 'So we're going to have to work with what we've got and trust she can pull this off. Because her window of opportunity is tonight, and if she plays her cards right then...' She trailed off for a moment as a dark cloud of worry settled over her. 'Well, then she's in there on her own.'

SEVENTEEN

Scarlet sat back and stared through her windscreen at the block of flats Isla lived in, mentally running through the plan for the hundredth time.

'Here she is,' she said quietly as Isla appeared. She straightened up and pushed her sleek raven hair back off her face. 'Thanks again for doing this.'

This was directed at Sandra, who she'd picked up just fifteen minutes earlier. Isla's smile of greeting faltered as she caught sight of the woman in the passenger seat, and Scarlet felt a prickle of guilt. Perhaps she should have picked Isla up first and warned her, but they were short on time, and Sandra's place had been en route. Sandra, completely oblivious to Isla's feelings towards her, waved and smiled breezily. The action lit up her face, making her look even more picture perfect than she already was, and Scarlet's sympathy for Isla increased slightly.

Sandra possessed the kind of natural beauty that was most commonly found on photoshopped magazine covers. With just a touch of make-up, her perfect tanned skin glowed like that of a bronzed goddess. At five foot eight she had – as Cath would put it – *legs for days,* and her slim figure curved gracefully in all the right places. Her warm smile and Bette Davis eyes drew people in like a moth to a flame, and her blonde waves always fell perfectly no matter what the day or weather. And while Scarlet was able to admire Sandra from the confident comfort of her own skin, she could understand why the woman got right under Isla's – and why Connor was still besotted with her, despite her making it abundantly clear that she didn't return his interest.

Isla slipped into the back seat, shutting the door quickly behind her. 'Hey,' she said cagily, her eyes darting between the backs of their heads.

'Hi, Isla,' Sandra replied. 'You look nice. I like that top.'

'Thanks,' Isla replied shortly.

Scarlet looked at her through the rear-view mirror as she pulled out into the road. 'You look great,' she echoed. 'Riccardo won't be able to resist.'

Isla's gaze slipped over to Sandra then back to meet hers. The query was clear.

'Sandra knows. And she's in on the plan too.'

Isla frowned. 'In what way?'

Scarlet grimaced internally. Isla wasn't going to like this development, but it was the best way to make things look natural.

'So, this whole plan hinges on Riccardo not thinking you have any link to us, right?' Scarlet slowed as she arrived at a red light and glanced at Isla. 'Which means you can't actually attend the casino night.'

Isla's frown deepened as she quickly back-pedalled through the thought process that must have led to this statement, and Scarlet watched the realisation click into place.

'Ahh, of course I can't.' Isla pursed her lips with a silent sigh of annoyance. 'To be there, I'd need to be with a firm and when I can't show one, I'd be blown. Shit—'

'It's fine – we have a plan. We've cut the upstairs bar staff and dropped to a skeleton detail on the floor, so there's no bar upstairs and no one to run orders.' The light turned green and she moved forward. 'Anyone who wants a drink will have to go down to the actual bar. Where you two will be enjoying a nice girls' night out. Sandra's your wingman.'

Isla didn't look impressed with this at all. 'I can handle this perfectly fine on my own, you know.'

'I know you can,' Scarlet assured her. 'But you'd look a bit suss sitting there on your own all night.'

Isla opened her mouth to reply, then seemingly changed her mind and closed it again, turning to look out of the window.

'At least you'll have someone to bounce plays off. I'll follow your lead,' Sandra offered tactfully. 'It's easier to set up a hook with two people. Plus,' she added, 'it's safer to go into things like this in twos.' Her smile dropped as she stared off into the distance. 'Riccardo's a nasty piece of work. Not someone you want to be alone with.'

'Mm,' Isla replied in grudging agreement.

The car fell into silence, and Scarlet felt the small bubble of unease in her stomach grow. She'd always felt like there was something off about Riccardo, something more than his hot temper and his greasy manner, but she'd still been shocked when she'd gone through Isla's file. *Was this really the only option they had?*

The car remained silent until they reached the factory car park, a ten-minute walk from the pub. Scarlet pulled up and twisted to face them both properly.

'Listen, the aim is just to find this room. The moment you do, you get out, OK?' Her troubled eyes rested on Isla. 'You get the invite, find the room and then scarper. We have no way of keeping up with you once you're up there. Cillian's round the corner, and Danny and Joe are watching the building from across the road. They have eyes on the lounge window, but that's it. If you need help, throw something out of it. A bottle, a glass, whatever you can find. They'll come up and do whatever it takes to pull you out, but that's a last resort, and it only works if you can get to the window.' She stared at Isla. 'Are you a hundred per cent sure you want to do this?'

Isla nodded. 'I'll be fine. It's our best chance against the Romanos, and someone needs to get this bastard.' Her expression turned grim and she shook her head. 'All those girls...'

Scarlet nodded. 'Yeah,' she said quietly. 'I know.'

'It might not even happen,' Isla replied. 'We're assuming he's going to want to party and that he'll be on the scout, but he might just be out for a quiet one.'

'He's definitely not out for a quiet one,' Scarlet replied with confidence. 'Any night without Mani gets loud. He never passes up the chance to go wild when he's off his leash.'

Mani kept tight control over his firm even in his supposed semi-retirement, and that included over his two sons. Not that Luca needed so much reining in these days, after Cillian and Connor had clipped his wings a couple of years back. These days he mainly skulked in his brother's shadow, no longer possessing the credibility to lead anything in the name of his father's firm.

Scarlet's phone vibrated, and she checked the screen. 'I need to go.'

'See you later then,' Isla replied, unbuckling her belt.

Sandra waited until she was outside, then she lowered her voice. 'I'll help her get in, then I'll stay nearby. You're sure she's up to this?'

Scarlet glanced out at Isla. 'She's up to it. But I appreciate you helping out. Keep safe, yeah?'

''Course,' Sandra replied, opening the door and slipping out.

Both doors shut, and Scarlet watched them walk away into the darkness, her hands tightening around the steering wheel. It wasn't often she got the jitters about a job, but then again, it wasn't often that the job held this kind of threat. She could face an enemy who was after their money or their businesses, or even their blood. Those battles were led and fought with strategy or anger or a mixture of both, and those were things she understood. Those were things they were all prepared to go up against. But this sort of threat was a whole other ball game. She turned the car around and pulled away.

Riccardo wasn't after money or power or revenge. At least not in the way most of their enemies were. Riccardo was just a depraved, sick bully who got off on hurting and sexually abusing women. *Lots* of women. Women who too often disappeared or never recovered their memories of what happened to them. This wasn't something she could understand at all. And *that* was the cause of the chill in her stomach tonight. Because one of the best lessons her aunt had ever taught her was that to beat an enemy, you needed to understand them. To go against one you didn't understand at all put you at an instant disadvantage, which made things downright dangerous.

Scarlet's grey-blue eyes stared into the darkness, for once a flicker of fear spearing their usual steel as she wondered, not for the first time, if they were making a truly terrible mistake.

EIGHTEEN

The smoke from Lily's cigarette drifted up into the air and curled around the second line of smoke from the one in Freddie Tyler's hand. He sat back in the chair opposite her, his brother Paul next to him, as the muted chatter from the casino night in the event space across the hall from her office filled the silence. Freddie's hazel-green eyes held Lily's gaze intently, his hard, chiselled face revealing nothing as he thought over the request, and accompanying offer, she'd just put to him.

Lily took another drag, waiting patiently. She and the Tylers went way back. Right back to when the pair of them had been just kids running around the estate and she'd babysat them, whenever their mother, Molly, had managed to get extra work in the evenings. Things had changed an awful lot since then of course. These days, the Tylers headed the largest firm in London. They were underworld royalty – respected by all, only opposed by fools. But they'd maintained a special bond over all those years. It was the reason she trusted them enough to share her plans. Even if they wanted no part of it, they would never betray her secrets.

'I've never had time for that side of the family,' Freddie said eventually, tapping his cigarette on the ashtray in front of him. 'But we occasionally do business with the nephews.'

Paul grunted an agreement and nodded slowly, lines in his forehead deepening as his dark brows knotted.

'There would be no risk of them or anyone else ever knowing of your involvement,' Lily replied. 'Mani will know about us of course. And their silence on that will be held under the same threat. But they'd never know you were there. We'll bind and blind 'em, have them ready before you arrive. So long as whoever takes them over keeps quiet, they'll never have a clue.'

A challenging twinkle appeared in Freddie's eye as he held her gaze, unwavering, and the corner of his mouth hitched up briefly. 'You know, every time you ask for a favour, I tell myself it can't possibly be more random than the last. And I'm always wrong. *Every* time.'

Lily grinned and took another drag on her cigarette. 'Well...' She blew out the smoke sharply. 'Technically this one ain't a favour.' Freddie hitched an eyebrow. 'On its own at least,' she amended.

'No,' he agreed, turning to his brother.

Paul tilted his head with an expression that showed he was on the fence. This one would be down to Freddie.

Freddie sighed and rubbed his eyes with his thumb and forefinger. 'You know what this will do to Ray, don't you? He'll never forgive you, Lil. I don't know what's going on with you two at the moment, but I *do* know he won't forgive you this.'

'Good,' she replied coldly. 'Maybe then he'll finally get the message.'

Freddie bit his upper lip and studied her for a moment. 'It's a great deal for us, and as a businessman I can't see any sense in turning you down. But as your friend, I urge you to reconsider what you're offering. I think you're making a mistake. Ray loves you, but he's a shark, and this is a big blow.'

'A very public statement too,' Paul added. 'That kind of thing can wound deeper than the actual blow.'

'True,' Freddie agreed. 'Especially for someone like Ray.'

Lily took another drag, holding it in before releasing it into the air slowly. She knew they were right, but she and Ray were already past the point of no return. Now she just wanted to hurt him. Hurt him as deeply as he'd hurt her. Except he didn't have any cherished family to steal away. His ego and his business were as close as she was going to get.

'You know the saying,' she said quietly. '*All's fair in love and war.* Well Ray waged war long before now. But you don't need to worry about that.' She swallowed the lump of bitterness and pain that formed suddenly in her throat. 'All you need to decide is whether you're in or not.'

Freddie looked at her sadly for a moment, then with a small sigh he nodded. 'Alright. We'll take the Romanos to the mainland and ditch them somewhere uncomfortable for you. Just get me details ahead of time. And as for your offer...' He shook his head. 'Well, like I said, I'd be a fool to refuse. After this is all cleared up, we'll sit down and iron out the details, but we're in.'

Lily nodded. 'Good. We'll sit down properly to negotiate the payoffs and limits, then your dealers can begin working our territory.'

The Drews had never dealt in the drugs trade before, or officially allowed other firms to deal on their turf. It still went on, of course, but on a much smaller scale than in other areas of the city, and on the odd occasion they'd found another firm's dealer trading, they'd always dropped them back to their bosses with a violently clear warning. But although Lily still wasn't a fan, the reason for her war against drugs in the area had gone. Ruby was dead, no longer running around chasing her next hit or high. And Lily wasn't naïve enough to believe she could keep drugs out of here forever. They were seeping in at the sides, more and more. At least this way she could regulate it. Control how much could come in and how often. And the payout they'd get for allowing the Tylers to deal there wouldn't hurt either.

Ray had offered her a similar deal, some time back, and she'd refused, not ready at the time to give up her stubborn fight against it all. After all their years together, and with their firms being so close, he should have been the one she made this deal with. It was his right, in many ways. To offer this to the Tylers instead – to *any* firm – was a snub of the highest degree. And a big financial blow for Ray. Hers was a lucrative territory.

A quiet knock sounded at the door, and George poked his head in. 'They're here,' he said gruffly with a nod of respect to the Tylers.

'Thanks. I'll come now.' Lily stood up and smoothed down her black knee-length dress. 'I apologise that I can't stop longer to seal this deal the proper way,' she said, opening a cupboard to the side of the room and pulling out a tray that held a cut-crystal decanter and four matching glasses. She placed it down on the desk. 'Please help yourselves and use my office as long as you like, then come join us when you're ready.'

Freddie nodded, reaching for the decanter. He popped the topper off and breathed in the scent of the amber liquid.

'Scotch. Single malt. Laphroaig?' he asked.

'Of course. One I decanted just for *you* actually.' She held his gaze with a small smile. 'But you already know that's my favourite. What *I* want to know is whether you're skilled enough to tell the age?' She winked at Paul then hitched an eyebrow at Freddie.

Paul chuckled. 'I'd like to see him try.'

A ghost of a smile lightened Freddie's hard expression, and he turned to Paul. 'You sound like you don't have any faith in my abilities.'

'I don't,' Paul replied with certainty. 'You know your malts, but I'd bet my last pound you couldn't narrow down to a year.'

Freddie raised his eyebrows. 'Alright then. How much?'

Lily perched on the side of her desk and watched, amused.

'Alright.' Paul grinned. 'I bet you a big bag of sand you can't guess it.' He pulled out a thick wad of notes and slapped it down on the desk.

'A grand, alright,' Freddie agreed. 'How about another for finish too?'

Paul narrowed his eyes then pulled out another wad. 'Alright – but, Lil, you have to write it down first so I know he ain't cheating.'

'Oh, of course,' Lily agreed. She quickly jotted down the details, then ripped the page out and handed it to Paul.

He slipped it away and fixed Freddie with a challenging stare. 'Go on then, smart arse.' He smirked as Freddie picked up the decanter. 'You ain't gonna have much to play with after this, you daft twat. But that's OK – I'll spot you a tenner. *If* you ask nicely.'

Freddie put his nose to the top of the bottle and swirled the whisky around gently, frowning into the distance.

'Vanilla... Lemon...' he said slowly.

'Is it whisky or cheesecake?' Paul asked drily.

Lily grinned.

'Bit of oak, and... Hmm. Leather,' Freddie finished decisively. Pouring out two measures he hovered over the third glass and raised an eyebrow at Lily.

She shook her head.

Freddie handed a glass to Paul, then sat back in his chair and waited for him to take a sip, before delivering his verdict. 'And *that*, Paul, is what a 1997 Laphroaig tastes like after being matured for twenty-five years in a single refill hogshead cask.'

Paul scoffed. 'Yeah, alright. Let's see, shall we?' He checked the paper Lily had handed him, and his face dropped in shock. '*No...*' he uttered. 'That ain't possible. *Really?*'

Freddie opened his arms wide and pulled an expression that said *I told you so.*

'Well *shit*,' Paul said, dumbfounded. 'That's bloody unbe-lievable.'

Freddie shrugged and picked up the two stacks of notes on the table. 'What can I say, it's a skill.'

'But *how?*' Paul asked with a frown. 'That's insane. You ever known anyone be able to do that, Lil?'

She walked over to the door with a chuckle, squeezing his shoulder as she passed. 'No. Still don't either. Freddie bought me that bottle for my fortieth. I tipped him off just before he played you.'

'Ahh, Lil, you're such a spoilsport,' Freddie complained.

Paul's eyes widened in accusation. 'You cheating bastard!'

Lily grinned and shrugged. 'What have I always told you, eh? You can cheat the shit out of anyone else, but you *don't* cheat family. Now give your brother his money back and go lose it out there on my tables, instead of in here to each other.' She tipped Freddie a wink, then slipped out and closed the door behind her.

'Come on then. You heard Lil – gimme my cash back,' she heard Paul demand.

'No! Ain't my fault you're gullible enough to lose your play money before we even hit the tables,' Freddie replied. 'But don't worry – I'll spot you a tenner. *If* you ask nicely.'

NINETEEN

Isla sipped her mocktail and stared resentfully at the reflection of the woman next to her through the mirror behind the bar. Why did they have to choose *her* of all people? She understood the logic of pairing someone up with her, but why the one person she genuinely truly disliked?

Sandra wasn't this great person she'd fooled everyone into believing she was. She was a selfish, spoiled brat who thought herself better than everyone else. It killed Isla having to watch Connor's lovestruck attempts to woo the woman. But it hurt even more watching Sandra rebuff him time and again so callously. Because he deserved better than that. He deserved happiness, even if that wasn't with her.

Her eyes darted nervously towards the door that led to the room upstairs, for the umpteenth time since Riccardo had walked in. What if he didn't come down? What if he just kept sending his men for drinks? She'd seen them twice already.

'... *two days* before her wedding and all! Talk about *pressure!*' Sandra prattled on beside her.

'Yeah, cool story,' Isla muttered sarcastically.

Sandra fell silent, and it was a few seconds before Isla realised she was studying her through the bar mirror.

'You know, you need to lighten up a bit,' Sandra said.

Isla bristled. 'And *you* need to mind your own,' she shot back.

Sandra frowned. 'It ain't an insult. You want to sit there all stressed out, go ahead. But moody mugs don't exactly scream *approachable*. So, if you want to catch Riccardo's attention when he finally *does* walk through that door, then *literally*, you need to lighten up.' She glanced down at Isla's mocktail. 'Why don't you have a proper drink? Take the edge off.'

'I'm not nervous,' Isla replied dismissively. 'This isn't my first rodeo with a man like him.'

Sandra nodded. 'Your ex. I remember.'

The familiarity in Sandra's words sent a barb of irritation through Isla's core, and she snapped. 'You don't know *shit* about my business.'

'I'm just saying I remember what you went through when you came here, that's all,' Sandra replied with a strained sigh. 'It was shitty, and you didn't deserve that. No one does. But bad as he was, I promise you that Riccardo's worse.' She'd lowered her voice and glanced towards the door. 'He's as bad as they get. You just need to stay sharp with him and never assume *anything*. OK?'

Isla's eyebrows shot upwards. 'You're giving me *advice*? You think just because you spent a few years as a hooker that you're the only one who knows how to handle a *bad man*?' She abruptly halted, feeling instantly guilty for the low blow.

Sandra's face tightened, and she turned back to the bar. She twisted her wine glass round by the stem, and a cold smile briefly flickered across her mouth before she tilted her head in acknowledgement.

'That's right, Isla,' she said in a flat voice. 'I *was* a hooker. I left all that behind a long time ago, but it's not something I'm ashamed of. So if that's what you were aiming for, you're out of luck.' She picked up her wine and tipped a good portion of it into her mouth. 'For better or worse, my life choices got me to where I am.' She turned to Isla now, her blue eyes cool and steady. 'And I *like* where I am. I like *who* I am and all.'

Isla lowered her gaze. 'I'm sorry,' she said awkwardly. 'I didn't mean that.'

'Yes, you did,' Sandra replied calmly. 'It's fine, Isla. Truths ain't something to apologise for. Not in a world full of liars.'

Isla opened her mouth to respond, but just then the door to the stairs swung open and a deep raucous laugh caught both their attentions. Riccardo swaggered through and made a beeline for the bar.

Sandra's hand gripped the top of her arm. 'Forget that now,' she whispered. 'All that matters is getting through this. And I meant what I said, Isla. *Stay vigilant.* Because whatever you think, I promise you... You really don't know what you're up against.'

TWENTY

Sandra laughed along with Isla at Riccardo's poor attempt at a joke, careful not to make eye contact as he moved his calculating gaze between the two of them. He was clearly weighing up which of them to go for, barely bothering to hide it as he made leery comment after leery comment.

Isla was holding her own now. After a moment of hesitation, she'd jumped into character like she'd been doing this her whole life. And perhaps she had. As she'd pointed out so aggressively before, Sandra didn't know much about her life at all. Now she flirted and flattered without pause, giggling away while Sandra stayed strategically behind her, on her bar stool.

Riccardo leaned sideways on the bar facing the pair of them, and he caught her attention with a tilt of his head. She looked up with a polite smile.

'You ladies need another drink. What you 'aving? Oi.' He turned towards Tommy, who was busy serving another customer and made a circle motion over the bar with his finger. 'Another round, maestro, when you're ready. Whatever these two want, two pints and four tequilas.'

'Sounds like someone's in the mood to party,' Isla said with a giggle.

Riccardo looked down at her with a smug smile, wiggling his eyebrows. 'I might just be.'

His gaze dropped to Isla's chest, and Sandra looked away to cover her disgust as he practically licked his lips. It was safe to say that Isla had earned her invite, and her concern for the spiky young woman swelled. Isla shouldn't be doing this. She had no idea what she was letting herself in for. She thought she did, but she was wrong.

Isla's ex had been violent, vindictive and controlling. A bully who got off on hurting her and who'd put her through hell. But he'd also had his own twisted version of feelings for her, by all accounts. He'd wanted her for himself, and her existence in his life was fairly public, so it was unlikely that he'd have ever actually killed her. On purpose at least.

But Riccardo had no such barriers. He didn't know Isla from Adam. He had no feelings for her, no public scrutiny to answer to. As far as he knew, no one of any importance would know she'd gone home with him tonight. And Riccardo enjoyed far more than a bit of violent rape.

He laughed again, and the sound set her teeth on edge. She grinned as if greatly amused and watched Tommy pour their drinks.

Isla thought she knew the worst of it. She didn't. What she'd dug up was bad enough, and when Scarlet had told her their plan and shown her Isla's findings, Sandra had almost warned her about the rest. But she'd stopped herself. She knew a lot more about Riccardo than they did, from her time as an escort, but there was a tightly bound code throughout the world of prostitution. When someone like him came along, they could spread certain warnings to protect each other, but no one talked outside of that circle. It wasn't done. They couldn't risk anyone from their line of work appearing untrustworthy. It put their business at risk and at times meant the difference between life and death.

But now she was here, watching Isla bait one of London's worst monsters into making her his next target, and she had no idea who he was. Sandra was scared for her. Genuinely scared. Mandy, the girl whose photos Isla had at the front of her file, hadn't just *gone missing*, like they'd told her. Mandy had been desperate. Mandy had known about Riccardo and had taken the jobs anyway. She'd accepted beating after beating, broken bones and internal damage, crying for the camera the way he wanted, because she needed the money – badly. But one day Mandy had made the fatal mistake of revealing that she had no family.

The last time she'd taken a job with Riccardo, there had been two of them. Tiff, the girl who'd made it out alive, never recovered from the ordeal. Sandra's friend had shared how Tiff had barely been able to relay what had happened, how she'd shaken violently as she'd whispered what she could before becoming incoherent and inconsolable.

Riccardo and two other men had beaten Mandy to death for pleasure. He'd told her in advance that this was how she'd die. They'd both tried to run, but it had been too late – they were locked in, and they'd killed Mandy cruelly and slowly, forcing Tiff to watch and getting sick kicks out of every second. The worse it got, the more Riccardo had enjoyed it, and after she was finally dead, he'd continued abusing Mandy's lifeless body for hours in the most unthinkable ways. Tiff had moved away a week later, cutting all ties.

Worry swirled in the pit of Sandra's stomach. What if he wasn't just looking to rape someone tonight? *Just.* The word ricocheted around her head, sounding more absurd every second. *Just* rape. What sick world did they live in that this was the better option? And how on earth was Isla going to get herself out of there once she was in? Sandra was supposed to leave once Isla got the invite, but she already knew she couldn't. She couldn't leave her alone with a devil she didn't know.

Tommy, the bar manager, placed the drinks in front of them and caught her eye briefly, reminding her that he was keeping watch on the situation.

Isla chatted on beside her. 'Well, Sally's knackered and has work really early tomorrow, so we just came out for a quiet couple.' They'd changed their names to be extra cautious. 'She wants to go soon though.'

'Yeah?' Riccardo leaned in a little closer. 'And what about you? You wanna go home too? Or you up for a party?'

'A party?' Isla asked chirpily. 'Where?'

'My place,' Riccardo replied. 'A few of us are heading back for a few drinks, few lines. You party, Amy?' he asked, kinking one eyebrow meaningfully. '*Party* party?'

'I party,' Isla replied with a grin. She turned to Sandra. 'You sure you want to go home?' She waited for Sandra to yawn as planned and state that she was too tired.

'Actually, I've changed my mind,' Sandra said instead, cursing her conscience. She'd rather be *anywhere* else, but here she was, jumping in with both feet instead. Because she knew she couldn't let Isla go through with this. She'd never forgive herself.

She pushed her breasts out, giving Riccardo a dazzling smile. 'This party sounds too fun to miss.' She held his gaze coyly.

Isla's jaw dropped, and she glared at Sandra as subtly as she could.

'I thought you were too *tired*,' she said with emphasis. 'And you've got work *really early*.'

'Sod it,' Sandra replied, brushing it off. 'I'll call in sick.'

A flash of resentment crossed Isla's face, and she whipped her head back around towards Riccardo. Moving to block his view of Sandra, she resumed her flirtation a little more exaggeratedly than before.

'I love parties,' she gushed.

His grin widened. 'Yeah? What else do you like then, party girl?' He leaned towards her ear. 'Do you like...'

Sandra couldn't make out the rest, but Isla instantly giggled and squeezed his arm. She watched with an internal sigh, barely registering Tommy's loud cough from further up the bar. The second cough caught her attention, and when she looked, he flicked his gaze pointedly to Isla's mocktail. Sandra dipped her brows very briefly in question, and he did it again before flipping his hand over below the bar level.

His meaning instantly became clear. Isla's drink was spiked. Sandra cursed herself for missing it. Riccardo must have slipped something in as he leaned over just now. Her insides grew colder. It wasn't enough for her to just go along to this party. She couldn't even protect Isla *here*. If Isla was in Riccardo's flat, Sandra stood no chance of making sure she got out unscathed.

'That settles it then,' Riccardo said. 'We'll finish these and head out. All of us.' He grinned at Sandra, and she returned the look enthusiastically.

'Great,' she said, reaching for her and Isla's drinks. 'Here you go, Amy.'

She grasped the tall glass and made to hand it over, loosening her grip just before Isla took it. It dropped, the bright purple liquid sloshing all down her front, soaking her clothes before the glass fell to the floor and shattered.

'What the *hell*!' Isla cried, jumping up and looking down at her wet, stained outfit in horror.

'Oh God, I'm so sorry!' Sandra cried, her hands flying to her cheeks.

'What are you *doing*?' Isla continued angrily. 'I'm *drenched*!'

Sandra jumped down from her bar stool and pushed Isla away.

'Excuse us a moment, gents! Come on – let's go sort you out.' She flashed the men a quick grin and steered Isla towards the ladies.

'Get the *fuck* off me, you lunatic,' Isla muttered through gritted teeth, yanking herself subtly out of Sandra's grip as they walked.

As soon as the door closed behind them, she rounded on Sandra with a snarl. 'What are you playing at? I *know* that wasn't an accident.' She narrowed her gaze and pointed her finger in Sandra's face. '*I* came up with this information, and *I* came up with the plan – *you* don't get to muscle in at the last minute and shove me out of the way just so that you can take the credit.'

Sandra batted Isla's finger out of the way and stepped purposely forward, forcing Isla to take a step back. 'Shut up, Isla. I ain't trying to take anyone's credit, I'm trying to do you a *favour*. Riccardo slipped you a roofie. I was saving you from being *drugged* for Christ's sake.'

Isla glared up at her, mistrust in her eyes, and Sandra tutted. 'Don't believe me? Here...' She grabbed the front of Isla's sodden top and scrunched a handful of the fabric together.

'Hey!' Isla cried as the action yanked her forward. 'What are you *doing*?'

'*Look*,' Sandra demanded.

She squeezed hard enough to release a few purple droplets onto the bright pink nails of her other hand. Almost instantly the pink began to fade to black where the liquid landed.

'This is a special polish – it shows up those types of drugs when you dip them in your drink,' she explained, but she could see from Isla's expression that she already understood.

She stepped back and ripped some tissue off a roll in one of the stalls to wipe her hand, then walked back to the sinks. She fluffed her hair and checked her make-up, before turning back to Isla, who was staring at her outfit with a look of deflated despair.

'Isla, you shouldn't go tonight,' Sandra said quietly. 'Once you're in there, you won't be able to just walk out, the way you think you can.'

Isla's expression immediately hardened. 'Just *stop*, Sandra. OK? I know you like to be queen bee and make sure that every man's attention is on you, but this isn't about that. Just let me do my job and get out of my way.'

Sandra's eyebrows rose, and she bit down on her tongue. A lesser person would have walked away and left Isla to it, after an insult like that. But that just wasn't Sandra. No matter how much of a bitch the girl was. Still, if she was going to succeed in saving Isla from herself tonight, she was going to have to switch tactics. She pulled in a deep breath and held her hands up.

'You know what, do what you want. Dry your trousers off under the drier – they ain't that bad. I'll find you a clean top. Scarlet keeps some bits upstairs in case she needs to change. She won't mind you borrowing one.' She nodded towards the drier. 'Go on. I'll be back in a minute, then I'll leave you to it. You're in now anyway; you don't need me anymore.'

'Oh. OK then,' Isla said, caught off guard by the sudden change. 'Thanks.'

Sandra smiled sadly. 'You're welcome.'

Isla turned towards the drier, and Sandra slipped out of the bathroom. Pausing for a moment to gather her courage, she lifted her chin, plastered on a smile, and sauntered back over to Riccardo and his men.

'Here she is,' he said, raking her up and down with his eyes.

She tipped her pelvis towards him and touched her hand to her chest. 'Yeah. Just me though, I'm afraid. Mardy arse in there changed her mind.' She rolled her eyes. 'One spilled drink and you'd think the world was ending.'

'Yeah?' Riccardo glanced over towards the bathroom, unconvinced. 'She seemed so up for it earlier.'

'Yep. Her mood swings harder than Tyson on speed. You can never predict where it's gonna go next.' She smirked.

'Ha! Women...' Riccardo chuckled. 'You're all fucking crazy, but we wouldn't want you any other way.' He leered at her, and she forced a laugh. 'You sure it's not that you just want me all to yourself?' he added, mostly joking.

'Maybe it is.' She picked up one of the tequilas and shot it back before slamming the empty glass back on the bar, careful to grab the one beside Riccardo rather than the one he'd placed by her bar stool. 'I guess you'll never know. Now are we going to party or not?' She touched his shirt and bit her bottom lip before walking past him towards the exit. 'I'm done here.'

Tommy tried to catch her eye, but she ignored it, too busy trying to quell her shaking nerves.

Riccardo exchanged a dark smile with his men and followed her. 'You heard the lady. Let's go.'

* * *

Lily laughed along with the rest of the table at the punchline of Freddie's story, but her attention was actually on the door. Tommy had just poked his head around and beckoned Scarlet out as she'd passed nearby. Seconds later, the door reopened and Scarlet's urgent gaze sought hers. *This couldn't be good.*

'Excuse me, gentlemen.' Lily stood up from her seat at the poker table and folded her hand.

She slipped out of the room and followed Scarlet through to her office. To her surprise, she found an angry Isla there, pacing the floor, a huge dark purple stain covering her front from her chest to her knees.

'What's going on?' she demanded.

'Sandra just took off with Riccardo,' Scarlet told her with a troubled frown. 'He roofied Isla's drink, so Sandra knocked it over her and took her to the loos to dry off. She said she was going back to keep Riccardo warm, but Tommy said she just led them all straight out. Told them Isla wasn't coming.'

'*Why*?' Lily asked, perplexed. 'When did this happen?'

'Five minutes ago,' Scarlet replied.

'And she's definitely gone?' Lily asked urgently, half turning back to the door.

'She's gone; I checked,' Isla said.

'What *happened*?' Scarlet asked. 'Did she say anything before she went? Anything at all?'

'No...' Isla hesitated with a squint. 'Well just that I shouldn't do this. But no reason why. Clearly she just wanted to pull this herself,' she added resentfully.

Lily's frown deepened, and she turned it over in her head. This wasn't like Sandra. She wouldn't jeopardise a job without good reason.

Her phone buzzed, and a text popped up from Sandra. She scanned it as Scarlet questioned Isla further then looked up grimly, silencing them both with her hand.

'Look, it's done. Perhaps something changed and she had to make the choice. Whatever happened, Sandra's on point now and we just have to go with it.'

Both of them stared back at her in surprise.

'Isla, I need you to go and update Cillian, then you can head home. Get cleaned up and get some sleep. We'll have a big day tomorrow. And don't worry. Plans change.'

'OK, call if you need me,' Isla said as she left, a trifle reluctantly.

Scarlet waited until the door closed before raising an eyebrow in question. Lily pulled the text up and turned the screen towards Scarlet.

'Things are more complicated than we thought,' she said heavily.

TWENTY-ONE

Sandra locked the bathroom door and grasped the sides of the sink, leaning heavily on it and staring at her reflection. There was a familiar haunted hollowness in the eyes staring back at her that she'd hoped never to see again in this life.

It had been a hard path that had led her to where she was today. After a cold, turbulent childhood in the care system, being bounced from one foster home to the next, she'd aged out with no family, no qualifications and no hope for the future. The only thing she'd had going for her was her looks. And they'd often been more of a curse than a blessing.

She'd been too young to understand that, when her first abuser had snuck into her room to take her virginity. He'd told her to stay quiet when she'd cried out in fear and pain, and she'd obeyed, frozen and terrified, as he'd raped her, his rough hands roaming her body, his sour breath hot on her cheek. She'd been just thirteen.

He'd been the first man to abuse her as a vulnerable child, but he'd been far from the last. She'd lost count of the number of foster homes she'd been moved on from after that. After her behaviour had spiralled sharply downwards. But she'd kept count of everything else. The number of abusers she'd suffered in care was seven. The number of times she'd asked for help was three. The number of times she'd been believed was zero. By eighteen, she'd become numb to it all, and by nineteen, she'd learned how to use her effect on men to her advantage.

The Drews had been the first people to ever give her a real chance. She'd started out working for them as a high-end escort, but she'd ended up finding genuine friends who cared about her. And when her chips were down, they hadn't turned their backs. Instead, Scarlet had offered her a job in the hairdresser's. And *then* she'd put her through her qualifications and helped her carve a whole new career. A whole new life.

The Drews had given her everything she held dear, and she owed them more than they realised for that. So although she'd stopped turning tricks three years ago, she would do it once more if she had to, for them.

Her fingers gripped the edge of the sink a little tighter, then she let go and stood up with a sniff. She needed to get herself together. Riccardo had already tried to drug her twice, and she knew she was going to have to play the next hour very carefully if she was going to come out of this relatively unscathed. It was just the four of them. Her, Riccardo and the two men from the pub. Music was playing and the cocaine was flowing in the other room. She'd declined Riccardo's repeated offers of cocaine and had caught the annoyance each time beneath his fake smile, which, unbeknown to him, had revealed one very important detail. The type of date-rape drug he was using.

There were two types easily available in this city. Others existed, but nine times out of ten it boiled down to either Rohypnol or GHB. Rohypnol was an all-nighter. It would knock a person out for up to twelve hours but could be tricky to administer. In liquid form only, it was easy enough to slip into a drink, but it had the disadvantage for the user of turning the liquid blue.

GHB only knocked people out for three to four hours; in comparison, however, it was a lot more versatile. In liquid form it remained colourless, but it also came in powder form and could be snorted, easily hidden in a line of cocaine.

Earlier in the pub, Isla's drink had been dark purple, so Sandra hadn't been able to tell, but his desperate bids for her to do *just one line* had made it quite clear.

A loud wave of laughter travelled through from the lounge, and Sandra glanced back into the mirror and pinched her cheeks one more time. Then, with a deep breath, she plastered on her best fake smile and opened the door.

'Ooh, what are those?' she enthused as she returned to the lounge and saw the round tray of tall shot glasses on the coffee table. They were filled with a shimmering amber concoction.

Riccardo's grin widened, and he immediately stood up, passing her one of the glasses. She accepted it, carefully positioning herself next to a tall potted plant.

'I call this liquid gold,' he said proudly. 'It's caramel liquor with vodka and this cocktail sparkle dust.'

'Oh, Riccardo.' Sandra giggled, tapping her hand on his chest. 'You're just full of surprises, aren't you?'

'I like to think so,' he replied, his intense gaze holding hers.

She stifled a shiver at the deadness she saw there. It wasn't just an absence of warmth; it was something flat and cold. Something deeply disturbing. Breaking away, she smiled at the other two men in the room.

The room Riccardo took women to definitely wasn't in this flat. Not that she'd ever suspected it was, but just in case, she'd enthusiastically asked for a tour when they arrived. Riccardo, delighted with the excuse to show off, had happily obliged, and of course there had been nothing out of the ordinary. Sandra had no idea what Isla had thought she'd be able to do when she arrived, but whatever her plan, it would have failed. Because there really was only one way to find the location of that room.

Riccardo needed to believe that whoever he was taking there was drugged. And once they were inside... Sandra firmly closed off the rest of that thought. It was too late to lose her nerve now.

'Come on then,' she suggested chirpily, lifting the shot. 'Let's do these together!'

The three men didn't need to be asked twice. Grabbing the remaining shots, the other man joined them. Riccardo held his glass up in the air alongside Sandra.

'Bottoms up,' he said. 'Here's to a good night.' He winked at his companions as they all chinked the glasses together, then the three men put them to their lips and downed the large shot.

Sandra carefully played along, touching her glass to theirs and bringing it to her lips, but as they all tipped their heads back, she expertly tipped hers into the plant pot and returned the empty glass to the correct position as their eyes moved back towards her.

'Mm, that was lush!' she enthused.

'Another?' Riccardo asked, kinking a dark eyebrow in question.

'No, no, I'd better not,' she said with a laugh. 'I'm already quite pissed actually.'

'Good,' he replied, his handsome dimples deepening as his grin widened. He took her empty shot glass. 'Let's get back to the music then.'

Riccardo moved back to the sofa and reignited the cocaine-fuelled energetic debate about what music genre was better than another. Sandra sat beside him, nodding along and pretended to listen. He hadn't cared that she'd declined the last drink, which was all the confirmation she needed. The shot had been laced.

She joined in with the conversation animatedly for the next few minutes, watching the clock on the wall. After ten minutes, she made a point of growing quieter. They began to watch her over the next five minutes as she started slowing her movements and shaking her head with a frown.

'You OK?' Riccardo asked.

'Mm,' she said faintly. 'I don't feel well.'

'Probably that last shot,' one of the other men suggested.

She nodded, keeping the action slow and slight. Two minutes later, she slumped back into the sofa, closing her eyes and opening them again as though it was an effort to do so. Through barely open slits, she watched the three men exchange a dark, excited look. She forced her body to relax, and another two minutes passed before one of the men questioned whether she was out.

Riccardo shook her arm. 'Hey, you awake?' he asked. He jiggled her again. 'Oi, hello?'

Sandra braced herself, knowing what was likely to come next. The slap was sharp and left a sting on her cheek, but she stayed limp without much effort. After years of abuse and then on the game, Sandra was an expert at mentally separating herself from pain. Her head moved from the force of the slap, and she let her body fall sideways into an awkward position, then waited.

'She's out,' one of them said.

'*Finally,*' Riccardo added, the fake joviality gone now. 'This bitch made it hard work.'

'I thought she might have been clued up for a second, when she didn't touch that first drink,' one of them said. 'Especially after that shit at the pub.'

'Nah.' Riccardo instantly dismissed the idea. 'She's as stupid as all the others. You know what these women are like. The bigger the tits—'

'The smaller the brain,' someone answered with a low chuckle.

'Let's go,' Riccardo ordered. 'I'm looking forward to doing this one.'

Fear crackled along Sandra's spine, and it took all her effort to keep her breathing even. There was a creaking sound as the three of them stood, then suddenly a pair of hands yanked her upwards, before she was thrown over a hard broad shoulder. Her stomach lurched as they started walking, and she forced herself to focus on the reason she was here, rather than what it was about to cost her. Because as they carried her out of the flat and the front door closed behind them, she already knew that her chances of getting out of here without paying that price were slim to none.

TWENTY-TWO

Isla paced around the flat she'd broken into several hours before, her arms tightly folded and deep frown lines etched into her forehead. This was the second time in a week that she'd let herself in somewhere unannounced and uninvited, but this time she was here for very different reasons. She certainly wasn't here out of concern, and the only feeling of warmth she held for the resident of this particular dwelling was a deep burning anger.

It was dark in the silent one-bedroomed flat, the only light coming from the streetlamps outside the windows. The yellow glow lit the place up enough for Isla to make her way around without too much difficulty. She'd kept the lights off, partly out of habitual caution but mainly because she wanted to take Sandra by surprise. She wanted to scare her, even if only for a second, before she had it out with her. It was a petty move, she knew, but she didn't care.

Pacing back through to Sandra's bedroom, she touched a tassel hanging from the lid of a perfume bottle on the dressing table, then sat with a sigh on the comfortable accent chair in the corner of the room. She picked at the material on the stuffed arm and pulled her phone from her pocket. It was nearly four in the morning. Why wasn't Sandra home yet? Had she gone straight to Lily perhaps?

After a moment of deliberation, she typed out a quick text to her boss, asking if she'd heard anything. The reply arrived almost instantly.

No, not yet. Get some sleep, I'll text you when I hear from her.

Isla put the phone away and gnawed absentmindedly on one of her nails as she considered abandoning her plan to confront Sandra tonight. After all, it wasn't really *tonight* anymore, at this point. It was nearly morning. And for all she knew, Sandra had gone somewhere else to sleep off the night's activities. For some reason that she'd later look back on and question, it never crossed Isla's mind that Sandra might not have returned yet because things had gone wrong.

Just as she'd finally decided to give up and go home, Isla heard the muted sound of keys jangling in the hallway outside the flat. She sat up and listened intently, holding her breath as the lock clicked open. Quickly jumping up she nipped to the bedroom door and half closed it, keeping it just open enough to see into the main living area beyond. This was *it*. This was her chance to confront Sandra and tell her what she really thought of her. She was *done* pretending she didn't feel the way she did, and she was done biting her lip while the other woman walked all over her and took whatever she wanted. Sandra had greatly underestimated her, and she was about to find out exactly how much.

The small flat flooded with light, and Isla listened intently, picking out the sounds of Sandra kicking off her heels and hanging her coat. There was a short silence, and she squinted tensely in the darkness of the bedroom. *What was she doing?* She couldn't see the entranceway from where she was hidden.

There was a clunk and a rustling from the direction of the kitchen, and Isla relaxed slightly. The fridge door opened and shut, then finally a shadow fell across the floor of the living room. Isla moved further back into the darkness and watched silently from the shadows as Sandra finally came into view. She moved slowly, and Isla's irritation rose with each unnecessary extra second she took crossing the room towards the sofa.

She finally reached it and turned to sit down, but as she did, Isla's eyes flew wide, and she let out a loud gasp. Sandra immediately leaped back up in fright, flying to the back of a nearby chair and grabbing a baseball bat concealed behind.

'Who's there?' she yelled, brandishing it in the air, her eyes blindly searching the tiny sliver of darkness that was visible to her of her bedroom. 'I'm armed and calling the police.' Sandra made to pull her phone out of her pocket, and Isla cursed, quickly darting out of the bedroom in alarm, her hands in the air.

'No, no, it's *me*! Sandra, it's just me.' *Shit*, she thought with a cringe as Sandra's face clouded with shocked fury. None of this was going as planned. But then again, looking at the state of Sandra, neither had the job.

TWENTY-THREE

Sandra lowered her aching body back onto the sofa and picked up the two frozen bags of peas she'd been about to apply to the worst of her wounds. She held one to the left side of her swollen face, wincing as the cold instantly stung the bruised and broken skin. The second bag remained in her hand as she glanced resentfully at her unwelcome guest. The last thing she wanted or needed was an audience right now. Especially this one.

'Go home, Isla,' she said wearily. 'I don't have the energy to fight with you tonight.'

She closed her eyes as the throbbing in her head intensified, and instantly she was back in that room. The room where she'd had to lie still and silent, while they raped and beat her. She reopened her eyes quickly, swallowing down the panic and fear that still fizzed through her whole body.

Isla still hadn't moved. Sandra silently begged her to just leave. She needed to clean herself up and drink enough vodka to force herself into oblivion in the hope of reaching a dreamless sleep. Not that dreams lay ahead. There was nothing but nightmares waiting for her on the other side of consciousness tonight.

Isla suddenly turned and disappeared down the hallway,

without uttering a word, and Sandra lay her head back feeling relieved. This was short-lived however, as the creak of the bathroom door revealed Isla hadn't actually left. A moment later, Isla reappeared, and Sandra sighed, irritated and fresh out of patience.

'Seriously, Isla, I ain't up for this,' she said, some strength returning to her voice. 'So your bitching will have to wait. I *mean* it. Do *not* push me right now.' She glared up at the other girl.

To her surprise, Isla simply nodded and perched on the coffee table in front of her. She placed a glass down on one of the coasters and reached up towards her face. Sandra pulled back with a frown then slowly relaxed once she saw the wet cloth in Isla's hand. Isla gently began to work away in silence at the dried blood covering Sandra's chin, then pushed the bag of peas away to take a closer look at the damage underneath. Her brown eyes roamed over the vicious wounds, her expression controlled now that she was over the initial shock.

'Where else?' she asked quietly.

Sandra shrugged, the effort making her wince. 'Everywhere really,' she replied.

'Here, drink this and turn around.' She picked up the glass and handed it over.

Sandra lifted it to her mouth and grimaced at the strong sharpness of the neat vodka but tipped it back all the same. It was what she needed. Staring blankly at the wall in front of her as Isla worked on the long gash that ran down her back, she waited for the vodka to take the edge off.

'Thanks,' she muttered after a while. 'Sorry for earlier. I thought you were here for a fight.'

'I was,' Isla admitted honestly. 'I'm not now.'

There was a short silence before she spoke again. 'What happened?'

Sandra closed her eyes, glad that she was facing away.

When she reopened them, she had to blink away the mist that gathered in her big blue eyes, and her brows knitted upwards helplessly for a moment.

'It stayed just the four of us. They tried drugging me a few times, and the last time I let them think they had. It was the only way to get in.' She swallowed, remembering the dread that had iced her stomach on that terrible journey across to his other flat. 'It's on the same floor, the opposite side, three doors up.'

'Where's your first aid kit?' Isla asked suddenly.

Sandra pointed to a box underneath the coffee table and waited as Isla opened it and located the little green bag.

'Riccardo locked us all inside,' she continued, pushing forward. She felt Isla's hands pause on her back. 'There was no way out, Isla.' Her tired voice suddenly sounded years older. 'There was never going to be.'

'Couldn't you have pretended to wake up?' Isla asked. 'Made out you came round early? Surely he'd have just let you go?'

Sandra exhaled sharply in a bitter, silent laugh, shaking her head. 'You don't understand.' She bit her lip. 'There's only so much I can explain. I'm bound by a code that you ain't part of. None of you are.' She looked down at her nails and picked at one of them. 'I know – *know*,' she reiterated strongly, 'that if I'd let him know I was awake tonight, I'd have disappeared. That's why it had to be me. If *you'd* got that far unharmed and – by some miracle – undiscovered, you would have pulled that move thinking it was your way out, because you're *blind* to how deep it goes. And you'd be dead now. No question. What you found out only scrapes the surface. There's so much more you don't know.'

'Then *tell* me,' Isla urged, sounding frustrated.

'I *can't*,' Sandra replied, equally as frustrated. 'Like I said, there's a code. And a woman is only as good as her word.'

Isla carried on tending to her back. 'I get that,' she grudgingly admitted.

'There was only one way,' Sandra continued flatly. 'Play dead, pay attention on the way in, let them do what they wanted and hope they don't work it out.' She felt the revulsion rise up inside her like a wave. 'Then act dumb after.'

It had been the hardest thing she'd ever done. Harder than she'd thought it was going to be. She'd known they were going to rape her. And much as she'd despised them, she'd known she could get through that. Better for her to take that bullet than for Isla to end up dead. Even faking unconsciousness through the abuse was something she felt uniquely prepared for. She'd learned horribly early in life how to detach while being hurt by men. But even the years of abuse she'd endured couldn't have prepared her for this. Riccardo's voice resounded, unbidden, in her head.

'Get her clothes off. It's time this bitch got what she's been begging for,' Riccardo had ordered.

She prepared herself for the blows, knowing they would come. The first few weren't too difficult to manage. A hand slapped her face, lightly, then harder, the sting getting sharper after the fourth or fifth time. Another hand squeezed at her breasts and grabbed the area between her thighs viciously. But then Riccardo got involved, and the violent depravity rose to levels she'd never expected. Her strength waned, and her fear intensified as things got worse and worse, but she knew she had to hold on. If she didn't, she was dead.

Reaching fever pitch, Riccardo grabbed her with a feral roar and flipped her over, slamming her face into the floor – hard. For a few moments, the world dimmed. The pain burst through her face like fire, and she realised, with a strange calmness, that she was about to pass out. Exhaling slowly, she prayed for the strength to remain silent just long enough to reach true unconsciousness. But somehow she remained awake. And as the savage attacks continued to rain down, she wasn't sure whether this was a blessing or a curse.

'So when you were in there, Riccardo, he...' Isla trailed off.

'Raped me?' Sandra asked flatly, not looking round. 'Of course he did. They all did.'

Isla's hand slowed, and Sandra lifted the glass of vodka to her mouth. She took another deep swig, grateful for the acidic burn as it travelled down her throat.

Sandra sniffed, forcing her mind to remain in the room she was in. She was home now. It was over.

'I had to pretend to be out for a few hours. When I pretended to come to, they quickly rushed me back and set me up to look like I'd slept with Riccardo out of choice. He acted surprised at my memory loss and tied it all up by telling me I'd fallen down the stairwell of the building and banged my head. Said we'd been mucking around and I'd lost my footing.'

She pulled a bitter expression. 'The shitty thing is, it ties it all up so neatly that I'd bet all the women he's done this to will have believed it without question. Because why wouldn't you? You get pissed, flirt with this hot guy, wake up to discover you hooked up – which explains why you're walking like John Wayne, but you can't remember it because you got smashed and fell down a metal stairwell – which explains why you feel like you've been beaten half to death. Because you wouldn't assume you'd *actually* been beaten half to death while being gang raped and filmed.' She made a sound of derision and blinked back the tears. 'He really is a piece of shit.'

'Well, he's about to get what's coming to him,' Isla said quietly. 'And all those women will at least get *some* justice, even if they don't know it.'

Several faces flickered through Sandra's mind. Grey lifeless bodies floating in rivers and rotting in bins far from home. Bodies so badly beaten they were unrecognisable. Bodies that would know no rest in the next life, after such horror.

'Not all of them,' she said quietly, to herself more than Isla.

'You said...' Isla hesitated. 'You said it had to be *you* tonight, because I didn't know enough to survive it.'

'I did,' Sandra replied, pushing away the ghosts of all the women who didn't make it out. 'I knew what he was capable of. What he enjoys. Knew I had to play dead or he'd have no problem disposing of me.' She sniffed. 'You'd have just got yourself killed. So yeah, it had to be me.' She exhaled heavily. 'Afterwards, I pretended to buy his story then left as soon as I could. And that's it. I don't want to talk about the rest.' She downed the rest of the vodka and placed the empty glass on the table.

Isla closed the first aid box, pulled the shoulder of Sandra's top back up and sat back. Sandra awkwardly turned and leaned back tiredly next to her.

'Sandra?' Isla asked.

'What?' Sandra replied.

'Thank you.' There was a long silence, then Isla shook her head with a sigh. 'I got you so wrong. I'm so sorry.'

Sandra studied the side of Isla's face and frowned thoughtfully. 'Why *were* you so convinced I was trying to one-up you?' she asked. 'In fact, what is it that bothers you about me so much in general? And don't lie; I think we're past all that now. I mean, if you can't be frank with me after breaking into my home, I don't know when you can.'

The corner of Isla's mouth hitched for a moment and then she looked down at her hands unhappily as she fiddled with one of her rings. 'You know, I've only ever had one relationship. Calvin. He was my first and only, well... anything.' She shrugged. 'I never met anyone before him, and then I was here, with the Drews.'

Sandra frowned. 'OK. So you've never slept with anyone else, at *all*?'

Isla's cheeks flushed pink. 'No,' she replied.

'Not even a one-night stand?' Sandra pressed. 'You've been here what, two, three years? And *nothing*?'

'No!' Isla repeated, a little testily this time. 'I've never dated, alright? I haven't got a clue where to even start.' She looked away, her cheeks flaming red now. 'Not that I even wanted to think about dating. After my last experience, it wasn't exactly a tempting prospect.'

Sandra tilted her head in acknowledgement. 'The dating pool *is* pretty feral. Even at the best of times.'

A thought suddenly occurred to her, and she shook her head with a look of disbelief. 'Hang on, you're telling me that *you*, with your one notch on the bedpost and self-confessed ignorance of men, were going to go home with someone you *knew* was a violent rapist tonight?' Her brows rose as she stared at Isla. 'As *bait*?'

'Well, I thought I'd be out before it got to all that,' Isla mumbled.

Sandra's brows rose higher.

'OK fine, when you put it like that, I guess it does sound stupid.'

'*Insane* is the word I'd use,' Sandra declared. 'Utterly fucking insane. Christ!' She shook her head. 'Anyway, what's all this got to do with your beef with me? I'm still no clearer.' She waited, trying to ignore the raw pain still throbbing angrily through her body. 'Come on, out with it, before we leave this odd little bubble and you go back to swinging hot and cold whenever I see you.'

Isla pushed her blonde locks back behind her ears. 'I didn't want to date because I refuse to put trust in someone I don't know. But then I started having feelings for someone I *already* trust and know.'

'Who?' Sandra asked. But as the word left her mouth, the answer suddenly clicked. 'Connor,' she breathed in surprise.

The rest of the dots all connected at once, and she let out a sound of realisation. 'Ahhhh, I see.'

Isla didn't respond, and Sandra's heart went out to the unhappy woman. Isla loved Connor. But Connor had been openly obsessed with *her* for years. It hadn't mattered that she'd told him point-blank that she would never go out with him, he still kept trying, never discouraged. And poor Isla had had to stand by and watch. Things all suddenly made much more sense.

Sandra shook her head. She could have helped fix this a long time ago, had she known. 'Connor doesn't *love* me, Isla. That's never been what it's about.'

'He *does*, Sandra,' Isla argued defeatedly. 'I've watched him. Seen him try to win you over time and again; he's absolutely head over heels for you.'

'*No*, Isla, he's *not*,' she repeated strongly. She pushed her free hand back through her long blonde hair and exhaled loudly. 'When I landed the job with the Drews as one of their escorts, I thought it was the best thing that had ever happened to me. *Genuine* protection, properly vetted clients, no pressure to do anything dangerous. It was the dream. A safe place that came with decent digs. I really thought I'd landed. Connor took a liking to me and would visit now and then. Paid me well for it too.'

Isla looked away, clearly not enjoying this information, but Sandra continued anyway. She needed to understand.

'I was a plaything to him. Something pretty and fun that was there whenever it took his fancy. Like a toy. And honestly, it wasn't even often. When I left for the hairdresser's, he asked me out, assuming I'd fall in his lap just as easy. But I'd gone straight, and I was serious, so I told him no, and he was really shocked.' Isla half turned back towards her. 'I don't think anyone's told him no in his life, other than his mother.'

They both grinned at this.

'He didn't know what to do with that. It drove him mad. I'd just laid out the biggest challenge ever – and then I was just *there* in the salon every day, right in front of him.'

She touched Isla's arm, and Isla finally looked up at her. 'It isn't *love*; it's obsession. And not even a particularly dark obsession. It's really just a game for him. Connor's a very strong, very hard man. What drives him, drives *both* of the twins, is an all-consuming need to win. At *everything*.' She shrugged. 'He don't love me. He don't even *know* me. He's just competitive and hasn't found any reason to drop the challenge. Maybe it's time he was given one.' She gave Isla a meaningful look. 'You need to tell him.'

Isla sighed. 'Actually I did, a few days ago. By accident.'

Sandra frowned. 'How—'

'It doesn't matter. But he knows. And he didn't say anything, so that tells me all I need to know.' She looked down.

'Well then he's an idiot,' Sandra replied with feeling. 'Because whether he realises it or not, you're exactly what he needs in his life.'

Isla shrugged and then sniffed, changing the subject. 'Listen, you need to text Lil. She waited up to check you got out OK.'

'*Shit*, yeah.' Sandra stood up stiffly, wincing at the fresh wave of pain the action caused. 'My phone died.'

'It's fine; I'll text her for you,' Isla offered. 'You should get some rest.' She stood up too and walked across the room to the hallway.

Sandra followed her through to the front door. 'Listen, Isla...' She turned around. 'Whatever happens with you and Connor, I'd like us to get on now.'

'Yeah, of course,' Isla replied, nodding.

'No, seriously,' Sandra pressed. 'This word is full of dickheads, and it's still a man's world, whether or not people like to believe it. And if the yous and the mes and all the other women of the world in between don't stick together or support each other, we end up with very little.' She held Isla's gaze seriously. 'Men come and go. It's the women around you you need to keep close. Trust me.'

The lifeless faces and distorted bodies of some of the prostitutes Riccardo had killed flashed through her mind once more. There were all kinds of sisterhoods running through the world beneath the surface. She had one of them to thank for the fact both hers and Isla's hearts were still beating today.

Isla nodded. 'Yeah. I hear that.' She reached out and grasped Sandra's hand.

Sandra squeezed it back. 'Go safe.'

Isla nodded then left, and Sandra closed the door with a tired sigh. She leaned back on it, thinking over everything that had happened. Tonight she'd learned that hell was real, but it wasn't at the centre of the earth. It was just a few miles away – and the devil's name was Riccardo Romano.

But even the devil could burn. And Sandra now had exactly what Lily needed to make sure he got everything he deserved.

TWENTY-FOUR

Benny's phone rang just as he pulled up to the abandoned ruin beside some disused railway tracks, where they were set to meet one of Ray's suppliers. He glanced at the screen grimly as he stepped out and caught Connor's attention over the roof of the car.

'I've got to take this. Go in – we don't need them getting antsy. You know the score.' He turned away and answered the call, walking over to the rusted overgrown tracks.

Connor closed his door and walked towards what was left of the old brick building, making a beeline for the gaping hole where a door would once have stood. He did know the score. Benny had made sure to prep him on the way over. He'd become pretty good at doing that lately, when there was no one else around, and Connor was grateful for it.

They were here today to pick up a shipment of cocaine. Or rather, several boxes of plastic mixing bowls. It was a new smuggling tactic some of the Colombians had recently adopted. A less risky one. They mixed the cocaine powder into melted plastic, used moulds to create simple household goods, packaged them as such, then shipped them across the world. It was almost impossible for authorities to distinguish whether or not a plastic item contained cocaine once it was in hard form, so it could be moved along the chain with very little risk. The cocaine was then extracted in a special facility Ray had set up, using acid to melt away the plastic.

Walking inside, Connor glanced around the mainly empty shell. Half the roof was missing, and what remained of the walls was covered by ivy and graffiti tags. Drifts of dead leaves had gathered in the corners and were littered with old tins and plastic wrappers, and the smell of damp decay lingered in the early winter air.

'Well, well, well,' came a deep voice with a thick Irish accent, from somewhere over Connor's right shoulder. 'If it isn't the prodigal son we have here today.'

Connor turned to see two men, one seated in a half-hidden alcove and the other standing beside him, his hands in his trouser pockets. The one seated was thickset with dark hair, heavy brows and a sly, calculating look only half hidden under his fixed smile. The other was tall and slim with dark red hair and a long, mean face. Connor took an instant dislike to the pair of them.

He smiled and walked over, sizing them up subtly. 'Declan O'Leary, I presume?' He addressed the stocky one, sitting down.

'And you're Connor Drew,' Declan said in reply. 'Or do ye go by Renshaw now?'

Connor didn't answer, instead hardening his gaze and holding Declan's coolly.

There was a tense few seconds as Declan stared back, testing the waters, but then he changed tack, holding his hands up in surrender. 'Drew it is.'

He stood up and walked over to the hole in the wall that Connor had entered by, looking over to Benny. 'Will we be waiting for him long, do ye think?' he asked, turning back to

Connor and pushing his hands back into his suit trouser pockets.

Connor caught the swift look he exchanged with the other man, and a small wave of warning prickled over his skin. Something was off.

'No need to wait at all,' he said. 'Let's get on with it, shall we?'

Declan raised his dark bushy brows with an amused half-smile. 'Straight to the point. I like it. So you're taking over these things now, are ye?'

Connor exhaled slowly as he tried to work out where this was leading. He decided to call their bluff and find out. 'Yeah.' He pretended to look around, pacing away a couple of steps so he could undo his suit jacket without it being too noticeable. His switchblade was in the inside pocket. 'You'll be dealing with me from now on. So anything you need to discuss, you know where to come.'

'Is that so?' Declan rubbed his chin and glanced at his companion again. 'Well, we've got the boxes round the back, but there was a couple of things we needed to discuss before making the exchange.'

'Yeah?' Connor watched them carefully, his sharp brown eyes locked on Declan's and keeping note of the other guy's movements in his peripheral vision. He caught the quick flash of fingers. Three and then three again. 'What's that then?'

Declan blew out a long, loud breath through his cheeks and shook his head. 'Well I'm sorry that you have to deal with this on your first day in the office, but there's been some changes, back down the line.'

'What changes?' Connor asked, his strong jaw setting into a hard line.

'There's been a lot more issues lately, getting this stuff over from Colombia, ye see. More boats than ever are being captured, their loads seized. The guys at the top are feeling the squeeze, d'ya know what I mean?' Declan spun the tale with an edge of woe, his silent companion nodding seriously behind him.

Connor nodded slowly, his anger beginning to bubble. 'And so?'

'So, unfortunately, the prices per kilo have gone up. Look at it as inflation.' Declan held his arms out helplessly. 'It happens in every market. When supply costs go up, the buy costs go up. It's the way of the world.'

'How much?' Connor asked.

'Six large, per kilo,' Declan replied.

'*Six grand*?' Connor replied incredulously. 'You want an extra *six grand* per kilo?'

'Hey, it ain't meself that puts the price on these things, friend. It's the damn Colombians.' He shook his head as if in sympathy with Connor.

A hint of a cold smile played at the edges of Connor's mouth as he stared at the man. 'Right. You said there was a couple of things. What else?'

'Well, see now, I saved the good news for last,' Declan said with a wide grin and a flourish of the hand. 'The bowls are only half the load this time. For the other half, I can give ye bricks, already processed. Straight coke. So there'll be no need to fanny around extracting it. I'll do that for ye, as a goodwill gesture. A welcome gift, so to speak, now that you're the main man in charge of all this. And ye never know,' he added brightly, 'I may even be able to do it again. We'll have to see what I can get a hold of.' He nodded and gave Connor a conspiratorial wink.

Connor nodded and glanced outside at Benny, wondering what was taking so long. He was slipping his phone into his pocket and walking over. *Finally*, Connor thought. He looked back at the two men with a brief cold smile.

'How thoughtful of you,' he said flatly, scratching his chin. Out of the corner of his eye, he saw Benny approach the entrance. 'But I just have one question.' He walked closer to Declan, as Benny rounded the jagged brickwork, and lowered his voice to an angry growl. 'Just how fucking stupid do you think I am?'

'What?' Declan asked, blinking.

'*What?*' Benny seconded, alarmed.

SLAM.

Connor shoved Declan with both hands, the action swift and hard, causing him to smack back against the wall. Taken by surprise, the man lost his footing and almost fell, but Connor caught him by the neck, squeezing it in a vice-like grip.

'You really take me for that much of a mug, do ya?' he roared.

'Fuck's *sake*,' Benny exclaimed with a sound of deep frustration as he jumped in to deal with the other guy.

They immediately began to scuffle, but Benny quickly gained the upper hand, as Connor had known he would.

Declan kicked out and attempted to twist away from Connor's grip. One hand fought to prise Connor's fingers from his neck, and he slipped the other behind his back, but Connor was too sharp to miss such an obvious move.

'Oh no you don't,' he growled, smashing Declan's fist against the brick until the blade fell with a clatter to the ground.

'You'll pay for this,' Declan hissed. 'You just wait.'

'No, it'll be *you* who pays for this one.'

Connor stepped back and released his grip, then swung a punch into Declan's face. The man flew across the floor, dust billowing up in a cloud around him as he disturbed the thick layer of filth. Benny threw his companion in the same direction, and there was a loud curse as he landed heavily on top.

'You wanna tell me what the *fuck* is going on?' Benny bellowed.

The two men hastily jumped up but were stopped in their tracks as Benny pulled out a revolver from behind his back. He aimed it in their direction, and they slowly backed down to their knees, looking furious.

Connor took a second to catch his breath, wiping his hand down his face. 'These cunts can't be trusted.' He eyed the gun in Benny's hand. He hadn't known the other man was tooled up, though he was certainly grateful for it now.

Benny made a sound of disbelief and stared at him with an expression that questioned whether or not he'd gone mad, but Connor just shook his head and then held Declan's glare with one of his own.

'It'll be *you* who pays for this fuck-up,' he reiterated, pointing a finger at him angrily. 'When you have to go back to your boss and explain how you lost a customer that takes half a mill's worth of product every couple of months.'

'*What happened?*' Benny repeated urgently. 'Seriously, start talking, Connor.'

'These cunts just tried to line their pockets with an extra six grand a kilo,' Connor told him.

'*What?*' Benny asked with a frown. 'Our rates are set at forty.'

'I know. They spun me a tale about the Colombians losing ships at sea and being hard up.'

That they'd taken him as such a fool angered him greatly. Back in the old days, that sort of thing had happened to the Colombians quite regularly. But now, thanks to the new advanced ways of smuggling product across, those issues had greatly *decreased,* not the other way around. Any idiot worth his salt knew that.

'They also tried palming us off with the cheap dirty shit they peddle themselves,' Connor added. Declan's eyes twitched with surprise. 'Yeah, you didn't think I knew who you were, did you? Well I do. So here's how it's gonna go now.' He stepped forward. 'Benny here's going to look after you while I go and load all those boxes into our car. Then we're going to leave with the boxes – *and* the cash – and you're going to toddle off home with nothing.'

Benny let out a long, irate sigh but said nothing and kept his gun pointed at the pair.

Connor glared at them. 'You can crawl under a rock or jump off a cliff, whatever – I don't really care. But I know exactly who you are, and if I *ever* see either of your mugs around here again, I will fucking kill you. You got that?'

Not waiting for an answer, Connor turned and marched out to find their car. The hot blood coursing through his veins felt good suddenly, like it was fuelling rather than frustrating him, now he'd finally released some of it. As he rounded the corner, he made a decision. He was done putting up with this shit. Being treated this way by Ray's men, Ray's allies – now Ray's suppliers. He was done.

It was about time people started realising who he was – and just how dangerous he could be, when he was finally pushed too far.

TWENTY-FIVE

The pub fell silent as Sandra walked in and took off the large sunglasses that had helped at least partially cover her bruised and broken face. Lily had closed for the afternoon to hold this meeting, and Sandra was the last to join. Scarlet and Cath had arrived first, then Isla, who'd given her a brief whispered rundown of Sandra's night. Cillian, Joe and the three Logan brothers had come next, followed shortly by Ben and Danny. The only two not here, who were in the know about this job, were Andy and George, but they were tied up elsewhere right now.

Lily pursed her lips at the sight of Sandra. It was every bit as bad as Isla had said. She sat back in her chair at one of the small round tables and took a deep drag on her cigarette as Cath rushed over, immediately clucking around Sandra like the mother hen she was.

'Christ almighty, that looks painful! Come, sit down. I'll get you a chair. Come on, love,' she said, pulling Sandra towards the large group of people sat on various chairs in a rough circle in the centre of the pub. She tried to help Sandra sit down, but Sandra gently squeezed her hand and moved it away.

'I'm fine, Cath, honestly,' she said. 'It's not as bad as it looks. I'm alright.'

Liar, Lily thought.

'Jesus Christ,' Scarlet muttered, shaking her head. She stood up and walked off behind the bar.

Cillian's eyes were glued to Sandra's face, his serious expression full of guilt. Lily understood how he felt completely. She carried that same feeling inside too. This was her firm. Sandra had gone in there knowing what was to come and she'd done it anyway. For *her*. She took a deep breath, her hatred for Riccardo burning like a hot coal in her chest. Perhaps banishment was too easy a sentence for him.

'Sandra, I...' Finn's voice cracked, and he hung his shaking head for a minute.

'What kind of man could do this to a woman?' Sean asked in disbelief.

'No man,' Cormac snapped angrily. 'That's not the work of a man; that's the work of a spineless scumbag.'

Sandra shifted uncomfortably and looked away from the sea of faces staring back at her. 'You're right, but let's move on, yeah? I got what you needed. So just make sure you pay him back for me.'

'Now *that's* something we can promise you,' Cormac replied firmly. 'Lil, I know we said we'd do this without inflicting any blows, but—'

'I know,' Lily said, cutting him off with a nod. 'I agree. We'll take him first and make sure he pays his dues before we carry out the rest.'

'Well, I insist that we take that job,' Finn piped up.

'Done,' Lily said quickly as Cillian opened his mouth to protest. He shut it again with a quiet sound of annoyance as she shot him a look that told him there would be no arguments.

Scarlet walked back over with a glass of water and a bottle of pills. 'Here,' she said, handing them both to Sandra.

'Codeine. Stronger than the shit you can get on prescription so just be careful.'

'And where exactly did you get them?' Cath asked her. 'I'm not sure I approve of that, Scarlet Drew.'

Scarlet tucked her long dark hair behind her ear and sat down next to Lily, picking up her glass of wine with an amused expression. 'Of all the things you've seen and heard me do, *that's* what you don't approve of?'

There was a light chuckle around the room, and Sandra visibly relaxed, clearly glad that the attention was no longer all on her.

Cath pursed her lips and folded her arms. 'You can flout the law and shoot whoever the hell you like, but you *shouldn't* be putting stuff into your body that a doctor ain't prescribed. You don't know *what* it could be doing.'

Ben tried to stifle the laugh that bubbled up, but it slipped out as a snort, and he half lowered his head as he let the rest fly.

Cath bristled and shot him daggers. 'Oh that's funny is it, Benjamin Ellis?' She hitched one dark, neatly arched eyebrow, and a devious glint appeared in her eye. 'I'd remember who's mates with your mum, if I were you. Stay on *my* radar and I might accidentally let slip about that dirty little piece you've got going on the side down the Treby.'

The laughing abruptly stopped, and his eyes widened in surprise and fear.

'Oh yeah, I know all about that.'

Lily tutted and rolled her eyes, regretting the second bottle of wine she'd had two Sundays before with Scarlet and Cath after the rest of the family had gone home. She'd told Cath that in confidence, and now the cheeky mare was using it to lord it over Ben.

Sandra popped two of the pills into her mouth and swallowed them down with the water, her eyes moving tensely between Scarlet and Cath. 'Thanks,' she said, slipping the bottle into her handbag.

'No worries,' Scarlet replied, taking another sip of her wine. 'So now that we've addressed the obvious, what did you find out?'

'It's a wide building; there are four flats each side of the hallway. Riccardo's in ninety-two, as you know, and the other one is number ninety-seven. It's three down on the other side, going away from the lift,' Sandra told them.

'Did you catch the door or locking system?' Lily asked, exchanging glances with Scarlet. They hadn't known Sandra was going to take Isla's place, so they hadn't been able to prep her.

Sandra nodded. 'I figured you'd want to know. It's the same door as all the others and he just used a key. Like a Chubb key. They've got more locks on the inside.' She stopped abruptly, and her expression tightened for a moment. 'But they're nothing technical. Just bolts,' she continued. 'It's a studio flat. One large room with a kitchenette in the corner and a bathroom to the side. There's a desk with a computer set up and the camera next to it on a stand. He's got these...' She squinted as she tried to describe it. 'They're like metal racks. Like you see in shop storage rooms. There were a couple of hard drives just sat out, but the middle shelf had boxes with date ranges written on them. I think there are more in there.'

Finn looked over to Lily, and she met his eyes with a grim expression that mirrored his. That was a *lot* of storage for something like this. *How many women had he done this to?*

'That's perfect,' Scarlet said. 'That's all we needed to know.' She glanced at Lily and waited for her to lead on.

'OK.' Lily took a deep drag on her cigarette then tapped it gently on the side of the ashtray as she blew out the smoke. 'Ben, Danny, you'll tag team on shifts with George and Andy watching Riccardo. He parties a lot, and from what we've seen so far, there's usually one or more women going in and out. We can't break in while there are girls there or he's got other company – it's too risky. We've had eyes on him on and off since we found out what they were doing to us, and he seems to crash out early once or twice a week on his own. We wait until he has one of those nights and we hit then.'

Cillian's face twisted into a look of disagreement. 'I'm getting married in a week. I can't afford to wait around and have this spill over. And we can't afford to wait until after all the festivities, because time ain't on our side. Plus, they might see the wedding as an opportunity to hit us while we're distracted.'

'That's a good point,' Scarlet agreed.

'What if we lure him out?' Isla suggested. 'If we haven't found a window by Tuesday, I'll text him. Say I got his number off Sandra's phone and that I was gutted we didn't get to hang. Invite him for some drinks and keep him busy in the bar for a couple of hours.'

Lily squeezed her gaze, not convinced. Last night had been a close enough call with Sandra. She didn't want to risk something else happening. Her gaze flickered over to the battered woman, and Cillian must have caught it.

'I'll watch her,' he offered. 'Keep her in sight the whole time.'

'No, I need you on point inside,' Lily told him.

'Then I can watch Isla,' Joe piped up. 'Unless you want me inside too?'

Lily bit her lip, mentally moving them all around in her head like chess pieces on a board. 'OK. If it comes to that, then, Joe, you're on Isla. Scarlet, you'll go in with Cillian to get the hard drives. It should be a simple in and out,' she added, seeing the worry on Cath's face.

Cath wasn't supposed to be here tonight. Though she was privy to most of their secrets and plots, she wasn't actually part of the firm, and there was a fine balance between things she would feel happier knowing and things she'd rather not. Cath fiddled with one of her small hoop earrings and tucked a strand of her thick dark hair back up into her neat French twist, gazing off into the distance.

Finn nodded. 'OK. Once you two have the drives, I'll be waiting for you to hand off, and I'll take them straight to Bill. I've spoken to him already about checking them over. We don't know what sort of encryption will be on there.'

'True,' Lily agreed.

'Assuming all goes well, once Bill's confirmed we have what we need, we'll grab Riccardo and take him somewhere he won't be heard.' Finn exchanged a look with his brothers. 'We need to teach this prick a lesson.'

Lily nodded, happy with how the plan was taking shape. 'When you're ready, we'll use his phone to summon Mani and Luca, pretend to be him. Once they're en route to us, Ben and Danny, you'll go with George and Andy to round up their closest men and his immediate family. Joe, you too. And tool up,' she warned. 'Take no chances. I'll iron out exactly who and where to hit them later.'

'How many are we talking?' Cillian asked, frowning.

'They only have three or four in their closest circle, max,' Lily replied. 'Just them and his wife. The rest will fall and run once the core is gone. But you won't be there; I'll need you with me.'

'Where do you want me?' Scarlet asked.

'With me too.' Lily looked at her, and she nodded. 'That will make six of us there for when Mani and Luca arrive. Overkill perhaps, but we need to make sure there's no issues securing them. We don't want to get that far only to stumble at the last hurdle.'

'The Tylers are on board, yeah?' Sean queried. 'They're ready to go?'

'They are,' she confirmed.

Finn's eyes narrowed thoughtfully. 'That was easy. This isn't a small ask. What did you give them?'

Lily half smiled, the action not reaching her cold eyes. 'A lot.'

Finn eyed her, waiting for more, but when she didn't give him anything further, he just nodded and moved on, respecting her silence.

'They'll be kept updated and meet us at the right moment. We'll load the Romanos bound and blind so they don't know of their involvement,' she told him. 'Then they'll ship them out and dump them somewhere difficult on the other side of the Channel. And that's where our involvement ends. The turf is yours to grab and secure however you see fit.'

She knew they'd already started making plans for that. A lot of the men who'd worked for them back when they'd been banished had moved to Spain, once there were jobs with the Logans there, but some who'd had too much to leave had stayed and kept a low profile. The Logans had been quietly re-recruiting them, ready for this takeover.

'I think that sounds like we have a pretty solid plan,' Finn replied, a smile spreading across his tanned leathery face.

'It does indeed,' Cillian echoed.

'I think this calls for drinks,' Finn said merrily, clapping his hands together.

Cath jumped up from her seat. 'I'll get the champers,' she chimed.

'I'll help you,' Cormac offered, following her over to the other end of the bar.

Lily's eyes rested on Sandra as the chatter started up between the rest of the group. She was in a lot of pain, though she was hiding it well. Sandra caught her looking, and Lily gave her a warm smile, moving to take the seat next to her that Cath had just vacated.

'We owe you an awful lot after last night,' she said quietly.

Sandra shook her head, brushing the comment off. 'Nah. It was me that owed you.'

'No.' Lily shook her head with a frown, knowing exactly what Sandra was referring to. 'You've earned everything you've got, Sandra. You're a hard worker, and that's why you were given that job and the following promotions. You don't owe anyone. I'm thankful to you for getting Isla out of a situation she didn't realise she was walking into. And for finding that room. Seriously.' She met Sandra's gaze. 'It could have been anywhere. While we thought it was close, it could have been a basement or the next building, or somewhere else entirely for all we really knew. And without knowing, we couldn't pull this off. My family would continue to be in danger, and I'd have nothing over them.' She looked away and shook her head. 'I don't know how I can repay you, but I *will*. I promise you that.'

The girl wasn't part of the firm, so her loyalty didn't naturally belong to Lily. Yet still she willingly gave it. Even to the point of taking the vicious beating and everything else she'd suffered last night. Most grown men wouldn't have been able to take that amount of abuse in the name of her firm.

Suddenly, a loud, outraged shriek cut through the chatter, and Lily's head shot round towards Cath, her senses on full alert. Her gaze reached Cath just in time to catch the hard slap she delivered to Cormac's face, the sound of it resounding through the room as everyone fell silent. Cath's face burned red with anger, and Lily stood up, her natural need to protect her sister-in-law kicking in – but before she could find out what was going on, Cath turned and fled, her bottom lip wobbling and the first few tears falling from her eyes.

She paused momentarily as she watched Cath disappear through the front door, and Scarlet overtook her, dark hair streaming out behind her as she flew like a banshee towards the man who'd caused such a reaction in her mother.

'What the *fuck* did you just do?' she demanded hotly.

Cormac, still rubbing his reddened cheek, pulled back from her warily, and Lily didn't blame him. Scarlet stalked towards him menacingly, a deadly look on her hard, beautiful face.

'Yes,' Lily seconded, walking over. 'I'd quite like to know that myself.'

'Cormac?' Sean asked tensely, moving to stand beside his brother.

Everyone else was gathering around them now too, exchanging anxious looks as the atmosphere in the room changed.

'I – well – ugh...' Cormac sighed and rubbed his forehead with an embarrassed expression.

'Well come on,' Cillian said strongly from over Lily's shoulder. 'Out with it – what've you done to my aunt?'

'Eh, easy, lad,' Finn said placatingly, stepping forward. 'Cormac?' He raised his eyebrows at his brother. 'What's going on?'

Cormac looked around at all the faces watching him and threw his hands in the air with a second, more irate sigh. 'Christ,' he muttered. 'I didn't do *nothing*! I think the *world* of Cath. In fact, I think so much of her that I asked her if she'd be interested in going out with me sometime. Alright? That's all,' he stressed, looking embarrassed and more than a little confused. 'We were having a good craic, I asked her out and then...' He trailed off and gestured towards the door, exhaling awkwardly through his nose.

Lily's eyes widened in surprise, and she turned to Scarlet, immediately understanding exactly what had happened. '*Shit*.'

They exchanged a grim look then darted towards the door together. Pushing through, they stopped just outside and looked around, but they were too late. Cath's taillights curled around the corner of the road in the distance as she sped away. She was gone.

TWENTY-SIX

Ray's face darkened until it was a deep shade of beetroot, the veins in his neck protruding so far that Connor was convinced he was about to have a heart attack. Pacing up and down behind his wide walnut desk in his home office, he ranted and raved, almost wild with fury. Connor's earlier confidence had now dwindled, and he cringed internally as he took the verbal beating.

'What the *fuck* did you think you were *doing?*' Ray demanded. 'Do you have *any* idea how hard it is to get a name up the chain once a link's been broken? *Do* you?'

Connor swallowed, forcing himself to stand tall and not flinch. 'No,' he admitted. 'But I'm guessing it's pretty hard.'

'It's almost fucking *impossible*,' Ray roared. He turned in a small circle, rubbing his hard, rugged face before facing Connor again and pointing a finger at him across the desk. 'You're fucking lucky,' he said in a low, dangerous voice. 'It took me all fucking day and several fucking favours that were owed to me, but I managed to make contact and smoothed this over. But it *cost* me.'

'How much?' Connor asked.

'*How much?*' Ray bellowed. 'That's all you've got to say to me, asking me how much your little tantrum cost me?'

'Yeah, I am,' Connor countered, holding his ground. 'How much?'

'*Fifty fucking grand,* you defiant little *shit.*'

Connor clenched his jaw, resisting the urge to punch Ray straight in the mouth. Two of Ray's closest men stood at the side of the room, watching this dressing-down, and he could tell they were enjoying every minute.

'So how exactly are you going to pay that off then, eh? Because you'll damn well pay for your own mistakes here,' Ray continued.

Connor shook his head. 'I already have,' he said calmly, holding Ray's gaze with a steely confidence.

'What did you just say?' Ray's frown deepened.

Connor glanced at Benny, who sat in a chair a couple of feet away, but he was listening in silence, his face resting on his fist and his eyes cast down. There would be no help for him there. He sighed.

'The fifty grand's a one-off, yeah?' Connor asked. 'And then you have a direct supply line with this new contact, I'm assuming.'

Ray didn't answer, but he also didn't cut him off, so Connor pushed forward. 'Those cunts were trying to add another six large to each kilo, which, for the twelve and a half you ordered, would have been an extra *seventy-five* grand.'

Ray's frown deepened further, but his anger seemed to be waning.

'On top of that, they were trying to switch out the top-grade coke you ordered for the cheap shit they cut with baby powder on the side. *That's* why I went for them. They were trying to screw you over. Screw your *firm* over. I was just doing my job.'

Ray sniffed and eyed him hard as he thought this over, then shook his head. 'Nah. They had to be testing you. I ain't had any problems with them before. You're new and they *knew* it. If you'd just pushed back and managed it instead of losing your fucking temper, none of this would have happened.'

Connor gritted his teeth. There was some truth in that, but he couldn't admit it. Not if he wanted to save what little face he had. He tried to think of some way to spin it to look better, but there wasn't one. He *hadn't* tried sorting it out calmly; he'd gone straight for the jugular. He opened his mouth, not sure exactly what was going to come out but knowing he had to say *something*, but was cut off.

'It weren't Connor they tried playing; it was *me*.'

Connor turned his head towards Benny in surprise. Benny fleetingly caught his gaze as he stood up, the warning to shut up and go with it clear. He stood beside Connor and faced Ray.

'*What?*' Ray asked, frowning in confusion. 'Why'd they go for *you*? Why now?'

When Benny had called Ray from the car, he hadn't shared details. It wasn't safe to talk specifics over the phone in their line of work. He'd reported that they had the gear but also the money, and that damage control was needed. To give his boss context while keeping it vague, he'd added that their bridges were burned and that Connor had struck a match.

'No idea.' Benny held his arms out then let them drop to his sides. 'Declan was acting pretty shifty at the last couple of drops. I didn't think much of it, but looking back, I think they were planning this.'

Benny stepped away from Connor, turning and openly sizing him up. Connor tensed but held his position.

'This one stepped in just as things were starting to turn ugly. I told Declan it wasn't happening, that he doesn't call those kinds of shots. Richie had me distracted, and Declan reached into his jacket, so Connor acted. Grabbed him by the throat and slammed him into the wall. Got the blade off him before he could do anything with it. *That's* when he told them to do one.' He met Connor's gaze with a nod and a look of approval. 'Your boy's got good instincts, Ray. Clearly gets that from you.' He held Connor's gaze. 'You have my trust and respect, Drew.'

There was a surprised silence, and Connor felt a rush of gratitude flush through his body. Benny's elaborate lie was a very risky move for him to make. Not least because if Ray ever found out it wasn't the truth, everything Benny had ever worked for would disappear. Trust was the most important asset to have earned in this game. Especially at the top. Without it, you were worth nothing. But he'd also just openly declared his acceptance of Connor, which was surprising to all of them in the room. There was a good chance that with someone as respected as Benny sharing proof of Connor's worthiness, others would follow. But there was also a chance it could cause his own alienation with some of the other men too. These were risks someone as smart as Benny wouldn't usually make, and Connor knew without needing to ask that he was doing it for Scarlet.

'Huh.' Ray placed his hands on his hips. 'Well, that certainly changes things.' He studied Connor critically, narrowing his gaze thoughtfully. 'Well done. You made a good call. I shouldn't have misjudged you.'

Connor shrugged it off. 'Don't worry about it.'

Ray walked over to his drinks cabinet and pulled out a decanter, pouring himself a large measure of the whisky within. He sipped this as he walked back to his desk, then pulled out his black leather chair and sat down, still eying Connor with an unreadable expression.

Connor swallowed, careful to keep his expression neutral. Why was Ray staring at him like that? Did he know Benny's words were a lie? Ray wasn't stupid; he could smell a play a mile off. But why would he have reason to suspect anything was up here? A bead of sweat formed between his shoulder blades and trickled down his back, but Connor stifled the urge to shrug off his jacket and loosen his shirt. Instead, he held Ray's gaze for a few moments then casually moved his attention to a picture on the wall just behind him.

'I need you to drop the money to our new contact,' Ray said finally, shifting his attention back to Benny after what felt like a very long, tense silence. 'What you have in the car and the extra fifty I'll give you in a minute. Make *friends* with the new guy. Make it work. We can't afford any more issues on this.'

'Yes, boss,' Benny said dutifully.

'*Both* of ya,' Ray added, moving his gaze back to Connor. 'Going forward, you can take point on the pickup arrangements.'

'Me?' Connor asked, surprised.

'Yeah,' Ray replied. 'You proved yourself today. Proved you can be trusted to do what needs to be done and that you've got a good eye on the ball.' Ray nodded. 'Jim, go get the bag with the money; take it out to Benny's car.'

'Yes, boss,' came the quiet reply from somewhere over Connor's shoulder.

'I'll ping you the location. Head over now,' Ray ordered.

Connor nodded curtly and turned with Benny, walking shoulder to shoulder with him out of the room and down the hall. Unbuttoning his suit jacket, Connor glanced back over his shoulder as they walked out into the bright sunlight of the crisp winter's day, to make sure they were alone.

'Thank you,' he said, the words quiet but heartfelt.

Benny continued staring ahead, his brow heavy and his face tense as they made their way over to the car. 'Just make sure I don't regret it,' he warned. 'Because this is either a step up or a fucking plane crash for us both.'

'I know,' Connor replied seriously, opening the passenger door. 'You won't.'

Jim trudged out behind them, and they waited as he threw

the bag of cash in the boot, slammed it shut and tapped on it twice before moving off down Ray's long, sweeping drive.

As they drove through the gates and onto the main road beyond, Connor smiled, finally seeing, for the first time, a small ray of hope for his future here.

TWENTY-SEVEN

Lily glanced at her watch again and huffed, irritated. Where *was* everyone? It was the Saturday before the shotgun wedding of the century and they were *supposed* to all be meeting at this ridiculously pink café twenty minutes ago, so they could go and find Billie a dress at the wedding boutique down the road. Billie had asked her, Scarlet, Isla and Cath to join her, having no female family of her own. Or at least none that cared to be involved in her life. But so far she was the only one to have arrived.

She eyed the fake cherry blossom tree overhanging the counter with a frown. *Why?* As if the pink everywhere else wasn't enough. Picking up her glass of tea – *glass* of tea, not a cup like you'd get everywhere else in the world – she sipped from it with a roll of her eyes.

Her phone rang, and she checked the caller ID before answering it. 'George. Update me.' She ran a hand back through her halo of tight blonde curls, but they bounced straight back as she lowered it again.

'Nothing new.' His deep, craggy voice sounded annoyed.

'He's just come out for the day, straight to the usual gaff for his coffee then set off with Mani and Luca.'

Luca. Resting back in the pastel-pink tub chair, Lily crossed her slim legs and smoothed her leather pencil skirt, glancing at the door.

'What's the deal with Luca these days?' she asked. 'Is he still just trailing round after them like a beaten puppy?'

'Pretty much. That kind of disgrace don't get forgotten easily, as you know.'

Lily twisted her bright red lips to one side. 'So *he's* still no threat, at least.'

'Nah. He ain't run anything but his mouth these last few years.'

Lily drummed her long, manicured nails on the arm of the chair. 'Keep an eye on Mani today. That old bastard's getting itchy, and word's starting to get round about the wedding. If he's planning something, we need to know.'

'Gotcha.'

'And swap out with Ben and Danny when you need to.'

Billie's bright blonde hair came bobbing past the front windows, her head turned towards the tall handsome man at her side. Lily's eyebrow hitched in surprise. 'I've got to go.'

She hung up just as the pair walked inside, grinning at each other over some joke, she presumed. They came over to her table, and she stood up to greet them.

'Cillian, what are you doing here?' she asked. 'This is a girls' thing – you ain't supposed to see the dress until the wedding.'

'I'm not stopping,' he told her. 'I just wanted to come see you before you guys went off.'

'Oh.' Lily smiled, feeling a warmth flood through her.

She was lucky in ways most mothers weren't at this stage of their children's lives, in that she still got to see Cillian almost every day. But even so, it still touched her heart when he came to see her just because he wanted to.

They sat down, and Lily glanced once more at her watch. 'Well, I'm sorry to say, everyone else is running late. I have no idea where they are.'

'Actually, we told you to come an hour earlier than everyone else,' Billie told her.

'Oh? Why?' Lily immediately grew concerned.

Billie bit her bottom lip and looked to Cillian, and that feeling grew.

'Cillian?' Lily turned her attention to him, searching his face.

'Well, er...' He shuffled awkwardly in his seat. 'We wanted to talk to you about something. Alone. Just us.'

Lily's skin prickled, and she looked around the small, busy café. Why had they chosen here, somewhere so public? This was going to be bad news. So bad they weren't brave enough to tell her at home. She felt a flush of fear rise hotly up her neck.

'You're moving away,' she accused flatly, putting her hand to her neck and looking around.

'*What?*' Cillian pulled his head back with a confused frown.

'You're planning to leave, aren't you?' Her voice rose slightly as she tried to work out what had triggered this. 'Because you're getting married.' She closed her eyes and mentally cursed.

'Mum!' Cillian exclaimed.

'What is it, the house prices?' she demanded. 'You *know* you don't have to worry about that. If you want to start your marriage off in a proper house instead of that bachelor pad of yours, that's *fine* – money's no object.'

'Lil!' Billie chimed in with a laugh, and Lily had a hard time keeping herself from launching at the girl who was suddenly trying to take her only remaining son away from her. 'No one's leaving!'

Lily searched her face, looking for signs of dishonesty, but there didn't appear to be any. Billie reached over the table and touched her arm in an unusual gesture of physical affection, but this didn't ease her mind one bit. Their relationship wasn't like that. What the *hell* was going on?

'I ain't going anywhere,' Cillian said strongly.

This *did* ease her mind, because she knew him inside and out and his tone was certain and true. 'Then will you two just tell me what the fuck is going on?' she demanded.

'We have something for you,' Cillian said, his tone as warm as the smile he turned towards Billie.

She reached into her large handbag and pulled out a slightly bent giftbag, handing it across to Lily. Lily took it with a cautious frown and opened it, pulling out the soft pink woollen knit blanket inside. On one corner, the name *Lily Rose Drew* was embroidered in white. Her frown deepened.

'Thanks,' she said slowly. 'It's very sweet, but Rose ain't my middle name.'

'No, it ain't,' Cillian agreed, smiling broadly.

'I have an identical one at home,' Billie said softly as Lily stared down at it again. 'I thought this one could stay at your house, for when she comes to visit.'

Tears filled Lily's eyes, blurring the pink and white into one, and a wave of incredible emotions that she couldn't even name washed over her so strongly it almost took her breath away.

'Oh my God,' she uttered, the tears falling down her cheeks. She turned her gaze up to Cillian. '*Really?*'

'Really,' he confirmed, his eyes shining with the threat of his own tears as he watched his mother's reaction. He cleared his throat and glanced away, only a composed warmth remaining in his eyes when he looked back. 'A baby girl, and we're naming her after you.'

'Oh my God,' Lily repeated shakily, fresh tears flooding out. She turned to Billie with a shocked emotional smile. 'I can't believe it! A baby girl. And you're sure about the name?' Her brow crinkled. 'You really don't have to do that...'

'Actually it was my idea,' Billie said. 'I couldn't think of a better name for this beautiful little thing.' She placed her hand on the small swell of her lower stomach, and Lily's mouth dropped open in surprise.

'How the hell did I not see that!' she declared. 'How far gone are you?'

'Nearly fourteen weeks,' Billie replied happily. She reached into her handbag again and pulled out an envelope. 'We had these done privately yesterday, along with a DNA test to check the sex. We just couldn't wait to find out.' She laughed.

Lily pulled out the images and gasped in awe. They weren't the simple black-and-white ones they'd had when she'd had babies; these images were much clearer, with a pale peach skin tone and real distinguishable features.

'This is amazing,' she breathed, taking in the little button nose and the tiny curled fingers. 'How do they get these?'

'They're 4D; it's a whole thing now,' Billie explained. 'They get the video up on a screen and you can watch her moving around and everything. It's incredible. They said we'd see much more in a couple more weeks. I was thinking we could book back in then and you could come with us, see her for yourself.'

Lily touched the little rosebud mouth on the picture of her namesake, already falling deeply in love. 'Lily Rose,' she breathed.

'I need the loo again,' Billie said with a laugh. 'Every five minutes it feels like! I'll be back in a sec.'

She walked off, and Lily reached across the table, grabbing Cillian's hand. Her bottom lip wobbled again, but she managed to control herself this time. 'I'm so chuffed for you,' she said with feeling. 'Are you happy?'

He nodded, and she could see the love shine from his eyes. 'Couldn't be happier. Billie's everything I ever wanted, and now I get another little version of her to love and look after. One that's part of me too.'

'Oh, Cillian.' Lily's eyes misted again as her heart swelled with pride and love. 'You're going to be an amazing dad, you really are.'

He looked away, the happiness dimming slightly. 'I don't know about that. I didn't exactly have someone to show me how to be, on that front.'

'Yes, you did,' Lily said strongly. 'You had *me*. A parent is a parent, Cillian. It don't matter whether you had the standard set, just a mum, just a dad, or *two* mums, *two* dads – what matters is that you had a parent who showed you how to love and care and protect.' She cast her gaze over his handsome face, stripping back the years from it in her mind. 'Not that I'm saying my parenting was perfect of course.' The corner of her mouth lifted in humour. 'But you always had love, care and protection. So I *know* you'll be just fine. The rest you'll figure out along the way. And I'll be right there to help you, whatever you need.'

Cillian squeezed her hand back with both of his. 'Thank you, Mum,' he said, the words coming straight from his heart. 'For everything.'

'Oh, my boy,' she said shakily. 'You never have to thank me for a thing. You're my life. And being there for you is my job. Something you'll understand on a whole new level soon.'

Another tear fell down her cheek, and they sat there for a few moments together in silence, hands held fast and hearts full to the brim.

'Everything OK?' The waitress waited expectantly, and though the woman had disturbed one of the most perfect moments of Lily's life, she was too happy to destroy her for it today.

'Yes,' she said instead, smiling brightly. 'Actually we're *more* than OK; we're celebrating. My son is going to become a father.'

'Oh, congratulations,' the waitress said, her vague smile showing her complete disinterest.

'We need champagne. Do you serve champagne?' Lily asked.

'We do! How many glasses?'

'Three. No – wait!' Lily caught herself quickly. 'Two. And a glass of your finest, er... apple juice, I guess. In a flute though.'

'Coming right up.'

The waitress moved off, and Lily turned back to Cillian with excitement in her eyes.

'There's so much to plan, so much to sort out. You need to *move*,' she said, deadly serious. 'I meant what I said about the house – money is no object. But you can't raise a baby in that flat. There's only one bedroom, for one thing.'

'I agree,' Cillian said. 'Billie does too. I've been looking at houses over your way. It wouldn't hurt to be a little closer after the baby's here.'

Lily's smile widened, but then she carefully calmed herself. She didn't want to be overbearing and put them off. 'Good idea. After the wedding, we'll work everything out so you're all set when you find the right place. Who else knows?' she asked.

'No one. We wanted you to be the first to know. *We* only found out a few days ago.' He laughed. 'Billie didn't realise until her favourite jeans didn't fit. I'm telling Connor tomorrow.'

The mention of her other son dampened Lily's mood, and she just nodded, looking away. There was an awkward silence.

'You need to sort this shit with Connor out, Mum,' Cillian said seriously. 'You can't punish him forever.'

Her eyes flashed as she looked back at him, but he didn't give her a chance to reply before continuing. '*No*, I'm serious. I don't understand what this shit with Ray is any more than you do. And it hurts me too. But you and I both know you love and miss him too much to keep giving him the cold shoulder for much longer, and my wedding is just a few days away. You *don't* want to look back on that day with regret because you were too stubborn to calm your temper a little earlier than you'd planned. And *I* don't want to either. So you'd better hear me now, Mum. *Sort it out.*'

Lily raised her eyebrows as Cillian's steely gaze locked on to hers. She knew he was right, but that didn't ease the spiky fireball of hurt fury the whole situation with Ray and Connor had set alight inside her.

Cillian's eyes softened. 'You don't want to end up like Billie's mum, Mum. A woman so bitter and self-absorbed that she'd rather cut off her child than just apologise and right a wrong. A woman who'd rather play the victim than be the parent she's supposed to be. You're *better* than that,' he said quietly. 'You ain't nothing like that woman. She's lost sight of what matters most in life, of what family really means. And because of that, her daughter – her beautiful, smart, amazing daughter – is getting married and having a baby, without a mum to help her through, the way mums are supposed to.'

'Well, she has *me*,' Lily replied. 'And I know it's not the same as having your own. I remember *very* well how hard it was having kids without parents around to help. So I'll be there for Billie – you know you can count on me for that. When she's exhausted and can't stop crying because it's all so overwhelming – and yes, that *will* happen; it's completely natural,' she added, seeing his face change. 'I'll be there to tell her it'll be alright. I'll send her to bed and hold the baby while she sleeps and sort your washing and make sure you both eat. Because you'll *also* be so tired you won't know what way's up.' She smiled. 'And we'll all get through it together. Because it's true what they say. It takes a village. And I would never let you raise this baby without one.' Her face clouded. 'That mother of hers should be bloody ashamed.'

'From what I hear, she's too focused on herself to feel anything like that,' Cillian replied. 'But don't change the

subject. What you're doing to Connor is wrong, and it's got to
end. *Now*, not in another couple of weeks when you finally cool
off. I know you're angry with him. *Be* angry with him. But be
angry to his face, for fuck's sake. Alright?'

Lily sighed. She knew Cillian was right, but it still needled.
And the comparison to Billie's absent-by-choice mother wasn't
something she appreciated at all. But she grudgingly took that
on the chin, not wanting to spoil such a special day with an
argument.

'I'll make it up with him when I see him,' she promised.
'Not that I forgive what he's done,' she added. 'He's betrayed
this firm on every level.'

'I feel the same, but he's still blood. He's still Connor.'

Lily nodded. 'He is. Nothing could ever change that.'

As she made the decision to end her cold shoulder, a deep
feeling of relief washed over her. She really couldn't have borne
another week without him. These last few had been hell.

'I'm not promising I'll be civil to Ray though,' she said
suddenly.

Cillian shrugged. 'Do what you like to Ray. Just keep it civil
at the wedding.'

'Deal,' she agreed.

The waitress reappeared with the drinks and placed them
on the table, walking away just as Billie arrived.

'Ooh, what's this?' she asked. 'Champers?'

'For us, yes,' Cillian replied. 'For you, the finest apple juice
money can buy.'

Billie's face fell and she sighed. 'Yeah, that sounds about
right.'

Lily laughed and lifted her glass. 'A toast,' she said, smiling
at them both. 'To the pair of you as you prepare to grow your
family. And to your beautiful daughter, my beautiful granddaughter, Lily Rose.' Her heart swelled once more, and she

looked down at Billie's bump. 'In the favoured words of *my* parents, may the road rise up to meet you, and may the wind be always at your back. May the sun shine warm upon your face, and until we meet, dear Lily Rose, may God hold you safe in the palm of His hand.'

TWENTY-EIGHT

Scarlet pulled up to the house and turned off the ignition, rubbing her face tiredly. It was nearly three in the morning. She didn't usually work on a Sunday, but she was so behind right now that she'd had no choice but to slip off after the big family lunch and get back to it. Time didn't care that Connor had gone; it ticked on regardless. There would always be more work fires to put out, more money to hide, more tracks to cover, whether she could keep up or not.

Scarlet closed the car door and entered the house as silently as she could, trying not to wake her mother, then kicked off her red-soled black stilettos, welcoming the soothing chill of the hall tiles beneath her aching feet. Her eyes were drawn to the warm lamp glow coming from the lounge, and as she peered in, she was surprised to find her mother curled up on the couch in her dressing gown, staring down at a framed picture in her lap.

'Hello, love,' Cath said quietly, looking up.

She'd been crying, her eyes puffy and red rimmed. A pile of scrunched-up tissues lay on the side table. With a frown, Scarlet walked over and sat next to her, shuffling up closer until they were shoulder to shoulder. She looked down at the familiar photo and laid her head on Cath's shoulder.

'I always loved that picture' she said, squeezing her mother's arm.

'Me too. It was such a special day.' Cath sniffed sadly and rested her head on Scarlet's.

Cath and Ronan stood together, all dressed up in red matching outfits, a gold tinsel wreath resting on Cath's dark shiny hair. Ronan's arm was draped around her shoulders, and they were staring into each other's eyes, laughing. Scarlet could remember taking the photo, capturing that perfect candid moment. It had been the best Christmas she could remember, full of laughter and love and lively merriment. She'd been just sixteen, blissfully unaware that it would be one of their last Christmases as a family. Ronan had been killed two years later.

'It'll be four years soon,' Scarlet said softly.

'I know. Still feels like yesterday.'

A tear slipped off her cheek onto the picture frame, and Scarlet stared at it for a moment, remembering the dark months after her father's death. Cath had almost lost herself completely back then, crying over pictures night after night and drinking herself into oblivion. But she'd come a long way since then. She'd learned how to live and move forward without Ronan.

Scarlet bit her lip. 'You know it's OK if you want to go on that date with Cormac.'

Cath immediately stiffened and folded her arms, shooting Scarlet a stubborn look of warning. 'I've told you – *and* Lil – I *don't* want to talk about it.'

'Well, maybe you should,' Scarlet pushed back, sitting up and turning to look at her. 'Because crying over pictures at three in the morning ain't a good alternative.'

Cath bristled, but when she opened her mouth to argue, a large sob escaped instead. Her face crumpled, and Scarlet pulled her into her arms, hugging her tightly as she cried, her own heart breaking along with her mother's.

'Mum, Dad wouldn't have wanted you to sit here on your own for the rest of your life,' she said. 'You're barely into your mid-forties and you've locked yourself away in this quiet little bubble like you're some old woman. But you're *not*. And...' She grimaced. 'And I won't be here with you forever. At some point I'll need a place of my own, and then what? I don't want you to be lonely.'

Cath pulled back and wiped her tears away with her hands. 'I know you'll go eventually, I do. But I just feel like – like I'd be *betraying* him dating someone else. Betraying his memory. When your dad and I got married, it was meant to be for life.'

'And it *was*,' Scarlet said, her voice soft. 'You *were* his life, and that life was a good one.' She reached up and tucked a fallen strand of her mother's dark hair back behind her ear. 'But that life ended four years ago. You can't carry on a marriage alone. You can carry the *love*, and the *memories*, but the marriage is gone.'

She winced as her words made Cath cry once more. 'I'm sorry, I don't want to upset you, but you need to stop living in the past. Dad will always be the love of your life and the person we all miss every day, and no one you choose to date will ever replace him. They'll just take a new role in our lives. Like a new friend. But, you know...' She pulled an awkward face. 'One with benefits.'

'Ugh, Scarlet,' Cath admonished, but she laughed, despite herself.

'Yeah, that was...' Scarlet wrinkled her nose and shook her head. 'No. OK. But you know what I'm saying. It's *OK* to say yes to a date. It's OK to like someone else. And it's OK to be honest with them too. Anyone worth dating will be under-standing and respectful of how you feel about Dad.'

Cath took in a deep breath and sighed tiredly. 'When did

you become so wise?' she asked wryly. 'I thought I was supposed to be the mother?'

'Well, I learned from the best,' Scarlet replied with a smile. She squeezed Cath's hand. 'The main question though, really, is how do you actually feel about Cormac? I mean, do you fancy him? He seems your type.'

'My *type*?' Cath raised an eyebrow.

'Yeah, you know...' Scarlet shrugged. 'He doesn't exactly look like Dad, but he clearly looks after himself, like Dad, and he's got that same hard moody look that hides the fact he's actually quite good fun.'

Cath laughed. 'Yeah, I suppose he does. He *is* nice, Cormac. And we've always got on.' But her smile faded as she looked back at the photo in her hands. 'I just don't think I can yet, Scar. I know it's been four years, but... I don't know.' She touched the picture.

Scarlet watched her sadly, wishing she knew how to help her mother move on. 'OK. Well, just think about it. And know that Lil and I both fully support you, whatever you do.'

Cath didn't answer. She placed the picture back on the side table and stood up with a yawn. 'I think it's time we were both in bed, don't you?'

'I do,' Scarlet agreed, yawning herself.

'Turn that light off, will you?' Cath asked, walking out to the hall.

'Sure.'

Scarlet's gaze lingered on the happy couple in the picture, her heart aching. Nothing seemed to last forever in this life, it seemed. Staring at her father's smiling face, she reached over and switched out the light.

TWENTY-NINE

Mani ended the call and resisted the urge to throw his mobile into the busy road next to him. With a small growl of frustration under his breath, he pushed through the front door of the small Italian restaurant and walked over to his favourite booth. Riccardo and Guy, one of their men, sat waiting, full steaming plates of the day's pasta special in front of them. Mani sat down opposite Riccardo with a great heaving sigh.

'So?' Riccardo asked, ripping off a piece of bread and putting it in his mouth. 'Any news?'

'Yes, your cousins have heard through the grapevine that the Logans are definitely in town,' Mani said grimly.

Riccardo and Guy exchanged a glance. 'And you're certain it was them who torched the house?'

'Absolutely certain. They wouldn't show their faces here without knowing that evidence was gone, and they couldn't know it was gone unless they'd *known* it was in that house. Though that's the part I still can't work out. *How* they found out.' Mani pinched the bridge of his nose. 'You need to be careful, watch your back a little closer for now until I can find out where they are and do something about all this.'

'What do they look like?' Riccardo asked thickly between chews, his mouth full once more.

Mani stared at his son's mouth, irritated by this. 'There's three of them. Irish, all quite tall. Blonde to brown hair. Finn and Cormac were broad; Sean was slighter. I haven't seen them for ten years but back then they kept themselves in shape and were handy with their fists. I wouldn't imagine much has changed. I know they hit the ground running out there, set themselves back up. They'll be around late forties, maybe fifty now.'

Riccardo made a sound of dismissive amusement. 'Old men then,' he said, grinning.

He shoved another piece of sauce-soaked bread in his mouth, and Mani lost his temper.

'For Christ's *sake!*' He slammed his fist on the table, his expression thunderous. 'How do you sit there stuffing your mouth at a time like this? Put that *down.*'

Riccardo did as he'd been told, clearly getting the message about how serious Mani was but still cocky enough to hold his hands up in a sarcastic display of surrender.

'I'm just trying to be sensible and line my stomach before we party later,' he said with a smirk.

'It's Monday night, for crying out loud,' Mani spat back. 'Do you ever *stop*? Seriously, when are you going to grow up and be *serious*, Riccardo?'

'Oh, I'm serious, Dad,' he replied. 'Serious about unwinding at the end of every long day. And I always get *everything* you ask done, so what else do you want from me, eh?' He held his hands out in question. 'Other than to look over my shoulder for old men from your past that is.'

Mani's eyes narrowed. 'You *fool*. You think you know it all, but you have no idea what the Logans are capable of, now that we've lost our leverage,' he hissed, his jowls wobbling as his face contorted in rage. 'And as for *age,* these men are nearly twenty years younger than *I* am, and *I'm* still running rings around *you*, Riccardo. You work hard, yes, but only pulling the strings *I wove* for you, in the kingdom *I* built, that's held up by *my* reputation.' He eyed his son hard, satisfied to see the colour warm his cheeks at this reminder. 'The Logans are in their prime – they're *dangerous* men, with everything to gain and nothing to lose. Do *not* underestimate them.'

Riccardo stared back at him over the table, his expression more serious now, the earlier smirk gone. He wiped his mouth with a napkin and rested back against the booth.

'Well, I *have* been keeping a closer eye on things lately, after Robert went missing,' he said. 'Things still don't add up there. And I've been followed a couple of times lately, but it wasn't the Logans.'

'Who?' Mani barked with a frown.

'The Drews.' Riccardo lifted his beer to his mouth.

Mani sat back, surprised. 'Who? When?'

'I've noticed a car following me a couple of times on my way here to meet you. The last time Guy was in his own car a couple of minutes behind. He caught up and followed it to the Black Bear. It was one of their newer guys. His name's Danny.' Riccardo took another sip of his beer. 'I think they know.'

Mani chewed the inside of his cheek. He'd felt so sure they didn't after testing the waters at the Drews' casino night. But then again, they couldn't be sure.

He sniffed. 'Lily's always been too straight to the point. If she knew, she'd want blood, and she'd want it yesterday.' He narrowed his gaze as he pondered it. 'But that doesn't mean she wouldn't change tactics.' He exhaled heavily. This should all have been over by now. The Drews should all be dead and gone, and he should be busy reaping the benefits. 'Whatever they're doing, we need to deal with them anyway. Perhaps we should move up the plan.'

Riccardo sat up again, interest in his eyes. 'To when?'

Mani thought it over. 'We'd only need a day, maybe two, to prepare and get everyone in place. We'd need to smooth over our alibis, ensure they're iron clad.' He thought it all over and suddenly a cold, dark smile spread across his face. 'Actually, I have a better idea. One that will truly pay them back for the devastation they've wreaked on this family over the years. Call your brother. There isn't a second to lose.'

THIRTY

Tuesday came around with no sign of Riccardo taking a break from his busy nightly parties. Some nights it had been just a handful of people; others he'd thrown a full-blown rager. Overall, as far as they could see, the man barely ever seemed to sleep. All would finally go quiet in the early hours, but that was when the rest of the building began to wake, and it was too risky to enter during the day. Anyone from the firm could come in or out, and they had no idea who, in the building, might be loyal enough to the Romanos to alert them to strangers sniffing around that floor.

Isla had texted, as planned, at breakfast time. By lunch, Riccardo had replied to her carefully worded flattery and agreed to meet her for a few late-night drinks after her fictional shift ended at ten thirty. By eleven, they were sat in a cosy nook in a small cocktail bar, being watched closely, unbeknown to Riccardo, by Joe, just two tables away. By eleven fifty-five, Scarlet and Cillian were in the side street opposite Riccardo's building in the back of Lily's car, dressed in plain black clothes and black caps pulled low, and with all they needed to pull the job on the seat between them in a duffel bag.

Lily looked over at the building and pushed away the nerves that naturally jittered at not just *being* in enemy territory – which was cause enough to put anyone on edge – but pulling a job on the very firm that wanted to kill them, right where they lived too. Or perhaps her nerves were due more to the fact she was sending Cillian and Scarlet in there and not joining them. Part of her wanted to go along, but the other part knew they'd be quicker and less conspicuous on their own. It would also mean no one was outside watching the door.

She sighed to herself and looked back at the pair of them in the mirror. Scarlet's big grey-blue eyes were trained on the building, her hard, pale face not giving anything away. Cillian was looking out of the window, his gaze spanning the perimeter uneasily.

'Just remember the front door code,' Lily said, picking up their earlier conversation. 'What is it?'

'Seventy-eight-ten,' Scarlet replied automatically.

'And then?' Lily prompted, looking back at them both in the rear-view mirror.

'Twelfth floor,' Cillian responded. 'Number ninety-seven. Chubb lock, for which I have these...' He pulled his lock-picking pins from somewhere and held them up, the glow from the nearest streetlight reflecting dimly off them in the darkness of the car. 'Then we're in.'

'Gloves on when we leave the lift, before the lock,' Scarlet added, just as Lily opened her mouth to correct that oversight. 'Then inside we grab as much as we can fit in here, as quick as we can, and leave.'

'In and out in fifteen minutes,' Cillian finished.

Lily nodded, satisfied that everyone was clear on what they were doing. 'Good. Call me when you're on your way down; I'll pull up outside.'

The clock on the dash flickered as it turned midnight. Scarlet opened her door and slipped out silently. Cillian slung the empty duffel bag over his shoulder and followed suit. Both doors slammed shut, then the two figures melted into the darkness, only reappearing again as they turned the corner at the end of the road.

Lily blew out a long, tense breath and leaned forward on the steering wheel, watching them with hawklike eyes as they approached the tall building, entered the code and disappeared inside. Sitting back, she rubbed her hands together and blew on them. It was bitterly cold tonight, but she didn't want to turn the engine on and draw any unnecessary attention to herself. She settled on crossing her arms and pushing them under her armpits. They were only going to be here for a few minutes; it wouldn't be long until she could turn the heating back on.

She passed the time by mentally following their journey up, allowing thirty seconds for the lift to arrive and a minute to travel up. She gave them two minutes to cross the hallway to the right door and for Cillian to pull out his pins. He'd need no more than a minute to pick the lock, but she waited until the clock ticked over to seven minutes past before she nodded, satisfied that they'd definitely be inside by then.

She watched the door, keeping her eye on the clock in her peripheral vision. Eight minutes past. Nine minutes past.

As the clock changed again, headlights came into view. She waited for the car to pass, not overly worried. The road here was a main route through the area, and midnight wasn't overly late for the odd traveller on a Tuesday.

But instead of passing by, the headlights seemed to slow, and as the side of the car came into view, it turned towards the building and pulled up right by the front.

Lily sat upright, all her senses alert and a frisson of fear running over her skin. The doors opened, and her mouth dropped open in horror. It was Luca with two of the Romanos' men. She grappled for her phone as they slammed the doors and jogged up the steps to the front door, hitting Cillian's number. It went straight to voicemail.

'No, no, *no!*' she gasped quietly.

She quickly moved to Scarlet's number, cursing out loud and hitting the steering wheel as that went to voicemail too. She tried both numbers again, twice, with the same result.

'*Shit!*' she cried, her panic now at full force.

Lily got out of the car, clung to the top of the door and looked around wildly, trying to work out what to do. She almost made for the building then drew back, knowing her appearance would only put them in more danger. She called Cillian's phone again and stayed on the line, waiting for the beep.

'Cillian, *get out,*' she cried. 'Both of you. Luca's here with two men, and I can't get through to your phones! He...' She trailed off, her eyes darting from side to side as she worked it through. 'He'll already be up there.' Her voice had turned deadly quiet. 'Shit, Cillian, call me. Tell me there's a way out. I'm calling for backup.'

She ended the call and immediately dialled Andy, who picked up in two rings. She wasted no time. 'Luca's here, they're inside and I can't get through to warn them.'

'We're on our way.'

The call ended, and Lily quickly dialled the next number.

'Danny, get everyone you can and get here *quickly*. Luca turned up...'

As she reeled off her urgent instructions, Lily's brain worked over the logistics, and her heart grew cold. Cillian and Scarlet had no idea Luca and those men were headed up there. The chances were that they were heading to Riccardo's home, but there was also a high chance that Cillian and Scarlet would be leaving the hidden flat at the same time. If Luca saw them, they were at an instant disadvantage. Even though Lily was gathering a small army to help them get out of there, they weren't in their own territory right now. And her men were half an hour away.

Her blood turned to ice. Half an hour was too long to be in the hands of an enemy, after being caught in the heart of their territory. Especially *this* enemy. What Luca would do to them just to get answers would be bad enough, but if he realised what they'd gone there to steal – the one thing that would destroy his brother's life – then it was all over. That half hour might as well be a century for all the good it would do them then.

If Luca knew that, he'd want the threat removed as soon as possible, which meant one of two things. He'd either kill them on the spot, or he'd take them somewhere private to do it. And in half an hour, when her men finally arrived, it would be too late. Cillian and Scarlet would either be en route to their own funeral, or all that would be left to collect upstairs would be their still, lifeless bodies.

THIRTY-ONE

Scarlet looked around the simple bedsit with a feeling of desolation and disgust. The walls, floor and ceiling were covered in black soundproofing foam tiles, as was the back of the front door, with the exception of the spy hole and handle. Bright spotlights beamed down from the ceiling, casting a cold grey light on the dark space. A large sofa bed stood in one corner; some ropes, gags and rags in another. She turned away, closing her eyes for a moment when she registered these, unable to bear the thought of how many women they'd been used on while he'd raped and filmed them.

'Don't focus on it,' Cillian said, noticing her reaction. 'Come – help me work out what's what.'

Scarlet nodded and walked over to the metal racks that held all the storage boxes. Cillian had already taken the laptop and the hard drive next to it, but there were many more. *Too* many, Scarlet realised. She narrowed her eyes as she studied the contents of the first box.

'I don't think these are all his,' she said slowly.

'What do you mean?'

She pulled two out of the first box and held them up for him to see. 'They're all date ranges on the labels, but there's different handwriting. And different hardware brands.'

'Could just be one of the others; Sandra said there were a few of them.' He looked away uncomfortably.

Scarlet looked back at the boxes and twisted her mouth with a frown. 'I don't think so,' she insisted. 'I think he's keeping these for other people too. Or buying them maybe. Either way, there's too many hard drives here to just be him. I mean...' She paused and looked at the specifications on the side of the small black box. 'This is five hundred gigabytes – that could easily hold a couple of hundred hours. And this one's a terabyte, which is double that space.'

They stared at each other for a moment, the implications of what this could mean registering with them at the same time.

'We need to get out of here,' Scarlet said urgently.

'Yep.' Cillian turned and grabbed the nearest box, tipping the contents into the bag. 'We'll figure out which are his later. Let's just move.'

Scarlet turned and helped him heap as many external hard drives as they could into the bag, then waited nervously as he zipped it back up. If Riccardo was part of a ring and all the drives were here, it could mean he wasn't the only one to use this room. They hadn't been keeping an eye on everyone else coming in and out of the building, only him. For all they knew, one of the others could arrive at any moment.

'Come on – let's go.' Cillian marched to the door and reached for the handle.

'Wait!' Scarlet rushed ahead and pushed his hand back. 'Let's check it's clear first.'

She put her eye to the peep hole and almost pulled back, but just then the lift doors opened in the distance. She froze and pulled a sharp intake of air.

'What?' Cillian asked, touching her arm. 'What is it?'

'It's Luca,' she breathed. 'And two others.'

'*Fuck,*' Cillian exclaimed, running a hand back through his dark hair in stress. 'Shit, are they coming in *here*?' He swung around and darted towards the small kitchenette, opening all the drawers in quick succession but finding them empty.

'I-I don't know.' Scarlet watched them. The closer they got, the faster her heart thudded against the wall of her chest. 'No. They've stopped. They're going into Riccardo's.' She felt a spark of relief, but it was short-lived as she watched Luca walk in and shut the door, leaving the other two to stand guard outside.

'Oh thank God,' Cillian said with a huge sigh of relief. 'Come on – let's go before he comes back out.'

'No, we can't,' Scarlet said with a feeling of dread. 'He's left the other two keeping watch outside.'

Cillian put both hands to his temples and turned around, looking like he was about to explode in either panic or fury.

Scarlet stepped back from the door and pulled out her phone. *Why hadn't Lily rung to warn them?* She frowned as she realised there were no bars of signal on the screen.

'Hey, check your phone,' she told him, looking back at hers with a confused frown. Suddenly, she looked up at the walls and the ceiling.

'No service,' Cillian confirmed.

Scarlet moved to the wall and ran her long nails into the groove between two tiles, gently prising one corner away from the wall.

'Fucking *copper*,' she spat.

'What you on about?' Cillian asked.

'Copper wire,' she repeated, moving so he could see. 'He's lined the room with this mesh to block phone signals.' She looked around the room and at the one sealed window at the side. 'Keep an eye on the peep hole; I'm going to check the bathroom.'

Cillian stood by the door and put his eye to the hole, and

Scarlet walked past the kitchenette towards the bathroom at the back, the only part of the flat separate from the rest. The outer part of the door was sound blocked, but the inside wasn't. She held her phone out, moving around the tiny space, looking for a signal and trying not to breathe through her nose. It stank to high heaven, the toilet ringed with multiple levels of grime and the floor beneath covered in patches of dried urine. Cringing, she hitched one leg up onto the almost equally as disgusting sink and reached up to the handle of the small window above it. To her relief, it opened, and she shoved it out as wide as it would go.

She hoisted herself up, kneeled awkwardly in the sink and leaned out. There was a flat roof not too far below, maybe eight feet. In the middle, there was a doorway, but she could see already that there was no handle on the outside. It would only open from inside.

Her phone began to vibrate in her hand, and she answered it quickly, relieved to have at least found a signal. 'Lil.'

'Jesus *Christ*,' Lily cried. 'Luca's up there.'

'We know. We're trapped,' Scarlet told her. 'He's in Riccardo's flat, but his men are in the hall. We can't get out.'

'Where are you?' Lily asked.

Scarlet looked around her with a wry lift of her brows. 'Well, the back half of me is still in the bathroom, and the front half is currently balancing out the window. There's a flat roof not far below; we can get to it, but there's no way off. Only an internal door.'

'Right.' There was a pause, and Scarlet could hear the sounds of her aunt moving quickly. 'It's a hotel,' she said. 'OK. Right.' There was another short pause, and Scarlet could practically hear the cogs turning in Lily's brain. 'OK, get onto the roof; I'll be there to let you out shortly.'

'How?' Scarlet asked.

'I just will. Get out of there and hide if you can, until I get there. Got it?' Lily replied.

'Yeah, OK.' Scarlet nodded, glancing back with a grim look of fear. 'But, Lil? Hurry. Things aren't as straightforward as we'd thought. Riccardo might not be the biggest worry we have right now.'

THIRTY-TWO

Lily took a deep breath and blew it out slowly as she mounted the steps at the front of the hotel. She'd never done anything like this before. She'd never had to. Pulling herself up to her full five feet and three inches, she marched to the reception desk with a confidence she didn't even slightly possess.

The night manager, a young man of around thirty, looked up with a smile, his expression utterly bored. 'Hello, how can I help?' he asked charmingly.

Lily raised her eyebrows and pursed her lips, pointedly running her gaze up and down him, attempting, as she did, to see if there were any guest names in sight on the desk. There weren't.

'You can *help* by taking me up to the roof, this *instant*, so that my *clients* can get back into their hotel room,' she demanded in her most authoritative voice.

The man blinked. 'Um, I'm sorry, what?'

'Your *roof*,' she repeated with a disdainful shake of her head. 'My clients have been stuck up there for an *hour*. They've been calling and calling the hotel number, and *no one* has answered.'

'They... There's someone on the roof?' he asked, a confused frown forming.

'*Two* people. *Two* people on your roof.' She glanced at his name tag. 'And unless you want a legal shitstorm to start on your shift, Michael, I suggest we get up there and let them out *pronto*.'

'I... The phone hasn't rung,' he said. 'I'm sorry, who are you? And who are your clients?'

'My clients are in room 103, and I'm their lawyer,' Lily replied. 'I *would* give you my card, but having been woken up at *midnight* after two very stressful days in court, the fact I might need one slipped my mind. But I'll tell you what *won't* slip my mind, Michael – the name of the person wasting my time with stupid questions, while a three-months-pregnant woman and her husband continue freezing to death on your roof, all because they made a wrong turn trying to find the ice machine.'

This seemed to do the trick – Michael's eyebrows flew up in a startled manner, and he finally stood up.

'Right. OK. Sorry though, I just... What were your clients' names please?' He frowned, trying to make sense of it all, but Lily pushed on, determined not to give him the chance.

'I told you, they're in room 103.' She tutted impatiently.

'But... their names?' Michael winced as she glared at him witheringly.

'If you don't already know their names, I'm not at liberty to tell you. This is an *extremely* high-profile case. I thought the hotel had been made aware.' She sighed loudly. 'Right, this really is getting too much now. I'm going to have to call this in.' She pulled out her phone. 'I just hope the judge doesn't pull you in for witness tampering. These two were put in here for protection, and now I find they're stranded on a roof, freezing, and you're standing in the way of me getting them back inside, back to safety.' She shot her head up suddenly, eying him hard.

'Or is that it? Oh my God... Are you working for *him*?' She stepped back, feigning alarm. 'OK, I'm calling the police—'

'No! Wait!' Michael held his hands out, his expression reminding her of a startled deer. 'I'm not working for anyone! Or – other than the hotel. Please, I just, let's go and let them in.' He hurriedly grabbed a large set of keys. 'Please follow me.'

Lily eyed him, pretending to weigh it up. 'OK. Let's go. But no more funny business. These two have been through a lot.'

'I... No, o-of course,' he stuttered. 'We want the utmost comfort for all our guests. I just don't know how they could have got onto the roof though.' He frowned as they entered the lift. 'You're sure this is the right hotel?'

'Of course I'm sure,' she replied. 'I dropped them here myself, and I just had a very tearful young woman on the phone describing very clearly that she was *on your roof*. I really hope this isn't your way of trying to shirk responsibility on behalf of the hotel.'

The lift doors opened, and she breathed a sigh of relief as he led the way down the rather tired cream-and-sage-green hallway. She wasn't sure how much longer she could keep up this level of tension before he began to cotton on to the fact it was utter bullshit.

'No, of course not,' he hurriedly assured her. 'It's just that...' His frown became pained. 'I don't know *how* they could have got out. It's locked.'

Lily pulled a face of sheer frustration behind his back. 'I have no idea how they got there. I'm a lawyer, not a psychic,' she snapped curtly.

They reached a short set of stairs and walked up to the door at the top. Lily had a hard time keeping the internal cringe from seeping onto her face as she saw the very big and very much locked deadbolt. Michael stared at it and then at Lily, and she turned to him with a haughty glare.

'*Well?*' she demanded. 'Are you going to wait until we have nothing to find but cold, dead bodies, or are you going to let my clients back inside?'

Michael opened his mouth as if to reply, but then closed it with a sigh and unlocked the deadbolt. Her heart racing as she worried about what she might find on the other side, Lily almost pushed him out of the way as it finally came loose, and pulled the door open wide.

She stepped out with one foot, keeping the other firmly inside and one hand on the door, and peered out into the darkness. Riccardo's building was in front of her, and she could see the window Scarlet must have been leaning out of before. It was the only one open. She looked around but couldn't see either of them for a moment, then suddenly there was a noise to the side.

Cillian appeared first, slipping around from behind the door where they must have been hiding. Scarlet followed, and she moved aside to let them in, closing the door quickly again behind them.

'Make sure that's locked *properly* this time,' Lily told Michael as he stared in amazement at the two people who'd just passed him. 'I'm sure the last thing this hotel needs is *more* scandal.' She swept past him and led Scarlet and Cillian towards the lift.

'Yes, of course.' He quickly locked it and hurried down the hallway after them. 'I'm so sorry for the stress this has caused you, ma'am,' he said, aiming his comment to Scarlet now. 'If there's anything I can do, anything I can send to your room, please let me know.'

She raised her eyebrows but simply nodded slowly, going along with it and glancing at Lily for clarification.

'Thank you, but that won't be necessary,' Lily said in a clipped tone.

'If you want a doctor to check you over, make sure everything's OK with the baby, I can call one in,' he continued, pressing the button for the first floor instead of the ground floor.

Scarlet's eyebrows rose even further, but she said nothing, staring ahead as the lift doors closed. Cillian stood to the back, keeping his head down and the bag as far out of sight as he could, though Michael kept glancing at it curiously.

Lily reached over and pressed the ground-floor button. 'There will be no need for a doctor, as I'm taking my client straight to the hospital to have her and the baby checked over. God only knows what damage this last hour has done.' To drive her point home, Lily slipped off her black wool cashmere-blend coat and slipped it over Scarlet's shoulders, rubbing them vigorously.

There was a silence as the lift travelled down, but Lily could see in the blurry reflection of the metal doors that Michael's frown was deepening, and his glances at Scarlet and Cillian were becoming more frequent.

'So you were looking for the ice machine?' he asked at last, directing his question at Cillian suspiciously.

'Yeah,' he replied. 'Never did find the damn thing.'

'Right. With your bag?' he asked, the suspicion stronger in his tone now.

The lift doors pinged open, and Lily placed herself between Michael and the others, propelling them towards the front door.

'Thank you, Michael. I'll be sure to mention this when we settle my client's bill, how helpful you were.' They hurried across the foyer. 'Please make sure my clients are not disturbed for the next couple of days.'

As they burst out into the street, Lily heaved a sigh of relief but didn't pause to enjoy it. They fell into step with each other and almost jogged across the road to where she'd left the car. She unlocked it, and Scarlet dived inside. Cillian nipped around to the other side and slung the bag in before doing the same. Lily was the last, starting the car and pulling away without pause.

As they rounded the end of the road back onto the dual

carriageway, she finally glanced back at them through the mirror. Scarlet stared out of the window, a bleak look in her eyes. Cillian stared back at her, his gaze troubled.

'What happened?' she asked quietly.

'It's more than just him and a couple of his mates,' Cillian told her. 'There's endless amounts. Scar thinks he's part of a ring. A big one by the look of it.'

'Right,' Lily said heavily. 'Shit.'

'Yeah, exactly. *Shit*,' Cillian agreed, rubbing a hand down his face.

They spent the rest of the drive to the meeting point in silence, as Lily tried to work out what the hell they were going to do. Because this changed things. They couldn't hold information like this in good conscience and let these people continue to do all they did unchecked. It was unthinkable. They needed to be stopped.

But if they did the right thing, then they lost their leverage. Which would put the Logans right back where they started, and with no protection against the Romanos when they came to take them out. Which left them with an impossible decision. Did they do the right thing? Or did they save themselves? It was an extra hurdle they really didn't need, and the choice wasn't simple. But it was one they now needed to decide on – and fast. Because now they'd set things in motion, there was no stopping it. Whatever way things went now, the countdown to the end had begun.

THIRTY-THREE

Finn parked in the next street to his actual destination, then slung the bag over his shoulder and walked quickly around, doing a quick 360 at the corner and shooting several glances over his shoulder to make sure he was truly alone. There was no one around, the rows of neat, well-cared-for middle-class houses all silent and in total darkness, as was to be expected at nearly two o'clock on a Wednesday morning.

The house on the corner of the next road was the only exception, a faint orange glow visible through the closed curtains of one of the front rooms. Finn took one more furtive look up and down the street then walked up to the front door. It opened as he lifted his hand to knock, and he stepped straight in, pushing it quickly closed behind him.

Bill Hanlon stood back and appraised him, a fond smile slowly spreading across his face.

Finn's expression mirrored his as he took in his old friend. The last ten years had aged Bill, the lines on his face a little deeper and his hair a little more sparse, but other than that, he still looked exactly the same, and seeing him in the flesh after so long away felt, like it had with Lily and Ray, like coming home.

'It is *so* fucking good to see you,' he said, with feeling.

'And you. I can't believe it's really been ten years since I last saw your mug in person,' Bill replied in disbelief. 'We have so much to catch up on, and Amy will want all of you and the family round for dinner when this is all over. For now though' – his expression turned serious as his eyes dropped to the bag on Finn's shoulder – 'let's get this sorted.'

'Yeah, let's,' Finn agreed, following Bill through to his office.

'I can't say I'll be sad to see Mani put out of business,' Bill told him, turning on the light and his computer.

The three monitors on the desk all lit up, and Finn's gaze swept the various pieces of equipment hooked up to them. A couple looked a bit like DVD players, but whether they were or not, he had no idea. The other boxes looked much more complex, and he didn't even try to hazard a guess as to what they could be. Bill opened a drawer and pulled out a second laptop, opening that on the desk too.

'I'll check them on here, in case they're carrying any viruses,' he explained, sitting down in his high-backed office chair. He pulled a second, smaller office chair up from beside the wall. 'Here, take a seat.'

Finn did just that, placing the duffel bag on the wide desk and unzipping it. He peered in and pulled out the two he was looking for. 'Here.' He passed them to Bill. 'They said they think the ones with this handwriting is him, but they think the others might belong to other people.'

'Oh.' Bill looked surprised. 'That don't sound good.'

'No,' Finn agreed. 'It really don't.'

They'd given him the basic rundown of what had happened when they'd handed it all over, and they hadn't had time to discuss it further, but he'd seen Lily's troubled face and had read between the lines. If this *did* turn out to be a ring they'd uncovered, that definitely complicated things. To what extent though, he wasn't sure. The only thing he *was* sure of was that he wasn't going back to Spain empty-handed. Whatever else they did, this leverage over the Romanos was too important for him to lose.

Bill plugged in the first external hard drive and a password request appeared on the screen. 'OK,' he murmured, 'let's do this.'

He cracked his knuckles and typed out a series of commands on the keyboard. Another box appeared and lines of text that made no sense to Finn flashed up, one after the other, in quick succession. The faster Bill typed, the faster the system's responses came back. After a while, Bill paused and reached over for one of the many technical-looking boxes stacked on a nearby shelf. He connected it to the laptop, and a second box flashed up. He typed out another series of commands then lifted his hands gently from the keyboard. The lines of text kept moving this time, and a few seconds later, both boxes disappeared, along with the passcode screen. They were in.

Several files appeared, and Bill clicked into one. A video began to play, starting with Riccardo backing away from the camera. A dark room came into sight, as did two other men hovering over a young woman seemingly passed out on the floor. With a grim look and a sound of disapproval, Bill clicked on a section of video two thirds of the way in.

As this section began to play, both Bill and Finn pulled back from the screen at the depraved violence suddenly in front of them.

'Jesus fucking Christ,' Finn exclaimed under his breath, looking away.

Bill moved forward and stopped the video, shaking his head with a look of disgust. There was a long silence, then he sighed heavily, pushing the playback counter up to the last few minutes and pressing play again. The woman was starting to stir on the screen now, and Riccardo was backing away. He stopped it, having seen enough to know how this one ended.

Finn leaned his elbow on the arm of the chair and rubbed his forehead, feeling physically sick at what he'd just witnessed, yet knowing this was only the beginning.

'From what we gather, there should be ones awake too,' he said reluctantly. 'And ones who might not have made it out.' He locked his jaw, his mouth forming a thin line for a moment. 'Lil suggested we check as many as possible. So we know for certain how much weight we have to use against them. We need enough detail to show we're not bluffing.'

Bill nodded, unsurprised, and clicked into the next video. This one was much the same as the last, as was the next, and the next. Each time they flicked ahead, despite only watching as few seconds as they could get away with, Finn felt more and more sick to his stomach. These were levels of depravity he'd never known could exist, and the things they were doing to these women – or *girls*; some of them barely looked like they were out of high school – were utterly evil, so full of rage and hate.

It was the fifth or sixth video they clicked on that began differently. This time there were two girls, both scantily clad – professional sex workers, if Finn were to hazard a guess. They were awake, smiling and flirting with the men in the room, trying to tempt them. When Bill clicked ahead, Finn had expected it to be less aggressive, but what they saw next chilled him to the core. Both women were terrified, beaten bloody and clinging together as the men surrounded them like hyenas playing with their prey. Riccardo's voice echoed through the laptop speaker, over the sound of their whimpers and sobs.

'You won't be leaving though, I'm afraid. These are your last few hours, sweetheart, so enjoy the ride.'

'What the hell...?' Finn breathed.

Bill moved the cursor to the next stop point and hesitated. With a low growling noise under his breath, he gritted his teeth and pressed down on the button. The two women's screams chimed out as the sight of one of them being simultaneously abused and beaten mercilessly filled the screen. She was barely alive, her voice so strangled it was barely even human.

The contents of Finn's stomach finally gave up the fight, and he lurched for the small bin under the desk, only just making it in time. As he heaved, the screams abruptly stopped and were replaced by a soft snivelling and Riccardo's low voice instructing someone to clear something up. A second later, there was silence.

Finn let out a long, loud breath of relief, slowly straightening back up as he wiped his mouth with the back of his hand. Next to him, Bill's expression was grim, the hand he was leaning on covering the lower half of his face.

Finn glanced back at the bin regretfully. 'Sorry,' he said. 'I've seen many things in my time: beatings, torture, murders – Christ, I was even at the business end when my Sara gave birth – and not one of those things even made me flinch, but that...' He trailed off with a sad shake of his head.

'Don't worry about it. I nearly joined you,' Bill replied.

Luckily the small bin was lined with a plastic bag, and Finn pulled the edges in, tying it up neatly. 'Where can I take this?'

'I'll take it out in a second. Let's just check this other one, see if this theory about a ring has anything in it,' Bill replied, unplugging Riccardo's hard drive and handing it to Finn.

Finn carefully placed it in the side pocket of the bag, making sure to keep it separate from the rest. It no longer mattered what else was there. While there were no doubt many more damning videos, this one hard drive alone held all they needed.

Bill's tapping resumed as he broke through the password screen of the second hard drive.

'I removed it by the way,' he said as his fingers flew over the keyboard. 'The password. If any of you need to get back into it, it will go straight to the files.'

'Thanks,' Finn replied, though he fervently hoped he never had need to look at those videos ever again.

He looked away this time as Bill quickly flicked through a couple of videos on the second hard drive. Bill didn't pause to properly decipher what exactly was happening in these ones. The basics were clear enough, and they didn't need any more details.

'So, it's the same place but different people. No one I've ever seen. I don't think they're one of us,' Bill said in a curious tone.

He reached over into the bag, looking at the labels with a frown until he found one with a different handwriting style. He plugged this in and repeated the same break through he'd used on the others.

As he flicked through those videos, Finn rifled through the contents of the bag and tried to work out how many different sets of handwriting there were.

'Different ones here too. Again same place,' Bill confirmed grimly. 'I don't think he's just part of a ring; I think he's been *running* it.'

Finn nodded, staring at the seven drives he'd laid out in a row. He hadn't even got halfway down the bag. There was no way Lily was going to be OK with ignoring this. There was no way *he* was OK with turning a blind eye either, though he needed to think up a resolution that covered them all. Some compromise that would mean they could still keep this as a threat to hang over the Romanos' heads, while making sure Riccardo wasn't able to do this ever again, and that the rest of them were stopped and damned in the way they deserved too.

He bit his top lip, thinking it all over, then looked over at Bill. 'I need to ask one more thing of you,' he said. 'If you'll do it.'

Bill swivelled his chair to face him, his expression guarded. 'Depends what you're asking,' he replied levelly.

'I need to separate all the drives with Riccardo and his men from the others. But it would mean going through them all. If you'll do it, you can name your price. I'll pay whatever you want.' He looked back at the bag. 'Because if we can separate all evidence relating to him, and if I can convince Lil it's the best way to go, we could still stick to our plan of ousting Mani and his firm for good, then drop the rest off at a station. Give the pigs an early Christmas present and stop these cunts doing that to anyone else again. And as for Riccardo, I'll make sure he never does this to another woman again myself,' he added darkly.

Bill looked at the bag then agreed with a nod. 'I'll do it. Double what we agreed, and I'll separate the two and sterilise the lot.' He gestured to Finn's and his own bare hands. 'Get them ready for the drop.'

'Thanks,' Finn said gratefully.

Bill stood up and fished the tied-up bag of sick out of the bin. 'Back in a sec,' he said before disappearing out of the room.

Finn took a deep breath in and exhaled, releasing some of the tension he'd been carrying around since they'd first agreed to this plan. It hadn't been their first choice, this particular route, but in the end, it had proved to be effective and fruitful. With everything so neatly stacked against him, Mani wouldn't be stupid enough to strike out at them. No one on their side of things would be harmed. The takeover would be simple – as simple as it *could* be anyway – and peaceful. Mani and all those close to him would suffer, and that suffering would be long and drawn out, sucking all the life and hope out of them for the rest of their days. And Riccardo would be the one to suffer the most. *That* was something he would personally make sure of, after all he'd witnessed in the last hour.

Suddenly remembering the bottle of rum he'd stashed in the front pocket of the bag, he unzipped it and pulled it out. The bright red bow was a little squashed, but he straightened it out as best he could and decided it didn't look too bad. Bill came back into the room and, with a tired half-smile, Finn held it out to him.

'This is for you,' he said. 'It isn't a drop in the ocean of what we owe you for the information you sent us – I don't think there's a gift in the world that could cover that – but it's a start. I hope you still love rum the way you used to. This is supposed to be one of the best, so I'm told.'

Bill took it with a look of surprise and then appreciation as he read the front of the bottle. 'A twenty-one-year-old El Dorado Special Reserve – yeah, that's one of the best alright!' He turned the bottle over in his hand, admiring it for a moment. 'This is gorgeous, but I don't know what I've done to deserve it. What's this information you're talking about?' He met Finn's gaze with a frown.

Finn stared back, confused. 'The envelope you sent me, to the factory in Spain,' he reminded him.

Bill's expression remained blank.

'With the details of where to find the body Mani hid from us all those years ago,' he continued.

Bill shrugged, looking utterly baffled, and Finn's confusion deepened.

'The *envelope*,' he repeated, his eyes searching Bill's face, sure that a light bulb was about to switch on somewhere. 'The details of Mani's aunt's house, and where the wall with the body was. You signed it off, BB.'

Bill was known by many through the underworld as Billy the Banker, following the daring bank heists of his youth. He hadn't pulled one in years, but he still signed off with the code initials BB when relaying messages to old friends.

Bill frowned, his face suddenly deeply concerned. 'I know what house you're talking about, Finn; I saw your calling card on the news. And when I read about the body in the wall, I figured it must be that, of *course*. It wasn't hard to connect the dots, but, mate, that's the first I knew of it.'

Finn drew back, the furrow in his brow deepening as shock rippled through him. He stared at Bill, and Bill stared back at him, each as confused as the other.

'But if you didn't send me that,' Finn said slowly, 'then who the fuck *did*? And why the hell are they pretending to be you?'

THIRTY-FOUR

Riccardo yawned on his way down in the lift, feeling irritated. He was tired this morning, but for once it wasn't for good reason. The date he'd had the night before had been a bust, the girl wasting his time with pointless prattle, leading him on for hours before turning cold and disappearing on him. *Stupid bitch*, he thought angrily. Clearly there was something wrong with her. What sort of woman flirted all night then suddenly changed her mind like that? *One that was sick in the head, that's what sort*, he told himself self-righteously.

Upon reaching the ground floor, he zipped up his jacket and stepped out into the cold. He needed a coffee. Instead of spending the night enjoying the delights of the girl's body, as expected, he'd had to sit and listen to his brother, coked up to the hilt, ranting on about all the things they were finally going to put right with this plan to take out the Drews. Which he'd done, nodding and pacifying Luca until he was finally calm enough to wind down – because he loved his brother. Or felt very protective of him at least. He wasn't sure if he actually knew what love was. Loyalty was much easier to understand. But either way, it certainly hadn't been the way he'd been intending to lose sleep last night.

Riccardo stifled another yawn and tried to shake the tiredness off as he jogged across the street towards the coffee shop where he always started off the day. A double espresso macchiato should wake him up a bit.

He quickened his step and shoved his cold hands into his pockets as he walked down the street, moving to avoid the crowd of teenagers gathered together on the pavement. He frowned, annoyed by how much space they were taking up. Glaring over at them as he tried to pass, he was surprised to see they weren't teenagers, as he'd assumed by their hooded tracksuits and low-pulled caps, after all. Some of them were older than he was. He registered one of the faces at the back, realising a moment too late that it belonged to a man working for the Drews.

He pulled himself up short, planning to turn and bolt, but it was too late. Several pairs of hands grabbed him, the group quickly swarming round and blocking him from view. As he opened his mouth to shout for help, a gag was shoved into his mouth, muting the sound to a gurgle. The side door of the van parked beside them rolled open, and they threw him inside, piling in after him and pinning him to the floor, face down.

Panic ran through Riccardo's body like an electric current, and he tried instinctively to fight them off, but there were too many of them. The door slammed shut, and the van lurched to the side as it pulled off into the road. Someone fastened a zip tie around his wrists, and another around his ankles, then whoever had been kneeling on his back eased off.

Turning his head to the side, Riccardo could see the large van was empty, other than two long benches down each side, where the group of men now sat, staring at him. His gaze darted between them all. Some faces he knew, all of them belonging to men who worked for the Drews, but there were three he didn't and it was these his gaze paused on as they pulled off their caps. These three men were older. Two were well built, clearly frequenters of a gym, the other more wiry. One was blonde, the others a bit darker. As he noted each detail, and the fact not one of them was worried about hiding their identity, his fear grew deeper, and his blood grew colder.

The blondest one leaned forward and grinned, the action cold and full of terrifying promise. 'Alright, sunshine?' he said in a low, gravelly voice. 'Do you know who I am?'

Riccardo stared back, his last hope fading as he realised his father's sins had finally caught up with him in the form of the Logans.

* * *

Finn Logan sat in the plastic garden chair and stared into the dark, soulless eyes of the man he'd witnessed on the videos in Bill's office just hours before and felt a level of revulsion he'd never felt for anyone or anything else before in his life. Not even for Mani. He sat there in silence, until he heard the van pull away and the barn door close after his brothers as they rejoined him inside.

Riccardo was tied to an identical plastic garden chair, facing him, just a few feet away. The back of that chair was secured to one of the supporting beams of the barn, something he knew Riccardo hadn't actually registered yet. If he had, he wouldn't have sat there so calmly, staring back at him with such defiance in his eyes. If he *had* registered that fact, he would have realised the reason behind it. He'd been in the game long enough to work out that simple sum, Finn was sure.

'Take the gag off,' Finn said quietly.

Sean moved forward and untied it, purposely banging Riccardo's head back roughly against the wooden beam. He let out a hiss of annoyance and narrowed his eyes at Sean's but otherwise remained quiet. He cricked his neck then lifted his jaw confidently, his gaze level when it met Finn's.

Finn let out a small sound of amusement, a hint of a grin playing at the corners of his mouth. 'You look like you're sat in the waiting room at the fucking dentist's,' he remarked.

Riccardo pulled a casual shrug-like expression. 'I might as well be,' he replied. 'How long are you giving him?'

Finn tilted his head to one side in question. 'What do you mean?'

'My old man,' Riccardo said. 'How long you giving him to cough up however much you're holding me ransom for? Just so I know,' he added, looking around with a sneer. 'I'm hoping not *too* long – this ain't exactly the Ritz. Fuck, this ain't even the *Holiday Inn.*'

Finn chuckled, sharing a look of amusement with each of his brothers. They stood either side of him, but Cormac stepped forward now, pushing his hands into his trouser pockets as he paced slowly back and forth, a half-smile still playing on his face as he stared Riccardo down.

'Is that what you think you're here for, lad?' he asked. 'Money off your da?'

'What else?' Riccardo replied, still seemingly unfazed.

It was a front, Finn knew. They'd all do the same in a similar situation. But the younger man seemed to still genuinely believe this was nothing to do with him. That he was just caught up in Mani's mess, and as such less likely to be hurt unless absolutely necessary. He watched, waiting for Cormac to drop the penny for him.

Cormac's smile faded, and when he glanced back at Riccardo, it was with a cold hardness in his eyes. 'What else?' he repeated, his deep voice dropping dangerously low. 'Let's see... You *could* be here to answer for what you did to our mate Sandra.'

Riccardo frowned, the confusion clear.

'Oh that's right, she was using another name that night. I can't remember what it was, but *you* should remember her.' He stopped pacing and faced Riccardo with a menacing glare. 'Beautiful girl, blonde, tall. You met her at the bar in The Blind Pig, before you drugged, raped and *beat* her.'

Riccardo's face drained of colour, and he began to shake his head hurriedly. 'No. Nah, I wouldn't do that. Mate, you've got this *all* wrong. I don't know what she told you, but that ain't how it went. We met in the bar, yeah, and we hit it off.' He raised his shoulders to his ears as he tried to shrug off the accusation. 'We had a great night. *Drank* too much, did a bit too much coke, things got crazy, but it wasn't like *that*. Seriously, I *like* the girl.'

'Yeah?' Cormac asked in a low voice that Finn knew meant the shit was about to fly.

He waited and wasn't disappointed. With a movement so fast Riccardo barely registered it was coming, Cormac pulled back his fist and slammed it into his face. The smack of skin on skin was swiftly followed by the secondary thud of skull on wood as the blow sent his head back against the beam behind him. Blood spurted out from his nose, which was now bent at a disturbingly odd angle.

Riccardo let out a shrill scream that lowered into yelps of pain as he struggled against his bindings. Both arms were still tied behind his back, each leg to one of the chair legs.

'*Fuuuuck!*' he yelled at the top of his lungs. 'You broke my *fucking* nose!'

'I wouldn't worry about it,' Finn told him. 'That'll be the least of your problems soon.'

He glanced sideways to Sean, who'd just pulled up a seat beside him, then stood up and walked forward. Cormac retreated, moving to stand behind the chair Finn had just vacated.

'The problem is, even if we *did* believe you over Sandra,'

Finn said, staring down at the bloodied trussed-up man, 'even if your version of things made that much more sense, it really would be hard to ignore that video you made of the four of you, wouldn't it?' He watched as Riccardo's eyes widened in surprise. 'You know, the one with you and her and your two mates in your little rape room across the hall?'

He stepped closer, leaning down until his face was on the same level as Riccardo's, just a foot or so away. 'The room you soundproofed to hide your victims' screams. Where you kept all those hard drives for you and all your other sick mates. I bet you thought yourself very clever hiding it there in plain sight, eh?'

Riccardo's skin turned a sickly shade of green, and his eyes darted around as he began to panic.

Finn leaned down, resting his hands on his knees. 'What's the matter? Cat got your tongue?'

He stared at the pale, bloodied man, his hands itching to form fists and be pummelled into his ugly, evil face over and over. But he held back, knowing that what was about to come would serve as a much more permanent punishment for the disgusting creature in front of him.

'I don't know what you're talking about,' Riccardo finally said, but there was little conviction in his tone. 'I don't know about any room or videos.'

'This ain't a court, boy,' Finn replied. 'You're not here to plead your case; you've already been found guilty. Of that and much, *much* more.'

He straightened up and glanced back at Sean. Sean nodded and slipped off, out of the barn.

'What do you want?' Riccardo asked, swallowing hard. 'I'll pay you whatever you want. I can't give you your turf back, because your pals, the Drews, own that now. You want my dad? You can have him. The old man's dead weight anyway. If that's what you want, I'll deliver him to you myself.' He was practically begging now. 'Just let me go. I'm not the one you have beef with.'

Finn stared at him with a look of incredulous disgust. He hated Mani, but that this rotten cancer of a man, this overgrown spoiled brat, would so willingly betray his own father, the man who'd given him everything he had, stuck in his craw. Those who chose a life in the underworld weren't always good men. Some were, some weren't; that was just the way things were, but the one thing they usually had in common was that they kept to a code. A code built around loyalty and respect. It was the only thing that really mattered, and if you didn't have *that*, you weren't worthy of anything or anyone. He shook his head in sombre disbelief.

Turning away, Finn wiped a hand over the lower part of his face and paced in a slow circle, glancing at Cormac with a look of question as he did so. Cormac peeled off and walked out of the barn to check on Sean.

'Where's he going?' Riccardo asked. 'And your other brother. What are they doing?'

'You're not dressed very smartly today,' Finn remarked, turning to face him again and eying the simple loose grey track-suit Riccardo wore. 'Where's your usual sharp suit?'

Riccardo frowned and looked down at himself. 'I'd just woken up,' he said defensively. 'I was only out to grab a coffee.'

Finn tutted. 'My father taught me that when you wake up in the morning, the first thing you do is make your bed and dress yourself properly for the day. You don't mess about being all scruffy. If you start the day scruffy, your mind *stays* scruffy. It's all up here, ye see.' He tapped the side of his head.

'Something certainly is,' Riccardo muttered.

'Oh, you think you're in a position to make jokes?' Finn asked, lifting his brows.

Riccardo fell silent, and Finn nodded slowly, watching him through narrowed eyes. The barn door clattered shut behind him, and he broke his gaze away, turning to see Cormac walk back towards them.

Cormac gave him a short nod as he reached them. 'Two minutes,' he confirmed.

'Two minutes until what?' Riccardo asked warily.

'You ever done a stint in prison, Romano?' Finn asked him, ignoring the question.

Riccardo groaned, closing his eyes with a look of despair. '*Please,*' he begged. 'I'll give you anything you want, but *don't* shop me in. Come on – what happened to honour among thieves?'

'Ha!' Finn exclaimed. 'That's a fine question coming from someone who was about to shop in his own *father.*' He exchanged a look of cold amusement with Cormac. 'Honour indeed...' he muttered. 'Don't worry – we won't be sending you there. At least not if your father does what he's told. No, I was just wondering.'

He turned and sat back in one of the plastic chairs, Cormac joining him a second later.

'It's a funny place, prison. My brother, Sean, he did a small spell, years back. Learned a lot of interesting new things. Like, did you know, for instance, that there's a whole code of punishments on the inside, for people who get put away for certain crimes? I mean, it might vary from prison to prison.' He shrugged. 'We only have the experience of that one. But when Sean told us about it, we thought it made a lot of sense.'

'We did,' Cormac agreed, nodding sagely.

Riccardo's gaze darted back and forth between them, his fear visibly increasing in his face and his breaths quickening. 'Listen, I ain't fucking around, OK?' he shouted. 'You've made your point – now name your price and I'll pay it.'

'Oh, you'll pay it alright,' Cormac agreed quietly.

'What are you *on* about?' Riccardo demanded.

'People who fiddled with kids, for example,' Finn continued, as though Riccardo hadn't spoken at all. '*They* get the worst punishments.'

'I've never touched kids!' Riccardo yelled. '*Never!*'

Finn nodded. 'But you have raped and tortured endless woman for fun though, haven't you? For no reason other than the fact you get off on it.' He couldn't keep the curl of disgust from his lip as he said the words. 'That was a punishable offence in that prison too. According to Sean's friends.'

Riccardo began shaking his head violently, struggling again to pull away from his binds. 'No, no, no,' he muttered. 'This is fucking *insane*. Those videos ain't what you think; they're just *role play*. I like it rough, *yes*, so those girls, they just play it out! And they *knew* I was filming. They agreed to it! You've got this wrong, guys, seriously, *listen* to me...'

The brothers simply watched as he struggled and bucked to no avail, ignoring his continued pleas. The barn door opened, and Finn stood up, looking at Cormac and jerking his head towards Riccardo.

'Get them off,' he instructed.

Cormac walked over to Riccardo and grabbed the loose tracksuit bottoms, yanking them down his legs as Finn walked over to Sean and took the plastic funnel from where he'd tucked it under his arm. He was careful not to upset the large steaming soup pot he was carrying in between both hands.

'What the *fuck* are you doing?' Riccardo bellowed at Cormac. 'Pull them back up, you sick fuck!'

Cormac ignored him, leaving his bottom half fully exposed and the trousers around his ankles. He walked to meet Sean, taking one of the handles so they could manoeuvre the pot together. Riccardo was screaming loudly now, in sheer terror, as he started to get the gist of what was about to happen.

'Holler all you want,' Finn said, shouting to be heard over the racket. 'Get it out. But no one will hear you. We're too far away from civilisation here for that.'

'*Ple-ease*,' Riccardo begged, openly sobbing now like the coward he really was. 'Don't do this.'

'It's too late for all of that,' Finn replied. 'Everyone has to pay their dues in this life. For everything you take, there's a price. For every action, there's a consequence. It's just the balance of nature.' He looked Riccardo in the eyes coldly. 'It's time to pay your outstanding debt to this world. And don't worry, you'll go on living afterwards. In a manner of speaking, at least. We'll not kill ye. But you'll not rape another woman again.'

Ignoring Riccardo's panicked pleas, he pulled a pair of thick leather gloves from his pocket and slipped them on, then held the wide plastic funnel over Riccardo's naked privates. Cormac and Sean tipped the clear boiling liquid through, careful not to spill any on their brother's hands, and after a moment of stunned silence, Riccardo's screams ripped through the air, ear-piercingly loud.

They poured slowly in a trickle, and Riccardo flailed around wildly as he tried and failed to escape the excruciating pain. Finn kept a close watch, aware they needed to keep the man alive if they were to keep their leverage over Mani. Because this wasn't just water they were pouring. There was no way Finn was risking the chance of only inflicting a skin wound that Riccardo could heal from. After what he'd seen on those videos – and of Sandra – he wanted to make sure the man could never function in that way ever again.

In that sense, this particular solution of ninety per cent sugar and ten per cent water added two particular benefits that boiling water alone did not. The first was that the boiling point was increased by thirty degrees, so it burned much hotter as they poured. The second was that the high sugar content made the liquid much thicker and sticky, so instead of rolling straight off and cooling quickly, the substance stuck to the skin, burning through and causing irreparable damage.

Riccardo's screams began to falter and then suddenly he passed out, his head slumping forward. Finn raised his hand and the others pulled the pot back, pausing the pour.

Finn looked down grimly at the steaming mess of syrup covering the man's privates. Already his flesh had blistered and broken, the damage growing deeper and more grotesque by the second.

'That should do it,' he said. 'Give it another five minutes or so before we hose it off. There's no way he'll be using that again any time soon.'

'I'll get the catheter and the clean-up kit ready,' Sean replied, turning away. 'We don't need him dying from infection, or we'll be right back where we started.'

Finn nodded and pulled out his phone to call Lily. Now that Riccardo was dealt with, it was time for their big finale.

THIRTY-FIVE

Mani called Riccardo's number as he drove up the dirt track towards the large wooden barn, tutting irritably when he didn't answer. 'Check those coordinates again,' he barked at Luca, who sat beside him in the passenger seat. 'This doesn't seem right.'

Luca took the phone from him and checked them on the map again. 'This is it,' he confirmed. 'The place he said to meet him.' He shrugged and frowned.

Mani pulled to a stop just outside the front and cut the engine, peering up at it with a narrowed, distrustful gaze. He made a small sound of annoyance and opened the car door, shuffling himself round awkwardly and pulling himself up to standing. Riccardo's text had said to meet him here, that he'd found a mole in the firm who was working for the Drews and needed to show them both the proof. He'd said it was urgent, that they were in danger and not to tell anyone where they were going.

It had made sense to Mani instantly. It certainly explained why their plan to kill the Drews after stealing their profits from the boxing matches hadn't worked. How they'd found out about

Robert, why he'd disappeared off the face of the earth. He'd picked up Luca and driven straight here, with not a word to anyone, trying to figure out on the way who it could be.

Luca walked round and met him by the door, looking around with a suspicious frown. 'Where's Riccardo's car?' He pushed a hand back through his thick black hair, resetting it in place absentmindedly as the wind disturbed it. 'Something's off. Maybe I should take a look around the back before we go in.'

Mani rolled his eyes and walked past him. '*Maybe* you should stop playing with your hair and imagining things like a little girl, Luca, and start thinking more like your brother,' he said scathingly.

Luca didn't respond, his eyes glazing over blankly the way they always did when he was reminded of how little his father thought of him now. He followed Mani towards the partially open barn door without another word, and Mani's attention returned to his elder son.

'Riccardo?' he called out as they reached the door. 'Where are you?' He pushed it further open, squinting into the darkness. His eyes hadn't adjusted yet, so he stepped in and looked around, Luca right beside him. 'Riccardo?'

There were stacks of boxes both sides of the enormous barn about halfway down, blocking his view of the rest of the space. Sheeting covered some of them; ropes dangled down from another. Mani walked forward with a humph.

'Riccardo, for the love of God, where *are* you?' he called impatiently.

A low groan came from one of the stacks of boxes, and he looked over towards it again, seeing the area a bit more clearly now that his eyes were adjusting. There, at the bottom, tucked almost completely out of view, was Riccardo, sitting on a chair, half bent over as if with his head in his hands.

'Riccardo!' Mani said with relief.

He moved towards him, the relief swiftly turning to dread

as he realised his son's arms were pulled awkwardly back out of sight. His gaze moved to the hospital gauze wrapped around his midsection and the tube leading out of it. Luca darted forward, and Mani swiftly followed, their immediate reaction to get to him. They both realised a moment too late that it was a trap.

Looking back as the barn door shut and the light was switched on, Mani swept his gaze over the people now walking out of the shadows and moving towards them. He exhaled heavily through his nose, his heart dropping, then turned back to his son, kneeling down and holding Riccardo's face between his hands.

'Hey, *hey*,' he said, slapping him gently. 'What did they do to you? Riccardo, what did they *do*?'

Luca swore, his hands on the top of his head as he grasped handfuls of his own hair in stress. 'I *knew* this was a mistake. I *knew* it!'

'Not *now*,' Mani hissed.

He tapped Riccardo's face again fearfully. He didn't understand exactly what they'd done, but he could see that his nose was broken, dried blood all down his face and his jacket. It wasn't this that scared him though: it was how unresponsive Riccardo was. He was half conscious, groaning and moaning pitifully, but he couldn't seem to keep his eyes open or raise his head. With a swell of rage, he stood up and turned to face them.

'What have you done to my boy?' he shouted, his gaze moving between Lily and Finn.

They were the leaders of their various companions. All three Logan brothers were there along with Lily, Cillian and the younger Drew girl, Scarlet. He idly wondered where the rest of Lily's men were, but his concern for Riccardo and their more immediate predicament quickly took priority. Lily was holding a gun, her steady gaze and aim both trained on him. Luca paced behind him mumbling under his breath in a lost panic.

'Don't worry, Mani,' Finn said, looking at him coldly, a hint of a cruel smile in his eyes. 'He'll live. We just gave him a bit of morphine to help with the pain and keep the fever away.'

Mani's eyes widened in horror. *What had they done to him?*

'You'll have him back in one piece soon. Or most of him anyway,' Finn added with a smirk.

'You piece of shit, you'd better not have done anything permanent to my boy,' Mani growled, shaking with rage. 'Or I'll—'

'Or you'll what?' Finn demanded loudly, cutting him off. He stepped forward and lifted his chin, looking down at Mani with contempt. 'Your days of threatening are over, Mani.' His words were hard. 'In fact, your days of doing *most* things are over. And if you want to leave here with your sons still breathing, you're going to have to listen very closely to what I've got to say.'

THIRTY-SIX

Lily watched Mani's small, mean eyes dart between her and Finn and could practically see all the scenarios he was mentally running through. His tongue poked out to one side, and he ran it slowly over his bottom lip as his round, puffy face contorted with rage and malice.

'How much morphine have you given him?' he asked, glancing back at Riccardo.

'Enough,' Sean replied.

Mani glared at him, opening his mouth to reply but then twisting his head away with a low growl. He glanced again at Riccardo, and Lily almost felt a spark of sympathy for him, parent to parent, but it didn't quite materialise. Not for the man who'd so coldly and clinically planned to kill *her* children. For him all she had left was vengeance.

'Here's what's going to happen,' Finn said. 'We're going to tie the three of you up, and you're not going to make a fuss.' Mani let out a bark of dark amusement, but Finn ignored it. 'Then we're going to send you off in a van where you'll stay until tomorrow night, at which point you'll be loaded onto a boat that will take you across the Channel.'

'The *Channel*?' Mani repeated. He drew his chin back until it was almost lost in the pudgy rolls of his neck, looking totally flummoxed.

'Yes, the Channel,' Finn confirmed. 'The three of you, along with your wife and some of your men, all of whom are being rounded up as we speak, will be dropped there and set free. From there you can do anything you want – *except* set foot back in England. You'll stay that side of the water and give up everything you have here, without argument, and you will never, *ever* return. Think of it as us returning the offer you once gave us, but with a few less benefits.'

Mani laughed loudly, staring at Finn as though he'd gone totally mad. 'And why the fuck would I do that?' he spat. He narrowed his eyes. 'You have no bodies of *mine* in the closet, nothing to keep *me* out of my own home, my own businesses.'

'Oh yes,' Finn said, snapping his fingers then pointing at Mani. 'That reminds me. You'll also sign over all your legal businesses to me. I took the liberty of having the paperwork drawn up in advance for you.'

He walked over to a backpack at the side of the room and jogged back over, unzipping it and pulling out a sheaf of paperwork. He waved it in the air then placed it on the floor beside him.

Lily watched, amused and surprised by how organised the brothers were with the paperwork. It had all happened so quickly she'd assumed they would work out how to clean up the chaos after they'd ousted the Romanos. She'd purposely not involved herself in the details of the Logans' takeover. They were pulling this job together for mutual benefit, but the aftermath was their business alone.

'Over my dead *body*,' Mani hissed furiously.

Finn just shrugged. 'It can be, if you'd rather. But be warned, your boys' bodies will follow.'

Lily handed the gun to Scarlet and took a step forward to

stand beside Finn. 'There will be no need for *any* bodies this time, Mani. Not yours and none hidden away in walls.' His gaze moved to meet hers, wary now. 'To answer your earlier question, you'll *do it* to save Riccardo from a lifetime in prison. One full of threats *much* worse than something as simple as death, once the other inmates find out all the things he's done.'

She watched the surprise and confusion light up behind his dark eyes. 'What are you *talking* about?' he demanded.

Behind him, Luca finally stopped pacing and froze, the fear clear in his face as the colour drained. She eyed him, watching as his gaze roamed around, meeting hers and instantly dropping.

'Luca knows what I'm talking about, don't you?' she said, her tone low and deadly.

He shook his head. 'Of course not!'

Lily sighed. '*Of course not,*' she mimicked under her breath. 'Tell me, Mani, how does a man as relentless and driven as you end up with two such pitiful wet blankets as sons?'

'Don't you dare speak of my sons that way,' he growled.

'Oh, I will,' she replied sincerely. 'They're spineless cowards, Mani. And *that one*' – she flicked her gaze over to Riccardo – 'is the reason you're about to lose everything.'

He glared at her but didn't respond, clearly worried now and waiting for the information he was still missing.

'Your eldest son has been running an underground ring of men who drug women, then rape and violently beat them, while filming it,' she told him.

'*What?*' he cried. 'No, he has *not!*'

'He *has*, Mani, and we have proof.'

She waited as Finn walked over and unlocked his phone to play Mani the short compilation clip Bill had put together for them. Mani's face paled and his jaw dropped open in shock as he gasped. As the clip came to an end, Finn walked back over, leaving Mani in a frozen state of shock. Mani put a hand to his head, then closed his mouth and swallowed.

'We have hundreds of hours of footage of Riccardo raping and beating the women he drugged. We also have footage of him raping and torturing women who *aren't* drugged,' Lily continued. 'But he didn't let those ones go with a web of lies and excuses, the way he did with the others. Those ones he beat to death on camera, *while* raping them.'

Mani flinched in horror, and she was glad. He *should* be horrified that he'd raised such a monster.

'He even told them he was going to do it to terrify them as much as possible in their last hellish hours on this earth. I can arrange for you to see copies of the full videos if you'd like more proof, but I wouldn't advise it. From what I understand, it's a very difficult watch.'

Mani turned white now, and as he looked away, she thought he might throw up or pass out, but he just closed his eyes and took a couple of deep breaths before reopening them. He locked eyes with Lily and clamped his mouth shut, exhaling loudly through his nose.

'So, you can go quietly and disappear off to a new life some-where in Europe,' Lily repeated. 'You'll never make contact back here again. You won't breathe a word about what happened here to anyone, not one *whisper* of our names or of who you once were. You'll restart as nobodies and keep your heads down so that we never hear even the slightest rumour of you again. You'll sign everything you own over and leave with nothing – but you'll have your family, your freedom and the chance at a fresh start. *Or* you can ignore any part of this, throw away this last chance and watch your son go off to rot in a jail cell for the rest of his life – *without* the chance of parole, I'd imagine, considering the level of violence and depravity – and wait to find out which day comes first. Whether it's the one where you get the call that your son's been gang-raped and murdered by his cell mates for what he did to those girls, some of whom were very young by the way.' Her gaze narrowed darkly. 'Or whether it's the one where you wake up to the feel of a knife in your stomach and one of our faces staring down at you in the dark, as what's left of your life slowly seeps away. Because if that's the route you choose, we *will* come for you, Mani. And there's too many of us for you to avoid forever.'

There was a long silence as Mani held her glare, fury and devastation warring behind his eyes as his natural instinct to fight was slowly overpowered with reason. She saw the moment he decided, the light dimming, the defeat quiet, and he suddenly seemed a lot smaller. Lily lifted her chin, silently claiming the win, then she turned to Cillian and nodded.

Cillian moved forward, and the Logans followed, Finn heading for Luca, who stood silently watching, unsure what was going on.

'Hey, whoa, whoa, *whoa*!' he yelled, trying to move backward and bumping against the wall of stacked crates next to his brother. 'Hey, get *off* me!'

'Luca, *shut up*,' Mani shouted over his shoulder bitterly. 'Just do as they say. We have no choice.'

'What?' he replied, looking horrified. 'Yes, we do.' He sounded as though he was trying to convince himself, rather than anyone else.

'No. We don't,' Mani said, not fighting Cillian and Cormac as they sat him in a chair and bound his wrists and ankles to it.

Cillian wrapped the blindfold over the top half of Mani's head, securing it tightly and glaring over at Luca, who was fighting Finn and Sean tooth and nail like a wild cat.

'Here, take this.' He handed over to Cormac and marched across to Luca, punching him square in the face and sending his head reeling back. 'All these years of hiding away like a mute fucking mouse and *this* is the time you decide to start fighting back?' he asked, his temper seeping through. 'You're *pathetic*,' he spat. 'Now *sit down* and *shut the fuck up*,' he demanded, grabbing the zip tie Finn had dropped to the floor in the struggle.

'Fuck you,' Luca replied, spitting in Cillian's face as he wrapped the zip tie around his wrist and began to pull it tight.

Cillian saw red, wiping the spit angrily from his face and drawing back his fist with a loud growl. He slammed it into Luca's face twice more in quick succession, feeling the cartilage break beneath his knuckles before the force sent Luca, and the chair he was bound to, crashing backward to the floor.

'Easy now,' Finn said, grabbing him with both hands by the shirt and swinging him round out of the way. 'Leave it – it's done. It's over.'

Cillian gritted his teeth, allowing Finn to move him without a fight, then he sniffed and raised his hands in the air, backing away. 'I'm fine. I'm good.'

Lily walked over to him, meeting his eye with a hard stare. 'You need to learn to control your temper at times like this,' she said, quietly enough that only he could hear. 'The times when you've backed them into a corner and they're goading you with nothing else to lose, because *that's* when people make mistakes.'

Cillian's jaw worked as he fought to keep a lid on the heat still simmering under the surface, and she leaned in closer, her eyes flashing. '*Hey*,' she growled. 'I *mean* it. *This* is the time cunts like that will try *anything* to get out of the corner they're in. *Do not bite*. Because you can't afford even a second of distraction. Got it?'

'Yeah, alright,' Cillian snapped. 'I've got it. That particular cunt just gets under my skin.'

Lily grabbed his face, turning it until his gaze locked back with hers. 'And under your skin is *exactly* where they know you're most vulnerable. Don't forget that.' She stared at him a moment longer then let go, turning away to stand with Scarlet as the rest of them finished securing and blindfolding the three men.

'They're here,' Scarlet said quietly. 'They just messaged to say they're outside.'

'OK, good.' Lily glanced at the gun Scarlet held down by her waist, pointed now towards Luca. 'You can put that away now. We won't be needing it anymore.'

Scarlet relaxed her grip and handed it back to Lily. 'This went well tonight,' she remarked. 'If only all our plans went as smoothly.'

Lily grinned wryly. 'We can only dream.'

Slipping the gun back into her handbag, Lily made her way out of the barn and round to the side towards the large dark van parked up with its back doors open. She could just make out the dark silhouette of a tall, broad man leaning against the side and the pinprick of light coming from the end of the cigarette held up to his mouth. The cigarette was lowered, and a cloud of smoke rose up into the air above his head. As she neared, his features became clearer under the dim glow of the crescent moon, and she smiled.

'Thanks for this,' she said, joining him against the side of the van and accepting the cigarette he offered her. She cupped her hands around it as he lit it for her, pulling in short puffs of smoke until it burned steadily. She leaned her head back and blew it out towards the sky, pushing back her mass of springy curls as she tried to roll the tension out of her shoulders.

'Was that Cillian I heard going off like a dodgy firework just now?' Freddie asked.

Lily bobbed her head to the side, shrugging her brows and taking another deep drag. 'Yep,' she replied as she blew out the smoke. 'He's come a long way, and he has a good head on him.

He just needs to learn to curb that spring reaction of his and he'll make a good leader one day. Him and Scarlet,' she added.

'Hmm,' Freddie murmured. 'And then you have Connor set to take over the ropes from Ray, I hear,' he said in a level voice. 'That's going to be quite the empire someday.'

Lily tensed, her eyes sliding sideways in an attempt to read Freddie's expression. He still stared ahead, his hard, chiselled face giving nothing away. She took another drag, trying to work out whether or not there were problems building here.

'Perhaps,' she said carefully. 'But no more than it is now. Ray and I have always been on the same team.'

'Have you?' Freddie turned to her now and arched an eyebrow.

Lily coloured, glad it was too dark for Freddie to see. 'OK, fine, not *always*. But we were for many years. My boys running the two separate firms will be no different. Hopefully a lot more peaceful,' she added wryly.

'No, I don't think so,' Freddie replied. 'You and Ray have always supported each other, yeah, but your firms were your own. Your jobs, your secrets, you remained independent.' He exhaled slowly. 'Your boys are two halves of one whole. They'll draw it together one day. Merge your firms into the largest underground organisation London's ever known.'

Lily bit the inside of her lip, a trickle of fear creeping into her heart. The Tylers were lifelong friends, but they were also underworld royalty. They ran this city and their word was *law*, for any firm who wanted to survive. And they took any threats to their reign very seriously.

'I don't think it would come to that,' she said, trying to play it down, unsure how else to proceed right now.

Freddie looked at her again, the hint of a smile playing at the corners of his mouth. 'Don't sound so worried,' he said. 'Your boys are good men. And when they inevitably take over one day, many years from now, no doubt, they'll do well. They have a lot of you in them. A lot of Ray too.'

'Huh,' Lily said, pursing her lips. 'Well that couldn't be helped.'

Freddie took another long drag and blew out the smoke slowly before answering. 'That ain't such a bad thing. For all Ray's bullheadedness, he's a clever bloke.' He pushed off the side of the van and flicked his cigarette away. 'Your boys will be interesting to watch, when they come into their own.' He nodded towards the barn. 'Let's get this lot loaded.'

Lily nodded, filing their conversation away to analyse later. 'They're ready to go,' she told him. 'It's all set for tomorrow?'

'Yeah. We'll drive them to the dockyard; park the van in one of my containers there for tonight. Paul's confirmed the rest have arrived,' Freddie replied.

'Where are they, in the container too?' she asked, wincing as she thought about Liana, Mani's wife.

'The men they brought in are tied up in one of the porta-cabins further down,' Freddie said, glancing over at one of his men as he stepped out of the front of the van. 'I had them take Liana over to Heaven Above. The girls have got her locked in one of the rooms upstairs.' He pulled a face. 'It's comfortable at least, and she'll be looked after well.'

'Thanks, Freddie, that's good of you,' Lily said, relieved that the woman wasn't suffering in the back of a container. It was unfortunate enough that she had to be dragged into all this at all, but sometimes collateral damage couldn't be avoided.

'No problem,' he replied. 'I haven't exactly done badly out of this deal,' he reminded her.

She smiled tiredly. 'Then we're both happy customers. As it should be. I'll go get things moving. You're coming to the wedding tomorrow, aren't you?'

'Of course,' Freddie replied. 'Wouldn't miss it for the world.'

Lily grinned and walked back towards the barn. It was

crazy to think in less than twenty-four hours her son would be marrying the love of his life, and she suddenly felt saddened that this was how he'd been forced to spend his last night as an unmarried man. He should have been enjoying a good old knees-up at the pub with his brother and his friends, or whatever else young men did before they got married these days. She knew he was spending the night at Connor's. Reaching the light of the barn, she looked at her watch. It wasn't horribly late. Maybe if he went now, he could still enjoy a few drinks with his brother.

The three Romanos were bound and blindfolded, ready to go. Lily looked over at Finn and gave him the signal to take them out to the van. This part was to be done in silence, as per Freddie's request. She'd already made Mani's silence about the Drews' involvement part of the deal, and she was pretty sure her threats were enough to keep that steady. But she could understand Freddie's reluctance to take that chance. He needed deniability, should anything go wrong and the word get out. Because while the Logans had every right to pull this job, the rest of them technically didn't. So this had to remain their dirty little secret.

Lily grabbed Cillian and pulled him aside while the others began to carry the first chair containing one of the three bound men outside. 'Hey, go home,' she ordered. 'Or to Connor's I mean.'

'No, Mum, I'm alright,' Cillian insisted, misunderstanding her. 'I've put a lid on it, I swear.'

'No, I know that,' Lily replied. 'I ain't talking about that. It's the night before your *wedding*. Go and relax, have some fun, sleep, whatever. Just forget all this for a few hours.'

She smiled up at him with love, still unable to believe her handsome eldest son was really getting married tomorrow. She could have sworn he only learned how to ride a bike yesterday.

Reaching up, she touched his cheek. 'When did you

suddenly get taller than me anyway?' she asked with a wistful laugh.

'About the time I stopped wearing nappies, I reckon,' he joked, grabbing her hand and squeezing it. Pulling it off his face he suddenly pulled her into his arms in a big bear hug. 'Come here, Mum.' He lowered his head and turned it to the side, resting his cheek on the top of her head. 'You're getting soppy in your old age, you know that?'

'I'm not *old*, you cheeky shit,' she murmured back. 'I'm still in my forties.'

'*Just*,' he reminded her, rather bravely.

Lily squeezed him fiercely, wishing she could keep him held against her heart like this forever. But she knew she couldn't. He wasn't her baby anymore. He was a full-grown man going off to start a family of his own.

She pulled away and looked up at him with a bittersweet smile. 'I love you, my boy. *So* much.'

'I know,' he replied, smiling back at her. 'And I love you too.'

Lily nodded then reluctantly stepped back with a sniff. 'Right,' she said. 'Go on. Just make sure you don't get bladdered and you get enough sleep so you ain't yawning at the altar, alright? Because if you do that, it won't just be me who'll be lining up to kill you; you'll have Father Dan to contend with too,' she warned.

He laughed. 'Alright. See you tomorrow.'

He walked away, and Scarlet appeared by her side. They both watched him leave, and to Lily's horror, she felt tears well up in her eyes.

Scarlet noticed and frowned in alarm. 'Shit, Lil, you OK?'

'I'm fine,' Lily snapped, turning away from the barn door. 'We just need to make sure that tomorrow is the *best* day of that boy's life, OK? Because he deserves it.' Her words were unnecessarily fierce, and Scarlet backed away cautiously.

'You've got it,' she agreed. 'I'm going to check they're doing OK out there.'

Lily wiped away the lingering wetness on her cheek as Scarlet disappeared, and crossed her arms with a sigh. Maybe Cillian was right. Maybe she really *was* getting soppy in her old age.

THIRTY-SEVEN

Billie smiled quietly, enjoying the noisy chatter around her as she sat in Lily's spare room having her hair styled at the dressing table. Having no family to spend this time with, she'd been thrilled when Lily had invited her to get ready here. She'd assumed Lily would want to have Cillian there, but Lily had dismissed the idea when she'd raised it, saying this morning was for the brothers to be together. Billie privately thought that the strain between Lily and Connor probably also had something to do with it, but she kept that to herself, just happy that Lily wanted to be part of *her* morning. She'd spent the night before watching films and pampering herself ready for today, along with Isla and Sandra, who were now suddenly firm friends.

Sandra pulled out the rollers, and loose curls fell down around her shoulders, softly framing her face. 'And you're sure you just want me to pin this bit?' Sandra checked, pulling a few strands up to the back. 'You don't want anything more fancy?'

Billie shook her head. 'Nope. That's perfect.'

Scarlet peered over from where she sat on the side of the bed having her make-up done by the make-up artist Lily had booked for them all. 'That's so pretty,' she said, trying not to move her mouth.

'It really is,' seconded Isla.

Sandra pinned it into place and smiled at her through the mirror. 'You're right,' she said. 'That is perfect.' She played with the back for a moment. 'It would be nice with a comb or something though. Have you got anything?'

'No, I didn't think to get anything,' Billie admitted.

'That's OK,' Lily said, walking into the room and around the bed towards them. 'I actually have just the thing for you to borrow.' She half smiled and tilted her head. 'Only if you want it, I mean. It was just a thought.' She shrugged and held it out.

Billie took the offered item from Lily and looked down at it. It was heavy, an antique-looking silver comb slide lined with pearls at the top, a single sapphire standing out in the middle.

'Oh, Lil, it's beautiful,' she said softly. 'And it's absolutely perfect, but are you sure you don't mind me borrowing it? It looks special.'

Scarlet leaned over to look, and when she saw what it was, she looked back at Lily with a knowing smile.

'I'd be *honoured* if you borrowed it,' Lily said firmly. 'It was my grandmother's. Her dad bought it for her as a wedding gift, to wear on the day as something blue. My mother wore it next, for her wedding, and then Cath wore it when she married Ronan.' Lily looked down at it with a smile. 'It's become a family tradition. All the Drew women wear it. Scarlet will wear it one day too, if she gets married. Not that you have to,' she added, catching Scarlet's eye with a laugh. 'I never did.' She turned back to Billie. 'One day you'll be sat here like this too, passing it down to Lily Rose,' she said.

There was a short silence as Lily stared at the comb and Billie tensed, looking around the room.

Scarlet frowned. 'Who?'

Lily gasped, clapping her hands to her mouth as her eyes

widened and met Billie's. 'Oh God! I'm so sorry,' she breathed. 'I don't know what I was thinking.'

Billie laughed. 'Don't worry, I accidentally let slip last night to these two.' She gestured to Isla and Sandra.

Scarlet's frown deepened, her dark brows knotting in confusion. 'Let *what* slip?'

Billie gave her an apologetic look. 'I would have told you, but we were going to announce it today at the reception.' She bit her lip with a big grin as realisation dawned on Scarlet's face.

'Oh my God, are you *pregnant*?' she asked.

'I am,' Billie squeaked happily.

'You're *pregnant*?' Cath screeched excitedly as she entered the room with a tray of tall beautifully displayed drinks, her jaw dropping dramatically. 'Oh my God, *Lily*!' she exclaimed, turning her look of delight towards her sister-in-law.

'I know,' Lily replied with a grin and a twinkle of excitement in her eyes.

'And it's a girl,' Billie added, knowing it was likely to be the next question.

'And her name's Lily Rose,' Lily added with a little animated wiggle in her seat, looking fit to burst with pride.

Cath gasped again, her jaw dropping even lower. 'Oh, wow! Ahh, Lil, that's so special. Ahh, to have a granddaughter named after you.' She pulled an emotional smile and placed a hand on her chest, balancing the tray on one arm. 'Billie, congratulations, love.'

'Thanks,' she replied as Cath walked over and gave her an awkward one-armed hug, the tray still balanced on the other one. 'We need to celebrate!' she declared, straightening up. 'And I have just the thing. Here you are...' She smiled and handed her a tall fizzing drink with blackberry-filled ice cubes. 'Oh no, wait...' She took it back with a small shake of the head. 'No, you can't have this. You *definitely* can't have this,' she repeated, widening her eyes as she looked back on them. 'I'll get you something else. Everyone else, help yourselves to these.'

Billie watched resignedly as everyone grabbed a glass. She couldn't complain. She had the best reason in the world to not be drinking today.

Cath sighed happily, grinning at her like a Cheshire cat and shaking her head. 'Honestly, love, it's fantastic news. And now you've said, it does make sense,' she added. 'I just thought you were getting a bit, well, you know...' Her eyes flickered down to Billie's torso with a look of sympathetic understanding. '*Comfortable.*'

'Cath!' Lily exclaimed, rolling her eyes with a tut.

'What?' Cath asked defensively. 'I didn't say there was anything wrong with that. It's perfectly natural when you're happy to let it all go a bit.'

'Christ almighty, don't listen to her,' Lily said with another roll of her eyes.

'What's wrong with saying that?' Cath asked, holding her arms out. 'It's true. We get comfortable, and there's nothing wrong with a few extra curves. I'm just saying I noticed, that's all.' She shrugged. 'Anyway, I'll make you a mocktail, love. You just wait here.'

She left the room, and Lily shook her head, dropping it into her hand with a chuckle.

An hour later, they were all downstairs dressed and ready to go. As bridesmaids, Scarlet and Isla wore matching rust-coloured satin sheath dresses, and Lily's mother of the groom outfit, chosen by Billie and grudgingly agreed to by Lily, was just a few shades darker, matching perfectly. Billie's dress was a floaty creation with an A-line skirt and a sweetheart neckline, soft gauze flowers sewn in a sweeping spray from one shoulder to the opposite ankle, and despite the fact she'd had just days to find it, she loved it so much that she was sure she wouldn't have found one she liked better even if she'd had all the time in the world. Wearing this dress and with all the finishing touches added, she genuinely felt like a real-life princess.

She clutched her bouquet of simple sunflowers interspersed with sprays of baby's breath and smiled widely as Cath took photo after photo of her on the stairs.

'That's it, love, just tilt your head a bit the other way now. Yeah, that's it,' Cath said, clicking away.

Lily came over and paused the little photography session with a hand on Cath's arm, the interruption a welcome one. Billie heaved a sigh of relief and stepped down towards her.

'Is the car here?' she asked.

'Not yet, love, no. It's about ten minutes away, but I'm going to go ahead in my car. Hope that's OK?'

Lily asked the question out of politeness, but Billie knew she was desperate to go and have a few minutes with her son before the wedding started. She smiled and nodded.

'Of course. I'll see you there.'

Lily walked away, and she hesitated a second before following her out to the front porch. 'Lil?'

Lily turned, her eyebrows raised in question.

'I just wanted to say... well, thanks. You know. For everything.' She pushed her hair back behind her ear awkwardly. 'I love Cillian, and I feel so lucky to be the one who gets to share his life,' she said honestly. 'But I also feel so lucky to have been taken in as family by the rest of you.'

Lily's face softened.

'You know I don't really have family. The family I do have are either absent by choice or we're not close.' She shrugged, pretending as she said it that it didn't really sting. 'Having you guys take me into your family has meant a lot. Especially you.' She mashed her lips together in an awkward smile, not used to being so open and vulnerable.

Lily took a step closer and squeezed her arm. 'Well, I feel lucky to have you in our lives too. Both for Cillian, and for myself. You're a special girl, Billie. And you're very much a Drew already. Wedding or not.'

Billie smiled, those precious words from Lily warming her heart. 'Thanks,' she managed, swallowing down the lump in her throat.

'Don't do it,' Lily warned. 'The make-up lady already left; we can't undo the damage if you cry.'

Billie laughed and nodded. 'True. I'll see you in a bit.'

She turned and walked back into the house and cradled her stomach, feeling a deep sense of peace. Today was going to be the happiest day of her life. Because as well as marrying the man she loved, she was finally getting something else she'd longed for for a very long time. Today she would officially become part of a family who actually *wanted* and *loved* her, and who she knew with the utmost certainty would shower the baby girl growing inside her with all the unconditional love and time and effort that she deserved.

Billie's lonely heart finally felt as though it had found a home here, in this family. And after all these years of wondering why she was so unlovable, and trying to ignore the hollow void where family was supposed to be, that simple acceptance was the most beautiful feeling in the world.

THIRTY-EIGHT

Lily parked her car in the church car park and walked around to the front. Father Dan stood outside, ushering the guests in and pointing them towards the seats. He smiled widely as Lily approached, taking in her dark rusty-brown satin outfit and jauntily slanted fascinator with a look of appreciation.

'Colour suits you, Lil,' he said. 'I don't think I've ever seen you out of black before. You look fantastic. And definitely too young to be the mother of the groom.'

Lily grinned and chuckled. 'I thought it was a sin to lie, Father,' she jokingly admonished.

'Oh, now, I'd never lie about a thing like that,' he replied with mock sternness.

He glanced back into the church, his smile fading. 'Listen, what's going on between you and Ray?' he asked, his tone a tad tense. 'He's been looking for you since he arrived, and he looks fit to kill.'

The priest's words sent a chill down her spine. In all the commotion, she'd almost forgotten Ray would be here today, and that by now he'd likely have heard of her new business arrangement with the Tylers. She followed his glance, the strange and frustrating mixture of longing and hatred bubbling up inside her, the way it always did when she thought about Ray now. Lifting her chin, she mentally prepared for whatever was about to come her way.

'Don't worry about it, Father. It's just business,' she told him.

'Yes, well...' He eyed her gravely. 'Just make sure that business doesn't spill over into the wedding.'

Lily's stare turned cold as she looked back at him. 'This is my *son's* wedding, Father,' she reminded him. 'I'd strangle the entire congregation with my bare hands before I let one of them ruin this day.'

He raised his eyebrows at this statement but just sighed in response. 'Your boys are in the back room, if you want to go through.'

Lily walked inside and slipped off to the back room before anyone could stop her. Shutting the door behind her, she turned and stopped still as she saw her two sons together in their matching navy morning suits. Their cravats were the same colour as the bridesmaids' dresses, a warm rusty autumnal colour, a few shades lighter than her own outfit. Cillian held two small yellow roses in his hand, two pins stuck between his teeth.

Connor looked at her, his expression open, and for a moment she caught a glimpse of the lost little boy underneath, before he looked away uncomfortably, with a studious frown, towards the corner of the room. Cillian, she noticed, put a hand out and touched his brother's side in a subtle gesture of support, and held her gaze expectantly.

Lily cleared her throat and crossed the room towards them with a fixed smile, feeling all sorts of different things. She'd missed Connor greatly, and Cillian was right, she couldn't have carried on without seeing or speaking to him much longer. Her children were the reason she breathed, her reason for fighting through every battle and every challenge. What was the point of anything without them?

Her anger had cooled now, if she was being honest with herself. She was still furious at Ray, but she couldn't stay angry with Connor. Instead, that part of her just felt frustrated now – and confused. That part of her wanted to lock him in a room and demand he tell her the truth, the real reason he'd gone somewhere so against everything he'd always felt and worked for. Because she *knew* he wasn't happy. She knew him better than anyone else in the world, with the exception of his twin.

Reaching the pair of them, she stopped, and there was an awkward silence. Connor shifted a half step backward, clearly unsure whether or not to remain by Cillian's side. Clearly unsure what reception he was going to get.

Seeing this, Lily suddenly felt a deep flood of shame wash through her. Her son shouldn't feel like that. Not with her. Not ever. She looked down, not sure how to begin bridging the gap between them, then Cillian's hand moved into view, holding out one of the yellow flowers. She took it and raised her head back up, refixing her smile.

'Well, you boys both look very sharp,' she said, breaking the silence.

'Thanks,' Cillian replied, pulling the pins out of his mouth. 'You look pretty amazing yourself.'

Connor glanced at her with a short nod. 'Thanks.'

Lily took the pins from Cillian, along with the other rose. 'Here, let me do these,' she said. 'You'll only stab yourselves and muck up your shirts.'

It was a flimsy excuse and they all knew it, but no one said a word. She reached up and pinned Cillian's first, smoothing his jacket down with a look of pride and love. Then she turned to Connor with a look of question. 'Can I?'

'Oh, yeah. Yeah,' he replied, turning to face her straight on so she could reach his lapel.

Lily pinned it in and smoothed his jacket too, looking up at him. He met her gaze and, after a moment, accepted the olive branch with a small smile. As the pair relaxed, Lily reached out and touched his arm. There was so much to say, but at the same time there was no need to say anything, so in the end she chose not to.

She took a deep breath in and stepped back, moving her gaze between her two sons and allowing the love she felt for them both to shine through.

'I can't believe it's your wedding day,' she said, looking at Cillian. 'It seems like only yesterday I was holding the pair of you in my arms for the first time.'

'Well, soon enough there'll be another little one for you to hold,' Cillian reminded her.

'*That's* what *I* can't believe,' Connor remarked. 'That you're going to be a *dad.*'

'I know – it's mad,' Cillian said with a wide grin.

'Honestly, hats off to you; you're braver than me, mate,' Connor replied with a laugh. 'Don't get me wrong, you know how happy I am for *you*, but I'd be shitting myself.'

'Why?' Cillian asked with a frown. 'It can't be that hard.'

Both Lily and Connor let out a short sound of amusement, but each, Lily soon realised, for very different reasons.

'What?' Cillian said. 'It's a baby. How hard can it be? Feed it, change it, keep it warm and give it love, *boom*, done.'

'*Boom?*' Lily repeated, raising an eyebrow.

'At *first*, yeah,' Connor agreed. 'But she'll soon grow, and she'll *keep* growing, until before you know it, she's a teenager.' He paused, giving Cillian a pointed look. 'How you gonna deal with *that* shitshow?'

Cillian's face fell as he realised Connor was right, but Lily just frowned and rolled her eyes.

'Connor, don't wind him up,' she admonished.

'I'm not! It's true!'

'You'll be fine,' she said to Cillian strongly. 'We'll cross that bridge when we get to it, but now ain't the time. Come on. Billie will be here in a minute, and *you* can't be fashionably late: that's *her* right as the bride.'

Cillian pulled himself together, and she ushered him through to the church. Connor fell in beside her and, as they walked through the door, she put a hand on his arm. He looked down at her.

'It really is good to see you,' she said with feeling.

His face softened into a smile. 'You too.'

Cillian beckoned him, and he continued following him through. Lily paused to close the door and had to stifle a gasp when a hand shot out from the side and pulled her behind one of the stone pillars.

Ray glared at her, his furious expression full of disbelief. 'Did you make a deal with the Tylers to peddle product through your territory?' he demanded.

Lily sucked in a deep breath and pulled herself to full height, glaring back at him defiantly. 'Yes,' she said with conviction. 'I *did*.' She jutted her chin out stubbornly and held his glare with a fire that matched his.

As she delivered the blow, he turned a dark shade of red, the vein in his temple throbbing dangerously fast and his expression shaking with pent-up fury. But while even most of the hardest men in their world would have cowered in her position, Lily openly basked in the glory of hitting him where it hurt. She gloated defiantly, refusing to be intimidated by Ray, the man who'd so stupidly thought he could get away with stealing her son from her.

'How *could* you?' he growled.

Lily smiled coldly, feeling the thrill of power in that moment. She leaned closer towards him. 'How does that feel, Ray?' she asked in a low deadly hiss. 'How does it feel to be betrayed by someone you thought loved you? Hm?'

She searched his face then suddenly took a step back as the painful ache set back into her heart. She didn't want to feel this hurt right now. She didn't want the reminder of how much she loved him, how much his betrayal of her trust had killed her. Looking away, she swallowed and composed herself.

'That deal isn't a patch on what you took from me, but I know it's hurt you,' she said, trying to keep the emotional shake out of her voice. 'And I'm glad.' She turned her gaze back to him. 'I hope it eats you up, knowing how much money they'll make and that you *never* will.'

Ray's nostrils flared, and the muscles in his jaw worked hard for a moment, but then he suddenly glanced over her shoulder and straightened up.

'Everything alright here, Ray?' Father Dan asked with a steely look. 'Did you lose your way to your seat?'

Ray exhaled frustratedly, looking back to Lily with a glare. 'This ain't over,' he growled before straightening his jacket and marching off.

Lily turned and watched him leave, exhaling slowly as her heart gradually calmed back down. Father Dan met her eye then turned away with a troubled sigh, and Lily was once more alone at the back of the church. She gave herself a few more seconds to compose herself, then lifted her chin and walked down the middle of the aisle to the front row, where Cath sat waiting for her.

'Where you *been*?' she whispered as Lily sat down. 'They're about to walk in!'

'I'm here now,' Lily whispered, looking back at the full church and nodding to all the people she knew. 'That's all that matters.'

The church organ started up with the wedding march, and everyone rose in their seats, ready for the wedding to begin.

THIRTY-NINE

Billie walked down the aisle, her arm tucked into that of her uncle, who was giving her away, and Lily looked back towards Cillian. His face lit up as he saw his bride, as though he'd never seen anything so beautiful, and Lily's heart swelled. She was so fiercely proud of her son, of the good man he'd turned out to be. He *deserved* this happiness. And so did Billie. She watched the girl now with a warm smile, grateful that of all the women Cillian could have chosen to bring into their family, it was her.

As Billie passed Ray's pew, Lily's smile tightened slightly. Lily could see his stormy gaze boring into her and pointedly ignored it – ignoring, too, the cold trickle of foreboding that slipped down her spine. She was ready for Ray. For this war that had been a long time coming. But there would be no fighting today. This day wasn't about them, and he would respect that whether he liked it or not.

Scarlet and Isla followed Billie down the aisle, graceful and elegant in their bridesmaid dresses. The small procession neared, passing the Logans, and Bill Hanlon and his wife, then the Tylers, who'd been positioned in the first pew behind immediate family, as a show of respect.

Lily gave them a furtive glance. Their conversation the day before had worried her. The Tylers were their closest allies and good friends, but business was business, and up until the moment Freddie had so pointedly brought up the subject, the fact her sons could one day be seen as a genuine threat to their longstanding reign in this city hadn't crossed her mind.

Both Freddie's and Paul's smiles were relaxed and genuine as they watched Billie pass, which eased her mind a little. She was going to have to keep a close eye on that situation, but if it *did* become an issue, it wasn't likely to develop until a point in the distant future. They would have time to work out how to navigate that road later.

As she watched them from the corner of her eye, Freddie reached into his pocket and pulled out his phone. He frowned before slipping it away again as Billie reached the altar. Lily turned to face the front, pushing her worries away, and focused on her son's wedding with a smile.

Father Dan cleared his throat. 'Please be seated,' he ordered. He smiled and looked around the church, his gaze resting on Cillian for a moment before he continued.

Lily's smile softened as he began the ceremony. Father Dan could be a tough nut, but he was a priest who genuinely cared for the people in his community. He'd known her children since they'd been born, had put the fear of God in them as they'd grown, trying to help mould them into good people. His happiness to be marrying Cillian today was genuine, and fitting, considering he'd been the one to baptise them. The morbid wondering of whether he'd be the one to bury them too crossed her mind before she could stop it, and she quickly shook it from her head. *What was wrong with her?*

She lifted her chin and listened to the reading Father Dan was now reciting. It was a beautiful piece about the beauty of marriage and the lifelong friendship and support that comes with it. Sweet words Lily knew she'd never fully understand herself. The concept was simple enough, but she'd never experienced life with someone there to lean on. She'd fought her way through alone since being orphaned at fourteen, with a young brother to raise and protect. She'd been the protector then and every day since.

A quiet buzz sounded from somewhere on the other side of the aisle, and she turned her head just enough to see back along the pews. It was Freddie's phone, she realised as he quickly silenced it again.

She turned back to the ceremony, watching Cillian as he gazed into Billie's eyes with pure love and trust. A small spear of sadness pierced her heart as she thought back to the days when it had been *her*, his mother, that he looked at with such trusting adoration. Back when he was young and he'd thought she knew and could do everything.

But that was the thing about motherhood. It was all so fleeting. You were gifted with this tiny human being that you cared for and nurtured and loved – that you moulded your entire life around. You were the centre of their universe and they were the centre of yours. And for a while it felt like that's how things would be forever. But they weren't. She sniffed and then brightened her smile as Billie looked over towards her.

Cath blew her nose loudly between emotional sobs, and Lily's brows furrowed into a frown.

'Cath, pack it in – they can hear you down the street,' she murmured quietly.

'I'm sorry,' Cath whispered. 'It's just so beautiful.' She sobbed again, drawing a few looks from the opposite pew.

'*Shush*,' Lily replied under her breath. She exhaled slowly through her nose, glancing at the videographer. She hoped he could edit that out. Everything about today *had* to be perfect. Cillian deserved no less.

'Come on, look.' She nudged Cath with her shoulder. 'They're about to say their vows.'

Cath's sniffs quietened, and Lily heaved an internal sigh of relief.

'Do you, Belinda Anne Archer, take this man, to love and to hold from this day on, for better, for worse, for richer, for poorer, in sickness and in health, until death do you part, according to God's holy law and in the presence of God and all the people here present today?' Father Dan asked.

'I do,' she said, her words heartfelt.

'And do *you*, Cillian Drew, take this woman, to love and to hold from this day on, for better, for worse, for richer, for poorer, in sickness and in health, until death do you part, according to God's holy law and in the presence of God and all the people here present today?'

Cillian smiled, his face bright with love. 'I do.'

'Who has the rings?' Father Dan eyed Connor expectantly.

'Ooh, yep, that's me!' He stepped forward and handed the rings to his brother.

'Grand,' Father Dan replied. 'Now, Belinda, repeat after me. With this ring...'

'*Belinda*?' Cath whispered as the vows continued. 'I didn't know her name was *Belinda*.'

'What did you think it was?' Lily asked, distracted by the sound of buzzing behind again. Glancing back, she saw Freddie silence his phone for the third time, his frown concerned. She wondered what it was as she slid her gaze away.

'I thought it was just *Billie*,' Cath replied.

Lily looked at her and she shrugged.

'And now,' Father Dan announced, raising his hands up in the air, 'to my *great* delight, I can finally declare these two young people *man* and *wife*.'

The church erupted with the sound of cheers and applause as Cillian kissed Billie firmly on the lips. Lily and Cath stood and joined in the cheers, Lily's face lighting up with happiness for the pair as they faced the congregation with smiles of joy and triumph.

The merry sounds of Mendelssohn's 'Wedding March' filled the air, and the newlyweds led the way back up the aisle. They stopped just inside the door and stood to the side, greeting everyone and accepting congratulatory kisses and compliments as people filed out.

As mother of the groom, Lily was the first in line. She smiled at Billie and straightened her veil. 'Welcome to the family, Mrs Drew,' she said, the words simple but heartfelt.

Billie laughed, her eyes still sparkling with pure happiness the way they had at the altar. 'It sounds so strange, doesn't it?'

Lily shook her head. 'I don't think it sounds strange at all. I think it's the perfect fit.'

She winked at her new daughter-in-law before turning to Cillian. She took a deep breath in and let it out in a swift sigh as she searched for the right words to say. His warm brown eyes met hers for a moment, then he pulled her into a hug.

'The second in one day,' she said with a light laugh into his chest. 'You need to be careful or people will think you've gone soft.' She sighed again, momentarily closing her eyes as she held on to the moment. 'You'll always be my baby,' she said, these words quieter than her others. Words that were just for him.

He hugged her a little tighter and replied with words that were just for her too. 'Of course I will. And you'll always be my mum. The best mum anyone could wish for. No one could ever take your place.'

Swallowing down the lump that formed in her throat, she leaned up to kiss his cheek then pulled back, forcing a smile. 'Come on, Cath,' she said, pulling her sister-in-law away. 'We're holding up the line.'

Stepping out into the bright sunshine, Lily blinked away her tears and looked up at the blue cloudless sky with a smile.

The wind suddenly switched direction, whipping her neck

with a biting chill and flicking her hair into her eyes. As she pushed it back, an old forgotten memory resurfaced. Another time, another fight with her windswept curls. A warning from her mother.

'Tis a warning sign, my wean. The winds of change come fast and fierce. Pay attention when they whisper and you'll not go far wrong.

Lily shivered and turned back to the church, shaking it off. It had been a long time since she'd thought of her mother's strange superstitions, and she wasn't wasting time on them today. Wind was just that. Wind. Today was a perfect day. A wonderful day. The kind of day her son deserved.

And nothing was going to ruin it.

FORTY

The atmosphere was lively as everyone slowly gathered outside the church. People lined both sides of the steps as Scarlet and Isla hurriedly handed out small bags of confetti, and the photographer double-checked his camera, getting ready for the money shot of the happy couple walking out.

Lily stood with Connor, watching the door, her smile relaxed as they waited. Opposite them, Freddie backed out of the crowd and walked away from the noisy church front to finally answer whoever was trying so hard to get hold of him.

Lily looked back towards the door with an expectant smile. '*This* is the most important photo,' she said excitedly, leaning her head back towards Connor's. 'The one as they leave the church and everyone throws confetti from the sides. I know Billie's hoping it's a good one so she can frame it, so make sure you throw yours really high to try and fill any gaps as it all falls. I imagine most people won't throw it high enough and that'll ruin the picture.'

Connor didn't respond, and she glanced back at him. He stared back, one eyebrow raised in amusement.

'Did you hear me?' she asked.

'I think Cath's starting to rub off on you.'

Lily's jaw dropped, and she narrowed her eyes. 'Just throw the damn confetti like I told you,' she snapped, turning back around.

'Listen...' Connor said, leaning in closer, his tone reluctant. 'What's going on with you and Ray? Apart from with me, I mean.' He moved to stand beside her, scratching the back of his neck as he glanced down the line of people on the opposite side. 'You can tell me to piss off if you like, but is there something I should know? I might work for him, but you're still my mum, and I know *something's* happened. He went *mental* last night out of nowhere after one of his watchers turned up. Smashed an ashtray through the glass doors of his drinks cabinet. Wouldn't talk in front of me, but he's been spitting feathers all morning, and he's looking at you like he wants to fucking kill ya, so *seriously,* Mum, if there's something you need to tell me, now's the time.'

Guilt flooded Lily's veins instantly as she realised what a predicament this would now put Connor in. When she'd offered the Tylers that deal, she and Connor weren't talking. She'd figured it wouldn't affect him with that clear separation, and that their reunion would be off the back of him returning to the fold. But now here they were, reunited, but still working on opposite sides of the line.

She followed Connor's glance down to where Ray stood with Benny. Half turned away, he had a dark frown on his face as he spoke urgently into Benny's ear. Benny nodded, his expression serious, offering the odd reply here and there.

Lily bit her lip and tilted her head towards Connor. 'I made a deal with the Tylers,' she said, glancing over her other shoulder to make sure no one else was listening in. 'I needed their help with a job and it was a big ask. I offered them a contract for the drug routes through our territory, in return.'

'*What?*' Connor gasped, his eyes widening in shock. '*Jesus,*

Mum...' He made a sound of exasperation and rubbed his eyes, glancing back over to Ray.

Lily grimaced. 'I'm sorry. At the time I arranged it, I didn't think it would affect you.'

Connor shook his head in disbelief. 'Well, clearly it *does*,' he said, irritated. 'What you gonna do?'

'*Do?*' Lily asked in surprise. 'Nothing.' She looked at him. 'This has been a long time coming, this showdown between me and Ray. Surely you can see that? He has *no* right to those routes; they're *ours*. It's up to *me* to decide who gets them, not *him*. Yeah, had we been on better terms, I would have given them to him, because it would have made sense, but we're not,' she said frankly. 'And if he feels so entitled to *my* territory that he's going to start a war, then I'm ready for it. Because it's about time he learned he can't just take whatever he wants.' Her chin lifted, and her expression hardened.

'Like *me*, you mean,' Connor replied coldly. 'Because I belong to you too, right?'

Lily looked round at him, taken aback by the expression on his face. 'That's not what I said,' she replied with a small frown.

'But it's what you meant,' Connor replied, his piercing gaze holding hers.

Lily stared back, his words not sitting comfortably with her. *Is that how she sounded?*

There was suddenly a loud cheer, and they both turned to see Cillian and Billie walking out of the church. She smiled, focusing back on them, knowing the moment was important to them. The photographer counted down from three, and they all threw their confetti in the air as the pair descended the steps. A shower of dried petals and paper filled the air as the flash went off, the happy couple laughing as the stuff landed in their hair and blew into their faces.

Connor slipped away as they reached the last step, moving

to stand beside Cillian and pulling him into a side hug. He said something that made them both laugh, and Lily watched, glad to see them together and happy again. Scarlet fell in beside Billie, pulling confetti from her hair as the photographer continued taking pictures.

'Everyone else on the steps,' he ordered. 'Come on, behind the bride and groom. Wedding party, you stay down here.'

Everyone started to move to where they were supposed to be, but Lily paused for a second longer, taking in the perfect picture in front of her. Her sons laughing together, the grin that creased Scarlet's face as Billie talked away animatedly, her hands gesturing wildly in the air as Scarlet gently pulled another petal from her hair. She suddenly wished she could capture this moment for the four of them, because perfect moments like this were so rare in this life.

Little did she know that it would become a moment that many people would look back on, in years to come, wondering if they could have done something different. Wondering if they could have made any difference to the outcome.

The sharp, deafening crack of a shot fired cut loudly through the air, and the happy chatter instantly changed to gasps and cries. Lily heard someone yell out her name, and she turned to see Freddie running back towards her, alarm in his eyes, but it was too late. She realised at the same time he did that what he'd been rushing to warn her about was already happening. The danger was already here.

Luca Romano swayed strangely from side to side across the road as he stalked towards them. His upper body heaved with deep, angry breaths of rage, his eyes dark, his face and clothes still caked in dried blood from when Cillian had broken his nose. He looked deranged, half mad with fury as he swept the gun back and forth across the crowd. The people at the top of the steps quickly swarmed back into the church, more than half of them making it before Luca lifted the gun into the air and let off a second shot of warning.

'Nobody fucking move!' he yelled. '*Nobody*. Next time one of you runs, I shoot,' he warned.

He waved the gun across the people left on the steps, then moved his aim down to Cillian and Connor. Billie had instinctively clung to Cillian's arm, but he firmly pushed her a couple of feet away now, keeping his eyes on Luca.

'Stay there, Bills,' he warned quietly.

'No,' she uttered, her tone terrified. She tried to step back, but Scarlet gripped her arm and shook her head.

Lily stared at Luca in horror, her heart beating so hard she could hear it in her ears as fear filled every pore in her body. *How the hell had he got out of the container?* His hand was shaking, she noticed, his focus on the boys, and she quickly eyed up the distance between them. She was the nearest person to him, having remained on the outer part of the pavement while everyone else had gone back up the steps behind the small wedding party, but she still wasn't close enough to get to him before he could get a shot off. She mentally cursed and quickly looked back towards Cillian and Connor, moving her gaze up to the small crowd of people still left on the steps as she tried to figure out her options.

She noted who was still there, catching Freddie's loaded gaze but moving swiftly on. This wasn't the time for the whys and the hows. Paul was beside Freddie, along with Anna and Tanya. Bill and his wife Amy were with them. Cos Christou, the head of one of the Greek firms in North London, stood the other side, with his wife, Haroulla. A huddle of Billie's girlfriends clung together, followed by Ray, two couples who were friends of Cillian's from school, and then Cath, Isla and Cormac. That was it.

Lily exhaled heavily and lifted her hands, stepping slowly

sideways into Luca's line of sight. Stepping into the line of fire, between his gun and her boys.

'You don't want to do that, Luca,' she said, trying to sound calm. 'Look around you. There are too many witnesses – you'll go away for good.'

Luca let out a short, sharp burst of laughter, as if her words were the funniest thing he'd heard all year.

'Lil, get the fuck back!' Ray called out from behind her.

Lily was surprised by the words of sentiment from Ray, everything considered, but she didn't look round. She needed to keep her focus on Luca.

'Luca, look at me,' she begged. 'Seriously. The police will already be on their way, and you don't want a life behind bars. I *know* you don't.'

'Oh, you *know*, do you?' he said, throwing his head back and laughing manically. 'You *know*! As opposed to a new life over in *fucking Spain*?' The laugher had stopped now, abruptly replaced by a seething hot anger.

Lily glanced back nervously at the group on the stairs. Ray squinted in confusion, and Cos Christou frowned, his curious gaze flickering around the group. She cursed internally. However they got out of this – and they *would*, she told herself – they didn't need other people in the underworld knowing what had gone down between them all.

'Mum, *please,* move out of the way,' Cillian demanded urgently. 'He'll do it. For God's sake just *move*.'

'Fine,' she shouted back. 'It *should* be me.'

'Lily!' Ray yelled angrily. She heard him curse, and for a moment, Luca's gaze flickered towards something behind her.

'Stay back!' he yelled. 'I mean it, Renshaw, *stay – the fuck – back!*' He let off another shot, this time in the direction of the crowd, and there was a short wave of screams.

Lily whipped round, her eyes wide with terror as she

searched for where it landed. A few of them stared up at the wall behind, and she breathed a sigh of relief.

'OK! OK!' Ray was just a few feet behind her now, his hands held up in surrender. 'I won't take another step, alright? But she's right, Luca, you don't want to do *this*. Just put the gun down and walk away. Whatever this is about can be sorted, but *not* here. This is a wedding for Christ's sake. It ain't done. You *know* that.'

Luca began to laugh again, the sound bitter and half mad. 'Oh I'm supposed to follow the rules, am I? After what *they* did? I don't think so.'

Ray exhaled heavily through his nose, and Lily glanced back at him.

'Ray, just go back to the steps, alright? This ain't your fight,' she told him, worried that his temper would break through and he'd end up getting himself shot.

'Back up to me and we'll go together,' he replied.

'Do what he says, Mum,' Connor seconded.

'No!' she exclaimed stubbornly. 'I'm not moving.'

'*None* of you cunts are moving anywhere I don't *tell* you to,' Luca shouted, baring his teeth as his expression contorted. '*You* though.' He pointed the gun at Lily. 'Move back to the side. *Now.*'

'No,' she repeated, her tone firm but calm.

'*What* did you say?' he asked incredulously. 'You think you have a fucking *choice*? *Move*,' he bellowed.

Lily stayed exactly where she was and took a deep breath. 'Luca, it's *me* you should be aiming that gun at, not my boys. *I'm* the one you should be blaming, if you're looking to blame someone.'

'*You?*' he repeated, narrowing his eyes at her bitterly. 'Oh I *do* blame you. But this ain't just about that. This is about *all* of it.' He glared at Connor and Cillian over her shoulder. 'You took *everything* from me. You stripped me of all I had,

made me a laughing stock in my own *firm*. My own *family*.'
Spittle sprayed from his mouth and hung from his chin as he
began to shake. 'I sat by and watched these last few years,
stuck in the *hell* you trapped me in, while you paraded
around this city acting like the big-bollocks you think you are,
having everything handed to you on a golden fucking plate,
while I got *nothing*!' he bellowed. 'I got ignored and ridiculed
and put at the butt of every joke – do you know what that's
like?'

He tilted his head to the side and took a step towards them,
and Lily's fear for the boys began to rise.

'*Do* you? Of course you don't,' he spat. 'All this time I sat
there and I did *nothing*, but *then*,' he said, a bark of incredulous
laughter bursting out. '*Then* you go and pull *this*. And I'm *done*
taking it. I'm putting an end to it. I'm putting an end to *you*.
Both of you.'

He leaned sideways trying to get around Lily, gritting his
teeth as he re-aimed the gun.

'No! Stop! It was *me*,' Lily shouted, her tone pleading. She
pointed to her chest, moving to block him once more. '*I* did that
to you, *all* of it. *I* ordered them to do all that to you for exactly
that purpose, to strip you of your cred because I didn't think you
were strong enough to get it back,' she admitted.

'What are you *doing* woman?' Ray shouted angrily.

'Telling the truth,' Lily replied, not looking back. '*I* did that
to you, Luca. They were just following orders the way you all
do. So if you want revenge, you take it on *me*.'

She held his gaze with a hard, level stare, already at peace
with what she was doing. She'd die for any of her children if it
meant saving them, and she'd do it gladly. That was her job. To
protect them, no matter what.

Lifting her chin defiantly, she stepped forward. 'You can
take me or you can kill me, but you will *not* touch my boys,' she
told him.

'You stupid bitch,' he said with a cold half-smile. 'You really think you can stop me?'

Darting to the side, he lifted the gun and aimed around her. Lily's heart leaped up into her mouth, and as he pulled the trigger, she dived instinctively into the space between the gun and her sons.

FORTY-ONE

Lily's feet left the ground, and she stretched out, trying to move as fast and far as possible with her body, but before she could reach the space she was flying towards, a pair of arms wrapped around her waist, and she was yanked sharply backward. She cried out in alarm, landing with a hard thump on the ground, tangled up in the grip of whoever had pulled her back. She pushed away, not allowing a second to pass between landing and fighting to get back up. Ray released her, and she catapulted across to her sons.

'Where'd it go?' Connor shouted.

'I don't know!' Cillian cried. 'Who's hit?'

His head swivelled quickly around at everyone before darting warily back to Luca.

Lily's first instinct was relief. Her boys were still OK. Her second instinct was to get back in front of them. She rushed forward, grabbing Billie's arm to manoeuvre her out of the way, but Billie didn't move.

'Billie, get...' Her voice trailed off as she caught the pale shock on the girl's face, and the realisation suddenly hit her that Billie hadn't been standing there a few moments ago. Her blood ran cold as her gaze flickered down to Billie's hands, which were pressed tightly over her stomach.

'You bastards really do *make things difficult*,' Luca raged. He re-cocked the gun with a resolute expression.

'Billie, *move*,' Cillian ordered, darting forward to shield her.

'*Stop right there!*' Luca yelled, suddenly distracted by Freddie and Bill, who'd taken the chance to slip down around the side, towards him. '*All of you!*' he screamed. Paul had slipped down the opposite side, as the brothers made their bid to close in on him, and Luca swung the gun wildly back and forth, trying to keep control.

'Lily,' Billie said, the word heavy with fear as she stared at her new mother-in-law.

'Mum, get her out of here. *Now*, while he's distracted,' Cillian said hurriedly.

Lily gripped Billie's arms as she suddenly swayed. 'Cillian,' she said in a low, urgent voice.

'*Now*, Mum,' he barked.

'*Cillian*,' she repeated, the sharpness in her voice finally making him turn around.

'What?' he asked impatiently.

Ray had stood up and was now inching forward, his arms raised as he tried once more to defuse things. 'Luca, listen to me. I don't know what's happened, but I *do* know there's always another way. Give me the gun, son, and you and I can go somewhere and talk.'

'Mum?' Cillian's eyes shot to Billie as her knees buckled, and she fell forward into Lily's arms. '*Billie!*'

His panicked cry caught everyone's attention as he pulled Billie out of Lily's arms and into his own. He tried to prop her up, but her legs gave way, so he lowered her gently to the ground, cradling her upper body against his.

A dark red stain appeared from under Billie's shaking hands, spreading quickly through her pretty dress and spilling over her white-knuckled fingers as she desperately held on to her stomach.

'No!' Cillian cried, the sound strangled. 'Someone call an ambulance! *Billie's been hit*! Billie, oh God...' He put his hand on hers, trying to stem the blood, but it just seemed to pour out faster. 'Hold on, OK? Just try not to move. You'll be alright, love, I promise, OK?' He stared at the slick dark blood as it began to pool on the ground then looked up at Lily helplessly.

Lily stared back at the pair of them in horror, at a loss for what to do. Ray was already on the phone, hurriedly giving emergency services the details. Someone called out that they were going to find some jackets or blankets to keep her warm. Two more people offered to help them, backing away carefully towards the church. Luca didn't try to stop them this time, the panic in his eyes clear. His eyes darted between Billie and the men who'd been trying to surround him. Swinging the gun around with a fearful panic in his eye, his hand shook even more than it had before.

'I didn't mean to hit her,' he cried out.

'Well, you *did*,' Connor snarled back, his face red with fury and with murder in his eyes. 'You stupid fucking *cunt*!' He took a step towards him, but Lily pulled him back.

'*Don't*,' she warned. 'You're who he's here for.'

'Luca,' Freddie called out to him, drawing his attention away. 'Listen to me. You know who I am...'

Lily breathed out in relief as Freddie kept him talking, leaving them to attend to Billie. Ice-cold dread spread through her as she quickly assessed the girl. Billie had been pale before, but she was swiftly turning a deathly shade of grey. Lily dropped to her knees beside her, in the rapidly expanding pool of blood, and reached over to grip one of Billie's hands. It was already cold to the touch. She closed her eyes for a moment, despair washing over her, then opened them again with a bright forced smile.

'You're going to be OK,' she told her, nodding encouragingly. 'Just hold on, OK, love?'

Billie's body began to shake violently.

Tears fell down Cillian's face as he sobbed, gripping her tighter. 'You *are*,' he told her. 'See? Mum says you'll be fine, and she knows her stuff, OK? So you just stay there. They'll be here soon. OK, babe?'

Billie nodded weakly, but Lily could see this was just for Cillian's sake. Billie knew how fast she was fading; Lily could see it in her eyes. There was just too much blood, and as Lily glanced at how far it had spread, she knew Billie didn't have much longer. Choking back a sob, she looked away, trying to hide it. She needed to *do* something.

'The ambulance – how long?' she shouted angrily.

Ray was right behind her, his phone to his ear. 'They're eight minutes out.'

'Eight?' she repeated faintly, meeting his eyes. He held her gaze, and she saw her fear mirrored there. He knew it too. Billie didn't have eight minutes. She made a sound of frustration. 'Tell them they need to move *faster*, *goddamn it*,' she yelled.

Connor ran his hands through his hair, his expression pained as he hovered beside them. 'What do I do?' he asked, looking at Lily for instruction.

Her eyes darted across to Luca warily. His face was stricken, and he looked scared as his eyes flicked constantly between Billie and the Tyler brothers on each side. They were still too far away to do anything, but they were keeping him distracted at least. 'Find a bottle of water,' she said quietly. 'Don't let him see you go if you can help it.'

He nodded and slunk off up the steps. Lily held her breath, but if Luca saw him, he no longer cared, as Connor made it inside without issue. Cath reappeared, passing Connor at the door and running down the steps. She dropped down by Billie's head, holding a rolled-up jacket. 'Cillian, she needs to lie straight. Lie her down; put this under her head,' she urged.

Scarlet was a few seconds behind Cath, squatting down with a glass bottle half full of something dark. She pulled the cork out of the top and held it out. 'It's all I could find,' she said. 'The communion wine. It's sweet; I thought it might help...' She trailed off with a helpless expression.

Lily nodded. She didn't have the heart to tell Scarlet it was too late for a bit of sugar to help anything now. Instead, she took the bottle and put it to Billie's lips.

'Here,' she said gently. 'Bit of Dutch courage to take the edge off, yeah?'

Billie dutifully took a small sip, but her interest was fading with her strength. Lily's sight blurred, and she swallowed hard. Cormac had arrived behind Scarlet and now held out a blanket towards Lily. She took it with a small word of thanks and was about to lay it over Billie, but Billie reached out her hand with a small shake of her head. 'Don't cover my dress,' she said, the words weak and stilted. 'It's so pretty.'

Lily's brow crumpled, and she pulled back the blanket, unable to deny her this simple request. Not now.

Cillian sat beside his wife, holding her slick, bloody hand and staring down at her with terrified, helpless eyes. 'Hold on, Bills, please,' he begged. 'You can't go anywhere. I need you.'

A tear fell from the corner of Billie's eye, slipping into her hair. 'She would have been so beautiful, Cillian,' she rasped. 'Lily Rose.'

He lowered his forehead to hers and sobbed, the sound raw and full of grief, and Lily's heart broke in two.

A dark silence fell, the only sound Cillian's muffled sobs, and time seemed to freeze over, trapping them all in this surreal nightmarish moment. But that illusion swiftly faded as Billie's body stopped shaking and she looked up at Lily with the ghost of a smile.

'I saved him, Lil,' she said, the words so quiet they were barely audible.

Tears stung Lily's eyes, and she nodded back, swallowing the lump in her throat. 'You did,' she managed.

But it should have been me, she added silently, guilt consuming her as she watched Billie's life fade away. Billie's *and* Lily Rose's. Two precious souls with their whole lives ahead of them. Two girls that were Cillian's whole world.

She bowed her head, no longer trying to stop her tears as they began to fall. It *should* have been *her*. *She* should have been the one to take that bullet. She was older, her children were grown, her main purpose in life served already. Her children would have mourned her, but they would've been OK. Cillian would have moved on with his life, his wife and daughter by his side. *Why hadn't it been her?*

The pain and fear suddenly melted away from Billie's expression, and she turned to Cillian with a peaceful smile. She opened her mouth as if to speak but then faltered. For one more moment, she held his gaze, then her smile fell away and her head slumped, as what light had remained in her face dimmed to nothing.

FORTY-TWO

'Billie?' Cillian said urgently, his voice shaking as he tried to get her to wake back up. 'No, no, no, no... This can't be happening. Come on, Bills, *wake up. Please*, babe, I can't do this without you.' He sobbed and stroked her face, but it was too late. *'Please!'* he cried. 'You *can't* leave me, Bills, you just can't...'

His words faded into his deep, pained sobs, and Lily fell back feeling empty and full of guilt as she watched her son cry over the body of his wife and unborn child. For once she had no idea what to do. She couldn't fix this. She couldn't make this better.

Everyone's attention had turned to Billie, but a clattering sound across the road now drew their gazes back to Luca. Lily's eyes searched the pavement, but he was no longer there. The gun lay discarded on the ground.

Shocked and angered that he'd had the nerve to slip away while the rest of them were distracted, Lily stood up and ran out into the road. Several of the others moved with her. Whipping her head back and forth, she just caught sight of the back of him as he rounded the far corner, running as fast as he could.

'*Shit!*' she exclaimed, grabbing fistfuls of her blonde curls and gritting her teeth with a growl of anger.

Ray walked over to the gun and picked it up, then he and Cormac shared a look before eying the end of the road.

'We won't catch up; he's too far ahead,' Ray said, reluctantly turning back to Lily. 'He's younger and faster than us, and he knows it.'

'Speak for yourself,' came a growl from behind them.

Lily turned just as Cillian grabbed the gun from Ray's hand.

'Hey!' Ray cried, taken by surprise.

'He killed my wife,' Cillian said, his voice shaking with fury and pain as he set off at a run. 'And I'm going to make him pay for it.'

'Cillian, *wait!*' Ray tried to run after him but stopped after a few paces, throwing his hands up in the air. '*Shit!*' He ran a hand back through his dark hair and turned to Lily. 'Where's he going? Where would they go?'

Scarlet ran over, Connor hot on her heels with a bottle of water in his hand.

'What happened?' he asked, staring after Cillian. 'What's he doing?' He glanced back at Billie, and his face paled. 'Oh God, no...'

'He's gone after Luca,' Lily said. '*Quickly*, go catch him! He shouldn't be alone; he ain't thinking straight. They went that way.' She pointed to where Cillian had just disappeared around the corner.

Connor shoved the bottle into her hand and immediately set off after him.

As Lily watched the second of her sons disappear, dread settled into her heart. Cillian wasn't in his right mind, and he was armed with a gun. There were too many ways this combination could end badly.

She turned back to Billie, her heart breaking a little bit more at the sight of her still body and ashen skin. Cath cradled Billie's head in her lap and, as she looked up at Lily miserably, she held something out. Lily took the antique hair slide and looked down at the blood smeared across the pearls. This wasn't how today was supposed to end. This wasn't how *any* of it was supposed to go.

Sirens finally wailed somewhere in the distance, and she sagged, the sound almost her undoing. They were too late now. They'd all been too late. Too late dealing with the Romanos, too late jumping in front of the bullet, too late answering the phone.

She looked up, her gaze searching for Freddie, and found him already watching her, his expression grim. She studied his face, questions swirling around her head. How had this happened? How had Luca got out? She closed her fist around the hair slide and walked determinedly towards him. It was time for some answers.

FORTY-THREE

Lily sat at the kitchen table and stared out of the window, unseeing. Cath sat opposite, arms folded, her expression grave. They hadn't talked much in the two days since the awful events at Cillian's wedding. They hadn't done much of anything except search for Cillian and wait for news.

Connor had returned empty-handed not long after he'd set off. Cillian had disappeared by the time he'd turned the corner, leaving no clue as to which direction he'd gone. No one had been able to get hold of him since. He'd simply disappeared off the face of the earth.

Lily hadn't slept a wink. Every time she closed her eyes, the fear that Cillian's silence was because Luca had finished what he started forced them back open. She'd been everywhere searching for him. Him, Luca, *any* of them. But she'd found nothing.

Freddie had told her that Luca had broken loose first, and that he'd then released the others. All the zip ties that had held them to the chairs had been snapped except one. The one that had strapped Luca's left hand. She'd known then how he'd got out. Cillian had been securing that hand back in the barn when

Luca had baited him into losing his temper. It was the oldest trick in the book. Luca had balled his fist as it was tightened, after ensuring Cillian was too distracted to notice, then waited until the time was right to slip his hand out and work himself free.

She guessed he'd only waited until the next morning so that the morphine was out of Riccardo's system. Luca had never been one to do things alone, always hiding behind his brother even before the twins had stripped him of his credibility. Which opened the question of where Riccardo was now. And Mani too, for that matter.

The calls Freddie had been receiving throughout the ceremony were from one of the dockhands. He was nothing to do with any of this, which was why Freddie hadn't thought the calls urgent. But he'd found the guard Freddie had left outside the container unconscious on the ground and immediately called him. Luckily, although generally straight, he was on the Tyler payroll to turn a blind eye to smuggled shipments. It appeared the Romanos had hit the guard over the head with a rock.

Freddie had admitted to her then that he hadn't thought any more than one guard was necessary, under the circumstances. The three men had been blindfolded, gagged and securely bound. It *should* have been a simple babysitting job, the guard there, mainly, to keep people from going *in* and stumbling across the bound men. By the time Freddie had learned what had happened, it had been too late.

Lily had accepted the explanation without question, realising, after hearing about the ties, that the blame lay with them. She didn't tell Freddie. She didn't tell anyone. In time, Cillian might realise it himself, but she hoped he didn't, and she certainly wasn't going to tell him. It would kill him, knowing that the person who'd set off this catastrophic chain of events was himself.

Freddie hadn't pressed the subject of who was to blame, simply telling her that however it had happened, he felt responsible. He should have left more men, he'd told her. And made sure the container was locked, not just bolted with the standard bolt that could be shifted from the inside. He and Paul had offered their help, promising to prioritise the search for Cillian and the Romanos until they were found. And they'd been true to their word, setting their men to task and personally spreading the word that anyone found helping the Romanos would be seen as an enemy of their firm, and that anyone who came forward with information would be rewarded.

The Logans and Ray's firm had also scoured the city, everyone pulling together, united in this, if not in other things. But as the hours and days carried on with no word, Lily's hope that they'd find Cillian alive was fading. How could he be alive? He had no phone, no wallet; he hadn't been home. And a small part of her couldn't help but wonder whether he'd decided to end things himself, whether he'd made the decision not to carry on without Billie. *That* thought terrified her the most.

Scarlet's low voice wafted through from the hall as she ended a call, then she appeared, rubbing her head tiredly, and hovered beside them for a moment.

'They need someone to go down, sort Billie's things,' she said, looking away. 'I'll go.'

'No.' Lily shook her head, ignoring the banging ache that now seemed to permanently reside there. 'It should be me.'

Her mind replayed the heartfelt words Billie had said to her before the wedding. The girl had been so grateful just to be there, to be part of their family. She'd been so excited for her future. Lily closed her eyes as a wave of grief washed over her, then she forced them back open with a deep sigh and stood up.

The front door creaked open, and her head swivelled towards it in hope. Ray walked in first, followed by Connor and Benny, who walked over to Scarlet and pulled her into his arms, kissing her forehead. Lily's eyes hovered in the empty space behind them for a moment.

'I'm sorry, Lil,' Ray said. 'No news.'

She nodded, looking away to hide her disappointment. 'I need to go,' she said flatly. Picking up her bag she paused to look at Connor. 'You're exhausted,' she said. 'Go upstairs and lie down for a bit.'

He shook his head. 'Nah, I'm heading back out. I just need a coffee.'

'I'll make you one,' Cath said, grasping the chance to do something useful.

Lily walked into the hall, picked up her keys and continued out to her car. As she pressed the button and her Mercedes bleeped back, the door reopened behind her.

'Lil, wait up a minute.'

She closed her eyes, feeling her heart drop at the sound of Ray's voice. She didn't have the energy for this. She didn't have the energy for *anything*, but least of all this. Pulling in a deep breath, she reached for the car door and tugged it open.

'Hey.' Ray caught up with her and pushed it shut again with a frown. 'Why are you avoiding me?' he demanded.

She sighed, irritated. 'Get out of my way, Ray.'

'*No*,' he retorted stubbornly. 'I won't.'

Lily stepped back and pursed her lips, raising her eyebrows coldly, then folded her arms and waited. Ray shook his head at her, clearly annoyed.

'What are you doing?' he asked.

'Trying to get in my car,' she replied flatly.

He gave her a withering look. 'What are you doing *to me*?' he clarified.

'Nothing, Ray,' she replied. 'I'm not doing anything to you. The same way you're not doing anything to me – right *now*. But that will change, won't it? When we find *him*, and *them*, and this is all over. Then we'll go back to being enemies again. And this little truce will be forgotten. So what's the point in pretend-ing, hm?' She pulled a shrug-like expression. 'There *is* no point, Ray. And I can't *do* that. I can't sit around and act like we're on the same side when we're not. You're here because you want Cillian found. *I* want Cillian found. We've put our differences on hold because of that temporary common ground so we can work together towards an outcome we both want, nothing more.'

'*Nothing more?*' he repeated, raising his eyebrows coldly. 'You and I have *always* been *more*, Lil. More of everything.' He blew a long breath out through his nose and leaned back on her car, looking away for a moment.

Lily stifled a sigh. She couldn't do this dance with him, not now. She'd loved Ray for thirty years, and every time they came to blows, it killed a small part of her. She'd weathered the heartache before, and she'd always made sure she was strong enough to withstand it. But this time she was too tired to put on a brave face. This time, for the first time, she felt like she might finally break if she let him in only to have to let him go again. So it was easier to just keep her distance and not set herself up for that fall. It was safer.

'When I found out you'd given that contract to the Tylers, I was furious,' Ray said, staring off into the distance behind her with a sombre frown.

'I can't hear this right now, Ray,' she replied, shaking her head.

'You *need* to hear this, Lil,' he replied, turning his deep blue eyes to meet hers. 'So please, just let me speak.'

Lily sighed and waited, knowing she had little choice.

'I was furious,' he repeated, his tone oddly calm. 'Not furious because I thought the right was mine, but furious because I knew you'd done it to hurt me. And it *did*,' he added. 'I can't lie. That contract's a gold mine, and you know it.'

She shrugged with a look of stubborn disinterest, and he shook his head.

'I was ready to have it out with you that day. I was ready to go tooth and nail, and I realised last night, it was because *anything* with you is better than nothing with you,' he continued. 'I'd rather fight with you than not have you in my life, Lil. So if that's what you want, then fine. Fight me. I'll fight you back, and we'll batter the shit out of each other until there's nothing left of us.' He stared at her now, the raw honesty written there in his eyes. 'But I don't think that's really what you want.'

Lily stared back at him, wanting to tear herself away but lacking the strength to do it. Hope and longing for him fought her natural sense of self-preservation and won, her mask falling away and revealing all the misery she felt beneath.

'*I* don't want to do this anymore, Lil,' Ray said, looking back at her sadly. 'What's the point?' He squinted over her shoulder. 'We've wasted so much time.'

Alarms began to clang around inside her core, knotting into the confused mass of emotions she was already barely keeping hold of. They rose now, like a tidal wave threatening to spill over, and she swallowed, not sure what to say. Not sure exactly what *Ray* was saying. Was he saying *goodbye*? Was he cutting ties with her for good? The thought instantly filled her with dread. She'd hated him lately; of *course* she had. But it was never really over between them. Or at least it never had been up to now. Maybe she'd finally pushed him over the edge. The thought left a hollow pain in her chest. She swallowed again, determined to see this out with strength, even if she had to fake it.

'Right. So you're saying goodbye,' she confirmed with a slow nod. She looked at the car, not trusting herself to hold it together if she looked directly at him. 'Well, you've got your message across loud and clear, Ray. You can go now.' She lifted her chin and clamped her jaw to stop the wobble threatening to give her away.

'*What?*' Ray frowned at her. 'Of course I'm not!'

Lily risked a quick glance at his face, but even this was too much. To her embarrassment, tears began to fall down her cheeks, and her chest began to heave erratically.

'Oh, Lil, for fuck's sake, come here,' he said, opening his arms.

'I'm not crying over *you*,' she snapped angrily, the words a complete lie. 'I'm just exhausted, and my son is missing, and Billie...' A sob escaped, and she clamped a hand over her mouth, horrified to discover she had absolutely no control over this anymore.

Ray grabbed her and pulled her into his arms. She fought him fiercely for a moment, the reaction instinctual, but he held tight until she gave in, no strength left to fight him anymore. Not when he was really all she wanted. She closed her eyes and leaned on his broad muscular chest, breathing in his musky scent as the tears streamed out. They stayed there like that, Ray holding her as she cried, for a good ten minutes. Then, after her tears finally calmed and she gently pulled back, he ran a hand over her curls and looked into her eyes with a serious expression.

'You know, the other day reminded me that nothing in life is guaranteed,' he said quietly. 'Not even tomorrow. I don't want to spend my last day fighting you. I *love* you, Lil. I don't care about that contract. It's just money. You're more important to me than anything. And I'll do or say or give up anything you want me to, if it makes you happy and it means we're OK.' He lifted a shoulder in a half shrug. 'Family is all that matters in this life. And *you're* my family, Lil. You always have been.' He moved his gaze around her face. 'And if you'll stop fucking *fighting* me, I'll be whatever you need. Because whether you believe it or not, I'm on your side. You don't need to keep fighting the world on your own. I mean, I know you *can*,' he added with a small grin, 'but you don't *have* to. Let me in, Lil. Because I'm so tired of beating down the door.'

Lily's eyes swam with tears again, and she wiped them away. It was terrifying for her, to consider trusting Ray enough to lean on him. But she could see he truly meant what he'd said. He was opening himself up and begging her to let him in, and she knew she owed it to him – and to herself – to at least try. She nodded.

'I'll try,' she said shakily. 'I will; I'll try.'

'That's good enough for me.' Ray pulled her to him and placed his forehead on hers. 'I'm going back out to continue the search. But when I come back, I'm staying here tonight.'

'I'm not really sleeping—' she began, but he cut her off.

'Exactly. Maybe tonight you will.' He kissed her forehead then walked off towards his car.

Watching him go, she then turned and slipped into her own car. Time stopped for no one, and there was somewhere she needed to be.

As she switched on the ignition, she caught her own eyes in the mirror and paused. For the first time in her life, the darkness there scared her. The haunted woman looking back wasn't someone she knew anymore. Wasn't someone she could predict. And there was something else in those dark depths. Something that told her just how close this stranger in the mirror was to becoming totally and dangerously unhinged.

As she backed out of the drive, she silently prayed that Ray came back to her with news of their son soon. Because if he didn't, she really didn't know what she was going to do.

FORTY-FOUR

Mani peered through the bushes at the house across the road. He was so close, but he was also aware that the Drews and the Logans would know he'd come here eventually. They could have people watching, waiting. He'd stood in this bush deliberating for half an hour, growing cold as the damp seeped into his bones. There hadn't been any movement on the road. No one sat in a car, no one, he didn't think, peeping out from a neighbour's window. It was as safe now as it was ever going to be. And even if he was wrong, what choice did he have?

They had no money, no resources that they could access and nowhere to go, other than the old garage they were hiding in. Their secret last resort that no one knew of but the immediate family. A place he now wished he'd kitted out with more thought.

The garage was in the middle of a row of garages. All it had inside was a mattress, a hoodie, a bucket, a crate of bottled water and a rucksack of snacks with long sell-by dates, most of which were now gone after two days of waiting there for Luca to return.

When Luca had broken them out of the container, Mani had urged him to reconsider. He didn't want to leave any more than Luca did, but he was smart enough to know that they'd been beaten. Their only chance at life was on the other side of the Channel now. But Luca wouldn't hear of it, his rage overtaking all sensibilities and Riccardo echoing the sentiment. Mani had been left with no choice but to go along with his sons. He couldn't exactly leave them alone. They were idiots, but they were *his* idiots. He had to try to protect them, even if that meant damning himself

Of course, that was the reason they were in this mess in the first place, and not for the first time, Mani wondered if life might just be better if he didn't feel so much responsibility towards his useless children. But there was no point in wondering. He did. And so he was here.

Peering down the road one last time, Mani grimaced and pulled the hood of his hoodie as far as it would go over his face. He hobbled out of his hiding place and rushed as fast as his legs would go to the large house across the street. His heart hammered in his chest, and he grew breathless as he made the short journey, his eyes wide and darting all over, sure he was about to be jumped and dragged away.

But no hands grabbed him. No shouts or pounding footsteps sounded, and soon enough he was at the front door, sweat dripping from his puffy red face. Glancing anxiously back over his shoulder, he rang the doorbell and leaned on the frame as he tried to catch his breath.

The door opened, and he hurried inside, almost knocking Maria over in his haste. He slammed the door shut then looked around for his nephews.

'Maria, go and get your brothers. *Quickly*,' he urged, flapping his hands at her in a shooing motion. '*Now*, Maria.'

She took in his dishevelled appearance, and her eyebrows

rose in surprise. 'Of course, Uncle. Why don't you wait in the library?'

'Eh.' He grunted in relief and nodded, then made his way there to wait.

Reaching the desk, he wiped the sweat from his head with one of the tissues from the dispenser there. Alex and Antonio arrived just seconds later as he eased himself into a chair.

Mani heaved a great sigh of relief at the sight of them. 'Thank God you're in.'

They walked over but didn't sit down, instead placing their hands in their pockets and standing a little distance away, looking oddly subdued.

'What's wrong?' Mani asked, his gaze moving from one to the other. 'Will you not sit?'

'What is it that you want, Uncle?' Alex asked, scratching his upper lip with a tense frown.

'Your cousins and I are in trouble. Your aunt too,' he told them. 'Riccardo has done some... some bad things. The Logans, the ones I spoke to you about, they and the Drews somehow got proof. The sort of proof that could put him away forever. They tried to ship us off to Europe, told us to start again there with nothing, or they would send the proof to the police.' Mani closed his eyes, cursing the two firms for the thousandth time. 'I had no choice; we had to agree.'

Alex nodded. 'OK. So how are you here?'

'They had us tied up. Luca managed to get free and released me and Riccardo. He wouldn't listen to reason, even despite his brother's state.' He saw the men frown. 'Riccardo is injured. They hurt him. Badly. I had to go along, try to keep them safe. I led them to a safe house of sorts, but when we got there, Luca stormed off with a gun, said he would kill them all and end our troubles.'

He grabbed another tissue and patted his head. The gun

had been in the garage too, Luca seizing it as soon as he'd seen the weapon.

'That was two days ago.' He looked up at the two men, genuine worry on his face. 'I risked a walk to a newsagent, saw news of the shooting on the TV. He shot Cillian Drew's new wife. The news says he left the scene and hasn't been found, but he hasn't come back either.' He could see by the lack of reaction on their faces that this wasn't new information. 'I need your help finding Luca. And we have no money or food. And Riccardo is in a bad way; he's burning up with fever. He needs a doctor, but I can't risk a hospital. If I could bring him here—'

'No.' Alex cut him off. 'No, I'm sorry, Uncle, but that is not possible.'

'*What?*' Mani's face darkened. 'What are you talking about? This is your *family*, your *cousin*. I am your uncle.'

'Yes, you're family. You're my mother's kin,' Alex replied. 'But these aren't family affairs; these are your firm's issues with other firms. Other firms you've pissed off by your underhand actions over the years.' He looked down at Mani with an expression of regret and disapproval. 'You went against our ways, so you're owed no protection. And I can't put my firm at risk by standing with you. I'm sorry.'

'You're turning me *away*?' Mani asked, astonished. 'You can't! I am your *blood*!'

'*You* are a liability,' Alex said strongly. 'And you need to leave. Word has gone around that anyone helping you is declaring themselves against the Tylers. I don't need that kind of attention here. I can't *afford* it either.'

Mani's jaw dropped, and he turned his gaze to his other nephew beseechingly. 'Antonio?'

Antonio shook his head. 'You did this to yourself.'

'I don't believe this,' Mani said faintly. 'I don't believe this. Where is your mother?' He moved towards the door. 'Elena?' he called out loudly.

'She's out,' Alex told him. 'But even if she were in, she's already agreed to this.'

Mani held his gaze for a moment, horrified. This had been his last resort, his only hope of getting help, of maybe pulling himself out of this mess.

Antonio walked over to the desk and opened a drawer, pulling out a thick envelope. He held it out to Mani.

'This is for you. It's enough to help you get away from here. We're taking a risk even giving you this, but like you said, you are blood.' He acknowledged this with a tilt of his head. 'So take it.'

Mani glared at his nephew, infuriated and devastated by the betrayal in his darkest time of need. He wanted to throw the money back in his stupid, self-righteous face, but he couldn't afford to. Instead, he snatched it from Alex roughly, glaring for a moment more before he turned and stormed out of the room. Maria stood down the hall, leaning on the wall, watching him silently. He glared at her too as he passed, knowing she'd heard every word, and then, without pause, he left the house. There was nothing here for him now.

He made it part way down the drive before he heard his niece call out. 'Uncle?'

He paused and looked back, a small hope reigniting. He'd never liked Maria, but she was still his niece. Perhaps her emotional female softness would prove useful for once. Perhaps she'd taken pity on him. That was something he could use. Something he could manipulate. It was why women were no good at business; they were too easily manipulated, letting their feelings override logic. He turned on a small smile for her, ready to play up to her supple emotions.

Maria smiled back as she reached him, a touch of warmth there, and his hope rose further. 'I couldn't let you go without saying a proper goodbye,' she said.

'Ahh, Maria,' he crooned sadly. 'I will truly miss you. We

may not have always seen eye to eye, but you always held a special place in my heart. It's that fire of yours.' He faked a chuckle. 'You remind me of my own mother, you know. Back when she was young.' He paused for effect then sighed. 'It is right that I should tell you that now.' He cast his eyes down. 'I don't think I will get the chance again.'

Maria put her hand to her chest, her warm smile softening. 'Ahh, Uncle, thank you. And I guess you're right,' she added. 'Now *is* the time to say all the things we need to say.'

She pulled him into a hug, and he froze. It was unexpected, but he quickly played along, squeezing her back and making a sound as though he found the action sweet.

'That's why I need to tell you now,' she said, putting her mouth to his ear and lowering her voice to a whisper. 'It was *me* who told the Logans where you hid the body.'

Mani gasped, and Maria pulled back, her red lips curling into a wide, triumphant smile, all warmth gone. Her eyes danced coldly as she watched him.

'I've waited a long time to see that look on your face, Uncle,' she said. 'And it was so worth the wait.'

'*Why?*' he asked. '*How?*' His mind reeled.

'I used to visit Great-Aunt Giulia when she was alive. I always felt sorry for her, stuck there all alone. She was lovely, always up for a chat,' Maria told him. 'Towards the end, she was agitated though. She knew she was dying and kept worrying about what people might find there after she was gone. She told me about the body and what you'd done. Asked me to help protect your secret.' She laughed now, amused.

'You're crazy,' he breathed.

'Crazy? No.' She shook her head. 'Angry? Yes.' She stared at him, naked contempt in her eyes. 'I've spent years being spoken down to and belittled by you, being treated like some house-maid in my *own home* when you visit, despite the fact I've been running this business alongside my brothers for years. A business far bigger and greater than yours.'

She stepped forward, and he took a step back, shocked by the look on her face. 'I've watched you cheat and lie your way through this game, losing the respect of every single firm around you, and yet still you walk around treating everyone like the muck on your shoe. You're a *joke*, Mani. One that everyone tired of a long time ago. *But*,' she said, tilting her head and pointing her finger at him, 'you're a dangerous one. You plot and scheme, and some of your dirty plays really do work. So I knew I had to go after you in the same way you go after everyone else. Behind your back. With smoke and mirrors; with *lies*.'

She stepped back, her face cold and composed, and Mani finally realised that he had greatly, *greatly* underestimated her.

'All I had to do was remove that one little stumbling block then sit back and wait for the Logans to bring you down. The Drews' involvement was an unexpected treat, and the *Tylers* making it their business was the absolute icing on the cake. I don't know *what* you did to piss them off so much, but it must have been bad. They shut you out of the underworld like that.' She snapped her fingers and pulled a look of amazement.

'You evil little bitch,' Mani hissed. 'How could you do this to me? To your cousins?'

'Easily,' she replied, not missing a beat. 'The pair of them are even worse than *you*.' She eyed him hard, and he saw the anger and disgust there.

She knew, he realised. She knew about Riccardo. Shame swept up his neck and into his face.

'And what about your aunt?' he asked, in one last feeble attempt to gain her sympathy.

'The Drews and the Logans are not like you,' Maria replied. 'They actually have scruples. They follow the code. She's a civilian, not part of the firm; they'll let her go once you're dead.'

He winced, and she stared into his eyes coldly. 'Goodbye,

Mani. This is the end of the line for you. You have nowhere to go, no one left to turn to and that cash won't last you long.' She swept her gaze over him one last time, then turned around and walked back to the house. 'Enjoy what little time you've got left.'

FORTY-FIVE

Connor stared at a greying piece of Blu-Tack on the wall of the truckers' café as he waited for Scarlet to return with the coffee. She placed a polystyrene cup in front of him, and he murmured his thanks as she sat down in the grubby plastic seat beside his. She stifled a yawn. They'd been out all night, their last stop being the depot for the second time. Not that Connor had expected him to be there. Cillian had no car; he wouldn't have been able to get this far. Not without help anyway. But who would have helped him without reporting back to them that he was safe?

'Where next?' Scarlet asked, rubbing the sleep from her eye determinedly and taking a sip of her coffee. She immediately grimaced and put it down.

Connor eyed his own cup and took a cautious sip. It was even worse than he'd expected, but he forced it down anyway.

'I honestly don't know,' he said, stressed. 'We've tried everywhere.'

Scarlet sighed and sat back. 'Fuck's sake. It's like all those times...' she trailed off and bit her lip.

Connor followed her train of thought. 'Like all those times

we went looking for Ruby,' he finished. 'It's OK, you can say it. It *is* a bit.'

Scarlet glanced at him. 'Sorry. I didn't mean to bring her up.'

'It's OK.'

As he said the words, Connor suddenly realised he meant them. He would never love that Scarlet had known about Ruby's death and had kept it from them, or that *he* now had to carry around that secret too. But he'd always understood why she'd covered it up the way she had. And now, with all that was currently going on, that whole situation didn't seem as big and all-consuming as it had before.

Since he'd found out Scarlet's secret, it had dominated his thoughts and flooded him with guilt every time he'd seen his mother or brother. He'd been unable to overcome it. But suddenly it seemed almost small. Suddenly, it wasn't some dark, gigantic weight slowly crushing him. Suddenly, when measured up against all they were now going through, it was just another piece of the past.

Now, all of that paled into insignificance next to his fear that they wouldn't find Cillian. Or that they'd find him dead. Connor couldn't fathom a world where his twin didn't exist. Finding him was all that mattered now, the past no longer important. He'd loved Ruby, but she was dead, and nothing could change that. It was time to move on. To remember the good times and focus everything else on the living. The events of the last few days had really put that into perspective.

'Ruby was always the master chameleon,' he said with a small smile, Scarlet's comment jogging some older memories of his sister. 'She'd share her hideouts with us sometimes, in the early days. We used to joke that if we ever needed to disappear —' He sat up abruptly.

'What?' Scarlet sat up too, searching his face. 'What would you do? Do you know where he is?'

'I think I do.' He stood up. 'Come on. Leave that.' He pushed away the coffee she'd been about to grab. 'He has to be there. He *has* to be.'

* * *

Twenty minutes later, they parked up in a quiet industrial road not far from Lily's house. It was a dead end, the two buildings each side fenced off with warning signs to keep out. Scarlet eyed them warily, stepping over the debris that littered the edges of the road.

'Where are we going?' she asked.

Connor walked to the corner of one of the fences, moving a panel to one side, revealing a gap just big enough to get through. He gestured for her to go through, and she reluctantly did, bending down to fit. He followed and silently led the way down the inner side of the fence for a few metres. Broken pieces of furniture and piles of rubbish littered the fenced-in space between the road and the building ahead, with its dirt-blackened walls and smashed-in windows.

'Are we going in there?' she asked, looking up at it.

'Keep your voice down,' Connor whispered, glancing up at the jagged-edged holes. 'And no, we're not.'

Scarlet fell silent, glancing up at the same place Connor had, wondering what was in there. Several metres down, Connor stopped and knocked on the side fence. He walked on slowly, knocking every step until the sound changed, then reached over the top, moving the panel aside.

Scarlet didn't wait this time, darting through to whatever was on the other side. She looked around as she straightened up and found herself at the end of a very large overgrown garden. Connor followed her through, pausing to replace the panel and refix the pin at the top that held it shut.

He overtook her, and they moved in silence through the bushes and weeds, and it wasn't until they were right next to the old brick building that Scarlet realised it wasn't just another weed-covered mound. The greenery had almost entirely engulfed it, but unlike the last building, this one still had glass at the windows.

'What is this place?' she whispered.

'A place Ruby found as a teenager,' he whispered back, peering in one of the windows. 'We put that pin lock on it so no one else would find it. It was actually the one place she never came to do drugs. I think she wanted to keep just one place of hers clean, you know?' He shrugged. 'Or not. I don't know. Maybe she just forgot about it.'

Scarlet smiled sadly. 'I doubt she forgot it,' she said, looking up at the building.

Connor picked his way through the brambles to the next window and peered into that one, drawing back quickly and spinning round. 'It's him!' he exclaimed quietly.

His expression was filled with relief, and Scarlet sagged as the same feeling flooded through her.

'Oh thank God,' she muttered. 'What's he *doing*?'

She made to join him, but Connor urged her back, moving away from the window. 'Come this way.' He led her towards the other end of the building to a door, wedged half open and covered with ivy, that wound through to the inside.

As they crept into the dark space beyond, Scarlet heard whimpers and cries of pain. She tensed, alarmed, but quickly realised the voice didn't belong to her cousin. She strained to see ahead, but the building was bigger than she'd thought from the outside, leading off in a wide T shape.

'*Pleeease...*' The long shakily drawn-out word trailed off into pitiful sobs. 'No more, *please*. I beg you.'

'I don't want you to beg,' snarled Cillian, his voice oddly low and slow. 'I want you to *suffer*.'

'I *have*,' came the reply from the voice Scarlet now realised was Luca's.

She felt a spark of satisfaction. He *should* suffer for what he'd done. But she was more concerned about Cillian, and she followed Connor across the large empty room to the corner that led off out of sight.

'It's not enough,' Cillian told him. 'It will *never* be enough.'

They turned the corner, and finally Cillian and Luca came into view. Connor stopped dead, and Scarlet's mouth dropped open in shock. Cillian turned towards them and blinked blearily, taking a moment to recognise them.

He wore just a vest that was now filthy above his suit trousers. His hair was all over the place, and his eyes were so puffy they barely still opened, caused by a mixture, Scarlet guessed, of no sleep, tears of grief and the large amount of alcohol he appeared to have consumed. He swayed drunkenly, Luca's gun in one hand and an almost empty bottle of whisky in the other.

'You remembered,' he said eventually, looking at Connor.

Connor nodded and walked forward slowly. 'Of course I did,' he replied. 'I'm sorry it took me so long.'

Scarlet stayed in step with Connor, stopping as he did when Cillian chuckled bitterly.

'I had a bet with myself that you wouldn't remember at *all*,' he said, spitting the words and swaying again, throwing his hands around wildly.

Scarlet eyed the gun, noticing it was cocked, and she stopped Connor with her hand as he tried to move on. He glanced at her, and she tilted her chin towards the gun.

'Well, I did,' he replied, looking at it grimly. 'Why don't you put that down for a minute, eh? You've got the bloody thing triggered.'

'I know I do,' Cillian replied. 'Whassamatter, you worried I'll shoot you?' His face crumpled up into one of withering disdain. 'You're my *brother*, Connor. You might be a fucking traitor; you might have left me here alone to deal with fucking *everything* – oops, no, sorry...'

He stumbled and almost fell, and Scarlet braced herself for the gun to go off, but somehow he righted himself.

'You left me *and* Scarlet to deal with everything.' He nodded and burped. 'But you're still my brother. I'd never hurt you. I can't believe you'd even think that.' He frowned and lifted the bottle of whisky to his mouth, tipping his head back to take a deep swig.

Scarlet and Connor moved forward as he waved the gun dangerously close to the wall, and she winced.

'Cillian please,' she begged softly. 'You're drunk; it's not safe.'

'And yet I'm not drunk *enough*,' he said, letting the last word out in a loud roar as he turned and threw the bottle of whisky against the back wall.

Luca cowered underneath, sobbing as bits of broken glass rained down over him. 'Please,' he begged. 'Help me.'

Scarlet looked at him properly, the sight making her feel a little ill. He was bound by old pieces of rope to a rusting metal bedframe pushed upright against the wall. Stripped to his underwear, she could see that his entire body was beaten and bruised. Cuts and burns criss-crossed his torso and limbs, some still bleeding, others not so fresh. His swollen face was barely recognisable, with his front teeth missing and his nose so flat it couldn't even really be classed as a nose anymore. His bound hands were both twisted at odd angles, and each finger had been broken.

Even despite what he'd done, and though she was glad he'd suffered for it, Scarlet felt a sliver of pity for the man. He'd endured three days of this torture.

'Cillian,' she said gently. 'You need to end this now and

come home.' She looked at him, silently begging him to hear her.

'*End* it?' he repeated, confused. 'No!' He frowned and pulled away from her, then began to laugh, the odd sound turning swiftly into tears. 'No,' he repeated, all of his pain coming through in that one word.

Tears welled up in Scarlet's eyes as her heart broke for her cousin. 'I know you're hurting, and you have every reason for that,' she said, stepping closer. 'But you need to know—'

'*No!*' he cried, cutting her off angrily. 'I don't want to hear it. I want you to *leave*. Go away, pretend you didn't find me. I'm not moving an inch; I'm staying right here, and I'm going to draw out the evil cunt's life for as long as I can,' he yelled, tears streaming down his face. 'And then...' He shook his head, looking upwards with the saddest expression Scarlet had ever seen.

'And then *what?*' Connor demanded hotly, walking over to him, no longer taking the caution to move slowly.

'*Back off,*' Cillian yelled.

Scarlet tensed, terrified that he'd turn the gun on Connor in this state, but he didn't. Connor stopped in front of him, and she quickly ran forward too, hesitantly placing her hand on Cillian's arm.

'No,' Connor said firmly. 'Not now, not *ever*, Cillian. Where *you* go, *I* go, remember? I shouldn't have left you. I'm sorry. I'm so sorry.'

Cillian suddenly seemed to disintegrate before their eyes, and he turned his head into Scarlet, almost falling into her arms. She steadied him and pulled him to her, looking over his sobbing head at Connor. Taking the opportunity to grab the gun while he was vulnerable, she prised his hand open, whispering comforting shushing noises to him.

'Shh, it's OK, shh, shh, shhhh. You're OK; I've got you.' She hugged him tightly, wishing she could take away his pain.

With the gun firmly in her grip, she nodded to Connor to take Cillian from her and moved back to safely disarm it.

Cillian suddenly seemed to realise what she was doing and pushed away from his brother, following Scarlet and nearly tripping over.

'No, don't!' he begged her. 'He killed them, Scarlet. He killed my Billie and Lily Rose.' His handsome face twisted up in pain. 'My family...'

'No,' she said quickly, realising suddenly that he didn't know what had happened after he'd disappeared. 'Lily Rose, yes, I'm so sorry,' she said gently. 'She's gone. But Billie's alive.'

'*What?*' He looked at her in horror. 'No... Why would you do that to me? Why would you *say* that? I watched her *die*, Scarlet; I was holding her in my arms for God's sake.' His anger was growing again, and Scarlet stepped back as he got right up in her face.

'She survived, Cillian.' Connor pulled him back.

Cillian yanked himself away roughly, but Connor just moved with him and grabbed him by the shoulders.

'Cillian, *look* at me,' he yelled. 'Look in my eyes. You *know* when I'm telling you the truth, and I *am.*'

Cillian stopped struggling, and Connor put his hands to the sides of his brother's head

'Billie survived. She's in the hospital. She's there and she *needs* you, mate. She needs her husband. She's in there grieving for your baby all on her own and worrying herself sick about you.'

Cillian's face opened up in shock as he finally accepted that they were telling him the truth. His bloodshot eyes moved over towards the direction of the door.

'You need to go to her,' Connor said.

'I need to go to her,' Cillian echoed.

'We need to get you sorted out though first. You can't turn

up to the hospital like that,' Connor continued, looking him up and down. 'Come on – let's get you cleaned up.'

'I'm fine,' Cillian argued.

'You're *not*,' Connor said firmly.

Cillian broke down in tears again, this time slumping onto Connor as he quietly sobbed. Connor looked over at Luca, then to Cillian, clearly trying to work out how to juggle both issues.

'I'll sort this,' Scarlet said quickly.

Connor glanced over to her with a look of uncertainty.

'Seriously, I'll take care of it. It's the least I can do,' she said, holding his gaze. They both knew what she was referring to, and it wasn't anything to do with Cillian.

He nodded. 'OK. Follow me out to the car though and come back with a crew. It ain't safe here alone.'

Scarlet laughed under her breath, amused. 'I'm the one with the gun, Connor,' she reminded him.

'True,' he conceded. 'But still.' He started walking Cillian out, glancing back at Luca. 'Finish this now and come back later to clean up. It'll be easier.'

Scarlet waited until the brothers had crossed the large space and disappeared before she turned back to the snivelling, broken wreck behind her.

'Please,' he whimpered. 'I need a hospital.'

Scarlet let out a sharp note of amusement. 'You think I'm here to *help* you?' She hitched an eyebrow, walking over to him with purpose and staring down at him in disgust. 'This isn't for you,' she said coldly. 'This is so my cousin can move on.'

Luca's whimpers turned into weak sobs.

'I'll end your pain but not out of kindness. I'll return later with people who hate you almost as much as we do. We'll pull your body down with *no* care, we'll talk about how much you deserved this and then we'll bury you somewhere no one will ever find you. You'll have no grave, no funeral, no casket. You'll just become worm food and the pathetic butt of yet another joke,' she added scathingly, 'until people forget you ever existed.'

She stepped closer to him, her hard stare full of hate. 'And *that's* what you get when you shoot a pregnant woman on her wedding day. For killing an innocent child before she's even drawn her first breath.' She lifted the gun to his head and cocked it. 'For killing a member of my *family*.'

She squeezed the trigger and shot him dead, then turned around and walked away without looking back.

FORTY-SIX

Lily put down the phone and cried tears of joy, not caring who saw her as she pulled up in the busy Soho side street. Parking on a double yellow line, she ignored the angry yell from a passing cyclist. The Tylers owned all the beat bobbies around these parts, and ticket wardens knew to steer clear. After stemming her sobs and taking a few moments to compose herself, she got out and knocked on the plain black door beside her. It was opened after a few seconds by a beautiful woman with long red hair who instantly grasped Lily's arm with a look of concern.

'Is there any news?' She pulled Lily inside and shut the door, ushering her up the stairs.

'Yes actually,' Lily said brightly, walking into the large empty bar on the next floor. 'They found him. He'd got Luca, put him through it from what I hear, but I haven't heard details yet.'

'*Damn* right,' Tanya said wholeheartedly as she slipped behind the oval bar in the centre of the room. 'He deserves everything he gets after what he did.' She shook her head sadly. 'That poor girl. To lose your baby that way – and on her wedding day...' She pursed her lips as she poured out three glasses of wine. 'How's she holding up?'

'Not great,' Lily admitted.

She glanced around at the many doors that led off this main room. It was a high whorehouse, and right now Liana, Mani's wife, was being kept in one of the rooms. It had been the only place Freddie could think of that was comfortable yet secure.

'She's in there,' Tanya said, reading her thoughts. She pointed to one at the end. 'We thought it would be quieter.' She pulled a face that revealed that it probably wasn't. 'Here.' She handed two of the glasses to Lily. 'She likes a tipple that one. Even if she's in a mood.'

'Thanks.' Lily took the glasses. 'Is it locked?'

Tanya shook her head. 'She won't come out. Tried once, realised she couldn't leave and what happens here, then ran back in. Hasn't dared budge since.'

Lily grinned then walked over to the room, pausing to knock before she entered.

'Go away,' came the curt response.

Neutralising her expression, Lily pushed open the door and walked inside. Liana sat in the corner of the room on a chair, her arms folded stubbornly across her middle. She looked surprised to see Lily but quickly tried to hide it. Her eyes darted to the glasses, lingering there for a moment, and Lily passed her one before sitting on the edge of the large bed opposite her. Liana took a sip of the wine, and Lily did the same, looking around the room with appreciation. The walls and ceiling were a midnight blue, gold accents highlighting the room all around.

'Nice room,' she said.

'Huh!' remarked Liana with a look of disgust. 'You know what they *do* here? How *dare* they put me here.'

'Would you prefer they tied you to a chair and left you in a container, like they did the rest of them?' she asked, lifting an eyebrow.

Liana narrowed her gaze. 'I would *prefer* that they did not *take* me at *all*,' she said, her Italian accent stronger now as her anger rose.

Lily nodded in acceptance. 'Fair enough. I'm going to keep this short. I know that you know why you're here, what the plan was, and why it's changed.'

'My boys escaped,' she replied with a triumphant gleam in her eye.

Lily nodded again. 'They did. But what they *also* did was piss off the Tylers, who've spread the word through the city that they're to be shut out. Even your own family have turned their back on them.' She watched Liana pale. 'They made some bad moves over the years; made too many enemies. They have nowhere to go now after Alex turned him away.'

'No, they wouldn't do that. You're lying,' she said nervously.

'It's the truth,' Lily replied calmly. 'They do a lot of business with the Tylers. They can't afford the fallout. And they never had much time for Mani. You know that.'

Liana touched her neck, her wide eyes darting all over Lily's face. Lily steeled herself for what she had to do next.

'You know Luca turned up at my son's wedding, don't you?' she asked.

Liana nodded.

'And you're aware that he shot my son's new wife, hospitalising her and killing their unborn daughter?' Something stuck at the back of her throat as she said it, her grief at losing her granddaughter before she'd even had a chance to meet her still raw.

Liana nodded again, looking away.

Lily pushed on, keeping her words simple. 'Cillian went after him, Liana. Luca's dead now.'

'What?' Liana cried, horrified.

Tears filled her eyes and spilled down her cheeks as she processed this news, and the wine glass in her hand fell to the floor. It smashed, the pieces of glass tinkling as they scattered all over the hard floor. '*No!*' she wailed, shaking her head. 'No, not my baby. Not my baby boy,' Liana moaned, biting her fist as the sound turned into a sob, and dropped her head into her hands.

Lily looked away. She wasn't sorry Luca was dead. She'd have killed him herself if she'd had the chance. But she knew Liana's pain all too well. Knew too that it would never pass.

'Riccardo is badly wounded and suffering greatly,' she said, moving on to the real reason she was here.

Liana's head snapped up as she realised what Lily was edging for, and she glared at her furiously. 'You think I'll tell you where they *are*?' she asked. 'Not on your life. Not *ever*. I would *never* betray my son. *Or* my husband.'

Lily watched her calmly, placing her wine glass down on the bedside table. 'They have no money, no car, no food, nowhere to go and no friends.' She paused to let it sink in. 'Half the city is out searching for them. Sooner or later we'll find them; it's simply a matter of time, and when we finally *do*, they'll likely be tortured and beaten for a long time.'

Liana looked horrified, and Lily leaned towards her. 'If you tell me where they are, I *promise* you that I'll make it quick and painless. It's too late for this to end any other way now, but you *can* make a difference to how they go.'

Liana's eyes refilled with tears, and she began to shake. 'I-I can't.'

'It's your choice. I won't force you,' Lily told her, sitting back. 'If it's a no, I'll return to the search and let nature take its course. But I want this *over*,' she said honestly. 'I'm *tired*, Liana. Aren't you?'

Liana's tears fell faster. 'And *me*? You'll make my death painless too?'

Lily frowned. '*Yours*? No. You'll be set free, as soon as this is over. I promise you.' She made a mental note to ask Finn to let Liana keep her house. It wasn't their home he was after; it was the businesses. And if the others were all gone, she would be no threat.

Liana closed her eyes, and Lily sat back, allowing her time to think it through. After a few minutes of silence though, Lily sighed and looked at her watch, standing up.

'I need to get back, so it's now or never, Liana.' Lily stared down at the woman. 'Do you want to help your family, or not?'

An hour later, Mani blinked as the roller door of the garage opened, and he held his hand up to shield his eyes against the sudden flood of sunlight.

'Who is it?' he called out anxiously. He kept blinking as his eyes adjusted then fell back against the mattress in relief as he realised it was just his wife. 'Ahh, Liana, it's *you*. How did you get away?'

'Mama?' a weak voice called out from behind him.

Mani moved aside to let Liana pass as she rushed forward.

'My boy, what have they *done*!' she cried, falling to her knees beside him and taking in his fevered appearance with horror. Her face crumpled, and she bent over to bury her head in his chest. 'I'm so sorry,' she wept. 'My boy, I'm so sorry.'

'For what?' Riccardo asked, his breathing laboured.

'Stop it, Liana,' Mani snapped. 'Pull yourself together for God's sake.'

Liana glared at him through her tears, then she turned away.

Lily watched, noting that there was no loving apology for *him*. She stepped out from the side, and as her shadow fell across Mani, he turned with a gasp. His eyes dropped to the gun in her hand then moved up to George and Andy behind her.

'Stand up, Mani,' she ordered.

He stared at her for a long moment then turned to Riccardo. His expression was bleak as he watched Liana stroke Riccardo's hair. She was sobbing quietly now, her head bent in defeat. He watched her for a moment more then nodded sadly, his expression resigned as he turned to face Lily.

He stood, stiffly rising to his feet using the wall to help him up. His usual air of self-importance was gone now, a tired old man standing where the devious fox she'd known used to be.

He met her eye. 'You'll make it quick?'

Lily nodded, more than happy to keep her word. Angry as she was for all he'd done, she had no wish to draw out his pain any longer than necessary. They'd won. It was over.

Mani nodded back. 'Send him on first,' he said, gesturing back to Riccardo.

'*No!*' Liana cried, staring up at Mani hatefully.

'Liana...' Mani tutted. 'Do you want the last thing he sees to be his father's death or his mother's loving face?' he asked her, lifting one thick bushy eyebrow.

Her bottom lip quivered, but her expression softened, and after a moment, she gave him one curt nod before looking back to her son. 'I love you, my boy,' she said brokenly.

Lily checked her silencer was on tight and walked into the small garage, wondering how Liana would feel if she knew what a monster her son really was. Not that she would ever tell her. All Liana would have now were her memories. It would be cruel to take those from her.

'Move back now, Liana,' Mani said quietly. 'Let the boy go.'

For a moment, Lily didn't think the woman was going to move, but reluctantly she pulled back, kissing his forehead one last time.

'Go find your brother,' she told him through her tears. 'I'll see you both soon.'

Lily pointed the gun at Riccardo's head and let off two shots in quick succession. He didn't try to move or struggle, too far gone from the infection that had clearly taken hold on his wounds to have the energy.

Turning to Mani, she arched an eyebrow. 'Any last words?'

He looked at his sobbing wife and made an awkward sound. 'Liana, she... What will she do?'

'Go back to her home and her life,' Lily replied. 'She's no threat without you.'

Mani nodded. 'OK. Well... Get on with it then.'

Lifting the gun, Lily held his defeated gaze for a few moments, then finally she pulled the trigger. He fell to the floor beside his son with a dull thump. Liana sobbed quietly into her hands just a few feet away. Lily untwisted the silencer and rested her gaze on her with a heavy sigh.

'I'll see that you get home with no issue.'

Liana slowly rose to her feet and turned to face her, her face stricken.

'I imagine Mani had a decent amount of cash at home, but if you need anything, you can call me, and I'll help you.'

Liana walked towards her slowly, staring into space as shock overtook her.

'Liana? Are you listening?'

There was no answer, and Lily sighed, turning back towards George and Andy to give them a list of instructions. As she let her guard down for that split second, Liana suddenly flipped the switch, grabbing the gun from Lily's hand and jumping back out of the way. She cocked it and held it out in front of her.

'Lil!' Andy yelled.

'*Shit*,' Lily cried, backing away slowly and raising her hands in the air. She almost instantly hit the side wall of the garage and froze. She had nowhere to go.

'Liana, put it down!' she ordered, despite knowing that she had no power now. Liana held all the cards.

'I don't think so,' Liana replied, her voice shaking. She swung the gun towards George and Andy, and they threw their hands up in the air.

'Hey, whoa,' they said, talking over each other in panic. 'Easy now.'

Liana swung it back towards Lily as she tried to creep out, and Lily cringed back in panic.

'Wait, *please*... You asked me earlier if I would make your death quick, remember?' Lily garbled, trying to connect to her somehow, her heart hammering in her chest as she stared down the barrel of the gun she'd just killed the woman's son and husband with. 'And – and do you remember what I said?'

Liana's face broke into a strange half-smile. 'Yes,' she said flatly. 'You said you wouldn't kill me.'

'Exactly!' Lily said, praying that she could somehow convince Liana to allow her the same, but as she looked at the bodies on the floor, she winced. It was unlikely.

'*Exactly*,' Liana repeated quietly, checking the gun was loaded.

'*Jesus*...' George groaned.

Lily closed her eyes and tensed, waiting for the shot to come, cursing herself for being so stupid. How could she have let her guard down like that?

She quickly pushed those thoughts away, focusing on the faces of her children instead. They were all she wanted to think of now, in these final moments. They were all that mattered to her. They always had been.

The shot went off, the sound booming around the small space without the silencer, and Lily jumped, waiting for the pain to kick in. The shot echoed off into silence, and then as the seconds ticked on, she realised she still hadn't felt anything.

'Er, Lil?' George said.

She opened her eyes and looked over to him and Andy. They were staring at the floor in front of her. She followed their eyes and, as she realised what had happened, her shoulders dropped, and she sighed with a mixture of relief and sadness.

'Why?' Andy asked, confused.

'She didn't want to be here anymore,' Lily replied quietly. 'Not without her children.'

She pulled the silencer back out of her pocket, looked at it for a moment then dropped it beside the dead woman. 'Don't clean this up,' she ordered. 'Let them be found. It will be put down to one big family tragedy.'

'Well, better theirs than yours,' George said grimly.

'*Ours*,' she corrected, turning to look at them. 'This firm is a family, whether you're blood or not. And don't you ever forget that.' She eyed them both. 'But you're right. Better theirs than ours.' She walked out of the garage. 'And it's about time we got back to ours. Because we won this one. Which means we can finally breathe again. And we live to see another day.'

As she looked back inside at the three dead bodies slumped in the filthy, blood-spattered garage and the tears still wet on Liana's face, she was reminded once more just how ugly winning could be in their world. But that was the life they chose. The life her children walked in. And so she'd do it again, for them, in a heartbeat. She'd do it a hundred times over, for them.

Reaching up, she pulled down the roller door and walked away from the Romanos for good.

FORTY-SEVEN

Lily sat beside her daughter-in-law, in the high-backed hospital chair she'd spent most of her time in these last few days, and reached over to give her hand a squeeze before sitting back. They'd taken it in shifts, never leaving her alone, but Lily had made sure she was there the most. Billie needed her. Lily might not have been her *actual* mother, but she was as close to one as Billie had, and she'd grown to love the girl dearly.

She'd made sure it was *her* who was there in the mornings and *her* who went to the flat to collect her things when she'd needed a change of night clothes and her wash kit. She'd gone to the shop she knew Billie liked, the one with all the organic creams, and had asked the shop assistant to find her the best things to help Billie heal. She didn't have much faith in the stuff herself, unsure how a few sprigs of lavender were supposed to cure this, that and the other, but she knew Billie did. And she remembered the kindness the girl had shown, years before, when Lily had sat beside a different hospital bed, praying for her own daughter's recovery. It was her turn to repay that kindness.

'Are you hungry?' she asked her. 'Or thirsty?'

Billie took a moment to respond, as she had ever since she'd woken up, as though her responses were on a delay. 'No thanks,' she said vaguely.

Scarlet looked up over Lily's shoulder from the other side of the bed and subtly caught her attention. Lily turned and saw Ray through the small internal window, pointing down the hallway. They were here.

'Back in a sec, love,' Lily said, standing up with Scarlet.

Billie didn't respond, her vacant gaze still resting on something outside, and they left the room just as Connor and Cillian arrived in the hallway.

'Where is she?' Cillian asked, peering through the window into her room.

Lily stepped aside and gestured to the door, not wanting to delay him any further from being with his wife. She'd gone to Connor's as soon as she'd been able, while he was still sorting Cillian out and sobering him up enough to come here. It had been a short visit but enough to put her mind at ease. They had a lot to discuss, but that could wait. He needed to be with Billie now. And she desperately needed him.

She watched him walk into the room and swallowed the hard lump in her throat. They had so much to go through still, the pair of them. But they were going to be OK; she knew they were. Together, they could get through anything.

* * *

The door shut, and Billie ignored it, keeping her gaze on the top branches of the tree across the car park that swayed in the wind. It was soothing to watch, in a numb nothingness kind of way. And nothingness was all she craved right now, the pain of losing her beautiful baby girl too raw and too all-consuming to deal with on her own. She felt hollow now. Empty, mentally as well as physically. Lily Rose had been a part of her. Billie had felt her grow; had felt the hard rounding of her stomach as she'd started taking up more space, and the little bubbles as she moved. They'd shared the same blood as it ran through their bodies, connected as one. She and her daughter. A tear escaped her eye and rolled down her cheek into her hairline.

Now Lily Rose was gone, her perfect little girl. The bullet hadn't hit her womb directly; it had entered just above, missing by an inch. The trauma to her body was what had triggered the miscarriage, after she'd passed out from losing too much blood. *Lucky* the doctors had called her.

Lucky.

Lucky that she'd not been further along. Lucky that her womb was undamaged. She could go on to have other children, they'd said, so calmly and casually, as if discussing handbags. She'd wanted to scream at them, ask if any of *them* had ever lost a child. Because she'd *loved* her daughter. She'd wanted her. And she'd been so cruelly ripped away from them.

She realised suddenly that whoever had walked in hadn't moved from the door. It sparked her interest just enough to make her turn her head, and when she did, her eyes widened, and her heart skipped a beat in her chest.

'Cillian,' she whispered, trying to pull herself up.

He was staring at her with so much love and devastation in his eyes that she couldn't stop her own face from crumpling. She burst into tears, her sobs deep and heartbreaking, and he finally moved forward, sitting next to her and pulling her into his arms as he broke down too.

'I'm so sorry,' he said, squeezing her tighter. 'I'm so sorry.'

She shook her head. 'No,' she said. 'No apologies. I'm just glad you're here now.' She broke off into tears again, and he kissed the top of her head.

'I'm sorry you had to do this alone,' he said.

She pulled away and looked at him. 'We lost her, Cillian,' she said in a small voice. 'We lost our baby, and they just keep talking about *me* and that *I'm* OK, and that we'll conceive again and they're just *ignoring* her like she was *nothing*.' She wiped her eyes, glad to finally be able to tell him, knowing he was the one person who would truly understand.

'Oh, Bills.' He hugged her to him. 'Lily Rose was *not* nothing. She was our girl. And we loved her, and we lost her. We *lost* her,' he repeated.

Billie nodded tearfully.

Cillian sniffed and wiped his own tears away. 'So here's what we're going to do. We're going to sort out a little ceremony to say goodbye. Something special. Something with the family, whoever you want there, or just us if you'd rather. We'll give her that.'

Fresh tears poured from Billie's eyes as she clung to Cillian, the tears of grief she'd been holding in since the wedding. She'd been waiting, she realised, to share them with the one person who would make things right. That would hold her together, the same way she would for him.

'Thank you,' she sobbed. 'Oh, Cillian... I'm so glad you're home.'

* * *

Connor walked back down the hospital corridor and handed one of the paper cups of coffee in his hands to Ray, taking a sip of his own as he followed Ray's gaze through the window to Cillian and Billie.

'How they doing?' he asked.

They'd been in there for an hour, just talking and hugging and crying. Getting it all out. Coming back together.

'Well, the crying's stopped,' Ray told him, sipping his coffee. '*Christ* this is shit.' He frowned down at it then took another sip anyway.

'Mm,' Connor agreed. He steeled himself and glanced nervously at Ray. 'Listen, I need to talk to you about something.'

Ray put his hand out. 'Er, let me stop you right there. I think I know what this is about.'

Connor exhaled slowly. This was going to be harder than he'd thought.

'You're gonna tell me you want to leave and go back to your mum, that about right?' Ray asked, glancing at him with a raised eyebrow.

'I wasn't going to put it like that, but yeah, pretty much,' Connor replied, tensing for battle.

'OK.' Ray sipped his coffee then fell silent.

Connor frowned. 'What?'

'I said OK,' Ray repeated. He looked at Connor and chuckled. 'Your face, it's a picture, honestly.'

'Is it a joke?' Connor asked. 'I don't get it.'

'No joke, mate.' Ray turned to face him. 'Listen, I'd love to keep you, but I get it. You need to be here. Cillian needs you. *Lil* needs you too, to be honest, though don't tell her I said that.'

He glanced over his shoulder to check she wasn't nearby then turned back to Connor with an unexpected warmth in his eyes. 'If you ever want to come back, there's a place for ya. And I hope you do, because I meant what I said about the future of the firms. But if you need to be here, *be here*. Life's too short. We need to do what's right and be with those we care about.'

Ray turned back to the window, and Connor just stared at him, the entire argument he'd spent hours putting together in his head going totally to waste.

'Right,' he said, facing the window. He glanced back at Ray once more, unnerved by this new version of the man. 'Right.'

Ray smiled, and after one last suspicious glance at him, Connor accepted it and smiled along with him.

EPILOGUE

The next six weeks seemed to pass in a flash. Billie's physical wounds healed well, and the doctors sent her home with another thoughtless load of well-meant comments that made her want to scream in their faces. But she didn't, because she had Cillian there to help light up the dark and carry the load when it was too much to bear. They held their special ceremony for Lily Rose in Lily's garden, the first night they could. They released paper lanterns and each read out something special for her, before lighting a candle and raising a toast to the smallest member of the Drew family who never quite made it home.

The newlyweds finally returned to their flat, promptly putting it up for sale. They'd decided it was time to buy a house so they were ready for when they decided – at whatever point that would be – to have their second child. Lily kept a steady stream of house viewings coming their way, all of which were within close distance to hers.

Connor moved back to his own firm, feeling an overwhelming sense of relief as his sense of meaning and joy returned to his life. He already knew he wouldn't go back to Ray. The idea was certainly logical, but it just wasn't for him.

He lived for his family. They might not always realise, but he was always watching out for them, looking after them both from a distance and by their side. It was what he was good at. And he didn't need anything more than that. Well, not *much* more anyway.

After he settled back in, he worked up the courage to finally ask Isla out. He'd thought about her a lot since she'd accidentally admitted her feelings to him that day in his flat. And the more he'd thought about her, the more he'd realised he *wanted* to think about her. The distance between them when he'd worked for Ray had highlighted how much they usually talked, and how much he'd missed those conversations. Isla had accepted his invite before he'd even finished his sentence. She'd also kissed him first before he'd had a chance to try his luck, on their first date. But he didn't mind too much. They were having a good time, and she made him smile. He liked that a lot.

After Connor's return, Ray started coming around the house much more, and when he wasn't there, Lily was usually found down in his territory. They started merging more of their jobs, and to everyone's surprise, it all ran rather smoothly. Lily's defences had lowered a little – not *that* much really, but she was working on it – and their relationship seemed to be stronger than ever.

The Logans took over the Romanos' territory fairly smoothly. After filing the paperwork to transfer ownership of all Mani's businesses to themselves, the rest had fallen in line quite quickly. There had been a few minor stand-offs, but nothing they hadn't been able to handle, and it hadn't been long before they'd moved Finn's and Sean's families back over, throwing a big Christmas party to celebrate their return.

Cath had finally decided to give Cormac a chance after things had settled down, and after a stern conversation in which she'd told him, very frankly, that she would always love Ronan, she would *not* remove any pictures of Ronan from the house and she would *never* accept him growing a moustache under *any* circumstances – and that if he didn't like any of that, he could sling his hook – things were going very well. He'd agreed with complete respect to all of her stipulations, hesitating only briefly on the one about the moustache.

Business had evened out now that Connor was back, leaving Scarlet and Cillian more than a touch baffled about how he managed to get so much done, when they'd struggled to share that same load between a number of them. It would forever remain a mystery, as Connor didn't even know himself, and as the year came to a close, things were once again booming within the Drew empire.

Scarlet had finally been able to release the guilt she'd been carrying around about Connor's exit from the firm, and the relief had been overwhelming. She still carried her secrets from the night of Ruby's death, but this was out of necessity rather than guilt. To keep her family whole, she had to protect them from the truth. Because that was her job. To protect them from anything that threatened their strength and peace – even themselves. And, for the most part, she was very good at it. She'd realised that, somewhere along the way. She'd been born for this life. Born to lead them all one day.

It had never really been a choice, the way the naïve young girl she'd used to be had once thought. Her veins were filled with the same fiery steel as her aunt's, the same deep instincts and love and loyalty. Scarlet was a Drew woman through and through, and she was right where she was supposed to be. Growing their empire and protecting the family at all costs. There would always be a next threat in their world, and Scarlet would always be ready for it. It was just who she was. It was in her blood. And though at times it was hard, she knew with deep certainty that she wouldn't want it any other way.

Christmas had been a jolly affair, held at Cath and Scarlet's for a change, full of food and fun and laughter. Scarlet had enjoyed seeing Cath laugh properly again, now she had Cormac around. It had been too long since she'd last been this happy. They'd enjoyed every second of the day, making merry and making plans, and then in the blink of an eye, New Year's Eve was upon them.

They'd gathered at Lily's house to see the new year in with a bang. The five couples – Lily and Ray, Cillian and Billie, Connor and Isla, Scarlet and Benny, and Cath and Cormac – all gathered in the lounge for a boogie as Cath put on her all-time favourite New Year's hits, one for each year she'd been alive. The song list was terrible, for the most part, but after a few drinks, nobody seemed to care about that. They pranced around the room, Ray doing his best knees-up dance to 'Baggy Trousers', exaggerating his moves as Scarlet joined in to rival him.

'You really think you've got it, kid?' he joked challengingly.

'*Kid?*' she asked. 'Oh-ho, OK, come on then, blue badge, let's see, shall we?'

'*Blue badge?*' Ray repeated in shock. 'How old do you think I *am?*'

'Ohhh, fighting words, Scarlet!' Benny called from the sidelines.

'Who you backing, Benny?' Lily asked with a devilish grin. 'Your boss or your girlfriend?'

'Err...' He scratched the back of his head, looking away. 'Was that the *door?*'

'Pussy,' Connor shouted as he ducked into the hall.

Billie smiled at the scene from the armchair, where she was curled up on Cillian's lap. Lily passed them and squeezed both their arms on her way out of the room.

'Who's up for Cath's frozen margaritas?' she called back over her shoulder.

There was a loud chorus of eager yeses, and Cath looked around at them all thrilled.

'Ahh, I'm glad you're up for trying them,' she said, beaming. 'I made them last night. Found a recipe in this new magazine. It says in there that it actually tastes *better* when you replace the tequila with this green stuff they make in France, absinthe...'

'Oh, no! No, no...' The chorus quickly started back up, everyone hurriedly changing their answers.

Cath humphed and folded her arms. 'Well, that's nice, ain't it? It don't hurt to try something new once in a while, you know.' She pursed her lips as Benny walked back in.

'What's that?' he asked, slipping his phone into his pocket.

'Nothing,' Ray told him with a grin. 'Cath made you a special cocktail, Benny; it's in the kitchen with Lil. Go grab it, yeah?'

'Oh, nice. Thanks, Cath,' he replied.

Isla snickered, hiding her face behind her hands, and the rest of them grinned.

Suddenly, Ray stood up and nipped over to the Christmas tree. 'Listen, boys, while your mum's out there, I've got a little something special to give her before we go into the new year.' He reached under and pulled out a small blue Tiffany box.

A tense silence fell across the room. Cath put her fingers to her mouth and turned to Scarlet in alarm. Scarlet bit her lip and glanced at Connor. Connor was staring at Ray, as was Cillian, their foreheads creasing into deep frowns.

'Ray, I don't think that's a good idea,' Connor warned.

'Why?' he asked. 'Things have been great lately. I think this is the perfect time.'

They heard Lily returning from the kitchen, and Cillian quickly caught his attention.

'Oi,' he hissed. 'Just *put it away*. *Don't do it*, alright? Seriously.' He gave him a look of warning.

'OK! Jesus, you'd think it was a bomb...' Ray raised his hands in surrender and slipped the Tiffany box into his pocket with a roll of his eyes.

Cath shuffled over to Scarlet, whispering frantically as Lily retook her seat across the room. 'What is he *doing*? He's going to *blow it*.' She bit her nails anxiously. 'Oh, he's going to ruin everything. He'll push her away again.' She made a sound of frustration, and Scarlet shushed her as Lily looked over.

'It's *fine*, don't worry. He won't do it,' she assured her mother, glancing worriedly over at Ray.

Benny sat down with his drink and took a sip, instantly spitting it out all over Lil's coffee table. She hid a grin as he stared at it, mortified.

'Oh God, sorry, Cath. Sorry, Lil. I didn't mean...' He trailed off as everyone erupted in peals of laughter.

Everyone except Cath. 'Yes, alright,' she snapped. 'I'll use tequila next time.'

'I liked it, love,' Cormac said, sitting next to her and pulling her into his arm.

She smiled. 'Did you really?'

'I did; I thought it was grand.'

Cath laid her head on his chest with a happy smile, and he caught Scarlet's eye over the top of her head. 'Awful,' he mouthed, pulling a pained expression and shaking his head.

She chuckled and looked away.

'Ray, what are you doing?' Cath's sharp question drew her attention back towards Ray, and her stomach constricted as she realised he was going for it.

'Lil,' he said, walking over to her with the little blue box. 'I have something for you. Something I saved especially for tonight.'

'No, no, no, no, no,' Scarlet murmured, horrified.

'I can't look,' Cath whispered, putting her hands to her mouth and watching all the same.

'Something a little bit special,' Ray continued.

He kneeled down before Lily, and her eyes flew wide in

alarm. Scarlet stood up then froze, not sure how to stop the train wreck that was about to unfold.

'Ray...' Lily said nervously.

'Will you take this gift, Lily Drew, from me to you?' He opened the box with a flourish, and her eyebrows shot upwards as she stared down at it.

'Oh, Ray...' She smiled and stepped forward, resting her arm on his shoulder as she took a closer look.

Everyone looked at each other in complete confusion. *What was going on?*

Ray turned back to them with a mischievous smile. 'You didn't really think I was that daft, did ya?' He held up the box, revealing the gleaming pair of diamond earrings inside.

'Oh you're *such* a tosser, Ray,' Cillian said, pinching the bridge of his nose. 'You really are.'

* * *

As the laughter erupted, Lily looked around at the people in the room, soaking it all in. It was good to hear them laugh. It was good to all be in the same room and on the same side. They'd all suffered blows this year. Some big, some small, some they'd never, even in their wildest nightmares, thought possible. They'd lost loved ones, battles, pieces of themselves they would never get back. But they'd survived and they'd grown. And their family had pulled together tighter than ever. There would be hard days ahead. There always were. But she felt blessed anyway, because no matter what else was going on in the world, they had each other. They had family. And at the end of the day, family really was the only thing that ever mattered.

A LETTER FROM EMMA TALLON

Dear readers,

And so the Drew family adventures have come to an end. For now at least. Thank you for taking this journey with me. I hope, through this series, that you laughed and cried, and you felt the deepest love and the darkest hatred at different times along the way.

If you'd like to join my mailing list to find out about my next book, please sign up here. You can unsubscribe at any time, and your details will never be shared.

www.bookouture.com/emma-tallon

Thank you for reading *Her Feud*. I really hope you enjoyed this final instalment. If you did, please do pop a review on Amazon. I read every single review, comment and message that gets sent – and hearing your thoughts about what you loved or gasped at, hearing you talk about my characters as though they're as alive in your mind as they are in mine, means more than I can say.

I'll be back very soon with some more gritty London underworld crime. You may have noticed the introduction of some brand-new characters in the course of this book. Two brothers and a sister with a rather complicated set-up – but I don't want to give too much away, so all I'll say is: Watch this space!

In the meantime, stay well, stay happy, be you and I'll catch you again soon.

With love,

Emma XX

facebook.com/emmatallonofficial
x.com/EmmaEsj
instagram.com/my.author.life

ACKNOWLEDGEMENTS

Firstly, thank YOU, reader. Without your support, I wouldn't be anywhere. I've only been able to make writing my career because of all of you, so I can't tell you how much every purchase, every review and every comment means to me.

A huge heartfelt thanks to my amazing editor (and fellow Slytherin), Helen Jenner, who uses her insane powers to help me turn my chaotic first drafts into the finished books you guys read. She puts up with 4 a.m. emails and reams of utter nonsense – mostly on the emails, some in the books – my terrible inability to hit an actual deadline and constant tendencies to go off on tangents, and she does it all with grace and style and kindness and great humour. Even after six years and fourteen books. She deserves a medal really.

Thank you to my two book besties, Casey Kelleher and Victoria Jenkins, for being there always, no matter what. Deadlines, plot holes, disasters and celebrations, they're the one solid constant. I love you guys so much and couldn't do life without you. Gladstone girls for the win.

And lastly, a little shoutout to all the staff at the Moxy for the decent coffee and for making it a fun and friendly environment to work in when the writing gets tough and I need a different scene. Half this book was written there, and no doubt some of the next one will be too. Cheers, guys!

PUBLISHING TEAM

Turning a manuscript into a book requires the efforts of many people. The publishing team at Bookouture would like to acknowledge everyone who contributed to this publication.

Commercial
Lauren Morrissette
Jil Thielen
Imogen Allport

Cover design
The Brewster Project

Data and analysis
Mark Alder
Mohamed Bussuri

Editorial
Helen Jenner
Ria Clare

Copyeditor
Janette Currie

Proofreader
Laura Kincaid

Marketing
Alex Crow
Melanie Price
Occy Carr
Cíara Rosney

Operations and distribution
Marina Valles
Stephanie Straub

Production
Hannah Snetsinger
Mandy Kullar
Jen Shannon

Publicity
Kim Nash
Noelle Holten
Myrto Kalavrezou
Jess Readett
Sarah Hardy

Rights and contracts
Peta Nightingale
Richard King
Saidah Graham